TIME AND TEMPERANCE

K. SCOTT FUCHS

TIME AND TEMPERANCE

First edition. December 31, 2023.

Copyright © 2023 K. Scott Fuchs.

ISBN: 979-8223945949

Written by K. Scott Fuchs.

Time and Temperance is dedicated first and foremost to The Lord, God, my Heavenly Father for all His love, grace, and kindness and for being the greatest hero and inspiration to me. With Him all things are possible and because of Him, this is possible. All thanks, praise, and glory to The Lord.

Also dedicated to the 2021 and 2022 National Champion Georgia Bulldogs.

For The Lord and Miss Lee

Kh. Scott Pm

ACKNOWLEDGEMENTS

Writing *Time and Temperance* was a long journey, it was one that lasted over five years. I would like to thank my supervisor Catherine Wynne for playing such an enormous role in not only helping me to complete this novel or a doctoral thesis, but also in my life. Thank you for your steadfast guidance, wisdom, and care, I cannot put into words what it truly means to me. Thank you to Martin Goodman for helping spurn where this novel came from and most importantly for giving me a chance; thank you for making me a better writer and helping me to better myself. I would also like to thank the University of Hull for playing such a huge part in helping bring this to life.

I would like to send a special thank you to Amanda Nicholson for helping design the cover art.

I would like to thank my friends and family for their support, some of whom took the time to read my work. I would like to thank them all for taking interest and for the love they have shown me, every step of the way. Thank you to Kevin Kuchmak, Andrew Nicholson, Cathy Im, Lesley Ayres, Martyn Robinson, Kerry Ann Whiteside, Tony Bolton, and my father.

I would like to thank Anne Bronte, Emily Dickinson, and Scott Joplin for being creative influences and role models I could learn from and inspire me to write.

Finally, I would like to thank you the reader who are kind enough to take the time to read these words with an open heart and mind. I sincerely thank you with the utmost appreciation and gratitude.

PROLOGUE

"Papa."

My eyes opened to large blue irises staring back at me which radiated with a gentleness, warmth, and love; they belonged to my eldest daughter Henrietta.

"I am sorry, did I wake you?"

"Just resting my eyes, sweetheart." I smiled at her.

"I am surprised Mummy and you don't have a full-on production about your romance, being one of history's greatest couples." Her lips slowly unfurled to a smile; her fair skin was accented by rosy cheeks, her defined jaw line and soft facial features wrinkled around her dimples.

Hetta's blue eyes are like her mother's and when she smiles, it was as if her mother was smiling back at me. The sight was one to behold.

"I suppose starting with a book will suffice." She extended her hand forward slipping a familiar leather-bound book was in her hand. Henrietta removed a hair clip and her long dark-auburn hair descended upon her orchid-print dress.

"Where did you find this, Hetta?"

"I stumbled upon it in Mother's things, whilst I was tidying your bedroom."

"You didn't have to do that." I sat up. "Thank you, darling."

"You seemed knackered." She sat beside me with her hands on her lap. Her excitement palpable through her twinkling eyes and bright smile. "I haven't read it." She inched closer to me. I looked

3

down at the cover, the title etched in traditional Victorian gold-leaf font.

"Do either of your sisters know about this?"

She shrugged her shoulders.

"So that probably means yes." I had a brief laugh. "Honey, this is a special gift to your mother, so it needs be to kept safe and it can't go missing, okay?" I placed my hand over hers and she nodded with more energy.

"Alright then, sweetheart...." I smiled at her and tapped her nose playfully, invoking a brief laugh from her. "Though you know much of it already, you can have a quick read through it if you'd like."

"I would prefer if you read it to me instead."

"I best get the girls then." I placed the leather-bound book down beside me.

"They are both having a kip..." Hetta grasped my hand. "I really want to hear this in your words, Papa.".

"It is a long story, Hen..."

"I got time..." She hung on my words with a twinkle in her eye, reminding me of when she was a younger and I read her favourite bedtime stories to her.

"Anything for you, my beautiful daughter." I stroked her cheek with my free hand. Her smile spilled across her from cheek-to-cheek; it was bubbly and full of life. I smiled back at her and she curled up against me.

"Though I think your mother would want me to wait until you're a bit older to read this to you..."

"Mummy isn't here right now, is she?" She rested her head on my chest.

I kissed her on the dome of her head and looked up toward the white mantle of our fireplace. Next to a framed black and white daguerreotype of my beloved's mother, stood a picture of her and I from our wedding day. She looked like an angel in white satin, her long dark copper-auburn hair flowing down toward her bosom and back. A flat-brimmed white sunhat with a navy bow and collection of lavender flowers flowing from the side of the headpiece. I was dressed more modestly, a simple white shirt, grey tie, and black suit. Unlike my beloved whose hair had been exquisitely arranged, I took the luxury of buzzing my hair and beard to a simple scruff. Her smile was as nearly as illuminous as her dress, a cream-coloured corseted gown that hugged her bust, matched by a long ivory lace overskirt that trailed along the floor. A narrow black brooch wrapped around her neck; her arms were bare but neatly tucked under a muslin veil and matching cloak that draped over her.

The joy escaped from the photograph. Mine shown in simply having my arm snug around her waist; hers in how tight she gripped a bouquet of roses whilst concealing the excitement that hid behind her gentle smile. And just like that, everything flashed in front of me.

Time and Temperance:

A Romance

VOLUME I

1.

C heshire, England 2017
The horizon was a faint orange and the moon glowed in the amethyst sky. A quiet road lined with beech trees snaked through a small town. Approaching a red-brick church set back on a hill, I stopped and made a sign of the cross. Headstones scattered through tall grass and a willow tree stood by the Tudor-style porch with a gas lamp. On an oak poster board were various notices:

Holmes Chapel Family Fair – Bank Holiday Weekend – 25th to 28th August

Goostrey Rose Day – 30th of June

Tatton Park Pop-Up Festival: 15th of July - August dates to be announced

Dunham Massey Antique Show and Folk Festival – 29th and 30th July;

The White Ribbon Foundation British Women's Temperance Society (BWTS) 150th Anniversary Concert Night at Lea Hall – 26th October – 7:00 PM

Community Choir – Every Monday 7:30 PM

Café and Connect – Every Wednesday Morning 9:30 AM to 12:30 PM.

I sauntered on, past more beech, elm, and oak trees. *Rachmaninov's 2nd Symphony the Adagio* was playing on my headphones as I took in the beauty of the old, most of which dated to the late 1800's as noted by their capstones. I adored Victorian houses, just like the literature and the music of the time. One captured my attention: a large red-bricked beauty with bay windows on either side of the house which formed two turrets that extended two stories. The windows were hooded with Corinthian column mouldings. It had a large black door, above which was a hooded window with a frieze, above that again three smaller hooded windows. My neck craned at the high-pitched blue-slate roof with its enchanting ornate black gables. The lights were on. What would it be like to live in such a place; to sit in the front room and look out from those large bay windows with all the light coming in, flooding the room up to its high-ceilings with brocade patterns?

In the front room was a portrait of a woman who appeared to be from the Victorian era. She had her hair up in a bouffant under a flowered hat, some loose strands had escaped underneath; it was auburn or light-brown with a sleek lustre. She wore a darker-coloured bodice with large ruffled sleeves and a long underskirt which flowed outward to form a bustle. It reminded me of a portrait of a woman that struck me at the Victorian Museum in Buxton. She had deep eyes and a soft complexion. Though not smiling, I could conceive that when she did, it would have been radiant. I imagined that perhaps she lived in the house way back then. I looked at the second-floor window and thought how lovely it must have been to come home to her. Such a woman could inspire me to be the best version of myself. That was always my dream. But this woman in the painting was from the past and I couldn't find her where I was.

I pulled out my phone and looked at the last text message from Rachel: *YOU MAKE ME WANT TO PULL MY HAIR FROM MY HEAD.* She hadn't always been like that. When I first met her, she was friendly and eager for us to spend time together. In a blur, everything deteriorated to where we were now and yet I had spent so much time trying to recover the person I had first met. Perhaps, it was all an illusion.

THE PHONE RANG, IT was half-past three in the morning: "Hello..." I was dazed by sleep.

"You alright?"

It was Rachel, her sharp Mancunian accent was quite relaxed.

"Yea, I'm good." I squinted as I sat up. "Is everything okay?"

"I'm at the club." Her words slurred.

"It's a Tuesday."

"Some lad wanted to dance with me but I turned him down...." She replied.

"Why would you even tell me that?"

"You want me to say yes to him?"

I had to walk on eggshells, especially when she was drinking. I didn't want to get into an argument because what she would do is say something horrible and then put the phone down and not call back. She knew I was sensitive; she knew this was a touchy time of year.

"Would you like me to come get you?" I yawned. "I'll bring you home, so you are safe..."

"I'm taking a taxi." She started laughing. I heard some men talking in the background.

"Give us a minute..." She spoke to the voices and hung up on me. When I tried to ring back, her phone was turned off. Straight to voicemail. I left a message, begging her to call me when she was back home. She didn't though, instead she rang the next afternoon saying she was on her way over.

Rachel should have arrived by four but didn't appear until twenty to seven. She barely kissed me when I reached out to do so; she still looked rough from the night before with bags under her eyes and her reddish-brown hair up in a bobble. Her eyes were bloodshot and her skin was flushed. Rachel was dressed down in a hooded sweatshirt with black leggings and a pair of white Nike trainers.

I got some pasta from the kitchen cupboard, turned on the oven, and poured water into a pan. There was no conversation, just an awkward tension filled by the occasional pops of bubble gum, a notification for a text message to Rachel's phone, her fingers clicking the keys, and the rumbles of boiling water in the pan.

"So, did you have a good time, last night?"

She laughed. "Is that a serious question?"

"Well, someone had to say something..." I crossed my arms and leaned against the wall. There she sat on the small black nylon couch with her arms crossed as well. "Look, you know today is a tough day for me right, so I am doing my best here..."

"Every day is a tough day for you..." She snickered defiantly. "Everything's a bloody anniversary of some morbid event..." Rachel closed her eyes and put her head in her hand. "Your friend shot himself, the car accident, your diabetes which you were younger than two when you got it..."

"I am not trying to get into a fight with you today." I shook my head. "I just wanted to spend the night, have a nice meal with you, and get through it..."

"Did you speak to a professional yet about the panic attacks?"

"Thank The Lord, I have another consultation on Monday." I turned around and stirred the boiling water, adding some pasta. "The initial appointment was like a freaking police interrogation."

"That's because you think everyone is against you."

I looked back at her over my shoulder, her ice-cold glare was fixed on me for a moment before it went back to her phone. "Well, they are."

"Right..." She held back her laugh as she crossed her legs. "So, when do you actually go for therapy?"

"It could be six months, unless I do something drastic."

"Flippin' hell..." She popped a bubble. "Are they taking the mick?"

"Nope... that's the way of it..."

"Well, here's hoping for the day that you won't have to wash your hands thirty-two times after you touch a work top."

This was the norm of late, speaking to me like this. She must have thought I enjoyed having to sanitise my hands every thirty seconds out of fear that I would inhale an influenza virus or start coughing from dust. It was not unusual though. I used to be mocked when I was sent home from school as a teen and ordered to be evaluated by a psychologist because my hands were bleeding so much from "over-washing." The thing is, I didn't enjoy this terror but it didn't make any difference to how I was treated. It was a long time ago now, but Rachel adopted the same attitude as so many others had done before.

I would be preoccupied for the evening if I drank from the same glass as someone, or was in close proximity to someone who wiped their nose and didn't wash their hands after it. She, on the other hand, couldn't care less about such things but then again, I had to worry about the diabetes. I couldn't give it an opportunity to get a shot at me. Diabetic ketoacidosis and retinopathy are no joke and the latter, in particular, terrified me to my core. Such events transpired from poor control and what can make the scoundrel go haywire? A pathogen, albeit only acutely.

Rachel's nonchalance made her my superior, somehow...Did she forget that when she was ill, I laid in bed with her to look after her, despite my obsessions and compulsions?

"You know what? There is no need for you to speak to me to like that." I stirred the pasta. "It is a condition which I am trying to get under control..."

"Shortness of breath and having heart palpations isn't a condition." Rachel pooh-poohed. "It's called not being a stress-head and getting a grip."

"You are the one who needs to get a grip..." I replied skittishly as I knew this could be a catalyst for a confrontation.

"You what?"

"I sense you are looking for a quarrel but I am not interested." I turned back and looked at her.

"Quarrel?" She rose to her feet. "There you are with your fancy words..."

"Quarrel isn't a fancy word, if I wanted to be more articulate, I would have said disputation."

She waved her hands. "You know what your problem is?"

"I am sure you will tell me". I opened the cupboard and pulled out a jar of passata.

"You're too full on." She shook her head. "You don't know how to have fun; everything is so intense with you..."

"Fun?" I chuckled. "Getting drunk in some random club on a Tuesday night is what you define as fun?"

"Better than sitting around listening to depressive music and hearing about your Victorian novels..."

"Very nice..." I shrugged the barb off. "... and who were those dudes that you were speaking with?"

"What does it matter?"

"I think anyone who had a partner who behaved as you did last night couldn't help but ask..." I put the passata jar down.

"Behaved?" She laughed. "You are not my parent."

"You know what?" I couldn't hold it any more, I was sick and tired of everything. "Forget all these innuendos..." I shook my head. "I want things to be good between us." I lowered the heat on the oven. "I don't understand what I've done. I get on great with your kids and I want to do right by you. But still you'd rather go out and drink, all the time?"

"Well, you don't drink with me, do you now?" She snickered again. "You're more concerned about how my mate's cat is getting on..."

"It's a cute animal." I threw my hands out. "You know I have a history of major depression, obsessive-compulsive disorder, and anxiety attacks?" I brought my hands back together. "Drinking is not in my best interest..."

"Here we are with the doom and gloom again."

She wanted to me react despite her aversion to my sensitivity, but I wouldn't bite.

"Who was watching the kids last night when you were out?"

"Piss off..." She laughed. "Don't tell me how to raise my children..."

"I am not, but still it is a valid question..."

"Spare any further lectures on your family values." She slurred her words as she looked at me with a palpable rage. "Along with your many obsessions with the nineteenth century...." The scent of vodka emerged from her throat when she yelled.

"A Victorian woman, that's what you want, init? That's what you came here for!" Her bloodshot eyes and steady pupils filled with fury. "One who could be wrapped around your filthy fingers while you worship the ground, she walks on..."

"Is it a crime to be affectionate to your lover?"

She waved her hand in my direction dismissively. "I have bad news for you, you won't be finding one of those in Manchester in 2017..."

"Who are you messaging?" I watched suspiciously. Rachel looked down at her phone and started typing.

"...If it were up to you, I'd be home at six and we'd be in bed by nine." She raised her voice. "Everywhere we go, you walk on the outside of the street and think that men should act a certain way at all times."

"Well what's the alternative?" I snapped back. "Acting feckless and getting wasted in some pub?! Leaving your kids at home while you're having a one-night stand with some wanna-be-tough guy piece of crap who is trying to copy a TV show he watched?" I raised my voice. "Is that how I am supposed to be?" I looked back at the bubbling water and stirred the pasta. "Cause I ain't like that nor will I ever be!"

"No, you cry at the end of *My Dog Skip*..." She taunted "...despite seeing the movie, a million-and-one times..."

"At least I am genuine..." I countered. "...not some fraud who pretends, they'd last five minutes at most in New York..."

Another text notification whistled from her phone. She smiled when she looked back down at her mobile.

I raised my hands to diffuse the situation. Rage would soon coil like a viper, if I didn't take a deep breath. I didn't want this; Truly, I wanted her to be happy and for us to be happy. I didn't want any more fighting; the bickering had gone on for too long and I could do no right. She was nothing like the woman I first met, it was as if I was chasing after a mirage that long since dissipated. When we were first together it was bliss, now I wanted to take the pan of scalding hot water and throw it through the wall. I took a deep breath.

"Why don't we cool down and talk about all this another time?" I opened the freezer door. "How would you like me to cook your steak?"

"I'm not staying..."

"What do you mean?" I shut the freezer. "We made plans, I bought food, and I am cooking you a meal..."

"You'll have seconds then, won't you?" She tried to get by at me and I reached to her stomach to hold her back from leaving. "Rachel, please..."

"Don't touch me!" She shoved me into the work top and stormed to the door.

"Do us all a favour will you? Get back in your time machine and go back to the 1800's." She mocked me. "Fucking bell-end." She slammed the door.

"Rachel, wait..." I gave chase. Despite her words, I didn't want her to go. Outside a small blue hatchback sputtered off onto the road and down the street. I clocked the plate details: *NB04 CCL*. I had no idea who was driving it and no idea where she was going. All I could do was watch the car speed away until it became smaller and smaller at the end of the road. Tears filled my eyes. It wasn't always like this, we used to stay up late and make love all night, talking for hours in between. We used to watch soap operas and make jokes about the characters. But not anymore....

Over the next two weeks, I got a bunch of text messages. She called me expletives, blamed me for everything, and said I made her act the way she did because she was not normally like this. Nestled in between these texts was kinder and gentler correspondence which led me to believe we could reconcile. She would cycle back between needing space and needing to see me. She referenced the better times and how she missed them but whenever I tried to steer back to that, the vitriol would be spewed again. It was vicious and endless cycle that wore me down. I was already struggling to keep the panic attacks at bay. I was exhausted even though I hadn't seen her since she had walked out.

One evening, my friend Martyn called and took me out for a drive through Longsight, not far from where she lived. I saw a blue hatchback parked outside a shawarma takeaway. It had the same reg. as the one she had left my flat in. Then Rachel emerged from the takeaway in a black coat, lit a cigarette, and leaned up against the car. Martyn and I were stuck in the commotion that is the A6, in the midst of stop-and-go traffic with cars travelling in a multitude of directions.

"I got to speak with her." I struggled to undo the safety belt.

"We're in the middle of traffic, mate!" Martyn itched his long red beard.

"I don't give a hoot!" I finally got free. "I need to put an end to all of this nonsense..." As I went to open the door, Martyn grabbed my shoulder.

"She's already done that for you..." He pointed.

A scrawny man in a New York Yankees baseball hat and red suede tracksuit exited the shop with a full plastic bag in hand. Rachel smiled at him as he came out and took a drag of her cigarette before the two kissed. They didn't know we were idling through the gridlock and that I was watching. Why would they even suspect such a thing? I was clearly the last thing on her mind. All I could do was stare and watch helplessly with a slacked-jaw and a lump in my throat. Betrayal dug its arrows into my chest.

Martyn's brown eyes fixed upon me as he touched my shoulder. I looked at him, my breaths started to grow quicker and faster.

"Was he the one she was texting?" My blood started to boil, I wanted to confront her and I wanted to bury that lowlife that was with her. "...he picked her up her from my flat." I turned to look at Martyn. "I am going to go handle this." I reached for the door and he grabbed me again.

"Don't." He shook his head. "Trust me, it's not worth it..." He patted my shoulder. "She's clearly not what you wanted..."

I looked at him, his words were almost prophetic. I was disarmed even when I looked back at the scene of the two engaging in tonsil hockey before they finally got into the car. Was I really so bad that she would sneak around with that scoundrel behind my back? Why didn't she just leave me if she was that unhappy? Why stick around and unleash the onslaught of cruel words and brutal taunts?

Truth be told, she was the "tip of the iceberg". It was everything else beneath that could not be seen which truly tore into me. Episodes, moments, sentiments building over the course of my time on the planet Earth which led up to that moment, encapsulated in her apathy toward me. Whether it be abandonment, abuse, stonewalling, or being discarded, this was the norm for me when it came to romance. I sought water from this heat and Rachel wished to offer me vinegar and salt with a hint of honey on occasion, so I could never replenish.

"I want a drink."

"But you haven't in ages..."

I stared into the red brake lights flashing on and off. I felt vacant, I felt alone, I felt like this is what I should be accustomed to. I didn't want to think anymore.

"Tesco..." I shook my head. "...or any pub." My neck reclined backward against the headrest. "...I need a drink."

And so, another spiral started...

2.

I woke up but couldn't get out of bed. I didn't want to...

I was awake but not refreshed. The night terror of the events that had unfolded filled me with pain. The disintegration of my relationship with Rachel was perhaps one of the lighter episodes compared to some of the flashbacks from other events that manifested in my dreams. I was stuck in my thoughts, stuck in the past.

I just wanted to go back to sleep and shut off. I didn't want to think because if I did, all I would think is that I am going to be stuck here forever. I'd either be dead early as I thought I would be or perhaps I could spend the next however many years alone and in silent suffering. After all, who would actually know? And who would actually care? People have said that a dark cloud followed me everywhere I go. Perhaps, the cumulonimbus clouds would push everyone away and the tempest would eventually consume me.

I moved my head and looked at the calendar pinned to the wall, I had forgotten what day it was, as they all seemed to blur together. I hadn't seen anyone; I hadn't talked to anyone. My birthday had come and gone and we were well past it, into autumn. All I kept wrestling with was the thought of death. When I looked at my phone and then the date on the calendar, I realised it was my friend Scott's birthday. I picked up the phone and dialled his number, I needed to get this out of the way today so I can go back to sleep or just lie on the couch and let the hours go by. I felt sick, I didn't want to eat but at the same time I could eat two Full English breakfasts. I watched the propellers in my floor fan spin; I found the noise soothing.

The phone rang.

"You all right, mucker?" He answered.

"What's up man?" I stretched my arm out. "I was just calling to wish you a happy birthday and pray you have many more, my friend."

"Cheers, mate."

You could hear his smile on the other side of the phone.

"I was hoping to hear from you actually..."

"Happy to speak with you too, man." I glanced out the window and through my arm back over the couch. "I don't know what your plans are but we can go shoot baskets or whatever you want to do when you are free, just let me know what works for you..."

The odds-on bet was that he would want to go to the pub and have a few, perhaps get a takeaway after to mark the occasion. I didn't feel like being around anyone at the moment, but it was his birthday and unlike me who didn't care much for my own, it meant something to him, so I wanted to do what he enjoyed.

"Actually, I'm in your neck of the woods. I could call in twenty minutes if you are about..."

"Ummm..." I tossed the duvet back and got of bed. "Sure...." I walked into the kitchenette and turned on the kettle. "I am a bit dishevelled though...."

"Aren't we all, mate?"

Half an hour later, he was at my door. We sat on the couch in the front room. No one said anything and soon it was filled with an awkward silence. There was an energy that consumed the quiet, as if something was meant to be spoken that was bubbling to the surface.

"So, what were you doing around this part?"

"Just finished a removal and had some time to kill before heading back to *The Duke* for the night." Scott pulled some rolling paper from his pockets. "...I'm not much in the mood for being social, as you know..."

"I can relate..." I put the television on. *Wuthering Heights* was paused from where I left it the day before. I hit play. *The Tenant of Wildfell Hall* and *The Lady of the Shroud* were on the coffee table. I tended to jump between the books because I struggled to concentrate on reading any one for too long, so going back and forth kept me engaged.

"So, I haven't seen you out for a while..." Scott dropped some tobacco on a flat piece of rolling paper. "In fact, no one's heard from you in weeks..."

"What do you mean? No one ever calls me anyhow..." I focused my attention on the television, my hand stretched across the couch. "If I don't call, no one calls." I sighed and gripped my bottle of Budweiser. "I am not stupid, man."

"I never said you was."

"Well then ask yourself, if I didn't call you today because it was your birthday and I just so happened to be available when you just so happened to be in the area, when would I have seen you?"

He dashed some loose tobacco into a rolling paper. "At some point, matey." He broke off a filter and placed it into the paper. "...I didn't give it much thought because I am not avoiding you..."

"In my younger years, kids used to bully me for being a juvenile diabetic, so I am used to being on my own and no one giving a fuck. In fact, I recall always asking people to hang out and they always had reasons why they couldn't and seldom did they ever ask me." I took a larger sip of beer. "...it's no different now..." I raised my hand with the bottle tight to my grip. "...so, whatever the fuck ever..."

"How many of those are you on, mate?"

"I am not drunk." I put the bottle down. "Far from it." I watched Scott's hands roll the paper over his tobacco back and forth as if he were making pizza dough.

"I'll tell you one thing though."

He looked up at me.

"When I was a teenager, my parents got divorced. In the build-up to my dad walking out, my parents used to fight every day. All hours, all night, and sometimes things got thrown out the window, my mom pulled a knife on my dad in front of me once, and even the cops had to come by a couple of times. I never felt at home obviously and was afraid to have anyone come around. But my buddy, Rich, he didn't care. We always checked on each other and yet we had other people in our lives and other commitments then. But still, we were always friends, and we still spoke on the Facebook phone long after I moved here." I clasped my hands together. "...nothing mattered other than making the effort to be a friend to one another..." A chuckle escaped me. "...so, like I said before about these other folks..."

"Have you chatted to him recently?" He licked the ends of his roll-up.

I froze for a moment and studied Scott as he continued to finish his rolled cigarette. My energy left me when I reminisced of our last conversation. "...He killed himself..."

Scott froze as well, holding the cigarette in his hand. Before he could say anything else, I interjected.

"...the day Rachel stormed off; it was the one-year anniversary of his death..."

"I'm gutted to hear that, mate. You spoke of him before but I didn't realise that..."

"It's all good, no one wants to hear that type of stuff round here anyways." I shook my head. "...it's too much for them."

"Well what else have you been doing?"

Scott hoped to ease the tone but I was still trapped in the moment, reliving the news when I received it. *I can't believe he did it*, and when the e-mail arrived, I had no idea what was being said until the course of events was ultimately revealed. He suffered from bipolar disorder and I knew full well everything that he was experiencing. Though there was a five-hour time difference, I would sometimes stay up until two or three in the morning so he could vent it all to me and settle before going to bed. So many were in shock when his body was found three days after he had apparently shot himself. No one knew until the stench of death filled his flat and permeated within the apartment house. Seemingly to so many others, this was a shocking horror that was unforeseen. I was heart-broken that it had to come to what it did but I knew he was suffering and sadly I saw it coming from a mile away, but there was nothing I could do.

The last conversation we ever had I told him I loved him but then he accused me of things in a heap of fury which resulted in him cutting off contact with me. I retaliated and did the same, stupidly. However, two weeks later, I just wanted to reach out to him and reason with him. I loved him and his friendship was far more important to me than who was right or wrong. I prayed for him and though he was unwell at the time and tried to push me away, as a result, Rich was still my friend and that's what mattered. All I wanted was him to be at peace and not suffer, he was truly a kind soul and his actions toward me were not like him, at all. Rich had an illness but the illness wasn't Rich. As I wrote the e-mail to re-initiate contact, the news was disclosed to me from a mutual acquaintance.

To the day, I blame myself for everything that happened though everyone I know told me that he was committed to what he did. I recall the $100 I wired him, a month before the incident. What if those were the funds, he used to purchase the bullets? What if I could have somehow stopped this and helped him? Despite these hypotheses, all I ever heard in return was that *even if you were around the corner, if he wanted to do it, you wouldn't stop him.*"

"Watching *Wuthering Heights*, yea?" Scott's question sewed into my reverie and brought my attention back to the television screen.

"I wanted to see how the movie compared to the book..." I watched on as Heathcliff, played by Tom Hardy, entered Thrushcross Grange. He was arguing with Cathy and she pulled him into the drawing room. "You know, I can relate to him..." I pointed at Heathcliff who picked a grape from the fruit bowl with an air of menace as Linton wept to Cathy about his entry into the house. "...I'd be pissed off too..."

"It's good to know you haven't let go of your Victorian obsession."

"Well you are not the first one to say that..." I laughed as I thought of Rachel's jeers, the last time that I saw her.

"So how do we sort this out?" He waved his hand at the television.

"A pistol?" A smile broke from my face. "...but they aren't legal in this country..."

"What ya like..." Scott rolled his eyes "What did you do for your birthday?"

"Come on, man..." I snickered. "I don't care about that stuff."

"But you turned 30...."

"And?"

He placed the rolled cigarette in his ear. "I thought given the significance, you might be more inclined to do summat..."

"Aren't you keeping it subtle yourself, this year?"

"Yeah but I enjoy the graft." He glanced out the front window. "I am having a few after my shift with Pete and Paula (the proprietor of *The Duke of York* who was like another mother to Scott)." He looked back at me. "Pop round, if you'd like..." A smile crossed his face. "We can celebrate your birthday too..."

"Dude, it's literally a marker that a year has passed and I am not dead..." I lunged forward. "How do you know in five years from now, it won't be worse?"

"Lovely." He chuckled. "How's the writing?" Scott picked up a purple notebook from the coffee table.

"Poems mostly and what not..."

"I know what it means to you." Scott passed the notebook over to me.

"It doesn't do much for me, anymore." I flung the notebook on the carpet.

"Was that necessary?"

I saw black spots for a moment.

"...Nothing really gives me much joy anymore, that's the problem..."

"Look mate, I'm going to be direct with you." Scott put the cigarette into his mouth. "I'm worried for your wellbeing. A couple weeks ago, Pete told me you were laughing about drowning yourself?" He placed the cigarette on the table. "Today you're joking about shooting yourself. How is any of this, even funny?"

I flipped the channel and the introductory music to the *Twilight Zone* started to play. "I got to check the score..." I looked down at my phone to check a score on a bet I made in college football. Scott looked up at the Georgia Bulldogs flag fixed to the wall above the couch.

"How are they doing?"

"We're undefeated." I took a sip from a cold bottle of Budweiser.

"Does that make you happy?"

"Yea..." I shrugged my shoulders.

"It doesn't sound it..." He shook his head. "You love that team, I thought you'd be off your bark."

"I am not just in a good frame of mind, at this point, so I can't enjoy it as I'd like to..."

The opening scenes of the episode showed a man sitting on a train glancing out the window at the snow. It was the episode *A Stop at Willoughby;* apt for the conversation.

"This is a good one right here..." I pointed at the television.

"Isn't this the one with the lad like you who wanted to go back into the 1800's?" He looked at me out of the corner of his eye.

"There's more to it than that..." I took another sip of beer.

"Yea, he threw himself from a train and killed himself..."

A lump formed in my throat; tears were forming behind my eyes. I felt lost and alone, in a whirlpool, struggling to tread water. I didn't even have the energy to engage in this deep of a conversation, I just wanted be to left alone; I wanted to go back to sleep even if it was something, I was no longer particularly good at doing.

Often, I woke up in the middle of the night and stared at the ceiling, asking myself is that how it was always going to be? The constant thought that raced through my head. I didn't care about turning 30 because I was already decaying from within. I wanted to cry but I couldn't do it then and there, that's the problem, many people can't deal with emotions. If I let it all out, they would probably take it the wrong way. I might as well be talking to a brick wall at that point. But ergo, maybe he would at least understand what I was trying to say.

"In his dream, he wanted to live in Willoughby because he was suffering and he just wanted to escape..."

"Is that what you want to do?"

"What kind of a question is that?" I got to my feet and he followed.

"Is that why you stay in this flat for days on end?"

"I don't like to be around people. No one understands me."

He put the cigarette back in his mouth.

"I am sick and tired of this crap." I took hold of the bottle and took a big swig. "Before she left me, Rachel told me I should go back in my time machine." My arms tensed. "Maybe, I should, as it would leave us all happier!"

"She didn't leave you; she was through with emotionally abusing you..."

"Is she emotionally abusing her new boyfriend?"

He shrugged his shoulders. "What does it matter?"

"Well what if it was me..." I itched my scruff. "What if I wasn't good enough?"

"That wasn't the issue, mate. It never is with her type."

"She wasn't my type..." I shrugged my shoulders and a laugh escaped from me. It wasn't a laugh of enjoyment but one of masked pain, to help me deal with the conflicts swirling inside me.

"No, she wasn't...." Scott chuckled. "But then again there is no one like that around here, mate." He pointed at the television of a woman walking across a lawn in a bustled skirt and a bodice with a parasol. She was a woman from the nineteenth century.

"Imagine if there was..." I laughed. "...could you imagine if I met some woman like that and I fell in love with her?" I glanced at the television and my imagination started to create scenarios that warmed my spirit, providing me a brief reprieve from this despaired and distraught state I was trapped in. "None of these idiots who say I am too nice and worship these assholes who hit them and have five kids to four different women because they watched *Beauty and the Beast*, one too many times when they were little..." I shut my eyes and took a deep breath to quell the rage building within me. "No..." I moved my head to the side. "...just a lovely lady like that..." I pointed at the television. "...arm in arm, as we go for a stroll on a sunny late afternoon..." A smile filled my face as I sat back down "...the thought of it seems incredible..." I placed my feet back up on the coffee table. "...Praise God, it would be a miracle; it would be a dream come true..."

"Well, I hope you do, it might just sort you out..." He put his coat on. "Anyways, I'm going to shoot off, mate."

"Alright then." I feigned a brief smile. "Thanks for coming..."

He made his way to the steps and he turned back to look at me. "I know you're lonely but that Rachel was never the answer, mate." He glanced at the television and the Victorian woman was on the screen standing by a bandstand, a smile broke from his face. "You'll be a different man the moment that you meet someone extraordinary and you won't even realise it." His smile grew wider. "It'll be a day you'll never want to forget." He chuckled. "...you might just write about it..." He made his way toward the steps. I watched him go and heard each of his steps down the stairs until the door creaked open and closed behind him. It was then I started to think about it all again. Everyone had careers, lovers, kids, as if they were a part of something grand and larger than them. And there I was, unable to make it out of the house on some days, melancholic and severely depressed. All I could do is drink and step out for a smoke, if I had the energy. Some days I was too lethargic to clean the dishes or mop the floors. This is not who I was but it is who I have become. I needed to find a way out, I needed to escape this reality.

I always wanted to be a writer but I couldn't even get on stage to share my work. It wasn't the fear of public speaking; I could do that in my sleep. It was being around people drunk and loud with false bravado. I wanted to fight them because I was sick of them and their lack of values. Out getting wrecked on booze and drugs when they had kids to tend to. People like Rachel who showed no affection to their partners and mutts who didn't even understand the concept of walking a woman to the door. But then again women like Rachel and many others didn't like it when I did so. I was an outcast and despite the grand acclamations that people offered to try to re-assure me, I could see through them. I could see the lies. Because despite the words, their actions contradicted them. I wanted to write a novel, but in the fog, I struggled to even form sentences on paper. I needed inspiration, I needed a spark, something to pull me from this crag of mire and sorrow. I prayed to The Lord, begging him to please show me the way out.

I collapsed onto the couch, clutching my head as I wept out loud but no one was there. I was alone in the dark and cold flat, feeling trapped. *Country Club* by Scott Joplin was playing in the background on the television. My heart started to beat out of my chest, my pulse throbbing like pendulum. I launched the bottle against the wall and it put a hole through the plaster. Upon the impact of the shattered bottle, I flipped the coffee table and went into my bedroom, slamming the door behind me. I had fallen dizzy and fell on top of the duvet with one of my legs dangling off the bed; I was done with this world.

Staring at all the pictures of the women from the nineteenth century, having a day by the beach or the older paintings of women in the National Trust houses: that's what I wanted; to be a gentleman and take care of a family.

I didn't want to spend the rest of my life as a miserable hermit that never fit anywhere; who was maligned and left to rot in a small, cramped, and chilly flat. All that feel-good stuff you read on the pamphlets, I felt as if it were utterly useless as it didn't apply to me! I must have been exempt and thus I had to do something!

There was a rather large and sharp cutting knife stored in the clutter in the kitchenette but I wasn't sure if it would get the job done. I could stab as much as I'd like but it'd take hours to bleed out, if it even worked. To be impulsive would have done more harm than good, I had to plan this so this was done right. I had to figure out a way how I could set myself free and be at peace. How could I even be thinking this way? Surely, a normal person would be terrified at the notion and yet I was in careful deliberation on the matter. Guilt washed over me; how could I even think of such a thing?

The remorse followed as a thousand thoughts continued through my head; I didn't really want to make such a destructive decision, I felt fearful that I didn't or wouldn't have a choice. I prayed to The Lord and asked He would forgive me and that He would help me. *Please stop the agony and help me sort through all of this; please stop the thoughts, so I can breathe.*

The noradrenaline had started to take effect and the dose was voluminous to counter the rage that had been surging within me. With my last ounce of energy, I reached to put on the alarm clock radio, classical music was playing. It was Beethoven's *Romance in F Major*. I was starting to drift away, my face pressing into the pillow as I started to settle. Finally, I curled up in a ball, turned over, and fell asleep.

3.

There was a knock at the door, my eyes flung open. A tightness filled my chest, pressing my body to my bed as I glanced at the window; raindrops pattered against it. I didn't want to get up, all I wanted to do was sleep, perhaps I could escape the palpitations; the sense of impending doom. *She Don't Care About Time* was playing on the clock radio, my fingers trembled as I reached tap off the clock radio.

Another knock, it had an elegant and rhythmic cadence. Nevertheless, all I could do is think about the menacing thoughts that started to stir in my head. I closed my eyes again with a hope I could flush them away. If there was no third knock, maybe I could make a run for it and escape from my flat and thoughts.

I JOGGED INTO THE RAIN and a steam of mist sprayed against my face with every stride I took. I sprinted onto the wet cobblestone street that extended to the block of flats where my friend Scott resided. Water trickled toward the sewers, splashing against the steps at the entrance to the block of flats. My fingers slammed against the buzzer panel. My eyes streamed left then right, no buzz, or answer on the intercom. I pressed the button again...still no answer.

I couldn't stand there and wait around. A sense of doom stalked me and I was trying to get away from it. My eyes prowled for a refuge. They halted at the sight of the footbridge that extended over a canal which led into grassy pastures. I threw on some headphones,

Debussy's *Arabesque No. 1* started to play, music fitting for the occasion. Then, I took the first step and did not stop. Hours had passed; I continued along the tributary and had no plans of letting up until it led me somewhere, I felt like I could breathe again. Until, I could find a place of relief.

I passed smokestacks, meadows, towns, and tunnels in a random assortment. The further I got from where I had started, the more I felt a combination of solace and uneasiness. It was an odd counterbalance that sent my mind into backflips. I couldn't be at home, I couldn't be alone, and I couldn't be with myself. Echoes of my thoughts haunted me at every turn. *"You were never good enough, you are nothing, you will always be alone, and you are going to die a horrible death."* These words meandered through my mind since I was young, when I learned about what could happen to me when I got older as a result of my diabetes. There are still other experiences that I struggle to still even think about let alone convey in any form of composition. All sprinted by as if they were a series of short movies; episodes in a chronicle; links in a chain fence that locked me in a cage.

As I passed Romiley, the skies cleared to an azure blue, and the sun bathed the footpath in warmth. The sound of drizzling rain against the foliage-filled trees was replaced by the chirps of the birds. The nasty thoughts in my head were subdued by the whistling of the River Goyt which meandered down the ridge. The mills, woodlands, and farms all went by in a blur until I came to a 200-year old aqueduct that provided a picturesque view of the hills, woods, and river below. I stopped for a moment to take in the kaleidoscopic view of red, orange, yellow, and brown scattered across the tree line.

I spat into the air and counted ten seconds before it landed in the river below. If someone were to jump to off, it would have been long enough for them to reflect on their decision. I read that often unless it is instantaneous, that falling from a height fills the actor with regret. The actors know they are plummeting to likely their death and regret jumping. I reflected and thought that would likely be the case with me, just like if I had stabbed myself to death in the bedroom, last night. I would know and have to come to grips with the fact that I did this to myself in the heat of the moment because I just wanted to pain to stop.

Nevertheless, tightness crushed my chest, my knees felt ready to buckle; I about-faced and took in a view of a farmhouse nestled between the arches of the adjacent rail viaduct. That must be lovely place to live, I thought. I envisioned it being like paradise if I were there with a woman that I was madly in love with and a baby girl that would be a resemblance of her mother. The thought brought a smile to my face as it seemed so foreign to me. My mind convinced me it was never going to happen and that I didn't deserve it. It all seemed like a dream to me, maybe something that could only occur in an alternate reality. In that moment, the temptation to jump off the aqueduct overwhelmed my mind; perhaps then I could find out if the theory held true. *Just do it.* The words repeated like a beating drum.

However, something compelled me to keep walking. I followed the compulsion, unsure of where it would take me, perhaps to a parallel reality where I didn't feel woozy, lethargic, panicky, and crippled by melancholy.

Just outside the town of Marple, I came to an empty bench that sat across from a rolling grassy clearing. Though it was a quiet stretch in the middle of nowhere, it loudly called my name. I took a seat and looked at the brick bridge that stretched over the canal and the stone cottage that stood behind it. Scott Joplin's *Maple Leaf Rag* was playing in my headphones and it fit the scene, as it felt as if I had gone back 100 years (in a good way). Nevertheless, I removed my headphones, and threw a Marlboro into my mouth. I lit the cigarette with a hope that it would help me overcome a nervousness that felt like it could pummel the greatest of warriors into submission. Feelings of hopelessness, helplessness, and peril had once again begun to stir. I had walked so far and had no idea how I was even getting back, not that I cared though. My eyes fled from the rolling lime green hill in front of me toward the water, searching for serenity in between the wind-blown ripples.

Geese glided across the top of the water in no particular formation, circumnavigating the autumn-coloured leaves that fell into the canal. The dark clouds, the chilling wind, and the intermittent rain that pursued me most of the day seemed to be a distant memory, even if my mind did not match the sunny conditions. My head throbbed as a vertigo filled me; I started to feel faint.

I plucked some pages of *The Lady of The Shroud* from my coat pocket and re-read the pages where Rupert declared his love for Teuta and his willingness to do anything to be with her. It made me think of *The Tenant of Wildfell Hall* and how I respected Gilbert Markham and his passion for Helen Graham. I longed to be in a similar situation. If only...

Steps clattered against the cobblestone path. I looked up toward the brick bridge that went over the canal and emerging from the shadows was a woman.

The pages fell out of my hand as I made eye contact with her; Her hair was long and flowing, dipped in a beautiful copper-red auburn shade. It fell down her back and toward her chest with the same elegance and grace that matched her steps. Her bright round eyes were a piercing blue that sparkled with life and hope. She had a fair, soft, delicate, gentle, flawless, and doll-like complexion. Her heart-shaped face was accented by defined dimples and cheeks sprinkled in a rosy colour. A cute Roman nose complemented a dignified yet warm smile whose charm and sweetness could not be concealed from behind her plump ruby cupid's bow lips. Her face looked like it would belong in a painting from the nineteenth century. Without a doubt, I had seen her in my dreams before. Her gaze itself, saw right through me; she was the most beautiful creature I had ever seen.

She moved graceful and elegantly, Schubert's *Klaivestruck No.2 D 946* played loudly in my head to score each step she took. The woman had a bell-shaped waist and a shapely hour-glass figure; perceptible underneath her white long-sleeve buttoned-up blouse and long navy skirt. She draped a violet wool coat over her arm which matched the bow that descended from around her neck. At that very moment, sunlight seemed to bounce off the exposed areas of her porcelain skin as if the sun were made to revolve around her, not the Earth. From head to toe, her beauty was matchless. The vintage and conservative aesthetic to what she wore only enhanced it.

Despite her overpowering magnificence, the woman had a calming and comforting presence about her, as if I was home wherever she stood. It was only minutes ago I was contemplating falling off the aqueduct and I was grateful I kept walking in this direction. Imagine if I hadn't...

"Lord, how does she even exist?" I exhaled the smoke in the opposite direction hoping it would dissipate before she walked past. Let her go past? I would regret that forever, I had to speak with her. I felt that I had been waiting my entire life to meet her, as if my soul could exclaim it from the top of the hill, across the canal. Normally, I can be very shy and timid but, in this situation, I knew I had to be bold and dig deep. She aroused all of the passion and ferocity, long buried within me, something I thought no longer lived within me.

A wind blew as she neared and those pages from the Bram Stoker novel flew into the canal. I asked myself should I ask her for directions and pretend to be lost (technically I was)? Maybe I should try the straightforward approach. Yeah! That always works.

The woman looked at me again and her glance had an uncanny ability to take my breath and make my heart feel like it was going to run out of my chest. Though I had never met her nor had I ever seen her before, I felt like I knew her forever. I had fallen head over heels for her and didn't even know her name. I had not said one word to her but I saw myself marrying this woman; truly it was love at first sight...

I hadn't even noticed that the cigarette started to burn between my fingers until I thought about taking a drag from being so overwhelmed by her presence. However, I had to stand tall, this was the moment.

I did a cross to The Lord and rose from the bench, dropping the cigarette on the ground before stepping on it. I couldn't back down, there was too much at stake here. I had felt a loser most of my life but on that day, I knew I was going to win or die trying, if there was ever a time to succeed, this had to be it.

"Excuse me, ma'am."

"Good afternoon." She stopped. "How do you do, sir?"

"Sir?" I raised my eyebrows. "Wow, your cordiality is humbling, Madame..."

She nodded her head slightly with a warm smile.

"I am okay, thank you for asking, and you?"

"Just off for a ramble." She flicked her eyebrows.

"Anyways, I am sorry to bother you but..."

She smiled. "I am not mithered, love."

I took a deep breath. "I don't normally do this kind of thing. But I saw you walking along here and I just wanted to say hello to you..."

She raised her eyebrows. "That is incredibly sweet of you." Her friendliness came through her smile. "Well, hello then..."

"I also wanted to tell you that you are honestly the most beautiful woman I have ever seen walking on The Good Lord's Earth..." I winced at the thought that the delivery was rushed and atrocious. Assuredly, she'd think I am some goon trying it on with her.

We locked eyes for a moment and I hoped she could read my mind and know I was speaking straight from the heart. I was already in the stage of planning to counter any contempt; in the event she was affronted. I was going to wait ten more seconds and if she said nothing, I would explain myself. As I formed my alibi, a white handkerchief fell from her hands.

"Allow me", I knelt down to pick up the handkerchief and placed it in her hand. The exchange in itself sent sparks through my veins. "I apologise for being so forward..." I looked into her eyes. "...you are very beautiful."

"I am flattered beyond measure, that was quite the compliment..." She looked at me out of the corner of her eye as she clutched the handkerchief. "...I take it this is how you greet all the maidens, yes?"

Her voice was like velvet to my ears. She had a very old-fashioned and polished accent. This woman did not sound like she was from Manchester; she sounded as if she were from an entirely different part of England. It was regal in how she spoke, it reminded me of Amelia Gabble from *Aristocats*.

"No..." I shook my head. "To be honest, I am a nervous shit most of the time." I covered my mouth. "Sorry, I didn't mean to curse."

She laughed and shook her head for a moment. "Preoccupied about vulgarity in the presence of a lady? I take it you are quite the gentleman then, aren't you?"

"I try to be..."

"You know that..." She pointed at cigarette which I stepped on before initiating. "is really poor for your health..."

"You are right and for the record, I don't litter either; I'll pick that up before I go..."

"Very well, there is a rubbish bin, right there." She smiled as her thumb pointed toward the receptacle.

"Normally, I don't smoke." I scratched the back of my head. "Just having a really bad day to be honest..."

"I am terribly sorry to hear that. I do hope it gets better for you."

I looked at her and took a deep breath. "It's gotten a lot better now." Heat rushed to my cheeks.

"You have a silver tongue." She blushed.

"I don't..." I laughed nervously. "...Look, I am sure you get this a lot but I was just hoping somehow that I could strike up a conversation with you, you'd see I am not a maniac, and maybe if I am so blessed I could take you for coffee and we can talk..."

She went quiet.

"...you seem like a really nice woman, so..." I shrugged my shoulders which I am sure were hunched from all the tension flowing through me. The woman peered at me as if I was a book, she was reading for the first time.

"Coffee?" She crossed her arms. "Where is your accent from?" Her eyes seemed to sparkle with interest. To my surprise and my delight, it appeared she was enjoying the conversation.

"Birmingham."

"Oh, come off it, if I were to estimate I would say you are from New York."

My eyes bulged, amazed at the pinpoint accuracy in her response. "How did you know that?"

"I have my ways." She smiled. "Perchance it was the manner in which you said coffee. It was awfully archetypal."

"You got me." I raised my hands. "I am not a fan of it because I sound like a mutant."

"Don't be daft. It's lovely, dear." She reached into her pocket, removing a sapphire-coloured butterfly bobby-pin. The woman swayed for a moment, appearing lost in a brief reverie as she clutched it. "So, what brings you up this way?" She placed the accessory back in her pocket, as if she were pausing whatever story was attached to the artefact.

"Just started walking and here I am."

"From where?" Her eyes locked in on me.

"Near Audenshaw."

"That's quite a journey, you must be exhausted."

"It all started with a load of classical music and a bit of Oasis mixed in..." I took of my glasses. "...next thing I know I am here speaking to you."

"You don't say." She chuckled. "Oasis are one of my favourite bands."

"I always loved *Hung in a Bad Place*..." My fingers wiped the lens of my glasses.

She broke a smile as if she were chatting with her long lest best friend. All I could do is stare at her, I felt as if I was going to lose my breath and thankfully it wasn't a panic attack or asthma-related.

"The lyrics really resonate with me, Madame." I forced myself out of the gawk to keep the conversation going.

"I can appreciate that as I have had the same experience." Her eyes softened to where she gazed at me with gentleness. "So, you walked here on your own?"

I nodded and looked down for a minute, briefly struck by shame and embarrassment. "I am on my own more than I like..."

"I've been alone for time now..." She looked into the water. "...I've grown accustomed to it." Her tone of voice accentuated the misery attached to the statement.

"I find that surprising considering you could light up any room you walked into."

"Thank you dearly..." She lit up as she looked back at me. "...incidentally, I've been New York before."

"And how did you like it?"

"I found that it was not as I had expected. Not to slate it and offer any offence." She put her hands up to make a stop sign to indicate she didn't mean to be condescending.

"None taken, it's a cesspool."

White teeth escaped from behind her lips until her fingers slowly cupped over them. Her shoulders jostled from the laughter.

"Besides what can top all this beauty we have around us here?" I waved my hands toward the sight of the rolling hills of farm land behind the canal.

"It is truly remarkable that in just twenty minutes on a train you can find yourself in the midst of Manchester. When I was a child, Rose Hill wasn't constructed yet so if you fancied coming around you would have had to hire a horse-drawn carriage."

I laughed at the incredulous remark. It seemed she had a penchant for sarcasm and hyperbole. "I don't know the history of Rose Hill Station, so I wouldn't know... "

"I suppose you can say, I have lived it." Her eyes twinkled back at me as she let out a brief giggle.

"So, you are from Manchester originally?"

"I lived in Ardwick when I was young but spent my formative years in London."

"And how did you end up here?"

A gloominess seemed to cast over her eyes then. "Ultimately, I was hired by a family to teach and look after their children."

"So, like a live-in nanny?"

She shook her head with a smile. "More like a governess." She looked back as if she staring back into the past. "Such a lovely family, they used to live over the hill there..." Her eyes stared into the canal. "The lady of the house treated me as if I were her own child."

"That's awesome, are you still in touch with them?"

"I outgrew my purpose..." Her eyes pained of loss until she feigned a smile. "Besides, I am a London girl at heart." Her eyes brightened. "I did have some exciting adventures there..."

"Well that explains why you sound like you are from the Victorian era..."

She paused for a moment and stroked her hair with a nervousness.

"That's mean to be a big compliment, Madame." I raised my hand. "Would you care to share any of your adventures in London that you mentioned?"

"...Do you know where they send all the hungry people in Warwickshire?"

Though she was trying to play it off, it was obvious that something suddenly made her uncomfortable, so I rolled with the joke. I shrugged my shoulders to elicit the answer to her riddle.

"Nuneaton." Her tongue poked its head from behind her ivory white teeth.

I laughed. "Should have sent them to Sandwich."

Her hair wrapped around her fingers as her eyes gleamed toward the sun.

"I am sorry we have been talking up a storm here but I don't believe I got your name".

"I am called Temperance." She curtsied with a slight bow. "Formally, Miss Temperance Grace Lee."

I told her my name and extended my hand towards her. She exuded the same grace when she took my hand, my knees felt like they were going to buckle. "Well, Miss Lee that is a beautiful name, very vintage..."

"Thank you. It has gone rather off-coloured."

"There is a street over in Ardwick named Temperance Street. They must have named it after you the moment you blessed them with your presence."

"Whilst I am honoured by the suggestion, I do not suppose that is the case I am afraid." Temperance smiled. "Incidentally, there is a street just off Hollins Lane that bears my given name. It is called Temperance Terrace, actually." She chuckled. "It hides in plain sight, much like myself." Temperance winked. "Not that I had a thing to do with its naming, of course..."

"I think they knew you were here..." I smirked. "I like it though, a nice alliteration ring to it..."

"To be fair, I prefer my Christian name that I acquired when I had seven years."

"Which is?"

"Elizabeth.

"That's the name of royalty, my lady." I nodded. "Also, one of my personal favourites..."

She brushed a stand of her hair which blew in the wind.

"...I am sorry if I am bit off the cuff by the way. I tend to say what I feel and I am bit of a hopeless romantic, so you'll have to forgive me. So many have told me to go in a time machine back to the 1800's. Only appropriate that now I meet a woman with a Victorian-era accent and a name prevalent during that period for that matter..." I chuckled. "...what are the odds of that?"

When I said that, she looked at me differently. As if I struck a chord with her, like I had known something about her that others didn't.

"...Truth be told; Victorian women are the greatest, I am their biggest fan."

She covered her mouth as she let out a brief laugh though I didn't mean to be comedic. "How many years have you?"

"I just turned 30, I don't look it nor feel it though."

"No, you do not at all. I would have estimated four and twenty." She looked me up and down. Electricity started to flow through my veins. Like the duck that made its way down the canal beside us, I too was calm on the surface but paddling like crazy beneath.

"Thank you very much."

"I doubt you will be able to guess mine." She swayed from the right to left as she crossed her arms.

"Turning 25."

"That's awfully kind of you."

"I know I am not supposed to ever ask a woman's age but now I am curious."

"Are you certain you wish to know?"

"Since there is so much suspense, now I feel like I have to."

"I turned 162 on the 15th of July." She had a really cheeky smile on her face when she said it. "Congratulations sir, you've finally met your Victorian woman."

"Well, let me tell you a secret." I looked left and right as if I didn't want anyone else to hear what I was going to tell her. "Truthfully, I've been around for like a thousand years, don't tell anybody, ight?"

"Oh, have you?" She bantered. "Having a laugh here, are we?" A smirked formed at her face. I thought to myself Miss Lee had a wicked sense of humour and found her utterly hilarious. I couldn't help but join in with the jokes.

"I used to be a firefighter in New York and they always told us that every time you put out a job, you get a hundred years added to your life..." I opened my hands and shot a playful smile.

"A millennia-old fireman from New York sitting near a field outside Marple. That's almost as incredulous as me being born in the year of our Lord, eighteen-hundred and fifty-five."

"I am not a firefighter, anymore..." I swallowed hard.

"Given your intonation, I gather you are very unhappy about that." Her eyes softened with empathy.

"I am a juvenile diabetic so I am disqualified from doing it over here."

"I see..." Temperance's eyes illuminated again. "So, have you come all this way to find me?"

I found it striking how Miss Lee could be polite yet direct; she could be demure yet fiery; she had an old-fashioned energy about her and seemed very genteel, yet there was a strength and resolve to her.

"Yep..."

Her eyebrows shot upward at the casualness and authenticity of my response. She grew reserved and her body language shifted, as if she were analysing me again. "...and you came all this way on your own?

I nodded. "And it was clearly worth it...." I opened my hand in her direction. A smile carved across her face when she looked back at me.

"...and since we know so much about one another Miss Lee, we best keep each other's secrets." A smile returned to my face.

"Please call me Temperance." She snickered. "Tempie, for short. Though none have called me that since I was a child..."

"Well, I must say Temperance, for a woman that has lived across three centuries, you age like wine..."

She rolled her eyes and stretched her arms, my eyes wandered down her chest toward her midsection until the snapping of a finger halted the diversion.

"Shouldn't you be looking up here, mate?" Her tone was stern.

"I am really sorry about that..." I raised my hands in defence. "...you have a really nice stomach..."

"I am chuffed that you are impressed by it."

"It looks strong too..."

She glanced downward toward her midsection. "I can't say I've ever been complimented in such a way before." Temperance looked upward with a childish grin on her face. "Are you for one tummy-buttons too?"

I was nervous beyond belief, hoping I could go with the flow and not make a mockery of myself as to thinking too much as to what say. "...I am...."

She raised her eyebrows. "I take it you fancy an innie then?"

"I am sure it looks fantastic."

Her returning smile proved evident that she was having fun in getting a rise out of me. I couldn't respond, instead I smiled back as I was all the more bashful.

"So, you are a hopeless romantic that wishes to court a Victorian English woman whilst also having a fetish for abdominal muscles." She rubbed her lip. "I must be the lady of your dreams, then."

"You are." It flew from my lips and I was quick to bite my lip after due to the tension created by my unrelenting compliments. I couldn't help it though, Temperance brought it out of me so effortlessly.

Nevertheless, in that moment, her playful smile and glimmering eyes softened. It was as if I said that something that went straight to her heart. "Well sir, I hope that is the only form of navel-gazing you engage in." She shined with a youthful energy which radiated from her eyes. "Otherwise you might miss out."

"You are right, Miss Lee."

"Temperance." She lowered her chin toward me.

"I mean Temperance...."

"Tempie..." Her innocent and youthful laugh filled the air, a delight to listen to as it was filled with joy and child-like merriment. "Apologies, I couldn't help but wind you up a bit. That does not seem all too difficult with you."

She was right, I am easily excitable. Needless to say, my heart was racing at this point.

"So where were you going before our conversation?"

"Are you referring to the course of events prior to your impertinent interruption?" She winked. "I am done ribbing you now,

I promise." Temperance stroked a strand of her hair. "I was finishing my walk and planning to nip into ASDA for a shop."

"If you have no objections, I'd be happy to walk you to ASDA." I placed my hand out so I could carry her coat for her.

"I am much obliged but I do not require an escort."

"To be completely honest, it's an excuse to talk to you some more."

Her cheeks sparkled with scarlet. "I see..." There was an ambivalence to her reply "...I am humbled really." She grabbed hold of her coat draped over her forearm which had begun to slide off. "And what did you wish to speak about?"

"Tell me something unique about yourself..."

"Are you certain you wish to venture there?"

"Definitely." I smiled. "For example, I am a writer, if I could do anything in the world it would be to write poems and novels, among other things..."

"I am so glad you said that." Her coat found its way into my hand. "I write too, you see." Her hand fell to her hip. "I have been working on a bit of an autobiographical project for donkey's years now."

"That sounds cool, have you shown it to anyone?"

"Gutted, I cannot say I have."

"Well if you would like to talk about it more, I am happy to listen." I extended my hand to her. "So, may I accompany you please?" I emphasised escort in a humorous accent.

She stared at me, her eyes squinting as if she trying to make out the small print in the book she was already reading. "Come along then." She replied with a demure accent.

4.

I reflected back to the horrible thoughts that had overcome me just minutes before I encountered Temperance. "I was feeling hopeless but now I feel as if I won the lottery."

"You are not hopeless." Temperance looked into my eyes like she had known me forever. "I would conclude that you hope more than most, care more than many, and are tired from a scourge of disappointment and heartache. It's evident you wear it all on your sleeve and your valour isn't strictly utilised in romantic pursuits either." In the gentleness that poured from her cerulean irises, I felt understood; I felt at peace.

"You seem to have the wisdom of a creature as old as time."

Temperance peered out me out of the corner of her eye, a brief tension filled the air.

"...along with an ability to read minds." I smiled. "Do you have superpowers, too?"

"Your assessment is practically spot on." Her cheeks reddened more as she smiled warmly. We continued onward down the canal and talked about some of our other hobbies and interests. We also had a vivid discussion on Victorian literature and it seemed Miss Temperance Lee was an expert on it. I found it enchanting considering she had the all makings of a heroine you would find in a Bronte Sisters novel.

After I accompanied Temperance to the ASDA, I walked her home and carried her groceries for her every step of the way. I didn't know what to expect as I took my first step onto a narrow lane that was hugged by a long line of two-up two-down houses built in the late nineteenth century. The lane ran parallel to a canal that meandered all the way to Derbyshire. In between the lane and the canal was a large emerald-coloured pasture where wood pigeons and black crows perched for a moment of respite. A footpath accompanied the canal, illuminated by Edwardian gas lamps. Across from it, a boat launch. Beyond the canal were more green fields that could be seen stretching for miles over valleys and hills.

"I'd like to thank you for today." Temperance stood at her gate and extended her hand to me. An agony overcame me; I didn't want to leave. I feigned a smile and looked into the canal for a moment.

"At first, I suspected you were a right charmer but you are quite chivalrous."

"I wish I were a charmer. Even now I am incredibly nervous speaking to you."

Her arm gripped my bicep. "Why? I am not going to maul you..." She looked out of the corner of her eye "...yet." A smirk unravelled her across her face.

"You know I would have been crushed, if you said no to all this." I laughed. "But then again, I don't think I would ever give up until you said yes..."

She raised her eyebrows.

"...nevertheless, thank you for giving me a chance..."

"I didn't think any of you lot exist anymore, likely aroused at the sight of a woman's ankles." Temperance's cheeks were flushed. "Albeit, navels in your case." She chuckled as opened the gate, I followed her to her front door with her grocery bags in my arms.

"I thought you were done messing with me?" I played along.

"Very well, no more comments from me concerning your knavish obsession with obscure body parts." She placed the key into a mortise lock and turned it to open the blue front door. Temperance turned to look at me and I stood at attention, hoping this wouldn't be a farewell after I carried her groceries in.

"Would you like to stay for a cup of a tea?"

Joy washed across me at her invitation, Temperance illuminated in response to the elation I could not hide.

"I'd love to." I clutched the grocery bags in hand.

"Come in, please." She stepped inside. "Did you know that this used to serve as housing for all the labourers that worked in a lime kiln that once stood across that canal?"

"...No, I didn't."

"I worked at a mill not much farther afield whilst it was still in operation."

It was fascinating to hear Temperance's anecdotes as it was like she was an artefact of the area, knowing the intricate histories from an intimate perspective.

"What was that like?" I placed the grocery bags on a floral pattern doormat and shut the door behind me.

"I don't give it much thought. It was ages ago." She placed her key in the lock and ensured the door was locked. "It burned to the ground, but it should have been shut. So many grafters were overcome with mercury poisoning..." Her steps thundered across the floor. "Lest we forget the trendy arsenic wallpaper found in many offices."

"Astonishing, since I thought arsenic wallpaper was banned prior to the twentieth century." I lifted up the groceries and surveyed the house. On my left, there was one door with a red placard on it saying "Water Closet". It looked as if it was taken off of a train that had been placed out of service decades ago. There was an oak staircase directly in front with one a door at the top of the steps which was also shut. I assumed that was her bedroom. To the right through the second door we came through was essentially one large room; divided into a sitting area, dining area, and kitchen area. A huge window was the focal point as it offered a flawless vista. When the sky was clear you could see deep into the hills and valleys for miles.

"Go have a seat over there, please."

"Thank you." I made my way toward a lime green sofa that was pitched against the wall. It looked like a piece of furniture that would be seen in a parlour or sitting room from a Georgian townhouse. On the wall, directly above the couch was a Union Jack that looked to be at least 100 years old but it was in extraordinary condition. The colour had faded a bit but there were no scuffs or tears in the fabric and it wasn't made of synthetic fabrics like most flags were made of today. This was all cotton with each stripe sewn on with larger threading. Despite the rarity and age of such an item, it was still in pristine condition.

To the left near the window, there was a matching dining table that sat four people. Across from me stood a bookshelf that displayed a bunch of memorabilia from events and places spanning 150 years. The first thing that struck my attention was an autographed baseball.

"Say, Temperance."

"Remember, you can call me Tempie darling."

"Do you like baseball?"

"I prefer footy me but that ball is a collectible."

"So, you collect antiques?

"That ball there is signed by a lass called Helene." She took hold of the metallic pot as it bubbled. "She signed it on the day she became the owner of the St. Louis Cardinals, you see."

"That was in 1911."

"I recollect the new departure that The Birds on The Bat were the first team in the all of professional sports to have a woman as its owner and operator. I felt inclined to offer my support to her...."

I inspected the ball closely; the colour had faded from the normal ivory white that baseballs had when they were fresh out the box. The ink was dried blotches of pigmentation on the ball's sepia shell. "It must have been hard to get your hands on this given that was over a hundred years ago."

She swung her hair around and shot me a smile. "It was not as difficult as you imagine."

I placed the ball back on the shelf and looked down at a crate of albums. The collection featured Pink Floyd, all four Led Zeppelin albums, along with Bob Marley and The Beatles. At the front of the set was *Abbey Road*.

"Are those records originals?" I glanced back at Temperance as she poured boiling water into two tea cups from a tarnished copper tea-kettle.

"Yes, I found them when I had a browse in the music store." She stirred the cups. "Quite a lucrative investment I made, me. I had not the slightest of inclinations that they would be worth a shilling when I purchased them."

"Well for that to be the case..."

"Never mind any of that for now..." Her feet scuttled across the floor. "...I recall you said you rapped when were in the shop earlier?" She placed a tray down on the coffee table. "You are a man of many talents it seems."

I glanced down at the plate of cakes, sandwiches, and crumpets. "That looks amazing. You sure know how to treat a guest."

She snapped her fingers which caused me to look up at the sight of two crème candles that were somehow burning. I didn't see her grab any matches or use a lighter.

"How did you?" I pointed at the candles.

"I am a magician." She reached for a cucumber sandwich. "Have a nibble."

I grabbed a biscuit.

"Oh dear, it's spitting again." Temperance glanced up at the rain that pattered against the window. "Hopefully, it clears off." She rose from the couch. "Since you were on the subject of music, do you mind if I put something on that I believe we would both like." She walked over toward the dining table and lifted a tablet off of it. "I tell you now, I have never seen such a remarkable invention before." Temperance pressed the tablet and it powered on.

"Is that a touch-screen?"

Temperance raised her eyebrows. "I was rather excited when I finally learned how to use this." She pressed the tablet twice and pointed her fingers at the speakers set up in opposite ends of the room. Music started to play.

"Was that another magic trick or do you have Bluetooth?"

"That's for you to find out." She grabbed another macaron off of the plate. Her hips swayed from side-to-side as she hopped on the couch.

My eyes travelled with her across the room. The chords for Oasis' *She's Electric* continued to play. "Ah yes, this song has...."

"...pure energy." We finished each other's sentence and stared at each other. My heart began to race again.

"Wouldn't it be cool if a woman could actually control electricity?"

"If only you knew." She winked.

"Would you like to dance?" I extended my hand to her. She took my hand with a warm smile and curtsied.

We danced across the sitting room floor, holding each other tight, and giggling like shy teenagers. At one point, she spun like a ballerina and then back to me. We bended downward and gazed into each's others eyes. *Morning Glory* started to play and my emotions became as intense as the opening riffs to the song. I pressed my lips against hers and we kissed.

Her lips had some form of a magical potion in them; they were warm, soft, and hypnotic as if they were a drug themselves. I felt like I was going to faint at any moment, I wanted to continue but Temperance pushed her hand against me.

"I am sorry..."

Temperance glanced at the floor as she caught her breath. "I cannot fathom that it even went that far; it shouldn't have."

"I couldn't help it, I felt like I was being drawn to you." I glanced out the window with both my arms placed upon my knees. "I don't mean to overstep any boundaries..."

"It's not that..." The tremolo in her voice revealed her nervousness. "...Never have I..."

"You've never what?"

She took a deep breath and let out a sigh. "You know..." Her shoulders hunched "...engaged in any form of face-making."

"Face-making? What is that?"

"Not even a brush." She sat beside me on the couch.

I leaned forward and cupped my hands, unsure of what she was hoping to tell me. "What are you trying to say?"

"I have never done this; I have never wed; I am fully in-tact." Her voice rose with each sentence.

"So, you are a virgin?" I leaned back.

She nodded.

"That's it?"

"You are not fussed?"

"Why would I be?" I grazed her arm. "That's the last thing I was thinking about..."

"I assumed you would have wanted more." She sighed. "From what I have always gathered, lads this day and age have a predilection for that sort of amorous congress."

"I am not that kind of dude. But I completely understand that you never had sex before because you haven't met the right person."

"Any person..." She corrected me more sternly. "Notwithstanding in my centuries of existence, I have never experienced any man attempt to court me properly. Grim isn't it?"

"I find that very hard to believe."

"If it were merely fiction." She sulked.

I couldn't imagine why anyone would pass up a chance at this woman even if she was really pushing the Victorian angle, which I admit other than to me would come off as eccentric. However, it made me foam at the mouth and she knew it.

"Temperance, you seem like a wonderful woman. You have such a gentle demeanour and clearly are a lady of high class and morals." I took her hand. "And I am glad that you are. But I didn't come here just to have a one-night stand with you even if you are completely irresistible."

"Thank you for your kind words and your discretion."

"I am glad that we have spent this time together." I smiled at her. "I just want to know even more about you..."

Concern came over Temperance's face, her eyes darted and peered out the window.

"Is everything alright?" I rubbed her fingers with my thumb.

She nodded with a smile. "Peachy." Temperance locked her fingers into mine. "Any roads, have you ever had rhubarb cider?" Her eyes flashed "it is a delightful confection..."

"No, but I would love to take you for one."

"Smashing." She jumped off the couch. "Give us a moment so I can throw on some more suitable attire. Hopefully, it doesn't leather it down." Temperance sped into her bedroom.

That night, Temperance and I walked down to a quaint country style pub around the corner from her home. Hours melted away like the two scoops of ice cream we shared. The serenity and the peace of being with her made time stand still; at the same token, it all went by in minutes. Fortunately, there was always an excuse for us to extend our time together. We conversed until 4:00 AM until I fell asleep on the floor. The next morning, we shared breakfast. Two weeks later, Temperance and I referred to each other as boyfriend and girlfriend.

We became virtually inseparable and did everything together. She met some of my friends and they all thought she was a lovely girl. She came with me when I performed poems and raps; some of which I dedicated to her. I helped Temperance with her errands, her chores, or whatever she else liked to do. We took long walks in the countryside, we went out for day trips, we kissed, we cuddled, and we made each other laugh. We always had a reason to be in each other's company and when we weren't, we were calling each other constantly or sending one another beautiful text messages. It was as if we were made for each other.

Over the time, I didn't meet one friend or family member of hers. I assumed she was a loner but it got to a point where I found it saddening, as it seemed she was actually reclusive. It made no sense to me either, a woman as friendly, charming, and vivacious as her seemingly alone in the world.

5.

I always enjoyed surprising Temperance with a bouquet of her favourite flowers: red roses, lavender, and orchids; it was always worth it to watch her ignite with joy. However, this time the flowers were going to be accompanied by three important words: I love you. I had been dying to tell Temperance. After all, I felt it from the moment I saw her. I had rehearsed all that I wanted to say to her, but overtures will be forgotten upon delivery; I just had to tell her how I feel: that I suffered in silence out of fear of scaring her. Yet, all I wanted was to throw my arms around her, look into her big blue eyes, tell her that she is the greatest thing to ever happen to me, and that I was head-over-heels in love with her. I had to tell her!

My heart pounded as I got out of the car and walked up the lane towards her home. Temperance looked down at me from behind the large window in her bedroom. She wore a ghostly white chemise and smiled at me with a welcoming warmth. I held up the flowers and she responded by making a heart shape with her hands. In that moment, I forgot where I was or remembered to even breathe. She blew a kiss at me and pressed her hands against the window. Her flesh smeared the moisture on the glass until she opened the door for me to come in.

An hour later we were working alongside in the river in the Etherow Country Park. I had planned to lead her to the far exit where there was a view of the valley, Compstall, and Marple. There, I planned to confess my love for Temperance. At that point, I didn't know what I was going to say but I knew I wanted to make the moment as special as possible, sharing it with the most beautiful woman in the entire universe. After that, I was going to take her for a meal at her favourite pub.

Temperance had plaited a part of her hair and let the rest of her crimson-auburn mane fall down her back. My beloved wore a white-coloured satin button-up blouse and a long crimson-coloured skirt. A brooch wrapped around her neck along with a long crimson bow. A single red rose tucked into her hair along with her blue butterfly hair pin. Three pink ribbons tied to the end of her plait. Over her attire, she wore my black bubble coat unzipped.

I swung Temperance's hand back and forth, smiling at her as I did so. "So, you know what you are going to have for supper?"

She giggled. "For starters, I am going to pinch your chips"

"I never got that you have the etiquette to criss-cross your utensils on your plate, refuse to speak while eating, and finish chewing before you cut your vegetables. Then you go and steal my food even when I offer to get you whatever you like."

"And I will always remind you to exhibit such manners."

"Is robbing my grub your way of punishing me?" I chuckled.

"Oh, by no means, Cherry Cake. I don't want my own." She answered demurely. "I fancy yours..."

"Weirdo." I rolled my eyes with a smile.

The footpath widened at a small field that sat along the river. Red picnic tables sat under the cover of birch trees, canvassing the green grass that descended into the rocky river bend. We were alone until we saw a familiar face, my friend Pete.

"Yo!" I put my finger up to the sky with my free hand.

Pete smiled at me as we approached as he pushed a wheelchair with his grandmother sat in it. Her hair billowed from beneath her tan winter hat. A red scarf flicked in the wind as it lay over a matching tan wool coat.

"What's up man? You good?" Temperance and I walked hand-in-hand until we stopped about ten feet in front of the two. Pete seemed pleasantly surprised whilst his grandmother looked like she had just seen a ghost.

"I should have expected to see the both of you, here." Pete smiled. "This is one of our favourite places to go out for a stroll." He nodded at his grandmother. "It's nice to see you out here with her and not up at the aqueduct alone, tormented, and lost in your thoughts."

Temperance's grip of my hand strengthened.

"Temp and I met not too far from there."

"And just like that Marple is no longer a place where your imagination runs wild or your thoughts get the best of you." He smiled at Temperance. "It's nice to see you, Temperance."

I looked at Pete's grandmother. Her dark eyes were fixed on Temperance in a peculiar way.

"Thank you, Peter, it is lovely to see you as well." Temperance curtsied. "Madame." She smiled at Pete's grandmother.

"Hi, Mrs. Davies."

"Hello there, son." She didn't take her eyes off of Tempie. The stare was so obvious that Pete and I both noticed it. However, my beloved did not.

"Sweetheart, I don't believe you have met Mrs. Davies before, correct?"

"That's right, darling." A slight breeze blew some loose strands of hair to the side of her face.

"I believe we have..." Pete's grandmother squinted. "Did you call her Temperance?"

"Indeed, it is a pleasure to earn your acquaintance." Tempie knelt down and extended her hand.

Pete's grandmother flinched. "I don't know if that would be a wise idea since lightning bolts come from your hand." She shot a coy smile.

My beloved became startled and confused.

"Don't mind her, she says wild things all the time."

Mrs. Davies cleared her throat. "Not this time, Peter. This one here has all sorts of supernatural abilities." Her cheeks quivered.

"Temperance, you wouldn't happen to be an illusionist, right?" Pete snickered.

She shook her head. "I've been a millworker, a hatter, seamstress, nurse, governess, and carer but never a performer. That is more up my better half's street." She chuckled but it was to no effect.

"Nana, do you remember how grandfather used to drive a lorry? My mate here used to drive a taxi in New York whilst he was also a firefighter." Pete rubbed his hand through his sandy blonde hair as he awaited his grandmother's reply. It was clear he was trying to divert the subject that was visibly disrupting Temperance.

"Does he now?" Mrs. Davies fixed her eyes on Tempie once again. She appeared a mix of confused, excited, and amazed. "...She looks identical to the Temperance I knew and she was also a nurse..."

Though Mrs. Davies' remarks were not any form of a taunt, my beloved looked terrified as if something buried had just been unearthed. This time, I tried to divert the conversation to ease the tension.

"She writes too you know, Mrs. Davies." My fingers gripped Temperance's waist tight. "Plus, she is incredible at drawing, she's good at playing the harmonica, and she literally sounds like an angel whenever she belts out a ballad."

"You sing?" Pete rocked his head back.

"A lick." She pinched her fingers. "I am not as he describes me. I mean he is a bloke that can form and rap a whole verse by feeding him a few words at random."

"The woman should be centre stage in concert halls. She has the voice to match her out-of-this world beauty."

"That wouldn't be too far off. She is not of this world." Pete's grandmother's eyes lit up. "She used to sing me to sleep when I was just a child."

"Nana, that would be impossible."

Temperance's eyes escaped toward a magpie that landed at the banks of the river. My eyes followed hers to the sight of the bird until a second magpie joined it. The nervous energy poured off of her. Perhaps, the attention was unwanted and overwhelming to Temperance as she was quite the quiet, humble, and modest type.

"Not with her." Pete's grandmother reclined backward. "She's ageless and immortal."

Temperance locked her arm in my mine; I took her hand and felt perspiration drip from her fingers; her pulse throbbed against my wrist. The nature of Mrs Davies' remarks was bizarre but clearly distressing to my lady, it started to anger me.

"What are you talking about, Nana?" He bent down.

"She is the one I was on about when you showed me a photo of them two." Light entered Mrs. Davies' eyes as she inched back to Pete, her grey and wrinkled finger shook as it pointed at my beloved.

Pete shook his head and smiled. "Right, you wouldn't happen to have a distant relative with the same name as you right? I know Temperance is not a common name but you look identical to someone she knew from 90 years ago."

"Does she look 115 years old?" I stepped in front of Temperance.

"I wasn't asking you, mate." Pete chuckled. "I was asking your missus."

"Look the conversation is clearly making her uncomfortable." My hand swept through the air. "Can we knock this off, please?"

"Peter, your mate knows all about it." Mrs. Davies smiled. "He is trying to protect her but there is no fooling me."

"What?" Pete itched his beard.

"I bet she told him about her powers and he is keeping it a secret..." A brief cough fled from her chest. "...these are madly in love with each other, it is awfully obvious. All you have to do is see how they look at one another."

I was suffering to tell her that I was in fact madly in love with her, in fact I was about five minutes away from finally doing so. I could have spilled the beans there but I wanted it to be really special. If Temperance actually loved me back...I wouldn't know what to do.

"You just wait..." Mrs. Davies cupped her hand outward. "He is going to throw all caution to the wind and bid for her hand in marriage."

"What an honour that would be." I replied sternly. "This woman is my best friend after all."

"As you are mine." Temperance's nerves cascaded away in a warm smile. "He is the bee's knees but don't tell him, I said that." She rubbed my finger.

"I am surprised she even has friends, given the secret..."

Temperance's smile and energy evaporated, as if she had just been hit in the gut.

Pete laughed. "My nan says you look identical to a nurse who eerily enough also had your name." His tone shifted to one of irritation. "She worked in a Paediatric Ward at MRI in the 1920's."

"She doesn't look like her Peter, she is her."

"If I may ask, what is your age Mrs. Davies?" Temperance bent down to look at her. And just like that she was composed.

"Ninety-eight, I imagine you won't remember me..."

Temperance reached toward Mrs. Davies' hand on the wheelchair handle.

"Promise not to shock me." She smiled at Temperance.

"Bless you Madame, I won't." Temperance knelt down and smiled warmly at her.

"When I was a little girl I was hospitalised with a case of influenza. There was a bad outbreak when I was seven and I fell poorly."

"I recall..." A murmur escaped under her breath. "About how severe the 1927 epidemic was. At one point, a thousand poor souls perished each week."

"Did you just do that arithmetic now?" Pete looked at Temperance for the first time as if something were off. "That's incredible."

She looked up at Pete. "When I was in nursing, the outbreak frequently discussed in the field for the purpose of quality control and risk assessment."

I glanced at Temperance out of the corner of my eye. Now, I was confused. Temperance had become so calm and grounded after being shaken just a minute ago.

"Obviously, Temperance does not look a day over twenty-four. Clearly, it is some crazy coincidence." Pete looked at me. "It's mad how there are people who have been here before us that bear a striking resemblance and sometimes even have the same name..." He arched his eyebrows. "By curiosity, how old are you Temperance?"

She looked up; the answer frozen on her lips.

"Twenty-eight" I interjected. "She's twenty-eight; Pete, I know with those bright eyes of hers that she doesn't look it..." Though I did not know her actual birthday at that point, I just knew it was July 15th and Temperance is an old-fashioned woman that didn't reveal her age.

Mrs. Davies laughed.

Temperance walked over beside me. "It is truly a delight to hear that someone could have such a positive impact on your nan, that she is remembering them nearly a century later." Her arm pressed against me followed by a reach of her hand.

"From what me nan told me about her previously, this nurse helped her back to health. There was a point where many feared she wasn't going to make it."

"She read me bedtime stories. She also carried around this hand-crank music box and played it to soothe me. I knew all about her powers, it was a secret between us." Mrs. Davies glanced down at the grass as it waived in the breeze. "I always wondered what happened to her and it plagued me to know she was well because she was so lovely to me..."

Pete smacked his side. "We did have a few brandies earlier, so I do apologise..." He paused. "From what I heard this Nurse Temperance was like a superhero."

Tempie clenched my hand. "I bet she is." Her cheeks turned to a rosy coloured. "Nurses generally are..."

"No, I mean the kids used to latch onto her arms all sizes: four, five, six, seven, maybe even eight stone and she would lift them effortlessly."

"Stronger than Vulcana, I tell you." Mrs. Davies interjected.

"She always ate her vegetables?" Temperance feigned a laugh. It was almost as if she were caught in a current and every time, she felt she had escaped it, something pulled her back in. Her smiles and laughs concealed her reticence, it was quite old-fashioned in how she so meekly yet reservedly played off Mrs. Davies' antagonisms, albeit they were clearly unintentional and bereft of any form of malice.

"This nurse was quite agile, athletic, and she could even throw her hat pins with pinpoint accuracy." Pete looked at the river. "She sounds like a real-life Wonder Woman."

Temperance drew her head close to me and covered her mouth. "...I am more like Catwoman or perhaps She-Hulk..."

I looked at her out of the corner of my eye and couldn't help but laugh. "You wouldn't go wrong either." I spoke softly into her ear and winked.

She tittered and patted my cheek.

"Her most remarkable attribute was her warm and compassionate nature." Mrs. Davies smiled at Temperance. "Most with her abilities would likely do unimaginable things. Not her though..." Mrs. Davies glanced at a grey squirrel dashing by the river bank. "...always so affectionate to children and animals; always so respectful to others..."

"So, what happened exactly, Nana?" Pete's hands slid into his pockets.

Mrs. Davies shrugged her shoulders. "She gave her notice, donated all her wages to the homeless, and vanished without a trace..." Mrs. Davies winked at Temperance.

The air went silent again though my lady's pulse thundered against my wrist once more. These fantastical remarks seemed to antagonise and unsettle her. The chimes of a cell phone broke the silence. Pete plucked a phone from his trousers. "It's Caz, she's waiting on us." He slid his phone back into his pocket. "We are going to have to set off."

"Let's leave them two lovebirds to it, Peter." Mrs Davies smiled at both of us. "It was nice to see you both." She turned her sights to Temperance exclusively. "Though it would be classed as scandalous in your day, I would be honoured if a lad eighty years my junior was devoted to me like he is to you, Temperance."

"Mrs. Davies, these remarks make my lady uneasy, so can you kindly stop inferring that she is over 100 years old, please?" I stepped in front of her. "...obviously, she is not..." I threw my hand back until I felt Temperance's fingers squeeze mine.

"It's all right dear, we are just having a laugh." Temperance forced a smile. "...You all know how this one gets, always wearing it all on his sleeve..." Temperance's shot a chastising glare toward me. "Little does he know that his chatty and cheerful expositions can be as prickly as nettles."

"Caz is getting really restless..." Pete pulled out his phone and fixed his eyes on the screen. Mrs Davies turned to watch him. "...we need to go..."

Temperance's fingers snapped to direct my attention toward her ruby lips. "Calm down."

I shrugged my shoulders and opened my hands.

"And on that note, I bid you both a good afternoon." Pete's grandmother smiled once more and adjusted her scarf. "I know you already do but you take extra good care of her. She is a special young lady."

"In a bit, mates." Pete turned the wheelchair turned around. Temperance's eyes became glassy, a frown had formed her face as we watched Pete and Mrs Davies disappear around the bend of the footpath.

"Whew..." She turned to look at me and let out a deep breath. "That was a close call."

"What do you mean?"

"That entire scenario could have gone awry..." Temperance squinted her nose. "No thanks to you, of course..." She clenched her hands. "...a bit of banter and you are wound up worse than a broken cuckoo..."

"I am sorry sweetheart, you seemed really on edge and I was just trying to put an end to it."

My beloved put her hand against her forehead. "I know, pudding..." Her hands gripped my jaw to hold my head in place. "You always mean well..." Her lips pressed against my cheek. In that moment, I forgot about all that just transpired. Once again, I was orientated toward my reasons for our visit.

"Shall we continue, then?"

"Actually..." She wiped some smeared lipstick off the side of my face. "I have become rather tired; can we leave it?"

I locked my fingers into Temperance's and pointed onward down the river. "The place I wanted to take you, it's just right there..."

Temperance licked her thumb and dabbed my cheek once more. "Another time, my dear, I no longer feel up for it..."

My heart started to race, I had this all planned out, I was nervous as it was but now, I had to re-think how to do it. I swallowed hard. "...there is something I need to speak to you about, it's important..."

Temperance continued to survey all of her surroundings, vigilant to detect any form of any early threat or hazard. "...can we speak about it later?" Her eyes seemed to wander and lock onto any that looked at her. Her skittish gazes were met with curious glances back in her direction. "I want to go have a lie down..." Temperance's skin grew wet from a sudden onset of a diaphoresis.

"Honey, are you feeling okay?"

Temperance's face swelled for a moment as her lips started to quiver.

"Sweetheart...." I stepped toward her with urgency and put my arms around her back to hold her. "...what's a matter?" My hands rubbed up and down her spine.

"Forgive my churlishness..." She looked down at the gravel that directed us toward the exit of the park. "I just need to let my hair down." Temperance took my hand and tugged on me with an unusual strength to guide me toward me the exit.

"Is there something you need to tell me?"

Temperance's froze in place, her eyes shot up and locked on me, bulging for a split second before they relaxed. "No..." She smiled and shook her head.

"Are you sure?"

Her disposition shifted once again, she was firm and flinty. "Did I mince my words?"

It was indeed, quite an unusual and alarming rapid change of emotions. Something was wrong but she was trying to have a stiff-upper lip about it and mask it with a smile. We did as she asked, despite my growing concerns and worries. I hooked her arm, she nodded demurely, and we continued on walking back to her home.

6.

Hours later, we huddled under a quilt on the couch in her sitting room drifting in and out of sleep. Flames from the electric fireplace filled the room with light and heat. Temperance's head rested against my chest as she lay still wrapped in my arms; my hands submerged in her hair that fell all over my mouth, nose, and arm. The waves of tumult from the events of the afternoon had since subsided, all was calm and still again. In the solace, I became pre-occupied with all the things that were yet to spoken about. I needed to tell her how I felt.

"Temp"

"Yes, my love?"

"I have something to share with you." I massaged her scalp with my thumb.

Her eyes opened with abruptness. "Before you do, perhaps we should have a bird's eye look at the situation."

"What are you talking about?"

"Never mind it." She shook her head. "...it's all codswallop, really..."

"If there is something you need to say..." My hand rested on top of hers. "you can tell me anything, Mama."

Temperance looked at me but said nothing, as if the very words spoken could open Pandora's Box.

"Shall I cook you a dinner with those roasties you are keen on?"

"Temperance, you don't need to avoid it." I cupped her hand. "I'm here for you, I love..."

Temperance sat up and raised her hand. Her powder-blue bodice expanded and contracted at a rapid pace, as if the silver buttons were ready to burst with each breath she took.

"What is it?"

"I cannot imagine how to explain it to you."

"Does this have anything to do with what happened in the park today?" I looked her straight in the eye and reached for her hand. "With some of the nonsense Pete's grandmother was saying about you being that nurse she used to know?"

"What if there was nothing nonsensational about it?" She gulped. "If it were true, would you feel differently about me?"

"I don't know how that could be true..."

Her eyes darted toward the fireplace.

"But if it were true, would you feel different about me?"

"No..." I slid my hand over hers. "...there is nothing that will change how I feel about you..."

She glanced at me from the corner of her eye. "I am confident that may not be the case after you hear this one."

"Try me." I patted her hand doing my best to conceal the fact my stomach was doing somersaults, desperate to release the three words which were pounding in my heart and begging to be let out.

"Very well, you've been warned." Temperance stood up and brushed a wrinkle off her sleeve. "I best fetch a few items so you can better understand..." She walked toward the door and shut it behind her. The flames crackled as her boots echoed against the steps.

What was this announcement? My stomach felt as it if were on fire and more ready to explode with each step she took as she descended the stairs.

Temperance returned with a wooden box and a tarnished brass key placed into the keyhole. She placed the box down upon the coffee table and re-joined me on the couch. "I have never done this before." Tempie took hold of my hands. "However, I don't want there to be anything between us." She took a deep breath. "Do you recall when we first met and you joked about me having superpowers?"

I nodded.

"It's true, I have been endowed with special powers." She turned the key and the box sprung open. Inside were a stack of sepia-coloured papers. Given their flimsy composition and visibly rough texture, they seemed to have aged and weathered.

"Go on, have a look."

I reached into the box and removed the stacks of papers. The first thing I came across were two drawings of horses, one was cream-coloured with fluorescent white eyes. Lightning poured out from its nose. The black horse was drawn in similar portrait style but its eyes were red. The stallion huffed a charcoal smoke from its mouth; flickers of ash poured from its mane.

"Did you draw these?"

"Yes, the white pony is called Daisy." Her finger slid across the paper. "That black one is called Sabre."

"These are exceptional."

"Thank you." She smiled briefly "However, that is not what I wanted to show you." Temperance moved her attention toward a collection of literature that remained in the box. I placed the drawings down on the table and took hold of the first piece of paper, I noticed the strokes of the text were of a fountain pen and written in an old form of script. After clearing what seemed to be hundreds of pages of memoirs front and back, I found a black-and-white photograph of a young woman who resembled Temperance in many ways. A tight floral dress hugged her curvy figure. Her facial structure reminded me of Tempie. The same cheeks, soft jawline, round face and eyes. Given the long hair and similar shade to Temperance, one would think it was a Victorian version of her. My beloved's eyes were filled with joy whilst this lady had eyes filled with mystery.

"Who is that?" I held the picture out for Tempie.

Her eyes watered. "Mummy."

"She is stunning. I see where you get your killer looks from."

Temperance sighed. "She's gone, now." She sniffled. "I still cannot bear to speak of it."

"I am sorry, sweetheart." My hand came to a rest over her trembling fingers. Her grip shook violently when she locked her hand in mine. When I looked back at the photograph, I thought my eyes deceived me. It said 15thSep, 1862.

"Is that date correct?"

Temperance glanced at the photograph and leered at me with a slow nod to confirm. I didn't know what to make of the claim, I thought it was maybe one of those Victorian vignette photos you could buy in Blackpool.

My eyes continued to scan the loose-leaf until the name Temperance appeared for the first time on a document stamped by a J.J Stanley, dated to January 1869 at St. Bride's Avenue, Blackfriars, London.

"This is a memory box of keepsakes." Temperance's grip grew tighter around my hand. "I have kept this along with a diary since I was a little girl."

"And it looks that you've written some stories as well?"

"To coincide with my entries, yes." Temperance pointed to a sepia-toned page that was dated 26th of May, 1863. "...I've dated them accordingly." Another page was dated to the 14th of June, 1901 followed by a memoir dated to July 1880 just before Temperance's twenty-fifth birthday; the anecdote once again pertained to St. Bride's Avenue in London. I read a few lines and placed the documents down.

"Apparently, you are quite the adventuress…" I glanced at her. "And you can control electricity…" A smiled unfurled across my face. "I know you joke about being a Victorian woman, but this is going too far now."

"Joke?" Her bloodshot eyes locked onto me as she leaned forward. "Before you have a go and tick me off as a nutter, have a look at this." She reached into the box and plucked what appeared to be another aged leaf of paper. However, this one was a certificate of birth dated from the exact day where she was supposedly born 15th of July, 1855. The certificate of birth was stamped by a woman named Penelope Hyde. The workhouse referenced as her place of birth existed. In fact, it is a point of interest in Manchester. The certificate was followed by another which cited Temperance's baptism and confirmation on the 15th of July in 1862 at Holy Trinity Church in Rusholme. That church also still stands today. The certificate reiterated her name along with the name she acquired from her confirmation: Temperance Grace Elizabeth Lee.

Another chilling discovery was a pay stub for Temperance Lee, dated from June of 1891 at Mellor Mill. This was the same mill that she referenced when we first met, now standing as ruins in The Roman Lakes Leisure Park. Her story was corroborated by the mill burning to the ground in 1892.

"I feared you wouldn't believe me."

"I want to believe you but this could be an elaborate hoax."

"Elaborate hoax, you say?" Tempie's irises turned from a deep shade of blue to a luminescent white in a split second. Upon the sight of it, I went pale. She leapt to her feet showcasing an agility that she hadn't displayed before. Temperance was athletic but this was supernatural how she easily kept her balance. Purple lightning bolts began to crawl up the side of her arms but it didn't burn her nor did it shock her; it was under her control.

"Temp..." I sat back as far as I could until the cushion pushed me back.

"Not so puffy chested now, are you love?" Her breasts rose and fell inches from my face. Temperance leaned over me as if she were ready to challenge me to a fight. I know many would have made a run for the door at the sight of this. However, I couldn't; I was still hopelessly in love with her, as ever.

Her eyes went blue again and Temperance sat smiling like she normally did; healthy, vibrant, and full of life. And there I sat speechless, as the electricity still danced around her fingernails.

"How do you do that?"

"You needn't be afraid my plum, I am merely hoping to prove that everything I have said to you is the unbridled truth." She snapped her fingers. Simultaneously, the microwave turned on, the television powered up, and music began to play. Temperance cartwheeled off the table and landed perfectly, it was then that it finally dawned on me that Temperance had superpowers.

"At least we've established, I was born in the year of our Lord, eighteen-hundred and fifty-five." She flicked her finger and the energy dissipated. Temperance plucked a hat pin from her thick mane of hair which was up in a large bun. She held the hair pin point up in her hand as she Temperance ripped the buttons of her bodice exposing a cream over-bust corset.

"Honey, be careful those can be sharp." I took a step towards her.

"And they can be rather nifty when you find yourself in peril." She took a deep breath. "This is going to hurt a bit but we best get on with it..."

Temperance turned the blade on her, but I put my hand on her chest in between the edge of the hat pin and her breast. She stumbled backwards and I fell forward.

"What are you doing?!" She spoke at length as I clutched her wrist and attempted to force the tip of the pin toward me.

"Let go of it." She strained, gritting her teeth, as her wrists reverberated. Our legs tangled up. I put one hand behind her back to protect her from falling. In that moment, her strength overpowered me with little resistance; a strength I had never seen in another person. Temperance yanked the pin away from me, the inertia of the pull caused me to stumble forward and the tip of the hat pin to puncture through the corset.

"Owww!" Her eyes bulged as she let out a moan, doubling over as the handle of the accessory protruded from her stomach, it may as well have been a dagger. Blood seeped from the wound, through the puncture in the corset, and expanding across her midsection.

My gut dropped.

Temperance placed a hand to the wound and looked down at it wearing a mix of agony and surprise on her face. It wasn't just a flesh wound; it was quite deep.

Panic filled me but I knew it had to come out of her. I reached for the handle and yanked the pin from her corset with urgency.

"Oof!" She grunted and gasped. I looked at the tip of the pin covered in claret.

Temperance curled up in a ball and lie on the carpet, taking in deep breaths, as she held herself. Blood stained the carpet beside her.

"We have to get you to the A&E..." Tears filled my eyes; I placed my hand over hers to apply pressure to the gash. My other hand shook as I threw the hat pin away from near us. "...Piece of fucking shit!" As upset as I was, I had to focus on taking care of her. I quickly rose to my feet. "I'll get some bandages so we can slow the..."

Before I could finish my sentence, I felt the full mass of Temperance cross my entire body. We fell toward the coffee table; I tried to take hold her and shield her from the brunt of the impact and take it upon myself but Temperance pushed off me and fell through instead, her back smashing through a glass candy dish and exploding everywhere into the collapsed table.

I lie on top of her as she inhaled and exhaled, her chest rising; when I looked down at her abdomen, the blood had seemed to slow. In that moment, Temperance turned me over and pinned me to the floor with little effort; her eyes glowed white; lightning flickered in her hair. A piece of glass had stabbed into her shoulder blade and she appeared unaffected or aware of it, for that matter.

"Stop." I put my hands up. "I am not trying to fight you, I love you!"

Her eyes turned blue once again.

"You what?" She appeared indifferent to the fact that was bleeding from various parts of her body.

"Sweetheart, you are hurt." I reached for a piece of glass that lodged in her.

"Argh!" Temperance yelped and swatted my hand away; her face was filled with pain. "What did you just say?"

"We need to bring you to the hospital."

Temperance dabbed her sweaty chest and forehead. "No..." She reached down into the box and looked over some of the aged papers in the box with the shard still protruding from her.

"We do not..." Temperance about-faced and smiled at me. The wound over her stomach had stopped bleeding. I was relieved that she had recovered but mystified as to how she did so, but still very much upset because I rather it would have gone into me instead.

"Ahh..." Temperance grimaced as she twisted the glass and slowly removed it from her back. "Ohhh!" She gritted her teeth and groaned until it was finally out. Temperance held her back as she took in a series of deep breaths. "That was a proper kick to the gut, but I've had worse..." She wiped her hands clean with a part of her petticoat and threw the glass into the wall like a dart. "That certainly brings back memories though..." Temperance held one hand over her wounded midsection. "Let me show you something, darling." She locked my hand in hers and placed it over a smaller cut on her arm from the glass; her hands seemed to warm with a palpable vibration. Ten seconds later, she pulled my fingers which gripped her tight away with her other hand. When she removed our hands, the bleeding had stopped!

My jaw sagged. "How did you do that?"

"If you had co-operated from the start, the demonstration would have been far more agreeable to me." Temperance giggled.

"I didn't want you to injure yourself..."

"I know that, dearest." She removed the papers from the table and placed them in my hand. "Have a look at these, it will all make sense."

"We should get you looked at..."

"Tis but a scratch, sweet." Her eyes glowed with affection. "Please do understand that none can know about this other than you, of course..." She pushed the literature further into my grasp. "Once this over and it will all make sense."

"There is still glass in your arms and back, my love..."

"I'll sort it; you need not worry..."

The papers fell limp once she let go as I remained in a state of shock. "Darling, must you continue to protest?" She kissed my cheek. "Now read this whilst I put on something a bit more appropriate for this occasion." Temperance flicked her hair and surveyed the aftermath. "We'll tidy up, later..." She bowed and curtsied. "If you'll excuse me." She walked toward her bedroom.

I held the papers and looked deeper into the box, at the top of the pile were a series of newspapers articles dated back to the mid and late Victorian era. '*Scantily Clad Heroine Saves Child from Drowning*', "*Valiant Vixen Subdues Mugger*', "*Dashing Damsel Performs Daring Feats in Morecambe*". My hands carefully weaved through the contents and discovered some more diary entries, some of which were stained with blood.

I placed the papers upon the table as my eyes turned to another photo dated to 1912, it was a black-and-white group photograph of several women posing outside the Manchester Royal Infirmary. I carefully gripped it and inspected it further: two rows of ladies stood shoulder-to-shoulder donned in black bonnets, white cotton blouses, and matching hoop skirts. After my sight navigated its way from one face to the next, there was one that jumped off the page in particular: Temperance's. They had the same innocence and gentleness, like when I gave her the bouquet of flowers earlier that day. I looked at another dated to 1898; Temperance sat on a chair with two girls, each holding a book. One looked near to her early teens, the other perhaps ten. The names *Vin and Ame* were written in faded ink but the handwriting matched Temperance's on the pay slip from Mellor Mill.

I glanced at another black and white photograph of two girls standing on the steps of a house, accompanied by a younger girl perhaps four or five years of age, along with two boys: one was a teenager, the eldest of the bunch, and the other appeared closer to the youngest girl. I assumed they were all brothers and sisters, behind them stood what I believe to be their parents. The boys had the same dark hair colour as the older man, the two older girls bore similar facial features to the woman stood behind them. On the back of this photograph, a message was still legible despite the material being over a century old: *Best wishes to our favourite governess. We will never forget you, Temperance.*

I could only examine these details for so long until I regressed into a state of shock. How is all of this even possible?

As I continued to comb through the contents of the box, I discovered a black and white photograph which appeared to be her Temperance with her hands behind her back, posing in a leotard after she had performed a feat of strength at Morecambe Pier. A latter description of her in action from a report in London mentioned she wore a lilac leotard tucked into leather tights with pink front lacing and a belt embossed with a pink T buckle.

Next, I discovered an IPN news article *Folk Heroine Defeats Champion Scrapper in Bedlam by The Sea*', what was unique about it was a diary entry was attached to it, which seemingly coincided with it. I left Temperance's original allotment on the table and read the article and diary entry instead.

7.

Though every twist and turn led me to a full stop, I retained belief that I could uncover the truth of my mother's disappearance. The trail led me to the resort town of Lytham St. Anne's, a pleasure pier was built there and it featured all the local amenities one could hope to enjoy on a trip to the sea-side. From the beach, it was an imposing citadel of pavilions, roundels, and ballrooms that appeared as if stood on stilts. It was irrefutable that the St. Anne's Pier was an engineering wonder of the nineteenth century. On a summer afternoon, I called to make a few inquiries in my continued investigation. This account details some of those proceedings.

"Good day." I curtsied as I held my emerald green overskirt to ensure it did not scuff the wooden planks of the pier. It is always important to exhibit good manners to complement good taste in how one dresses. I wore a matching hat that I fixed to my hair and two black ribbons draped down the back of my bodice. I also donned a red bow around my waist and another from a cameo which extended down from my neck.

Two men stood behind a wood booth in which Jeweller was written on the façade in large black lettering. One of the men stepped forward, a stout man in navy corduroy trousers and a burgundy vest over a starch white chemise. A black cravat descended over his chest. His brown handle-bar moustache matched his top hat.

"Madame". The jeweller tipped his hat whilst another man stood against a display case with his hands behind his back. The man was dressed in identical attire to his colleague but maintained a stoic *disposition. His green eyes monitored my every mannerism and movement.*

I looked into the display cases at the various hair clips, brushes, and brooches on display. All were polished gold and silver with gems of contrasting shades and colours. My eyes darted left and right until they landed on a familiar sight. "I've called to purchase this." My finger hovered over a blue butterfly hair pin that I never thought I would see again. The mere sight of it made the journey worthwhile, it was a gift Mother gave me when I was a girl.

"I am sorry, but the one isn't for sale."

"Then why is it on display?" I stroked the back of my head. Quite a peculiar response, indeed. It only prompted me to raise another query. "A Mister Broadhurst is the purveyor of this item, is he not?"

The jeweller and his colleague both shot each other a look. "And who may I ask do I have the pleasure of addressing?" A burly man with neatly-combed jet-black hair emerged from a cloud of cigar smoke. His face was rough and weathered, hidden behind a well-tamed handle-bar moustache.

"A woman who has come a long way to buy this off you..." I watched them cautiously, concealing my apprehension behind my amicable demeanour. "It has the initials T.G.L. engraved on the back, yes?"

"That's right." He crossed his arms. "How do you know that?"

"It was mine once, when I was younger." I smiled sweetly. "It was gifted to me by my mother and bears extraordinary sentimental value, you see..."

"Is that so?"

"Declare your price and I shall meet it." I looked left and right, noticing two men that watched the discussion whilst impeding the way to the exit from the pier. Three more men congregated near to the pavilion also observing the dialogue from a distance.

"I am certain you can meet the number..." The man removed the hair pin from the display case and emerged from the booth. "Augustus

Cuthbert Broadhurst." He doffed his hat in acknowledgement. "It is a pleasure to meet you."

An arm pressed against my back, it wasn't forceful but assertive, demanding me to acknowledge its presence. The two men that accompanied Broadhurst stood at my left and right flank "Would you care to talk a walk with us?" A portly man three inches shorter than I, latched his hand to my bicep. "...We can have a word about the item and finalise the transaction." Broadhurst smiled at me and extended his hand toward the pavilion.

This turn seemed rather troubling and I was not eager to continue this engagement any longer. I looked up at the pavilion, a white hulking edifice with multiple teal gambles set against a sloping black roof. A balustrade frieze wrapped around the exterior of the building painted in a cherry hue. A white spiked iron railing complemented the running trim which matched the cast iron fencing that surrounded the pavilion. My chest expanded, full from a tension that overcame me. There were opportune venues and occasions where I could use my powers yet still protect their secrecy. This was not the appropriate time to be enticed to test those waters. Verily, I hypothesised I could use agency and deportment to pardon myself from this perceived intrusion.

"You are a busy man; I don't wish to take up your time." I replied. "Surely we can negotiate the transaction here and now without any stir?"

"Will you come this way, please?" The jeweller wrapped his hand tighter around my arm. "If you shan't co-operate, my colleague Mister Campbell will take great pleasure in bashing your gigglemug all over this pier."

Campbell cracked his knuckle and smiled at me for the first time, extending his hand toward the pavilion. The audacity of these miscreants to threaten a lady in public. Despite such an appalling gesture, I obliged. Perchance, this could all be sorted out as one massive misunderstanding.

I looked at Broadhurst from the corner of my eye and nodded once to signal my complaisance.

Broadhurst bowed his head.

The boots of the three clinked against the wood panels of the pier twice until I was overcome by a sweet smell that fatigued me. It unsettled me, as I didn't believe any substance could bring forth such a phenomenon. I convulsed as two soaked rags dabbed each of my cheeks, smearing toward my nostrils.

"Unhand me at once!" I flexed my arms and heard a tear, followed by the sound of the two men crashing onto the deck. The aroma was still sweet to my tongue, the pier had spun a bit but I was able to look down and see my top had split from when I threw those men from me. Broadhurst smiled at me and I wondered as to why. When I looked down, I had seen that some of my lilac undergarment was showing. This was the last thing I had hoped for on many accounts. With urgency, I covered myself and evaded Campbell who attempted to tackle me, I side-stepped him and he tumbled into one of the men who I threw off of me. Broadhurst sprinted towards the entrance of the pavilion. I had a choice: follow him and try to get back the hair pin or flee the pier. The latter would be easier to achieve than the former but I had to recover what was left of Mother, also he might know what became of her; so, I followed him.

The remaining henchmen drew their weapons and gave chase. It didn't take long for me to catch up to the waddling Broadhurst, but when I turned a corner one of his hired hands emerged from the shadows and whacked me across the stomach with a snooker stick. My corset bore the brunt of the attack and shattered the instrument in two. I felt no effect from the blow, but it's startling effect caused me to stumble forward into the arms of another henchman. He smothered my face with a rag coated in the obscure agent. My strength started to leave me when another pressed to my nose. I convulsed and fixed my eyes to the gas chandelier descending from the ceiling which spun more with each inhalation. My knees started to buckle as if my feet were ready to give out.

"Take control of her!"

A third rag covered my nostrils from a blurry apparition

"Quickly!" Broadhurst shouted. "Before she recovers!"

I had to do something; My arms started to spark but it was to no avail when a train might as well have hit me from behind; the rest of my pursuers had caught up to me. The trampling mass of men drove me to the ground where they piled onto my back. I was too weak to toss them from me; the assailants kept the rags soaked in the debilitating substance pressed to my face throughout the arrest; I could breathe nothing else but the sweet fragrance and feel nothing but my face against the carpet with several knees pressed into my spine. Soon after, all went black.

Some time had passed but finally I could hear one of Chopin's Nocturnes humming through the walls (Op. 32, No. 2 in A-flat Major to be exact, as it one of my favourites). When I opened my eyes, the first thing I saw was my hair pin twinkling in the hands of Broadhurst. The second was more frightening: I was stripped down to my leotard.

I was subdued, bare, and exposed; my identity was supposed to be a secret and I had been granted such gratuities until then as none had ever seen me in my costume unless I had wanted them to. However, all my clothes worn to the pier had now been confiscated.

The room was largely empty, dark with no windows, lit by red globe gas lamps fixed to the walls covered in white and gold foliage wallpaper. The ceilings with patterned in a brocade carved into each of the panels. Two steel balls were chained to each of my ankles weighing heavy on my thighs. Few would be able to stand with these hindrances, but I could manage; I dare say I could even take a few small steps. My mouth was stuffed with my scarf, my hands bound together by rope, and my arms detained by the large man whose clutches I had fallen into when I collapsed. The only thing they did not confiscate was the pins concealed in my bun and plaits. Beyond doubt, they would be instrumental should I attempt an escape. However, it would prove difficult until my ankles were freed. Prudence was essential in this matter.

"It's called chloroform." Broadhurst tossed an empty green jar against the wall, smashing it to pieces. "Though your tolerance is far greater than anyone I've used it on previously, it always does the trick." He walked closer and bit on the cigar. "You must be Temperance." A circle of smoke circled around his nose. "I understand you to be a clever girl." He chuckled. "Yet you were idiotic enough to dare deceive us regarding the nature of your visit." Broadhurst's tone raised. "It is fair to conclude that it wasn't solely for an accessory for your hair." A faint hint of whiskey masked his breath as he held a few strands of my hair in his hands under the candlelight. "So here is how this works..." Broadhurst stepped toward me in a menacing fashion. "I will ask the questions and you must give me the answers." He took another puff of the cigar and blew it in my face, bereft of any formal etiquette. Despite the insult and injury given, I did not react.

"Should you be flippant my associates will take great pleasure in disciplining you..."

I looked to my left and right, Campbell and the Jeweller flanked Broadhurst, standing close to me. It was regretfully obvious that these men had full intention of hurting me without any show of remorse.

"...am I clear?" He reached for the scarf.

I nodded and he removed it from my mouth, I could taste the damp air again. The large brute that handled me, severed the rope, and let go of me. He remained an ominous shadow as he stood close behind, accompanied by other henchmen of similar build to the jeweller who enthusiastically punched his hand and cupped his fist. I paid no mind to it, as all I needed now was to be freed from the remaining bondage. If Broadhurst would unshackle my legs, I could do as I pleased to dispatch the threat. Perhaps employing a diplomatic approach would encourage him to do so.

"Is all this necessary?" I spoke in a soft tone.

My call for diplomacy was answered with Campbell's fist curling into my stomach.

"Hmph." My breath escaped me as I doubled over for a moment.

"I ask the questions, here." He flicked the ash from his cigar next to my boot. "Your mother is called Abigail, correct?"

I did not reply.

"You can answer."

"I will do when you tell me precisely where I should tell you to get off..."

Broadhurst chuckled at the affectation, I knew it would result being hit, but temptation overruled discretion. Before I could brace myself or flex my abdominals, another punch landed in my midsection; another grunt fled my lips.

Campbell's fist smashed into my abdominals again.

"Oof!" My grunt grew louder as I bent over and held my stomach. Though Campbell were a little man, his punches were awful to take even if I possess strong abdominals.

"Let's try this once again." Broadhurst cupped my chin and clenched on my jaw. "Your mother is called Abigail, is she not?" He released my jaw to let me speak.

"I take it you already know the answer..." I formed the words in between my breaths.

The villain clasped my hair and pulled. "It seems you have inherited her attitude as well as her looks." Broadhurst twisted the hair in his hand and tugged harder, the force tore at my scalp. "I was due a night with her for seven quid but instead she disappeared to who knows where." He flung my head to the side. "My old pal had associations with your mother and he too has vanished without a trace..." Broadhurst puffed on his cigar "...in fact the last day he was seen he was apparently with her..." The cigar rested between his pearly white teeth.

"Are your referring to Pride?"

Broadhurst smirked at the mention of the name. "No...but there are all sorts of crazy tales about him..." He spat. "My mate was called Envy; Him and I used to organise some cash bouts with your mother..." Smoke wafted into the air. "But given your desire to mouse about, I am certain you already know that." He took another puff of the cigar. "It is fascinating that should you mention Pride..."

I paused to think about how to reply, fearful of the consequences of any wrong response; As words formed on my lips Broadhurst nodded to the brute behind me. His henchman pulled on my hair to force my neck to an unnatural angle, straining my back and throat. My visceral moans became a sultry serenade to their ears.

Broadhurst nodded at the lout to release my hair. "So, did you come to ask us, if we know where your Mummy is?" He spoke in a mocking tone and laughed; his henchmen followed his lead. "If I knew her whereabouts, why would I tell you?" Broadhurst dropped his cigar. "That overpriced convenience fleeced me and I intend to exact my dues."

"Ahh..." I let out a gasp as the ache subsided. "Evidently, you are an expert in the market so I sought your advice." I snickered knowing full well that I would pay for the remark. However, I was not assuaged since he dared dishonour Mother. Campbell fired a punch into my core, dropping my hands to where I had been hit whilst winding me in an instant. A third henchmen struck me between the shoulder blades, sending pins and needles down my spine. The brute placed his thumbs under my armpit and pulled my arms away to open my midsection for more damage, The Jeweller took liberties and fired a painful combination of punches into my stomach and face, sending my head in opposite directions. The collection of blows elicited a chorus of groans and screams from me.

"Mind her face." He pulled The Jeweller's fist down and backed him away. "We need her looking smart."

At this juncture, my insides felt as if they were tossed in a mangle and it started to hurt to breathe; I expected to receive more punishment, but instead came a series of soft knocks at the door.

"Ah yes..." Broadhurst stepped on the cigar. "That must be Del." He walked toward the door and opened it. "Hello!" His voice exclaimed with exuberance as a woman strolled in wearing the clothing I donned to the pier. Her face looked similar to Broadhurst's, her eyes were hazel as opposed to his brown, her hair a honey wheat shade comprised of ringlets that dropped toward her thin frame.

"My dear sister." They kissed each other's cheek. "It's so good of you to come." His hand took hold of her gloved white hand.

"The pleasure is mine, dear brother." She sauntered in followed by a maid of similar build who wore a black chemise and white bonnet. Her menacing black eyes set in her clear pale skin, the most distinguishing characteristic.

"Temperance, allow me to introduce you to my lovely sister, Adelaide..." Broadhurst shut the door behind her.

"Delia for short." She curtsied and bowed. "I have heard so much about you..." Said she.

The two smiled at each other, sinister grins unravelling across their faces.

"I do say, that your style is impeccable." Delia smiled and walked towards me; her maid followed to my rear. "That is a splendid costume for such a marvellous physique." Her fingers brushed against the side of my cheek. "Tis a shame, you wish to meddle in our family's operations." She twirled a loose strand of my hair in her finger and ran her thumb against my neck toward the top of my breast. "I feel as if I would adore you otherwise." Delia's eyes glanced down toward my cleavage as I breathed heavy. "Such a heaving bosom." She removed her gloves and cupped my bust. "A woman knows the best way to handle another woman."

Delia rubbed her hands against my bruised stomach. "How is that, Pepper?" Her fingers crawled underneath my garment; she dug her hands into my abdomen enough to make it burn but then massaged away any ache. "Is that better?" Delia started to kiss my neck. "Now tell us why you came here, truly..." She pulled her lips back, her face encroached upon mine. "...did Mother send you to square her debts?"

"Are your seductions designed to cajole me to tell you a tale contrary to the truth?"

A crack filled the room following by a sharp pain that tore through the flesh of my back causing me to shriek. When I glanced back the maid held a belt in her hand.

Delia laughed as she clamped down on my breast, twisting mercilessly filling with me a crushing pain that left me reeling. "You are missing that bulletproof corset now, I bet..." Her smile widened as I screamed out in anguish as she applied more pressure. I could drive her back with an electric burst, but I didn't bite just yet.

"So, tell us, Little Temperance!" She released the hold. "What brings you to merry old St. Anne's?"

"I came here to purchase my butterfly and hoped you would tell me as to how you acquired it..." I gasped as I pressed my hand against where the skin had now turned black and blue. "Ooooh." I groaned, gritted my teeth, and sucked wind hoping all of it would quell the painful storm raging through me from the vicious attacks.

"My niece found it whilst we were playing on the beach. A woman that appeared not much older than you or I, laid claim to it stating that it belonged to her niece actually."

"But that's impossible, my mother purchased it brand new." I winced. "thus, the bespoke engraving on the back..."

"Well I guess Mummy lied to you too..." Delia guffawed. "...needless to say, when I showed this to Gussie, he recognised it immediately." She smirked over at her brother. "And we knew if we advertised this it would

be a matter of time until you turned up and confirm for us whether these wild tales that were circulating were in fact true..."

I placed my hand to stomach and Delia watched carefully. "What tales?"

The back of her hand smacked across my face, splattering my hair over my forehead. "Don't you mock us, you!"

"Excellent strike, sister." He bowed to her. "I understand my sister's disgust toward your pleading ignorance, as none believe you." Broadhurst took two steps as his feet echoed against the floor. "You see despite Abigail's disappearance and her daughter's apparent death, word spread of a woman that from description looked similar to Abigail and performed all sorts of spectacular feats, particularly in London..." He held the butterfly up to the light. "...what is confounding is that there was no previous record of this woman..." Broadhurst stepped between Delia and I, backing her way with a tenderness and chivalry about it. "This mysterious maiden became the heroine of Ludgate Circus." He grabbed my cheek. "She stopped crimes, she was an esteemed acrobat, and she could even wrestle alligators with ease." Broadhurst swiped his moustache. "She could lift more than any lad in any exhibition she took part in and she wore tarty body-hugging lilac-coloured tights identical to yours." He chuckled. "She even has your name." Broadhurst simpered. "What compelled us most was the odd rumours going around that your mother was apparently equipped with supernatural powers, as well..."

I kept a straight face and said nothing.

"And then it all dawned upon us..."

Delia smiled. "We know who you are, Pepper..." She raised her hands. "...and we want to know how you acquired your abilities."

"I don't have any powers..."

Another smack filled the room as leather from the belt gnashed its teeth into my back and caused me to yelp in agony as blood trickled down my spine.

Broadhurst a fired a left and right hook into my stomach near to my ribs; grunts flew from me freely. His punches were the softest of the bunch but they were amplified by the damage his sister and his pack of terriers had already done from battering my abdomen.

"I am not having these theatrics." Broadhurst patted my head as I held myself, placing my hand down against the floor as I was driven to a knee. Despite struggling to stand, I started to recover from pressing my hands to my body to expedite my reprieve.

"Until Delia arrived, I am surprised that we've managed to hurt you." He cackled. "I am equally shocked that you hadn't tried to lever the lot of us..." He placed his hand against my cheek. "It is well documented that you are quite the ringster, some say incredible." Broadhurst reached into his breast-pocket and removed a billet from The Incredible Temperance Escapes from Snake Pit and an article from the Illustrated Police News of a foiled robbery at Covent Garden. At that point, all I could do is look away in dismay.

"I've also read that when you have boxed or wrestled for sport, you were the victor by decisive margins or your triumphs were flawless outright, one after the other irrespective of whether your foe was man or woman." He placed the literature back in his breast pocket. "When I learned of your accolades, I contrived the notion that perhaps, I can find a way to use this to my advantage." He spat. "Whether it be profiting from these talents, tracking down your mother perhaps, or at minimum making back the money she pinched off me." Broadhurst ran his fingers against his lip and chin. "So, I bided my time and waited for the opportune chance. This pathetic jewel that you hold so dear served to be the perfect bait..." He spoke to his henchmen. "After all, it literally brought you to me, wearing a bow."

"We have arranged a showcase." Delia cracked her knuckles. "I had these created when you were resting." She pressed a white flyer into Broadhurst's hand as the roughneck released the pressure to my back.

"Don't you mean when I was poisoned?"

"Come now, Temperance..." Broadhurst shook out his hand. "...If we are going to collaborate together, we must be on amiable terms." He rubbed my cheek. "There is no need for such brash accusations as you will be handsomely rewarded for your efforts."

"I am a minted woman." My fingers dabbed my lips to rub away the trickling blood from the earlier slap. "I have plenty of money in my accounts."

"Then you'll have more. "Delia smiled.

"And we can deduct the price of the accessory from your wage." Her brother chimed in.

"I should dismantle the lot of you."

A boot crashed into my left glute; a dull pain pulsated through my flesh.

"Ouch!" I glared back at the third henchmen cackled admiring his handy work; my backside throbbed from the strike. "That is going to leave a mark..." The back of my hand pressed against my glute, which felt hot to the touch.

"Only temporary." Broadhurst watched the swelling form on my glute. "...it is obvious you don't want anyone to know the truth about you." Delia walked over and grabbed my shoulder.

"Your back is no longer bleeding." She glanced down "...it's as if you were never gashed at all." Delia glanced back at her brother. "I would dare say that is superhuman, Gussie, wouldn't you agree?"

"Indeed, dear sister." He kept his dogs at bay with a steady hand. "Alas Temperance, it would be ill-advised from your point of view to let things slip." Broadhurst finally handed me the flyer. "...should you be more agreeable then your secret will be safe."

"I have never met a spin merchant, the likes of you." I surveyed a black-scale sketch of a woman with a parasol with a shapely figure in a unitard staring down a hulking bareknuckle boxer and a ghoulish midget was set beneath a headline written in Serif font. It read The

Incredible Temperance versus Bram "The Crippler" Beresford and Little Gibface.

"*Little Gibface?*" *I returned the flyer to Broadhurst.* "*That's an awful moniker.*"

"*Justifiable when you see what he looks like...*"

"*I best go check on the little one...*" *Delia put her gloves back on and snapped her fingers. The maid came forward with a box and placed it into her brother's hands.* "*...whilst you finalise the arrangements with our new colleague.*" *A slight nod was directed from her toward Broadhurst.* "*It was lovely to meet you, Temperance.*" *She smiled at me and then pressed her cheeks to her brother's as they parted with a kiss. The maid stepped to the door to open it.* "*Be good for my brother, you hear!*" *The sounds of fanfare and chatter poured into the room.*

Broadhurst looked at his men. "*You can leave us lads.*" *Each one of them moved rank in file to the open brown oak door until Campbell grasped the brass handle and shut the door behind him. It was now Broadhurst and I, alone in silence.*

Broadhurst struck a match and puffed on his cigar twice before bringing into a rest in a silver ashtray. "*We were going to sanction a bout between Bram and someone in his class but then you graced us with your presence.*" *He rubbed his hands together.* "*Thus, the opportunity presented itself.*" *He strolled over to a varnished wood side table and lifted a copper toilet mirror to remove a set of keys and a tin box.* "*The dwarf is Beresford's right hand, hardly a challenge.*" *The chain jingled as he locked the door.* "*You are a crowd-pleaser, Miss Lee...*" *He swiped his moustache with confidence. It was the first time he used my surname, added leverage in his blackmail campaign.* "*Those are my dear's sister's words precisely...*" *Regretfully, the revelation that Delia knew it as well changed the dynamics extensively.*

"*...a commodity, an attraction of sorts.*" *He reached into his pocket and held a small goblet of oil.* "*Even the children love you; your skills, your costume, your style, and your elegance.*" *Broadhurst placed the* container in my hand. "*Due to your popularity, there are many that will fancy a punt on you winning a match against The Crippler.*" He took a step closer. "*We need to orchestrate a strategy to maximise our earnings on such a prognostication.*"

"*So, this is a stitch-up?*" I rubbed oil across all areas of exposed skin, bringing a cooling and refreshing sensation to where it touched. Should Broadhurst find himself getting handsy, this would work to my advantage as the oil makes it easier to control my electricity.

"*Not by the least.*" Broadhurst gawked at my skin which glistened from the substance. "*I will handle the books but you keep it entertaining and minimise use of your powers. Some back and forth action with some suspense, will really excite our guests.*" He bit his lip. "*Is the oil there to help you slip into that tantalising skin-tight outfit?*"

"*It has other purposes.*" I stretched and ran my hands up and down my skin. The pains had subsided, I felt restored and recovered. "*...I anticipate you will soon find out, as to what.*"

"*Intriguing.*" Broadhurst opened a box which held several surgical tools, including a syringe, a vial, and a fleam with a jagged point. "*You are impervious to injury and illness.*" Broadhurst removed the fleam and shut the box. "*And yet you still feel pain.*" He held the device in front of me and stared at me with a menacing grin, until he placed it down on the table. "*My sister and I are eager to learn how we can attain these invulnerabilities you possess.*" Broadhurst turned my face from side to side.

"*What are you doing?*"

"*Conducting a physical examination.*" Broadhurst took a step back and surveyed my body as if it were a fresh shoulder of mutton he purchased at the market. "*Flex your muscles.*" He grasped my bi-cep. "*Go on.*"

A strange request but I obliged. I flexed and my arm bulged with rock from beneath my soft ivory flesh. Broadhurst moved his hands down to my wrist and then up my thighs with a rare gentleness he had not shown throughout the encounter.

"Truly, you are solid as a rock."

"It's from doing so many callisthenics." I responded smug and condescending.

His hands traversed my waist until they gripped my buttocks. "How is that you do not thousands of suitors fawning over you?" Broadhurst squeezed one of my glutes, particularly hard. I had never experienced such depravity before, I was in disbelief and at a loss for words.

His hands reached up to grab my cleavage. Broadhurst cleared his throat and pulled the straps down to expose my breasts. "I know you are not supposed to touch these but how could I resist such a well-endowed and shapely bosom..." He placed his hands under my breasts.

"A tad tardy, considering what your sister has already done..."

"I am terribly sorry, Miss Lee, that was unbecoming of her." The villain continued to pull the leotard down to my hips. He admired the handy work of his henchmen who left my torso full of red and purple markings.

Broken chords of Lizst's Hungarian Rhapsody 10 sweated through the wall, it seemed to halt the fiend in his progress for a moment.

I looked side to side, hoping this was all some bad dream. What was this coward planning to do to me? He already beat me and touched me in a way, no woman should ever be. All this for a hair accessory that I would have paid him any price! For that I deserved to be humiliated, attacked, and violated? Right there and then, I could kill him, and it couldn't have happened to a more pleasant gentleman, but then what? My thoughts were interrupted by cool metal slithering between my thighs. "You are a proper bit of frock." Broadhurst smirked as his fingers meandered up my leg. "Let us see if your fairest flower has been plucked." The cold metal of the compressor drew closer to my groin; I wouldn't let him commit a most unholy sin. I smacked his hand away and the instrument flew from his grasp onto the floor.

Broadhurst jabbed me and a mist of spit flew from my lips, as my head cocked backwards. "So, I take it, you haven't been ruined!" He clenched down his hand, squeezing my cheeks to my face. "In that case, allow me to issue a new proposition." He unbuttoned his trousers. "...if I can have you now, we can forgive your mother's debt, and you can have your hair clip back too..."

"Fine." I cried out.

He let go of me, my response seemed to have both disarmed and stunned him.

"You don't wish to be saved for your wedding night?"

"No..." I let out a deep breath and clutched my jaw for soreness. "Please forgive my reaction but I did not want such a significant moment to be initiated with chilled metal penetrating me." It was difficult to maintain composure as I never loathed anyone more than this man.

Broadhurst bowed his head once.

"However, if you desire to make the most of it, unshackle me." My hand rested at my hip. "As a gymnast, I am extremely flexible." I fluttered my eyebrows.

Broadhurst licked his lips and bent down to my ankles; A set of keys fell beside my boots. "I am not going to have any trouble with you, am I?" He looked up at me.

I shook my head concealing my hidden glee, I finally had him where I wanted him. Electrocuting a room full of henchmen whilst my feet were shackled would be a tall order. But striking this man on his own whilst not detained would be easy peasy.

Broadhurst broke the lock and guided my legs out of the chains.

"Come closer..." I placed his hands around my back. I moved my head to breathe into his ear "... never touch me again, you vile reprobate." Electricity formed around my arms and the force drove him back.

"Ahhh!" He squealed as he was overcome by a pool of sweat. "What man would even look at you, let alone wed you?"

I spat at him. "Delighted, it shan't be you."

Broadhurst huffed with rage and reached for the fleam. "You little bitch!"

My hands dove into my hair to clutch a hat pin. The imminent skirmish was interrupted by a series of knocks followed by the door flying open.

"Boss!" A younger man walked into the room not seen before. He was a late adolescent with a dark complexion and fully developed beard. His brown eyes went darker at the sight of me covering my breasts. Confusion navigated his lips at the image of a fleam in his boss' hands. "Your daughter..."

Broadhurst looked down. His movements were languid and tepid, as if he were a little boy caught red-handed. There is an idiom that men never wanted to get caught doing wrong to a woman but given the fact this cretin had a daughter; it was an even more colossal blunder. He looked up at me for refuge from his embarrassment but I offered none. I smiled as I pulled my leotard up over my body.

He walked over to the side table, placed the fleam down, and removed a paper bag from a drawer.

"Give these to Ada, will you?" He extended the bag toward the other man at the door. "Tell her to be a good little pixie for Auntie Del and that Dada loves her." The bag crinkled in his hand. "Please be careful with these, she does love her marshmallows."

The man nodded. "I will do."

"Thank you." Broadhurst stroked his hair.

"She also said she is excited to show you what she learned on the piano."

"Excellent, I cannot wait to hear how my girl got on with her practice." Broadhurst's sincerity was palpable for the first time. "I will be there shortly; I just need another minute with our guest." His hand *diverted toward me but I kept an ice-cold glare upon him. "She will be performing for us in the ring and I must ensure she has all that she requires." Broadhurst reached to his pocket and removed my butterfly clip. "Can you also give this to Gib, please?"*

The man looked strangely at the hair piece and shot a peculiar glance to me before resting on the sight of Broadhurst with his crotch buttons still undone.

"He will be partnering with our femme Phenom, here." He reached for the door handle and started to close it. "Many thanks, Francis."

Francis appeared befuddled as he watched the door close. Broadhurst turned around and stroked his hair.

I crossed my arms. "I wonder what your daughter would have made of what transpired in here?"

"She will never learn of it." Broadhurst buttoned his trousers.

"Equally shocked, that she is in such close proximity to this tip."

"I am all she has." Broadhurst glanced into the toilet mirror. "This is the only way I could ever see her when my work takes me away from home." He let out a brief a smile. "The joy I feel when she arrives in the coach and the sorrow I feel when she leaves."

"How many years has she?"

"Ada-Lou is six." He glowed. "The greatest part of my day is when I open my arms to her and she runs to me on the balls of her feet." Broadhurst listened onto the piano notes that pinged into the room from an adjacent chamber. In that instant, he appeared to be any other father speaking proudly of his daughter. I longed to know what that was like. It was an odd juxtaposition. Broadhurst had shifted from a merciless barbarian to one that could almost pass as an amorous soul.

"And do you believe she would condone your behaviour, this afternoon?"

"She has nought to do with this."

"Would you like her or your sister to be treated in the same fashion, as I?"

Broadhurst's fist slammed against the side table. "Upon my word, you wretched hedge-creeper..."

I placed my hand over my mouth, holding back a laugh. Such immaculate vocabulary...

"Delia is a well-bred lady."

I snorted.

"Adela has a father and had a mother who was an upstanding woman, none of these descriptors apply to you."

"Oh, my dear me." I laughed. "Has it ever occurred to you that you could spend more time with your daughter, if you sought a better profession?" My smile widened. "A flapdoodle that gets his jollies off by molesting woman, how shameful and despicable." I shrugged my shoulders. "Surely, your late wife would agree?"

Any semblance of remorse and shame shown by Broadhurst melted away in an inferno of anger. He paced toward me with his fists curled. "How dare you insult Louisa!" Broadhurst swung his fist wildly at me but I ducked and swiftly applied a rear chokehold. He flailed his arms in desperation until his head fell deeper into the submission.

"It's never a fair fight when it's actually fair, is it?" I taunted him as my arms remained locked in place until Broadhurst stomped on my boot. "Ouch!" I clenched down harder. "You'll have to do better than that." Then, he resorted to an unexpected and underhanded tactic, the heel of his boot smacked upward into my groin and I saw stars. I cried out from the hard strike and released the hold immediately, folding up like an accordion. I pressed my hands to where I was struck my hands to soothe where he kicked me.

"Don't you lecture me on ethics!" He grabbed my ear and pulled on it, as I was doubled over, hissing; moaning; and labouring to catch my breath. "I do it for the same reasons your mother did what she did." He pointed down to me whilst I held myself, gritting my teeth, as the throbbing sensations that ripped through me. "To make sure both Ada and Delia are never without."

I clenched down on Broadhurst's finger with force and he let out a whimper. "Endearing rationalisations from a criminal." I stood upright again and twisted his wrist which caused him to scream louder. "Did you know at this very moment, I can fracture this in three different ways, if I chose to?" My eyes glowed fluorescent white. "And some would argue I should do for that dirty trick you just pulled."

For the first time, Broadhurst trembled in fear. "Alternatively, I can take my leave and we shall never speak of this again." I shoved him back into the side table. "Unless, you prefer to finish this spar with me?" My hands pressed his head down as he arched his back against the table. "I would thoroughly enjoy that."

Broadhurst howled as his hands swam across the top of the table, taking hold of the fleam. My eyes watched as his fingers clung to the instrument, I slammed my hand down to pin it in place. A moment later, my arms went numb when Broadhurst jabbed two fingers from his free hand into my arm pit which made me fall forward into him and render me vulnerable. As I pressed against him, the fleam dug into where my neck met my shoulder.

"Owww!" I yelped and pressed my hand to the blood, this in turn opened me up for more punishment as the device dove into the exposed area of my midsection near to my rib.

"Awww!" I screamed as it dug into my flesh.

"Ohhhh!" I shrieked as the fleam stabbed into me, narrowly missing my rib cage and lodging in place just above the preceding wound. Blood poured down my shoulder and puddled in my leotard. Broadhurst slithered out from me pressed against him. His hand grabbed the back of my head and guided it forward until it crashed against the face of the desk.

I slumped over, my body tired, sweaty, and burning from all the damage I took; I couldn't take much more. His boot smacked into the back of my thigh, a mild blow by comparison but it banged my wounds against the edge of the desk which filled with me fresh bolts of pain.

Broadhurst reached for the door handle to complete his escape. It was to no avail as I clutched him and overpowered him, forcing him back down onto the table.

"Flee if you must Mister Broadhurst, but there is no use." Electricity formed at my finger-tips.

"If you kill me, you will be a wanted woman for the rest of your days." He gripped the end of the fleam lodged in me and jerked it; I hissed in pain. "Even your supernatural attributes cannot prevent that." He twisted the device further into me.

"Owww!" I barked out in anguish.

A grin formed across his face at the sight of my suffering. "You know as well I do, Miss Lee..." He pushed and twisted further; I groaned louder. "...that you cannot afford that."

I gripped a hand around his chest. "You initiated all of this commotion." I pinned him down in place. "And I've had enough of your shenanigans."

Broadhurst raised his hands to signal peace. "If you orphan my daughter, there will be no hope for you. As the woman, you will be blamed by default...""

Sadly, there was much verity in my enemy's argument. Should the predicament become more precarious, the law would side with him. Moreover, though I loathed the slattern, his daughter was innocent, I couldn't take him from her. Sweat seeped into the wounds producing excruciating and pulsating sensations. The instrument felt as if it were gouging deeper into my insides with every movement. Nevertheless, despite all the pain Broadhurst caused me, sensibility was paramount. I let go of him.

"Fortunately, no offences have been committed as of now." He adjusted his collar. "And it will remain that way, should you agree to our partnership."

I moaned and staggered with each step I took as I held my midsection. "You really hurt me; you know." My hands trembled as I plucked at the fleam. "Ahh." I groaned, whimpered, and winced as I attempted to free the instrument, until it was finally removed. I gasped with relief when my hands cupped the wounds. "Naturally, you can fetch my butterfly and put an end to this needless controversy..."

Broadhurst watched as the blood slowed from my wounds. "We can make an enormous profit off of this showcase alone." His hands reached for the door-handle. "You can either retrieve your accessory in the ring and settle your mother's delinquency..." He stepped into the corridor. "...or you can leave now without it, have your secret exposed, and both my sister and I will ensure you become known to the pennies for assault and attempted robbery."

My hands sparked into a purple flash; I had entertained enough of his threats.

"Before you lose your temper, Temperance..." He looked astonished that I could generate the electricity whilst blood trickled down my arm from the stab wound to my lower neck. "Consider that should you choose the latter, eventually you will be apprehended, you will be sent away to an asylum, if not thrown in a gaol, and then you will have plenty of time to explain how you shrug off knife wounds..." He guffawed. "...if course, no one splashes you with Holy Water..."

"What are you speaking of?" Heat tingled in my cheeks.

"I have looked further into your affairs and I am certain it will rid us of you..." Broadhurst grinned. "...Since it apparently it works on your mother." He placed the tip of his boot against the door.

"What if you are wrong?" I placed my hand to my shoulder to quell the ache, gritting my teeth as I let out faint moans whilst doing so.

"Chances are I am not, since the apple never falls far from the tree." Broadhurst smirked. "...and I am certain there are some undesirables that would love to learn of this information since..." He twisted his moustache. "...you always emerge victorious and ultimately leave unscathed." Broadhurst focused on my arm wound which had nearly sealed. "How would that change though if the secret was revealed?" A smile returned to this face. "Should you co-operate with us; none will ever find out..."

I could not confirm whether what he said he was actually true or not. Regardless, this was the last thing I would want spreading about even if no one believed him and it were entirely untrue. The villain knew who I was and that was a danger in itself.

Broadhurst's eyes locked on my healing wounds once more. "...so how did you acquire your many talents, Miss Lee?"

"I can't honestly say as to how." I lowered a strap of my leotard and exposed my breast and core to this heathen. Whilst it was an undeserving delight to this scoundrel, flesh to flesh palpation would expedite the recovery. And so, I pressed my hand over the wet blood which still seeped from my sweaty abdomen. Relief started to fill me.

"I believe you..." His eyes blinked in a rapid cadence for a few moments, deliberating his next move like a chess master. "And I believe it would be wise to expand our collaboration to allow me to analyse these gifts of yours more thoroughly..." He nodded. "That could be equally advantageous for the both of us." Broadhurst licked his lips. "We anticipate your cooperation in that endeavour, as well..." I reached for the strap and brought my leotard back up over my body, as a show of defiance before pressing each of my hands to the nearly-healed wounds initially caused by him.

"...Please take a few minutes to doll up for your big show." He bowed his head and closed the door.

I could have burst through the door, made my way through whatever opposition crossed me, and faced all the potentially calamitous consequences that could accompany such a move. However, that wasn't what was most weighing in my mind or motivated me. I couldn't forget about my butterfly because was it was the only thing I had left of my mother. – T.G.L.

8.

I PN Report - *A Recapitulation of the Incredible Temperance v. Bram "The Crippler" Beresford and Little Gibface.*

The buxom beauty was delighted to entertain the many fans in attendance that travelled near and far to see her in action. Proprietor A.C. Broadhurst extended the invitation to the luminary lass on short notice, Temperance was nonetheless delighted to accept. Broadhurst led the proceedings and orchestrated the introductions of the scheduled adversaries. Little Gibface was first to the ring, followed by the heroine herself. Regaled as the Feminine Champion of the North West, the Incredible Temperance emerged into the Moorish Pavilion prim in plum, her svelte physique on display for all to marvel in. Many of the young lads cat-called the lovely maiden as she dazzled audiences in a low-cut sleeveless leotard that contoured to her curvy and busty build. Her skin was coated in a sleek oil, smoothing out all of the edges of her arms, legs, back, and derriere which the attire accentuated and flaunted. Her hair was plaited and down her back, anchored by several hair pins that kept her flowered bonnet in place. Despite her glowing and elegant ensemble, blood stains and slight tears near her abdomen gave her costume a rustic aesthetic. The heroine doffed her hat and was greeted by the official tasked with administering the match-up.

The Incredible Temperance attempted to negotiate a truce between her and her dwarf opponent. Several times, she declared no desire to hurt him or his partner and only wished for him to hand her a butterfly hair clip in his possession. Those in attendance nor Little Gibface himself were eager to broker peace talks. The midget taunted the crowd favourite as she chased him around the ring, referencing her accomplishments in saving children from drowning in under toe and single-handedly restoring peace at a riot. The Incredible Temperance blocked a kick that followed and placed Gibface into a headlock. Thereafter she absorbed two elbows to the stomach which had little effect. Gibface's desperate strikes were all the more futile against Incredible Temperance's flexed abdominals. She countered with a hip toss sending him to the ground.

The adversary charged forward but Incredible Temperance pushed Gibface to arms' length with no resistance. She remarked that he must be having a laugh, before lifting him off the ground with one hand. Once again, she demanded her coveted possession but a defiant Gibface retorted with lewd remarks. The Incredible Temperance slammed him down and incapacitated him, making it an easy victory. After rummaging through Gibface's pockets, the butterfly hair clip she sought was not discovered.

The Crippler entered the ring and revealed he was the possessor of the artefact. She attempted to negotiate with him but he would have none of it. In a game of cat and mouse, he pursued the Incredible Temperance around the ring as the tigress cartwheeled, back-flipped, and executed all forms of acrobatic techniques. The audience showed their appreciation when she landed outside of the ring after somersaulting from the top rope preceded by tight-walking it in an exhibition of masterful agility and dexterity. Beresford was not impressed and Temperance was ordered back into the ring, if she hoped to re-gain her trophy. The two grappled and wrestled but it was Temperance who controlled the ebb and flow. The Crippler found himself overpowered very quickly by The Incredible Temperance. She smiled and giggled as she evaded his attacks, only to counter them with successful defensive manoeuvres. The display of supremacy continued on for several minutes until the Incredible Temperance moved Beresford into one of the corners. At this point, bookmakers present were pricing the lady wonder as a 1/10 favourite. None rushed to bet her since the returns would be minimal; but none would wager on The Crippler, since Temperance was so dominant. She asked the pinned Beresford for the jewel and hoped he would concede to a draw on the occasion; Beresford declined, stating he would "never compete with a girl."

The referee interjected and scolded the Incredible Temperance. It was obvious, the official was looking to sway to momentum away from her as she was well in control for the whole of the event. In the midst of pleading her case to the referee, Bram poked Temperance in the eye and kicked her in the midsection which doubled the feminine champion over; Beresford dropped an eye-watering elbow on the dome of her skull; a throbbing knife which radiated down the heroine's spine and disoriented her. Beresford grabbed Temperance by the strap of her leotard and forced her into the corner, driving his shoulder into her before pressing his palm against her face and raking into her eyes. The Crippler snuck a hard punch to her ribs, under the heart just above an area of dry blood on Temperance's leotard which she also wore to the ring: the origins of which remain a mystery! Covertly, Beresford threw a couple more punches into Temperance's kidneys, her groans summoning a casual intervention from the referee. The official finally broke up the combatants and Beresford expressed his dissent with these actions, in the midst of their argument; a revelation: Little Gibface returned to the apron! He also took liberties, clutching the hair of The Incredible Temperance and pulling hard with a torque that arched her back against the turnbuckle. A chorus of boos filled the pavilion, Beresford shot a look at his partner and embellished with the official to engage in further pleasantries with the referee to give Gibface more time to weaken their opponent. The midget snuck through the ropes and launched a vicious toe kick to Temperance's abdomen, the steel toe of his boot punching into her diaphragm and under-bust. "Ewwf!" She grunted and coiled; Gibface followed up with a searing slap to her breasts which elicited a shriek from the feminine wonder, forcing her to place her hand to the discoloured region of her bosom and catch her breath; He came with another kick to the midsection just over her navel which forced Temperance to grunt loudly, squat, and drop her hands over her stomach. Gibface's assault followed with an elbow to the face and a hoof kick to the groin in which Incredible Temperance shrieked and held her lady parts before falling to her knees. The underhanded attack prompted the boos to roar and nearly drowned out Temperance's grunts and moans from each blow as she received them in succession; Gibface did a lot of damage and was successful in hurting and significantly weakening the heroine; he escaped through the ropes and left the heroine fallen on fours, prime for the plucking for Beresford who yielded to the referee to take advantage. On the outside of the ring, debris was thrown at Gibface who revelled in his dirty work.

The Crippler stomped on Temperance's fingers.

"Ahuhh!" She cried out and sat up-right holding her hands as she grimaced in pain. Beresford clenched his hands down around her hair and lifted her vertical, before gripping his hands firmly around Temperance's throat to deprive her of oxygen and force her back into the corner where Gibface materialised for the first time on the apron to legally enter the bout. The referee counted to five and broke up the chokehold; then Beresford unceremoniously landed a well-placed knee into the soft of Temperance's abdomen and drove whatever wind remained in her out, in a thunderous grunt before he tossed her to the ground like she was a dirty dish rag.

The strategic strikes by her antagonists at this point had severed supremely effective as it dropped Incredible Temperance to her fours, hissing and wincing as she massaged her abdomen where she had been struck with a hope it would quell the pain.

The collaborators gestured to spectators to cheer for them with the hope they would gain support; few would oblige. Beresford continued to clap on the apron as his partner approached Temperance who was on fours with one hand pressed to her stomach. The dwarf hopped up and *smashed his axe-handle arms down over her back, crashing her to the mat.*

Whilst she lay on her stomach, the adversary stomped her in the small of her back and her buttocks. These strikes seemed to infuriate Temperance and catalyse a second wind, inspiring her to rise with expedience. Gibface fled at the scene and this roused the audience to cheer as he ran to make the tag and Beresford entered the ring. The Incredible Temperance was able to generate some quick offense with a few strikes until The Crippler clapped her in the ears when she went to grapple him. He followed it with a biting punch across her face which drew blood from her nose and sent a spray of mist across the ring. Beresford took advantage of the opening and lifted Temperance high off the ground before slamming her down on the mat to drive the energy out of her. This was only the prelude to the pandemonium...

Beresford ambled toward centre of the ring as Temperance was on lying on her back, one arm sprawled out, the other lying over her stomach. "It's time for you to get back to the kitchen, chick." The Crippler clenched his big palms down on her hair and yanked her up to a vertical position. The bare-chested hulking man wrapped his arms around Temperance and squeezed her, suffocating all of the air from her ribs and stomach. "Women should be seen and not heard, it's right for you to pack it in." Beresford lifted her off the ground again and tightened the vice-grip bear hug on her.

The audience glowered and heckled at the sight of Temperance groaning and straining from her ribs being compressed inward. She struggled to breathe and the lion's share of body blows she had received earlier likely enhanced her peril.

"Incredible Temperance, four to one to win by knockout" A voice called out to takers who wanted to believe she could overcome her opponent despite appearing to be on her way to a submission defeat. "Offer on for the next ten seconds" Men scoured to place their bets; Broadhurst watched on, apparently entertained by the sight. A smile

unravelled on Temperance's face after the announcement. She stretched and pushed apart Beresford's arms, releasing the bear hug, and rolling to the mat. Perhaps, she had been acting all along!

The auditorium was brought to a silence at the effortless display of supremacy by the orchid enchantress. She stared down Little Gibface whose devilish face stood reticent in the midst of the feat. There was no ghoulish grin or fang-like teeth protruding from his lips. There, he was genuinely terrified.

"You two have had your fun." Temperance dabbed her nose. "It's time to put an end to this dog and pony show." Her hands clasped around Beresford's genitals and he screamed in agony. Little Gibface waddled between the ropes and charged at Temperance in a last-dash hope to save his partner. She threw Beresford into Gibface and sent his top hat flipping into the air as he collapsed on the mat face-down, his long brown beard and black overcoat draped across the ring. Spectators cheered and clapped in cadence to show their support for the heroine.

Temperance punched Beresford in the face, kicked him in the gut, and threw him over her head crashing his shoulders down on the mat, as she bridged her legs. Beresford shook off the effects but before he could find his orientation, Temperance clubbed him on the back with her bare fist and wrapped her bicep around his throat, drawing the oxygen from his lungs. She reached down and lifted The Crippler over his shoulders as if he were a sack of potatoes and slammed him on top of Little Gibface. Temperance threw a punch across his jaw for safe measure, putting him to sleep on top of his companion. Both were unconscious.

Broadhurst turned to his sister and one spectator close to the two reportedly heard him say "The lass won so effortlessly" and after struggling to read his lips perceived him to say "Think of what this will cost us."

Thereafter, the sister of the host known as Delia affectionately, placed her hand over her brother's clenched fist, his fingers recoiled when she slipped a glass vial into Broadhurst's open hand. The host's frown *turned to delight when he smiled at his sister and kissed her hand. He then summoned a man who stood in the aisle; his most distinguishing feature being his long salt and pepper beard.*

Temperance reached into the pocket of Beresford's trunks and removed the butterfly bobby-pin. She placed it in her hair and donned her bonnet. Elation filled Temperance as she curtsied and bowed to the applause of on-lookers, blowing kisses to the many that cheered. She swiped her forehead clean and pressed her hand against her cleavage. She continued to smile, dripping in sweat, and breathing heavy from her exertions.

Broadhurst placed his hand around the man he summoned to speak into his ear. The man removed his bowler hat and nodded his head. The compere slipped the vial into his associate's hand and patted him on the back. As the man made his way toward the ring, the master of ceremonies called out to him once again. His response in this instance, could be easily deciphered from his lips.

"SEND IN THE SNAKES"

Broadhurst's sister giggled and clapped her hands, clutching her brother's arm harder; perhaps excited by the prospect of another series of theatrics. Soon after, a brood of vipers was released in the ring which prompted the enchantress to go from enemy to friend of her two fallen combatants and further invoked bedlam in the audience. In a dramatic effort, the Incredible Temperance dragged both Beresford and Gibface from the ring, narrowly escaping the clutches of the cobras that lunged at her, one snake's venom-soaked fangs missed her by centimetres. A barrel roll served as her means of evasion.

A contingent of security personnel encroached upon the ring and the Incredible Temperance delighted spectators with another marvel, as she levitated in the air with a pink cape materialising around her neck. She plucked a hat-pin from her hair and hurled it at one of the rogues, the subsequent action dislodged a pistol from his hand and caused it to discharge on the floor. Spectators were aghast at the sound and charged to the exits, creating congestion all ways out. The Incredible Temperance was left to fend off the gang that surrounded her. Fortunately, she was able to find some assistance from Little Gibface who released several mongooses into the ring to battle the snakes. He saluted the heroine and hid under the mat from her adversaries that showed discontent with his desire to help The Incredible Temperance.

She launched two lightning bolts at two men on the outside of the ring and rendered them unconscious. The crowd started to flee its seats at this point, realising this was no longer a part of the act. The referee of the bout attempted to subdue the Incredible Temperance by tugging on her cape and bringing her to the ground. However, his attempts were met by her flinging him to the side like he was a toy. The lilac-clad adventuress removed the cape as two more attackers converged upon her but she easily defeated the duo with a series of gymnastic techniques and skilled hand-to-hand strikes, culminating in her lifting both men at once with each of her hands. Another two men tried their luck and once again the Incredible Temperance manipulated electricity and tossed another hat-pin with precision accuracy to mitigate any immediate threats. Three more attackers tried their luck and three more were defeated easily by Temperance who choreographed a series of defence manoeuvres to subdue them.

From there, a gun fired and a bullet crashed into the mat of the ring, another against the ring-post, with the Incredible Temperance cartwheeling and dodging each. The gunman responsible was also the lad that equipped the mysterious glass vial of what appeared to be water. Two bolts of lightning escaped from Temperance's finger tips and forced both the gun and vial from his hands. Thereafter, Temperance shattered the vial of water with a hat pin cast from her mane. The actor's confidence shattered alongside it, as if the water were a conduit of success in the struggle. However, I.T.'s icy glare indicated that she had no time for commiserations as a flurry of electricity descended upon her adversary, scorching his waistcoat, and knocking him out. Temperance leapt into the air, flipped, and somersaulted through the tiers toward the exit, as more gunshots rang out behind her.

9.

I read a few more lines from the IPN Report before I could have crumbled it in my hands out of pure anger, I am surprised I had made it that far...

According to reports and from Temperance previously, she could fall from heights and only suffer bruises. She could cast lightning, scale tall buildings, and throw hat-pins; She possessed superhuman strength, she could levitate, and knife or bullet wounds were like paper-cuts to her. I didn't doubt any of it, but I loathed the idea of any of those things happening to her. It was as if my OCD and depression joined forces and took steroids, as such intrusive thoughts often tormented me when it came to her. I had night terrors and all sorts of trance-like reveries of her in danger, materialising against my own will. My comfort was found in the fact that they were just thoughts despite how disturbing because in those occasions, I could glance at Temperance and know she was safe. However, this was a diary entry of a previous experience and I hated the notion of anyone groping, insulting, or hurting her and not being there to stop it. Because if I was there to stop them, these amoebas would have been dealt with in such a way...

"When I find these animals, I am going to eat them!" I smacked my hand. "They want to take it to that level?" I paced back and forth, hyperventilating with each step. "The woman I love? We'll see who takes the glory from this field." I stopped for a moment and glanced at a croquet club; a smirk rolled across my face.

"That will do." I took hold of it and glanced at the kitchen, I considered grabbing a knife from the drawer but at this point, all I could do is shut the lights and stare out into the night, squeezing the club violently. I shut my eyes and tried to compose myself with deep breaths until the scent of hyacinth tickled my nose, it smelled like the body oil Temp wears. That was all I needed to part ways with trying to control my anger, my eyes flew open with haste.

"Let's go get these pancake-eating mutts."

I didn't know where these people were or where I was even going, but I wanted a piece of someone. Someone had to pay for harming my beloved. I may as well have been blacked out.

Suddenly, the door opened and lights came back on; there stood Temperance wearing the same costume in the faded black and white image in the box; the same as described in what I just read: a lilac-coloured high-cut Lycra leotard that contoured to her toned core and every curve of her body. Her toned thighs were oiled along with her biceps and chest. Her busty breasts looked ready to pour out from a low neckline. The garment was like a second layer of skin revealing her chiselled abdomen and the outline of her belly button; Her long red hair fell down her back in a long plait. Never had I seen Temperance show that much flesh in my entire time I had been with her, and I have no shame admitting I was incredibly aroused.

"What on Earth is going on in here?"

The club fell out of my hands. "Woah..." My lips fluttered. "I'm sorry if I was yelling..." I stuttered as she took a step toward me. My beloved placed her hand over her mouth to hold back laughter.

"I take it you are not so sceptical anymore..." She stroked her hair.

"I never was to begin with..." A contrasting boyish smile materialised on my face, as my heart pounded through my chest. I was no longer angry but bewitched by the combination of carnal lust and passionate love for this woman.

"Do you like my costume?" She smirked as she twirled few strands of hair in her fingers.

"You look amazing." I bit and chewed on my thumbnail. "No belt and front lace leggings though?" I made a stupid joke to ease my nerves and the overall tension in the room. Temperance went quiet and looked at me peculiarly for the reference, glancing over at the box for a moment before turning back to look at me.

"I think it's too hot in here for me to wear those..." She batted her eyebrows once.

"If it's too hot in here, it's strictly because of you." I tugged on my collar and continued to bite on my nail, somewhat muffling my words.

"Pardon?" She knew what I said but she was being playful.

"I said I was right about your abs too..."

She looked down and back at me, then she rolled her eyes. "You are an eccentric creature."

"I was just reflecting about the time we first met." I waved my hand in her direction. "Your costume proves I was right."

"Though this is revealing it bodes ergonomic purpose as it allows me to move freely and enables my skin to stay cool whenever I turn up the amperage..." A white flash sparked from her eye. "A corset and crinoline wouldn't be advantageous with respect to the stunts I perform." She threw her hand at her hip. "The only drawback is that this kit tears rather easy and doesn't offer much protection." Temperance cringed. "Fortunately, I have my healing capabilities as you saw from the previous incident just before..." She briefly turned exposing her shoulder blades, the back of her arms, and the exposed skin on her back. "...See..." There was no scarring, blood, or bruising; no sign of glass in her either. My eyes wandered down at her massive and round glutes which protruded from the leotard. I have no shame in admitting I wanted to grab her and make love to her on the floor right then and there, but my mind darted back to what I just had read; then my lust for Temperance was overpowered by my love for her and subsequently the rage returned: I was clamouring to throw down with the idiots that threatened her and tried to beat her.

"So, who put their hands on you?" I cracked my knuckles. "I am making a list."

"What are you on about?" A look of concern rolled across her face. "Fiddle sticks, darling. Have you become niggled?"

She grew anxious that she had done something wrong until she glanced over again at the stack of papers lying beside the box. "I see you didn't read what I told you to. If you had read what I instructed, you would ascertain as to why I wear this along with the full reach of my skills..."

"Well what I read gave me a full understanding of both." I huffed. "Are they still in St. Anne's now?

My voice raised and her eyes shot at mine at the mention of the town. "Is that what you read instead?" She leered at me and glanced up at the ceiling. "So that's what the club was for." Her hands rested on her hips. "...Oh dear..."

"Why did you write it?"

"To corroborate my story in case anyone dare contest the chronology of what occurred."

"Who would do that?"

"It no longer matters now." She was visibly agitated as this had clearly not gone to plan, Temperance closed her eyes and held her head in her hand.

"Is it those idiots?" I stepped closer to her. "Because I promise you, I'll head over there and smoke every last one of them mother-!"

She hushed me with the sensation of her fingers pressing against my chest from beneath white open-fingered gloves. "Good luck finding those, since that was a long time ago."

"Well then I'll settle the score one of their grandsons!"

"As if you would lower yourself to such a level." Temperance kept her hands pressed her against my chest with a gentle touch. "you are better than that..." She stroked my cheek. "It's alright now, Bon Bon."

"No, it's not." I exhaled violently. "St. Anne's isn't far at all, all I gotta do is get down to the M60 and I will be there in an hour." My veins throbbed. "And when I get there, I will wipe that no-good scum off the face of the Earth, you just wait!"

"Why are you shouting at me?" Temperance wrinkled her forehead. "I am not at fault..."

I was so belligerent that I lost sight of the fact that I was yelling at the very person that inspired this passionate fury.

"I am sorry, honey." I sighed. "I am just furious at the situation." My fingers shook "I would have given anything to stop them..."

"How could you have?" She cupped my hands. "It was long before you were a glimmer in anyone's eyes." Temperance picked up the article. "That IPN report is from a time where the Alexandra Limp was a trend..." Her eyes fixed upon me. "The ballroom and the pier are nothing more than glimpses into a by-gone era..." She placed the article back in the box. "...there is only one thing that still remains from that time..." Temperance looked around the room as if she were lost and here for the first time. "...me..."

"I just can't bear the thought of anyone hurting or violating you." I bit into my lip perhaps with a hope of drawing blood. "It makes my skin crawl, I can't help the fact that I will always defend your honour and want to protect you and take care of you, anyway I can..."

"And you have done wonderfully..." She caressed my cheek. "Hitherto, a single hair has not fallen from my head whilst you and I have been together."

"I wouldn't let that happen without all-out war."

"Never have I doubted that." She smiled as her thumb grazed my knuckle. "Nonetheless, I defeated the maladroit and hardly broke a sweat..." Her hand stroked my fist. "You did read onto the end, yes?"

"Honestly, I rather not think about any of it." I scratched the back of my head. "I can never forgive myself for what happened just before, either..."

The innocent child-like laugh that I loved about her filled the room. "Do you see any bruises or scratches on me?"

"No and I never want to..."

Her tone got seductive. "So, I was going to ask you..." She glanced down at her oiled busty bosom which looked to escape from the leotard and shot me a seductive smile. "How do my breasts look in this?"

I started to shake, not from rage, but a timidity that came from being in the presence of such a beautiful entity. At the same time, I admit I was overwhelmed by hormones and urges. "Perfect..." I gulped and stuttered. "You have amazing boobs, honey..."

"These are excellent for storing things when I am on the go." She ran her finger into her cleavage and smiled at me. "So much for women being powerless without pockets, aye?" Temperance clearly knew what she was doing to excite me; my heart started to race and a buzzing sounded in my ears. "That's not the only thing I was thinking but I can see your point..."

She slapped my arm and I flinched. "I was having a laugh, dearest..."

"Sorry..." I let out a deep breath. "...I am just a little fixated on how hot you look."

"Is that so?" Temperance sat on my lap, her body drawing closer to mine as she threw her finger against top of my head. "So why worry about running after them lot when you could be here with me instead?"

"Are you trying to seduce me?"

"Pooh! not by the least." She placed her hand to her chest. "...can you be seduced?" My beloved twirled her hair. "Am I doing well?"

Temperance had lost her moxie for a moment again, as if her confidence were riding on my reply.

"You have done so much more than that already..." I held my head for a minute until I shook when she touched me. Temperance beckoned me close to her, she took hold of my hand and placed it on her abdomen. She whispered into my ears. "How is that, Butterscotch?"

I started to hyperventilate and clutched her back with my other arm tight. Her lips pressed against my cheek. "To be fair, I admit it is adorable that you were so brassed off." Her warms hand cupped against my curled-up fist. "I promise, if anyone wants to give me a never-say-die, they are all yours." Her lips moved down to press against my knuckle. "With you, I know I am safe as houses and no one will hurt me though I do not require your assistance." Temperance smiled sweetly. "I will leave you to it just as you told off those lads that night, we were walking back from Wetherspoons. I must admit though that I am inclined to sneak a lightning bolt when you are not looking, of course." A giggle snuck from between her lips. "But I'll stand behind you and let you protect me."

"You are my queen, Temperance." I kissed her forehead and moved my head back to smile at her. "I love...." My lips were silenced by her fingers pressing them close.

"Come now, let's have a seat..." She clutched my arm and we moved over to the couch. "You must understand that I am essentially immortal. The only conceivable way someone can do me in is douse me with Holy Water, though I never fancied myself demonic." She sat and I followed. "If I get punched, stabbed, or shot it may injure me but I will heal..."

"And still I will never let anyone or anything hurt you..." Blood rushed to my knees as I was attempted to sit up until Temperance once again forced me back down to a seated position. It was incredible to witness how her strength overpowered me with ease, despite being enraged.

"Do realise that if you were to jump in front of a bullet for me, you may very well likely die as opposed to me screaming ouch and bleeding for a short period of time." She cupped her hand. "...as previously demonstrated..."

"I don't care." I stared into her eyes. "You are sacred to me."

My beloved looked back, her pupils constraining as it detected the determination that poured out of me.

"And if you lose your life as a result?" Temperance looked at me as if she were going to melt.

"So be it." I shrugged my shoulders. "It'd be an honour to go out that way."

"You have no idea how much I love...you being with me." Her pace of response accelerated gradually. "This is why I would have much preferred you have learned of my healing abilities with a hat pin or scullery knife. I anticipated it would give your head a wobbler; you were close to losing the plot earlier." I stared blankly at her, still trying to process all that was occurring. Was this actually happening?

"One can only envisage what would transpire in a differing context..." Temperance pressed her hands to my temples and massaged them. "...I reacted with similar fury and astonishment when my Mum explained her powers to me after she were wounded."

"Look, Temp..." I sighed. "...I have been needing to say something for a long time, it will explain everything..."

"Before you do, you must also consider that with my powers I also never age and I will always look like this, for you." She threw her hands on her hips and posed as if she were modelling. "So, quit being such a mardy bum." Her hands pressed to my temples as she sucked on my lip. "...Here I am looking like a dish for you and you rather fixate over cobblers."

"How did you get these abilities, sweetheart?" I initiated a kiss and we kissed some more until she pulled back.

"We best save that for the diary, there is no need to chunner on about this any longer." Her leotard creased and flattened with each breath she took. "...but you must know the truth...in the event, you were to fall in love with me."

My eyes shot up at her, temporarily breaking free from the bewitching trance Temperance put me in.

"...I want you to know everything about me, just as I know everything about you." Her grip intensified. "I wore this for you so you can see I am not merely telling tales and more so..." Temperance rubbed the back of her head as if doing so could coax the words out. Though she had all these supernatural abilities, my beloved was very vulnerable in the moment.

"...right, this is very difficult, because..." She swallowed really hard. Her eyes were large and glossy with affection pouring out of them. They appeared ready to spring forward and embrace me but held back from a fear that they would not be caught. "...because...I...love you..."

My jaw dropped. What I had hoped to achieve all evening, she had done so effortlessly. Nevertheless, I couldn't have imagined three better words that could have been said. Blood rushed through me, my sinuses were no longer compressed, and my head was no longer dizzy.

"...I am in love with you..." There was a sense of panic in her eyes, and I imagine looking back at her, outwardly I appeared bewildered. However, for the first time it was pure ecstasy. I wanted to jump up and kiss her. But my mind wouldn't let me, it always had a way of trying to spoil the moment. *Why would she love me? How could she?*

"But I am a guy that doesn't deserve to be loved. I have a drinking problem, I struggle with depression, I have panic attacks...."

"They are no different than your diabetes and you've have done really well to overcome those conditions. But you must know, I will always stand beside you and there wasn't a speck of truth in what you just said about yourself, petal."

Tears filled my eyes, what beautiful and kind words from such a wonderful woman. They pierced my heart but she didn't stop there.

"I have never felt the way I do about anyone like I do about you. I have fallen arm-over-teakettle for you."

"Me?" My finger smacked against my chest. I couldn't believe what I was hearing. This was even more of a revelation than the confession of her supernatural powers.

"Yes, you." Her lips pecked my hand. "Base over apex."

"Are you sure you didn't make a mistake?"

"No, silly sausage." My hands shook from her leaning against me and laughing at my statement.

"But what about the diabetes? I mean I always thought was going to get me at a young age."

"What does that have to do with my loving you?" She rubbed her face against my hand. "And anyhow, I can fix that..."

"What about the fact that I don't even fit in anywhere?"

"I do not believe I am in a position to comment on that one..." She locked her hands in my fingers and kissed them.

"Come on Temperance, there is no way you could possibly love me..." I twitched." ...you know what I am saying, right?"

Her palms cupped over mine. "No, I am a tad confused by your waffling..." I felt her touch pull away. Temperance's fingers dove in between her knee and her boots. A folded piece of paper came out in between her index and middle finger. "Could you read me the last two lines of this poem?" Her hand extended toward mine until I grasped it. "I reckon you are familiar with the author of this."

I unfolded the piece of paper and scanned it. The scent of Temperance's sweat combined with the sight of my handwriting placed me into a state of surprise. "I don't mean to be nosey but I discovered this when I dusted the bookshelf in your flat..."

It was a poem I had written. I looked up at her and squeezed my cheeks.

"...whilst you were in the loo washing your face..." Her hand pressed against my shoulder. "Could you read it, me?"

I looked down at the poem, my hand started to tremble until I felt her fingers wrap around it, then it steadied.

"*Shall I continue? You implore me to extend. Encourage me not to worry, it's better than giving in. I pray for your virtue, for your word always true. I shall be buried in misery, if I am torn down by you.*"

"When I read those unsettling words, I wanted to hold you so tight that you would never feel so broken again..."

I didn't know what to say or do, the entire thing didn't seem real. Why would a woman as grand and as magnificent as her ever want to hold me?

"...I promise you that I will always be there for you. Just as I have done, whenever you have had a case of the morbs or anything else." She tugged on her boot. "You can always find sanctuary in my arms, butterscotch."

The stereo turned on and mysteriously it began to play *The Favorite* by Scott Joplin. Tears escaped my saggy eyes, moisture filled my nose, my lips quivered, and my throat felt heavy.

"My abilities are a bit unhinged now." She swallowed. "That was supposed to play when I came out." Temperance stared at the speakers as static-filled notes filled the room. "Joplin is your favourite..." The back of her hand stroked my cheek and caught a tear. "Hopefully I won't have to flog it too long before you understand you deserve to be loved..." Her hand rested on the side of my face. "...don't we all?"

I couldn't hold back my tears from her.

"...I am not getting gobby either. This is why I willingly disclosed all my secrets to you." She flicked her hair. "...And I wore this attire because I want you to be the first chap..." Temperance whistled from a nervousness seemed to consume her. "...how shall I say this?" She looked away skittishly. "...I want you to be the first and only bloke to carry me into the bedroom and tear this off of me." Her tone of voice softened to a sensual timbre once she re-gained her confidence. "Then you and I can make love all night until we collapse in each other's arms."

"Me?"

"Is that all you say?" A playful smile parted her lips. "Me?"

"I mean are you sure?"

She nodded. "Unless, you do not want to."

"Oh no, I want to." I fidgeted with a smile. "Very badly."

Her hand crashed over my mouth.

"Then have me." Temperance slid a strap down. "Unless I was mistaken, I heard you say you love me earlier..." She looked down at the ground. "However, I fear that reaching such a conclusion may have been presumptuous and these sentiments may be unrequited..."

Temperance could destroy me more than anyone I had ever known and she didn't have to electrocute me to do so. All she had to do was be gone one day and it would be over for me. But I had to leap to the stars to catch her and if I found myself tumbling to the ground, I'd smile as I splattered across the pavement.

"On the day I met you, I was contemplating taking my own life..." My fingers lifted her chin. "...But now I hope I can live forever, so I can always be with you."

The words expanded Temperance's eyes. "I believe we can actually arrange that."

"Temperance Grace Lee, I have been dying to say this to you for a long time coming..." My hands clutched both sides of her face. "...I love you! I am crazy about you; I am helplessly in love with you."

Huge smiles unfurled across both our faces. "Praised be to The Lord, He gave me you who makes me go to sleep with a smile on my face and something to look forward to every morning..."

Temperance beamed. "Really?"

"Now you are the one asking questions?" I laughed and poked her belly-button to get her to giggle and ease her tension some more.

"Right, you are."

"I was afraid that you didn't feel the same. I just didn't ever think I'd see the day where something like this would happen to me. I always thought I'd end up dead in a field somewhere."

"Please don't say such dreadful things." Her arms invited me to come into them.

"But you changed all of that, you have filled with more peace, happiness, and hope than I could ever imagine." My arms slithered around her waist and ribs. "You are the greatest blessing to ever happen to me; I loved you from the moment I first saw you and I am with you until the end of time, if you will have me..."

Her eyes glowed. "Of course, I will..." She gleamed. "You love me; I must be dreaming..."

"I sincerely hope this is not a dream. If it is, may I never wake from it." I stroked her hair. "I love you; I love you; I love you!" My lips went on a rampage pressing against her cheeks, nose, and lips. "I want to tell you all the time how much I love you, honey bee."

"And I love you, my Butterscotch." Temperance closed her eyes as I closed mine. Our lips were moment away from sharing a kiss until the opening chords to *Here Comes the Sun* echoed through the speakers. We both looked over at the stereo as lightning began to slowly creep up her arm. "I told you one lie..." The harmonium and acoustic guitars continued play in the background. "This is my favourite song." She smiled and glanced down at the purple and blue lightning which seemed to bounce with the melodies playing through the stereo. Strangely enough, it did not touch me even with my hands and arms around her. "I always imagined having a daughter and singing this to her." Tempie swung her hair.

Her voice was nothing short of angelic. I never heard her sing like this before but it was worth the wait. She hit every note and effortlessly harmonised with the melody. The music seemed to come out of her eyes; I stood frozen, in awe of her.

Electricity bounced off of her porcelain skin in rhythm with her cadence, as she sung the chorus. Though I believed it wasn't possible in that moment I fell deeper in love with her.

Joy poured out of her as she attempted to sing the next verse. However, I wouldn't let her get to the next line, I embraced her tight and pressed my lips against hers. She met me with force and threw her arms tight around me. I grabbed a hand full of her hair as we continued to kiss. My hands moved toward the side of her cheek as her nails dug into the back of my shirt; her teeth clenched on my lip as I ran my hands up her midsection and bosom.

Temperance nibbled on my earlobe and breathed into my ear, grabbing the back of my head as my lips worked their way down her neck to her breasts. The two of us pulled away to stare into each other's eyes again. We locked lips with more intensity and Temperance jumped on to my hips.

"Make love to me," she whispered in my ear and tugged at my shirt, as I pressed her against the wall, sucking on her neck as I lowered a strap of her leotard. She panted and gasped as her hands wandered toward my belt. Our lips never parted until we made our way up the stairs into the bedroom and disrobed each other.

Temperance looked at me as if I were a painting in a museum and stroked me as if I were the finest of linens. I gazed at her with a similar wonder, how her hair fell down over her back and marvelled in all of the lovely curves of her body, all of the smooth definitions of her arms, abdomen, legs, and hands. I pulled her close and felt her warm and silky skin rub against the hair on my legs and stomach.

Our tongues flicked back and forth like a game of tennis as we savoured each other's lips. We indulged the flesh and the curves of each other's anatomies; our hands, teeth, and lips traversing every inch of every thigh, glute, abdomen, and private part until finally, we were both one for the first time. Temperance screamed as warmed blood poured on me; I was afraid that I hurt her but her clamping down on my shoulder and gyrating her hips would signal that she enjoyed the experience. Her strength and passion met mine and there were many ecstasies that bellowed through the night which were louder than the clang of the bedposts against the wall, the howls of the wind, or the snow pelting the windows.

We made love for hours which seemed like mere minutes. The icy stillness was overpowered by sweat-drenched heat as we expended all our energies, engaged all of our bodies, and filled each other with our passions until we could not anymore. We collapsed in each other's arms both trying to re-catch our breath until we fell asleep in our tight embrace. In the morning, we made love three more times until we finally found our way into the living room and delved into Temperance's diary.

VOLUME II

10.

*I*f I was to tell you about me, I would have to tell you about my mother. With great pride, I declare she was more than my mum, she was my hero, my best friend, and my elder sister. I am her; she is me...she like me, is a mystery.

To provide you with a true lens into the course of events, I would be averse to merely furnishing leaves from my diary exclusively to serve as an adequate memoir. Therefore, I will also narrate events related to Mother in linear form when appropriate.

This is a story; this is our story. Henceforth, let us commence this tale from where it all began. – Miss Temperance Grace Lee, 19 March, 1884

TREMORS FILLED ABIGAIL'S body as she sat on the lip of the wooden bed frame. The bed sheets were all white, untouched, and unused. The duvet remained on top of the bed with two matching pillows propped against the headboard. Tears trickled down her cheeks, forming small puddles on the faded tile floor. Her auburn hair scattered onto her grey combinations. All of the noise of the infirmary was drowned out by Abigail's contemplation. The chatter, commotion, and footfall were an afterthought. *What next?* The only words that echoed through her mind.

"What is your date of birth?" A sober voice interrupted Abigail's train of thought.

"17th of October..." Abigail gazed up and squinted into the sunlight. "Eighteen-Hundred and Thirty-Eight."

A doctor scribbled notes; Over his wrinkled face, his glasses remain unmoved like his expression. His black wool frock coat shined under the sunlight that beamed through the large windows. Once he finished writing, he carefully removed his eyeglasses.

"Do you have any other children?"

She shook her head.

His tone did not change, still lacking emotion. "So, this is your first child?"

Abigail sniffled. "...yes...." She glanced back and forth.

"And who do you live with?"

Abigail looked up at the ceiling, a sudden fear of punishment gripped her. Sister Alice could never know...but every remark seemed like a gamble that could bring forth such a possibility.

"No one, I am an orphan..."

The doctor raised his eyebrows.

"Miss Lee, when you first arrived you didn't strike me as a lass, we'd find wandering the streets..." The doctor sported the same apathetic glare he donned just moments ago. "Are you from around these parts?"

The question brought her back to a field on the outsides of Evington on a cool autumn morning and the recollections of when she was finally brought home to the nunnery after the incident.

"No, I am from Manchester way."

"Manchester, you say?"

Abigail nodded.

"Why did you journey to Leicester?"

It was only yesterday that Sister Margaret surreptitiously lent her the money for the journey to find help away from the vicarage, if she was with child. All the haunting thoughts that raced through her head in her travels were staring back at her. She had to come up with another quick response.

"I have a mate down this way who invited me to stay at hers until I got sorted..." Abigail stuttered. "Unfortunately, I started to exhibit these symptoms and reluctantly..." She gulped "...I came here under her guidance."

"And how does a homeless orphan become intimate friends with one such a great distance away?"

Abigail tensed; her heart raced. She took a deep breath as the response formed on her tongue.

The doctor studied her and raised his hand. "I was curious to know." He put his glasses back on. "But do tell me, when was the last time you copulated?"

It started with a gossamer gown and the use of a make-shift rope composed of bedsheets to scurry off to *The Shambles Pub*. What was supposed to be a rite of passage for every sixteen-year-old lass, somehow led to this.

She couldn't remember his face, only his red hair and grey plaid vest. It began with him buying her a drink, the next thing she could recall the raindrops kissing her cheeks. Abigail could still see the bruises formed on her pale flesh; the bites over her neck; and the scratches over her breasts; She could recall her soiled gown, also stained by grass; she could still feel the vertigo and the piercing sensitivity to the caws of magpies, matched by the sight of her stockings, her pants, petticoat, and boots all scattered about the meadow. Then there was the breeze that kissed her groin, a foreign experience that chilled her bones; the indiscernible sticky substance dried on the inside of her thighs which filled her eyes with tears. The feelings of shame, embarrassment, resentment, and humiliation returned to her. And yet, even then, Abigail still did not know how she got there.

A loud scream pierced through the room and disturbed her reminiscence. Two nurses stood over an elderly man that convulsed in his bed. Sweat poured down to his chin and soaked the balding area between his grey thatched hair.

What would she say now? What should she do? She still didn't know. Abigail was immured in fear and confusion whilst the doctor stood over her waiting for an answer which finally formed audibly.

"...on my day of birth."

Abigail glanced back at the doctor as he took more notes.

"And since the father is unknown, the child is clearly an unfortunate."

She scowled. "You need not put it so crudely."

"I have a lot of patients to tend to..." He cleared his throat. "...I will have you remanded to the infirmary in Crumpsall."

"Crumpsall?"

"Since you are a Manchester lass, I am sure you are familiar with the ward there..."

She forced a smile but never had actually been to either Crumpsall or Manchester. Her stomach turned in knots.

"...The Union is for women in your predicament. You will be looked after and once you have given birth; you can acquire further accommodation for the both of you there."

"But I am not seeking accommodation."

The doctor took a large breath through his nose. "Well we cannot have you or your bubby out on the cold streets in the dead of winter..."

Abigail gulped. "What would it cost me?"

"A courtesy of the state."

"Is this a workhouse?"

"That's one way to define it." The doctor glanced down at Abigail from the bridge of his nose.

When the thought of a workhouse came to Abigail's mind, she was filled with the image of dirty floors, overcrowded rooms, and bowls of cold gruel. It was no place for anyone; it was no place for her child. In her reverie, the doctor had made his way toward the exit.

"Wait!" She leapt from her bed. "I believe we've gotten off on the wrong foot."

The doctor turned around.

"I am actually well off, you see."

"Are you?" He smiled. "Is that why, you came here?"

"None would believe me if I told them I could not remember the father, I was stupefied." Her eyes watered up. "I will be disowned."

"Are you implying that someone forced themselves upon you?"

Tears trickled down Abigail's cheeks.

The doctor showed no remorse in his ice-cold glare. "Did you notify the authorities?"

She remained silent.

He said nothing, as if her behaviour confirmed something he already knew. The doctor turned and took one step toward the exit.

"There was no evidence to make an accusation."

"Your account has an uncanny way of contradicting itself." He spoke at length.

"Please, you've got this wrong..." Abigail's white socks slid across the floor that was stained in all types of bodily fluids. She winced in pain as cold steel smashed into her knee. "Bloody bedpost!" Abigail kicked the frame in retaliation. The sheer force of her blow caused the cot to lift off the ground for a brief moment.

"That is enough!" His voice thundered and froze Abigail in place. "...now unless you wish to be assessed for hysteria for as well, I recommend you refrain from having another outburst and take advantage of the charity offered to you."

Abigail held her head as her tears collected in the palms of her hands.

"You are one of the best-dressed vagrants I have ever encountered and your character aligns with every practitioner of the great evil that stepped into here previously..." The doctor shrugged his shoulders. "... but the good people in Crumpsall will make no inquiries..."

Abigail was cornered as her choices were reduced to the workhouse or returning to the nunnery she fled and bearing the wrath of the consequences. In either scenario, Abigail wasn't going home.

11.

The skies were overcast and the wind howled. Strands of Abigail's hair danced in front of her eyes and fell backward behind her. Mist splashed against Abigail's face, she squinted, focusing on taking the next step in front of her, prudently hoping to avoid puddles of dark mud that seemed to devour her boots. Her thighs ached from walking against the steep incline of the grassy hill which seemed to have no crest. Finally, Abigail reached the brow of the hill and surveyed the landscape; It looked a lot like where she had called home; it looked like Evington.

Abigail's crimson satin cloak flicked in the wind, she took hold of the garment and pressed it against her to shield her body-hugging crimson bodice from being soaked. A rustle ripped through the sounds of the rain.

Abigail about-faced. "Who is there?"

No response.

When Lady Lee turned back to take a look at the valley, the sky was a charcoal black. Fire had spread across all of the lands in front of her; its embers glowed extra bright in the sea of smoke. The scent of brimstone and sulphur blanketed the fresh and crisp country air of Leicestershire.

"Oh, my goodness." Abigail placed her free hand over her mouth. "I should go for help."

"Mummy," The voice of a young girl called out.

Abigail looked left and right. There was no sign of the source, then she felt a small hand grip at her side.

"Mummy."

Abigail looked down into the blue eyes of a young girl stared up at her. Her plaited copper-red fell over a white chemise and drooping grey skirt. Her eyes transformed from a sparkling azure to a lightning white.

"What is it, darling?"

The girl didn't say anything but only pointed in the direction of the smoke and the fire. When Abigail took her sights off of the little girl into the direction that she pointed towards, a young woman stood in front of her.

Like the little girl, she too had the same piercing sky-blue eyes and long copper-red hair that instead fell down her back. She was fully developed; her fair skin carved into a shapely, svelte, hour-glass figure that was squeezed into a lilac leotard that clung to her athletic physique. Her arms were toned with definition, falling toward her curvy hips, and pressing against her thighs etched with power, strength, and femininity. She had an elegance in her posture, class in her mannerisms, and a grace in her disposition.

"Who are you?" Abigail crossed her arms.

"I am you and I am her."

"I beg your pardon, love?"

The woman said nothing. She turned to grab a bow and an arrow. Lightning briefly flashed from her hands and the arrow had caught on fire. The fire consumed the head of the projectile but did not even spread to any portion of the bow. She pulled back on the tension cord and released the arrow, sending it high into the sky in the direction of conflagration in the valley below, her back muscles tensed and relaxed with its release. There was noticeable bruising on her shoulder blades along with a tear in her suit nearest her navel. A few dry patches of blood specked over her abdomen. The woman turned around, swinging her hair in a gentle flick.

"I always preferred hat-pins, me." She smiled at Abigail. "I have superb precision when I cast them."

"Who are you?"

"I am you and I am her." The woman pointed back towards the little girl.

"If you were my daughter, I would forbid you to wear such provocative attire."

"Pooh..." The woman yawned and waved her hand in front of her mouth, unamused nor stirred by the remarks. "...and where do you suppose I have acquired my inspiration for such fashion from? Sister Alice?" The lady smiled with a warmth and a playfulness. Her sweetness started to pour from her eyes.

Silence filled the air until another voice spoke.

"Temperance is a virtue, but pride is a sin." Abigail recognised the voice. Behind her stood her a friendly face that filled her with solace. The same friend from the night of the incident.

"Ernest, are you acquainted with this woman?" She gazed across at the damsel who bore an eerily striking semblance to her in complexion and facial structure.

Ernest wore a long white shirt with a grey vest and matching pants. A gold pocket-watch chained to his black leather belt; it did not tick; it always stood still. He wore a black top hat with a glistening brim. However, his most stunning accessory laid resting in his right arm. Wearing a white bonnet and a pink combination, an infant slept peacefully despite all that was going around it. "The choice is yours."

"What is?"

The grey and black that filled the skies from fire and stormy weather dissipated into a pastel blue. The skies had filled with a blinding sunlight.

"The choice is yours..." Ernest showed no change in his solemn expression. "Miss Lee."

"Why are you calling me, Miss Lee?"

Once again, she felt a tugging at the side of her skirt. Just like before, it was the little girl. "Miss Lee." She waved and pointed toward the woman who stood in front of her.

"I am Miss Lee" The woman winked at Abigail. "Temperance is a virtue, Madame." She curtsied.

"Abigail!" Another voice cried out to her, this one seemed foreign to her. She looked around in all directions.

"Abigail!" The voice repeated again but she could not locate the source

"The choice is yours."

"What is?" Abigail opened her hands.

Her eyes opened.

"Abigail." Hot vapours from a hard cloth rag spilled across her head. A woman stood over her wearing a white apron, blotches of blood were scattered across it.

"What happened?"

"Do not be alarmed, all is right."

"I don't understand, I..." Abigail yawned, still groggy from awaking in such an abrupt manner.

"Thank The Lord." The nurse kept the warm rag pressed against Abigail's forehead. "Can you hold that for me please?"

Abigail took hold of the rag and kept in place against where her head throbbed. The nurse poured a glass of water from a pitcher. "We nearly lost you during delivery due to the fever and blood loss."

Abigail sat up, disoriented and still unsure of where she was.

"Steady now, dear." The nurse took the rag and handed a glass of water to Abigail. "We assumed that the whisky would have tempered the bearing pains but all it did was cause you to bleed more profusely. Fortunately, we were able to stabilise you after you had lost consciousness..." The nurse gleamed. "...you've given birth to a healthy baby girl."

Abigail smiled. "I have a daughter?"

Joy flowed out from the nurse's eyes. "She is a right beaut too. Clearly, she takes after her mother."

Abigail let out a deep breath and laid back against the pillow. She stared up at the ceiling, feeling disoriented but all the more overjoyed. Another nurse entered with a baby wrapped a blanket in her arms. The face of the child could not be made out, until the nurse gently placed it in Abigail's arms. She gripped the child tight and then she cried. Abigail brushed away the blanket to study its little lips, button-shaped nose, and its eyes still shut. She glowed with ebullience as she cradled her daughter; studying her pink and soft skin.

"Isn't she adorable?"

Abigail kissed the child's forehead. "All that anguish I have endured is straight as an elm if this is the end result."

Abigail could not take her eyes off the baby, ecstasy consumed her. She immersed in her daughter's subtle movements, her minute stretches, and jostling of her petite head to find the most comfort against her mother's bosom.

"Miss Hyde will produce a certificate of birth of you. The registrar should have it to you later today."

Abigail kept her eyes on the baby as it stretched its arms toward her, letting out a slight yawn.

"What shall you call her?"

One name crossed her mind, flashing like a bolt of lightning. "Temperance..." Abigail stroked the dome of the baby's head. "...Temperance Grace..." She curled her index finger and gently rubbed its cheeks.

"Temperance Grace Lee, born 15th of July, in the year of our Lord, eleven-hundred eighteen fifty-five at eleven minutes past eleven."

12.

Mother always told me, she regretted not keeping diary as it could have chronicled some major events her life and give her a chance to reflect on them. As such, she purchased me a book of loose leaf so I can always have something to hold onto from my younger days. Though I was so much older then and younger than that now, this is a memoir of an afternoon in May of 1863.

"Poppet!"

"Coming, Mum!" I scampered out of bed into the sitting room.

"Would you like a brew?" Mummy gripped a metal kettle that hissed with vapour.

My mother was a stunning woman. It was early in the morning and she appeared so elegant in a set of combinations with her hair up. At the time, Mummy was four-and-two years of age; she had deep blue eyes and fair, flawless, porcelain skin. As such I always thought it was an honour to be said that I looked like her and in many ways was a miniature of her. Many said I spoke like her, used her terms, and also had Mum's wit, class, and sense of humour. The only discernible difference was our hair. Mum was a dark auburn whilst I had a distinct auburn-cinnamon shade.

Mummy opened an oak-coloured cupboard and took out two white teacups. After she prepared the tea, she stepped away from the kitchenette to the sitting area behind where two green couches were positioned around a brown coffee table. The flat was not large by any means, it consisted of one room that had basic kitchen fittings, an area to sit, and a table near a large window where we had our meals together.

On clear days, the emerging skyline of smokestacks, factories, and mills could be seen in the distance. Opposite them, the tree-lined suburbs of Levenshulme and Reddish were always visible. Mother marketed her archery skills there and offered lessons to those who could afford to make a hobby of it. She did it with the hope she would find a potential suitor. Unfortunately for Mother, she never had any success and I couldn't understand why.

Rain pelted the windows on that spring afternoon and thick fog encroached on the view. All that could be seen is the large park which stood across from our home. It was an emerald oasis and private refuge from the coal-black reaches of Manchester's City Centre for all the residents that lived around it; it was called Ardwick Green.

I walked over toward the couches and saw my copy of Jane Eyre sitting on the table. I reached for it, pulled my combinations tight to me (which matched Mother's), and threw myself onto the cushion of the couch.

Mother placed the two cups of tea upon the coffee table and sat next to me. She kissed me on the forehead. I smiled and cuddled close to her.

"How are you getting on with that, lovely?"

"I cannot understand this word, mama." I pointed at a line in the text.

"Opprobrium." She ran her hand through my hair.

"What does that mean?" Her cheek rested against Abbie's breast.

"It's when someone is nasty and disagreeable."

"Like when you didn't agree with the lady down the hall making noise in the middle of the night?"

Mummy laughed to herself for a moment. "That's correct, Temperance."

"Some of these words are difficult, Mummy."

"Well, it is important that you know them darling." She looked up at the pine rafter. "Sometimes people try to use big words to hide the truth from you and make it hard to understand the facts."

"They could do but I like the part where Jane saves that Mister Rochester from the fire." I closed the book. "I wish I could do that."

She took the novel out of my hand. "You can do anything you desire, beautiful." Mummy reached over and handed me my cup of tea. "Do you remember who was starting all those fires?"

"That Bertha did." I took a sip.

"Yes, and that was a very naughty deed." Mother reached for her cup of tea. "Don't you get any ideas now." She pinched my cheek.

"Why do you think she would do something like that, Mum?"

"I suppose that Rochester wasn't a saint himself." She took another sip of tea.

"I don't think I'd want to marry him."

Mummy's smile kissed the cup. "Quite a pity, people do such wicked things, don't they?"

"You don't, Mumma." I put my tea cup back on the table and placed my head on her chest. "You are always good."

She embraced me. "Aww, thank you my dear. You know how to flatter me."

My nose started to itch and tingle until I let out a sneeze. "Pardon."

"I hope you are not getting sick." She rubbed my nose.

"Mum, why do people do bad things?" I sniffled.

"That's a complicated question, poppet. It does not matter as long as we both realise it is important to be kind to others." She reached into my hair once more and pulled her finger out when it came into a clump. "Tempie, we need to sort your hair. Shall I plait it for you?"

"Yes, please." I sat up. "Can I do yours too?"

"Of course, you can." She smiled. "We can clean the cistern first and fill that old iron tub with some hot water and have a bath."

"And we never have to leave our bedroom!" I clapped my hand and sneezed once again.

"Bless you, dear."

"Mummy, why would Bertha put a house on fire?"

"She was angry." Mother placed her hand on the back of my head and rubbed it for a moment. "She was locked in an attic on her own. That's a really naughty thing to do. I reckon Bertha thought the fire would stop anyone else from being mean to her."

"But people did mean things to you, Mum and you never put anything on fire."

She laughed. "Heavens, no. I suppose if I did, we would have to shout the fire brigade and some dashing lad would have to come save us both."

"Even the lady that you boxed for three quid."

"Temperance Grace, what are you on about?" She grabbed my shoulders and looked into my eyes. "Where did you hear that?"

"Mister Arthur."

"What else has he been telling you?" She scowled.

"He said that you are a fit dish."

"What did he say?!" Her eyes bulged.

I didn't understand that he was using vulgarities to describe her. I thought it was an honest compliment in retrospect.

"He also said you are good at bows and arrows, knitting, cooking, cleaning, and being a pew-jile-ist."

"I believe the word you are referencing is pugilist, dear."

"I found out it's another word for boxer." I made a fist and giggled. "I am going to be the next women's champion in bare-knuckle boxing and batter lads just like you." I flexed my arm muscle. "I would be great at it, see..."

Mother squeezed my arm. "You are a strong lass, it's obvious when we have our romps." She shook her head and smiled. "...but you best stick to reading your books, darling."

I grabbed Mummy's arm and squeezed her muscle. Once she felt my fingers on top of it, she flexed. My eyes bulged as my fingers expanded around the bulge. She did that to amuse me and it always worked.

"I wish I could be as strong, pretty, and clever as you."

She blushed.

"And you did this in your corset?"

"Yes, but it slows me down. It's armour that protects my body should I get hit." Her hand cupped my chin. "I could be injured, otherwise."

A frown formed on my lips at the mention of her being injured. Mother slipped her arm around me to comfort and reassure me. "You must understand Tempie, it was poor of me to do."

"Then why did you do it, Mummy?"

"Papa Ernest was delayed in sending us funds. I had to do what was required to make sure you and Mister Ruffles [my stuffed toy elephant] had a warm bed to sleep in."

"...Please don't fight anyone again, I can sell my toys instead..." I threw my arm across her and placed her head on her. "I don't want anyone to hurt you."

"Such a sweet girl." She stroked my head. "I promise you, my lovely. I won't." Mother looked over at her collection of gowns and dresses lying on the maiden, all vibrant colours and pastel hues. Though Mummy was not what society called a "well-bred woman", she purchased a full wardrobe of bodices, corsets, petticoats, overdresses, hats, bonnets, and chemises that would lead one to believe otherwise. Needless to say, all of these items accentuated her beauty.

"Can you tell me more about the workhouse?" I looked up at her. "I can't remember it."

"Well you wouldn't my dear, you were just a small little thing." Mummy chuckled. "You only had six months when we left." She rose to her feet. "We left in the dead of Winter." Mummy put her hands on her hips. "That mean Miss Hyde wanted to take you from me but I wouldn't

let her." She glowed as she looked down at me. "I have a few things saved from there I can show you."

Mother exited into the bedroom and moments later she returned with a folder, *Abigail E. RW6 (With Child – Lee, Temperance G.)* written on the face of it in bright red. Below it, a random assortment of numbers stamped: *1855-25-07-04.*

"What does all that mean?"

"It references the day we were placed there, the 25th of July, year of our Lord, Eighteen Hundred and Fifty-Five."

"What was it like there?"

"A small cold draughty room with a flimsy iron-framed cot and a small wooden crib that you barely fit into. The floor panels were made of a dark larch wood that were scuffed in dust and dirt. You wouldn't want to tread barefoot because you could get a splinter which led to infection. Five minutes without footwear could lead to weeks of being bed-ridden." The folder draped in Mothers' fingers "I've seen it happen. Why do you think we keep this place neat and tidy?"

I smiled at her and listened on.

"We shared a clay chamber pot. It was the traditional periwinkle coating on the outside, lined with hay inside. I was always reminded that it was my duty to clean it as we were not staying at a coaching house. We had one quilt and one set of combinations which you soiled often since there were never enough nappies. In the winter, you could hear the inmates exchanging jokes whenever they had to shovel the snow but they were soon interrupted by one of the porters reminding them that it was not time for leisure and idleness."

"That sounds like slavery."

"Don't tell the Members of Parliament, they will argue that this is for the public good." Mummy chuckled.

She opened the folder and removed a certificate of birth with my name on it, I noticed Miss Penelope Hyde had signed it. Mother looked *down at the document, reminiscing as if she was reliving my birth all over again.*

"So why was Miss Hyde mean? She was at my birthday."

"She was a Matron's Assistant. Part of her duties was performing clerical work for the registrar." Mummy looked over at me. "Like all the other women that worked there, she was covered in black draping garments that covered her from neck to toe. Her hair was tied up and tucked beneath one of those cup-like white bonnets. That woman's boots used to thunder against the floor wherever she went. She had this distant gaze that showed how disinterested she was in the people that came in there." Mummy took a sip of tea. "She was no different with me. When I was declared fit for work, I was forced to make a decision."

"What decision, Mumma?"

"I had two weeks to decide whether to stay there or go. If I stayed there, they were going to separate us. If I was going to leave, I had to find work to support the both of us. The trouble is, no one would employee me because I had you out of wedlock." Mummy took another sip of tea. "Miss Hyde used to tell me that a chaste woman is an angel but should one lose their purity, you might as well be condemned to Hell."

"You are right, Mum." I looked down at the folder that trembled in her hand. "She doesn't sound very nice."

"She told me that I should put you up for adoption if I wouldn't sign you into an apprenticeship. Basically, I had to hope a good family fostered you or one day when you were old enough you would be shipped off to one of those sod-awful cotton mills." Mother shook her head. "I wouldn't let that happen." Mother cringed. "Penny as she was called always reminded me of the conditions of our accommodation and thus if I didn't like them, I could try my luck in Ashton-under-Lyne or Stockport."

"So, what did you do?"

"I wrote a letter..." She picked up another piece of loose leaf. *"...to an old friend."* Mother slid another letter across the table. *"Have a go at reading it, Tempie."* I picked up the letter and started to read.

"Dear Abbie,

It is always a pleasure to hear from you. I am delighted to hear that you have safely given birth to a lovely baby girl. Perhaps, one day when things are more settled, I can meet Temperance. We have certainly come a long way from that bitter morning, you returned to the inn."

"What happened?" I glanced up at Mumma, still innocently unaware of the topic of conversation, at the time.

"Carry on, you are doing fabulous." Mother replied in an expressionless manner, unmoved by the nature of the question.

On the last occasion that you had written to me, you had told me you were placed into the state's custody in Manchester. I see from the correspondence address that you are still under their care in Crumpsall. Upon reviewing what you have disclosed to me, it seems that you and Temperance find yourselves in quite a conundrum.

I would be keen to offer you and your daughter a place to stay here but I don't believe that would be in either of our best interests. A while back, Alice called hoping to learn of your whereabouts, I of course denied possessing that knowledge with respect to your present predicament. If Alice were to turn up whilst you two were here, one could only imagine how that would play out." *I stopped reading for a moment. "Mummy who is Alice?"*

"That's for another conversation, sweeting." She rubbed my back. *"You are doing well, keep going."*

I do understand that some are very dogmatic in their ways. Since you have left, some are regretfully, more bound to believe in the falsehoods and rumours concerning your pregnancy than the actual course of events." *I once again halted at this sentence. "What does that mean, Mum?"*

She pointed back toward the next line of the letter. "...However, these are the same lot who are always too concerned with how things appear as opposed to what they truly are.

I know what happened that night and there isn't a day that goes by that I don't find myself wishing to have stopped that gal-sneaker. I knew his intentions toward you were anything but pure and though I warned him that I had my eye on him, I could not detect his tampering with your drink. He must have covertly slipped in a substance when my back was turned which caused you to black out and enabled him to..." *Mother's hand pressed over the letter.*

"Skip that part, darling..."

I looked up at her with confusion. "...does this have anything to do with me?"

Mother gently nudged me to read from where her finger landed.

"I told you that I would always be there for you Abbie and nonetheless long to aid you two lovely ladies in the best manner possible. Enclosed is ten pounds, I hope that will get you both off to a good start in the "Cottonopolis" as they refer to Manchester. It seems you have more opportunity there anyhow. Whilst I am certain you have had your difficulties acquiring a steady wage, I am also confident that it is only a matter of time before you find success. Remember, you are an exquisite young woman and blessed with all sorts of talent and ability. Anyone who does not recognise this is nothing more than blind, lame, and foolish; perhaps they are all three.

The inn has been quite profitable as of late, should you require any more assistance please do write us and I would be happy to send you more funds. I have a daughter and granddaughter to look after and it's the Christian thing to do.

Warmest affections,

Ernest."

My eyes twinkled extra bright after reading that letter. "He's so lovely..."

Mother took the letter from my handle with a gentleness and placed it back into the file. "Anytime I needed money, all I had to do was write him and he would be quick sending it to us..."

I kicked my legs and listened to the story with enthusiasm.

"When I collected the tenner from his letter, I had to be sure that Miss Hyde didn't know or she would have taken it off me." Mother's eyes bulged. "But your mother had the last word with her when she prepared the discharged papers." Her eyes lit up as she smiled at me. "Thanks to his generosity, we were able to move in here right away." She looked over toward the door. "Speaking of which, can you see if the post is under the door?"

"Yes, Mummy." I hopped off the couch toward the door, a long trail of auburn-cinnamon hair followed me across the room. "There is nothing there, Mumma."

"Thank you, darling." Concern started to grow on Mother's face. "Quite odd as it's not like him to take so long to respond."

13.

16 *May 1863 -*
Days passed and still there was no correspondence from Pop Pop.

"*Tempie, dear!*"

"*Yes, Mummy.*"

"*It's time to go, my love.*"

"*Coming...*" *I called back.*

As I ran in, an envelope appeared under the door. "*Hold fire, poppet.*" *Mother ran her finger against her shimmering gold-coloured corset clad to her body. She had let her hair down which fell back against the white chemise stuffed under the corset. Her heels echoed across the flat as she walked toward the envelope. Passing the large white sunhat left on the dining table, along with a matching bodice that complemented her scarlet overskirt lying adjacent to it. Mother grabbed the sides of the brown envelope that sat in between the copper catch of the door and the marigold floor mat.*

To the Attention of Ms. Abigail Elizabeth Lee, inscribed in a large legible font, drawing a sense of urgency to the document. The return address belonged to a solicitor.

"*Loughborough?*" *She opened the door to see if the post man was about, perhaps he could provide more details into the origins of the parcel. However, the corridor was an empty and dark catacomb. A scarce twinkle of light filled the stairwell and reflected modestly against brass doorknockers fixed to each of the living quarters on the floor. Mother ran her finger through the seam of the envelope to break the crimson seal. After that, she stepped out into the corridor and shut the door behind her.*

FROM THE CHAMBER OF W.C. Thomasson, Principal Solicitor Representing the Estate of J. Ernest Tomlinson.

"Estate?" Abigail's chest rose and fell with increased speed.

To Mistress Lee,

We write you today as executors of the will of the deceased Mister Josiah Ernest Tomlinson, an individual who we have come to understand you had developed close relations with.

"Deceased?!" Her hand patted against her forehead.

It is with our deepest sympathies that we regret to inform you of Mister Tomlinson's untimely passing, the cause of which appears to be self-murder. Mister Tomlinson's body was discovered a week ago in the front bedroom above a public house he operated. The mention took her back to that bitter morning when she sprinted to *The Shambles*, desperate for answers. She knocked relentlessly, trembling when Ernest finally answered the door. She didn't know what to expect but he invited her inside, cooked her breakfast, and offered her some fresh clothes that used to belong to his daughter. As Ernest prepared a bath for her, she sat in that very room. The walls were painted in a gentle yellow that glowed from the early sunlight entering through the windows, piercing through white curtains that danced in an occasional breeze. She sat atop the bed which hadn't been slept in for ages but the oak frame was still polished and the white bedsheet neatly done. The cream-coloured quilt was folded, with four fluffed pillows resting against the headboard, and a stuffed elephant with a friendly smile resting against them. It was the bedroom of Ernest's daughter, Clara. *"On his person, we found a letter stating that he wished for you to be the heir to the enterprise and total sum of his assets.*

Whilst we understand that Mister Tomlinson regarded you as his daughter, discernible through your correspondence with him and the memoranda he collected of your visits, his wishes cannot supersede a previous arrangement originated in his previous marriage to his late wife. The primary beneficiaries enlisted were Mister Tomlinson's wife Evelyn, his eldest daughter Sophia, and his youngest daughter Clarissa. All of whom died prematurely from diphtheria in 1851. Unfortunately for Mister Tomlinson, he never endeavoured to destroy the previous contract and thus nullify the existing will.

It is likely that Mister Tomlinson buried the preceding arrangement in his grief and spontaneously created a new document that could not have been legitimised in a court of law. Alas, we are forced to review the former document on file which vaguely declares next of kin, in the event Evelyn, Sophia, or Clarissa were unable to inherit. Moreover, whilst we understand that you were Mister Tomlinson's daughter in heart and spirit, there is no formal documentation that establishes Mister Tomlinson as your parent. Hitherto, it would be strictly on the bounds of circumspection that we can name you as the aforementioned next of kin, albeit there is no paperwork to reinforce such a premise. Therefore, in complying with the terms of his will, Mister Tomlinson's next of kin as directed would be the sole son of his late wife's only sister. We have engaged in negotiations with the bequeathed with a hope of ameliorating your circumstance.

It has also been determined that Mister Tomlinson was an administrator of a trust that was established for what we perceive to be a child born to him in a Manchester workhouse. The clandestine nature of this account also suggests that the child itself is illegitimate. Whilst the account in question cannot be transferred to the custody of Mister Tomlinson's nephew, it can neither be withdrawn to compensate you. However, we are still investigating this matter further as the details surrounding said account remain a mystery. If any relevant developments should emerge in our enquiries that pertain to you, we will be sure to contact you in due course.

We appreciate that this news is a misfortune that you did not wish to learn of, the grim revelation of Mister Tomlinson's demise would be a great challenge for any to acquiesce. Once again, we extend our condolences. Please correspond with us, if we can be of any additional assistance to you.

Very truly yours...

"You look scrumptious today." Her reading was interrupted by a man who stood across from her in the corridor. He was about five-feet seven inches and wore a khaki-coloured vest over a white shirt. His black bow-tie dangled from beneath his starched collar. Under a tan flat-brimmed hat, his menacing brown eyes locked onto Abigail.

Tears trickled down her cheeks. "Thank you."

"You are quite the ravishing beauty." He rubbed the side of her corset.

"Keep your scruffy hands off me, Arthur."

"What the devil is wrong, Abigail?" He reached for her hand; she jerked her arm away.

"Just let me alone."

Arthur followed Abigail into her flat. "I only want to help."

"I have an idea on where you can start..." Abigail about-faced with a vexed glare. "Quit reciting lustful overtures to my daughter..." Her voice rose.

"Your daughter is a lovely young lady." He removed his hat, revealing his short black hair. "I am merely complimenting her mother."

"Do not attempt to deceive me Arthur, you haven't the slightest bit of sincerity." She gripped the letter tight in her right hand. "Regretfully, I am forced to postpone our catch-up since I have to focus my attention towards how I am going to pay the rent..." Abigail opened the door to the flat and attempted to shut the door, until Envy's hand served as an impediment.

"I can lend you the cash." He reached into his pocket and removed a wad of notes. "How much do you need?"

"No, thank you. Be a part of your next cheeky flutter, I will not."

"It worked out well for us, previously." He placed the money back in his pockets.

"I also promised my daughter that I would never box again, as it frightens her. So, thank you for your offer, but kindly I refuse."

"Even if you have a clear proficiency for it, you know you are far too pretty to be getting into scraps, anyhow."

"Many thanks, can you go now?"

"May I finish what I had to say?"

"You have thirty seconds and I have started counting."

"I am gobsmacked that there aren't a hundred blokes calling at your door every day to court you." Arthur eyed her up and down as if she were a juicy piece of meat, a steak served with some chips and an ale.

"There have been a few but once they learn of Tempie, all bets are off, right?" She tilted her head to the side with a mischievous smile making it quite evident that Abigail quite enjoyed dropping the pun.

"The way of the world, in it? Doesn't change the fact that they are bleeding ridiculous. No one would ever suspect you had a child." He rubbed her forearm. "You have amazing skin, beautiful eyes, and your body is magnificent..."

"Charmed, I am confident your love interests are swooning at such sweet words..."

"Is there any fault in saying I lust for you? That's the problem with everyone, they don't say how they feel."

"How profound and philosophic." Abigail snickered and attempted to shut the door.

"What I would do to have you..." Arthur placed his hand in the way.

"Regretfully, you shall not..." Abigail attempted to shut the door again but once again the antagonist prevented such an event.

"No, no!"

"Do I have to shout the authorities for intrusion? Or perhaps you are eager to wager on a dust-up between you and I?"

"How much do you need, Abbie?"

She stood between her flat and the corridor. She leaned against the door frame, glaring at Arthur with expansive breaths. He watched her breasts rise and fall with each respiration, looking like a dog stuck in heat. "My eyes are up here, love." She directed Arthur's attention away from her chest by pointing towards her eyes. "Perhaps if I let you touch these; you will sod off..."

"I will lend you twenty quid."

"And what do you ask in return for such a generous contribution?" Abigail crossed her arms to cover her breasts. He approached her with caution and placed her hands around her waist, moving closer towards her as if he was going in for a kiss. Abigail did not budge nor elicit any reaction.

"You." He whispered in her ears.

"Me?"

"Aye, you. For a night, maybe two."

"Is that all?" She shook her head, playing along with a heavy dose of wit and banter.

"I don't know if I'd ever get tired of shagging you." He reached behind her; she slapped his hand away.

"I will drop my knickers at such purple prose, the lotties must be salivating..."

"If you won't let me have you, perhaps we can turn your looks into a profitable venture for both of us."

"Are you asking me to be a tart?" She whispered as she mocked his remarks.

"Think long and hard. I reckon lads would pay a hundred quid to smash your jam."

Abigail cringed at the terminology; she retreated toward her flat and slammed the door in his face.

"My associate and I will get thirty percent each, you take forty. Easily you can be on a couple quid for just a few hours of work. Good luck finding that round here with all the strikes on and the cotton shortage." His voice carried through the wood of the door.

Abigail opened the door wide enough where she could converse with Mister Envy without obstruction. "I am unsure of what I am more astounded of your creative entrepreneurial acumen or your grotesque objectification of women. Do you actually believe I would have it?

Arthur tensed up and did not respond.

"When you are ready to answer me, I am all ears. I am not really the sort of woman that has her jam smashed as you vividly put it." Abigail condescended with a cheeky smile which transformed into an aggressive glare. "So, thank you but no thank you, I am not interested, filthy minger."

"Are you willing to reconsider that if we raised your cut to half?"

Abigail shook her head.

"The way I see it; you don't have much of a choice in this scenario. Even if it is just a couple of nights, you and I both know that will assure allocation..."

"Assure allocation? Look at you with your ten guinea terms." Abigail glowered at Arthur with disgust.

"You know freckles appear under your eyes when you get angry."

"So, go have a Randy about it you dirty scrote!"

He laughed and leaned back. "Fifty-five percent to you, final offer..." He tipped the brim of his hat and walked down the corridor into the shadows. "Give us a knock when you are ready."

Abigail slammed the door which caused a crash that resonated across the hallway.

I HEARD MOTHER YELLING outside in the corridor and cried out to her several times hoping it would give her reason to get away. When she had stepped out, I went into the bedroom to make the bed. I knew she had returned when I heard the front door slam behind her.

"Tosser." She threw the letter on the floor.

"Mummy!"

"I am coming, sweet." Mummy entered the bedroom.

"What's happened with Papa Ernest?" I fluffed a pillow.

The mention of the subject caused her to tear up. She couldn't answer.

"What's wrong, Mummy?"

She swallowed. "I do not know how to say this..."

"What is it?"

"Papa Ernest is dead."

"Dead?"

"I am afraid so, peach." A tear trickled down her cheek.

"No, Mummy!" I threw my arms around her as she started to sob.

She shut her eyes and held me. "He cared for both of us, greatly."

"Why did he die?"

Mother pulled away to regain composure. In a circular motion, she rubbed my shoulders. "How do I explain?" She wiped my nose with the back of her hand, as I was now crying, as well.

"There are some people in this world who become very sad. Though they might have a lot of reasons to feel that way, they arrive at a point where they believe that the only thing that would help is..."

"Dying?"

"If I could pray for one thing it is that you never have to learn of why someone would be driven to such a point. Sadly, it's often the gentlest of souls that seem to be chased by that ugly black dog."

"A black dog ate him?" I covered my mouth.

Mummy brushed back some strands of hair that fell over my eyes. "Long story short, I suppose you can say it is just that."

"But George the bulldog over the road is black and he always licks me when he sees me. I do not understand..."

She broke a brief smile.

"The black dog is a metaphor for melancholia, sweeting."

I looked down at the floor, also upset I didn't know the meaning of the analogy. "...What made him sad? I thought we made Pop Pop happy?"

"It's a terribly long story to gab about..." She pressed her lips against my cheek. I looked down and imagined what could have made him, so sad; Suddenly, a thought burst into my mind. "Does this have anything to do with what you didn't want me to read about in the letter?"

"No, darling." She pressed her hand to my cheek.

"Because I know that a pelican didn't drop me off as a late birthday gift for you..." I looked up at her and bit my thumb, sucking on it to distract me from the sorrow.

Mother squinted her eyes at me, seemingly inquisitive as to how I could arrive at such a conclusion. "What would make you say that?"

"Cause..." I ran and grabbed my doll from the couch. "...when you gave me Hortie on my sixth birthday, it was to celebrate." I clutched the doll against me and stroked its long brown curls. Her blue painted eyes twinkled to match her narrow black serpentine smile. "...but you don't celebrate your birthday even though I was a belated gift for it..."

"Belated..." She smiled "...that's a good choice of words, poppet." She grew unsettled but she tried so desperately to conceal it.

"...you would celebrate your birthday, if that was the case."

Mother looked down.

"...also, if a pelican left me at the workhouse, wouldn't Miss Hyde have stolen me from you like you said she tried to?"

"Tempie dear, how else would you have gotten here, if it wasn't the pelican that brought you to me?"

"Please don't lie to me, Mumma."

Tears formed in her eyes and she sat back. Once again, she tried to cover them up but there was no use, as she appeared ready to weep.

"I think you and Pop Pop told me about the pelican whilst you kept a secret about my father." I coughed into my sleeve. "...since I never met him..."

"Pop Pop is your father..."

"No..." I shook my head. "He's your father, so he can't be mine too..."

"Temperance, he chose to be a father to me, much like with you..." She pressed her hand to nose briefly. "...He loved very you much."

"And I loved him the same but that's not the point, Mummy...."

She was aghast though it was hard to determine exactly what she was feeling. Mother nevertheless seemed to be somewhere else, recollecting a series of events and watching them unfold before her very eyes.

"Mummy..."

She turned to look at me.

"Please tell me what really happened."

"I don't know if this is the right time..."

"You can trust me, Mummy." I took a step towards her. "Shouldn't I know the truth?" Tears started to swell in my own eyes. "...it's not good to keep secrets from each other..." I clutched my doll tighter and bit on my thumb again for relief from the excitable and nervous energy which consumed me.

A tear broke from her eye and she cupped my cheek, letting out a faint sniffle before she sighed. "...I've always wanted to protect you, Temperance." *Her hand smudged my cheek.* "...I never wish to withhold anything from you, my love."

"Then, tell me, Mummy." *I took her hand.* "...I can ask Hortie to leave us, so it's just you and I."

She glanced down and smiled at the doll briefly. "She can stay." *Mother swiped away a tear and composed herself.* "I was hoping you wouldn't have to find out this way, until you've matured more and were a tad older." *She plucked a handkerchief from the table beside her.* "You are only seven, after all..." *Mother blew her nose.*

"I am nearly eight, thank you."

Her finger flicked against my shoulder.

"Oww!" *I cried out from the sting.*

"Don't be cheeky, Temperance."

"I am sorry, Mummy."

"Let's go have a seat." *Mother reached under my arms and picked me up, moving us both over to the couch.* "There is no easy way to narrate this for you." *She placed her arm around me.* "As it's not something I speak about." *Her stare returned to her.* "...and yet I think about that day all the time, every detail; every moment. I remember what I wore the night of, awaking in that field the morning after, and rushing through Evington past that old Baptist Church to Pop Pop's inn." *She looked over at the front door.* "It was the incident itself which I still cannot recall."

"Tell me it, as you remember." *I clutched the doll with both arms and listened on.*

She peered down to me. "You are too young for that, I'm afraid."

"Please..." *I placed my hand on her skirt.* "...it may help you as much as it would me..."

Mother pulled me close to her and kissed the top of my head. "I want you to make me a promise then..." *She cupped my cheeks, I nodded back at her. "...promise me that you will always remember that no matter what I tell you that I would do it all again, if it would lead me to you." She pressed my head against her bosom. I nodded again and embraced her tight and so she gave me one more kiss before chronicling the events of that fateful day.*

Her curiosity and vim for being free from the walls of the vicarage compelled her to put on her finest clothes and sneak off to the nearest pub to commemorate her turning one and six. There is where she met Pop Pop for the first time and she ordered a pint. Sat next to her was a dashing lad at the bar that she had never saw previously. He was charming, gallant, had a way with words, and was nearly as intoxicating as that first pint of brown ale that Mummy sipped on. In a rapid blur, she became overwhelmed and felt the need to relieve herself in the outhouse. When she returned, her condition worsened. This charismatic lad who Mother recalls having the same shade of hair colour as I, escorted her out. In the chilled autumn night, he offered her accommodation for the evening, as she feared being disciplined severely if she should return thoroughly 'squiffed', as she put it. The next thing she could remember was awaking in a field alongside a dirt road on the outskirts of town. It was there, that I was conceived.

Mother's detail was rich, she told me all of the sights, sounds, smells, and sensations she felt Though it were many years ago, her anecdote would have left one to believe they were there with her, as it happened; perhaps they could live it as she did.

Her tale boded similar qualities when she described her engagements with Pop Pop (called Ernest) who tended to her all through that 'bitter morning', as both previously defined it. He comforted her; he consoled her. However, Mother was reluctant to leave his inn as she feared her 'wig would be dashed' or to put it simply, she was afraid she would be beaten when she returned to the vicarage. Nevertheless, Pop Pop re-assured her, it would be otherwise. He was also a surrogate father to Alice and thus was quite persuasive with her.

In this instance, he encouraged her to show grace, care, and mercy. Ultimately, he was the reason why her punishment was less severe than she anticipated. Whilst no physical peril presented itself to Mum, she was still locked in her chamber for ten days, albeit she had barely any energy to leave her bed for many weeks after the assault.

Every day, she relived the event but yet she had no one to speak with, nor did she have the inclination to speak about it; it wasn't apropos according to her or according to the words of one she refused to name: the portion for being a sinful temptress.

Once Mother had finally started to put some semblance of the incident behind her, she experienced early signs that she was with child. Fearful of the reaction to revelation, Mum fled the vicarage seeking refuge and help, elsewhere.

At the conclusion of her recapitulation of the events surrounding my conception, we embraced each other tightly and cried in each other's arms until we drifted off for a brief kip. My eyes an opened hour later to the sound of wind whooshing against the window panes. I lurched my head up and looked at Mummy who yawned and stretched her arm, patting my back to alert me to let her up.

"Oh my, dear me..." She yawned again. "...it's nearly time for tea." Mother rose from the couch and I followed.

"Mum, can we have trifle tonight?"

"I don't know if today is a good one for that, dearest."

"You always surprise me with treats from the confectioner when something sad happens." I glanced up at her. "I thought it would lift both of our chins after what happened to Pop Pop." My eyes turned downward. "...and after the story you told me..."

"That's not the issue, my love." Remorse and guilt seemed to overtake her. "...I am not sure I can afford the treacle for us, tonight..."

"You always know what is best, Mummy." I pressed my hands to her leg. "Can I clean the floors for you?"

Mother didn't answer, she seemed lost in thought for a moment, in an intense analysis of important decisions racing through her mind. The remorse and guilt that had just lay siege to her had been replaced with an idea which sprung back her energy.

"On second thought, I best nip out before the confectioner shuts..." Mother bent down. "Since we are having strawberry trifle tonight." She tickled me with a hope that it would elicit a giggle from me.

I clapped my hands with excitement. I admit Mother loved to spoil me, she told me many times she wants to give me everything. She also said it was a delight for her to put a beaming smile on her little girl's face. I was always grateful for that and always wanted to make her equally happy.

"I will tell you what you can do..."

"Yes, Mother." I stood at attention.

"I would like you to wash yourself up, have a change of clothes, and then you can ready the table for tea, darling."

"Sure!" I sprinted off toward the bedroom with sheer joy bursting through my smile.

Mummy placed her hand on my shoulder to signal me to stop. I about-faced and watched her stroll toward the table and take her bonnet, a clean chemise, and a long crimson cloak that draped over one of the chairs. She put her hands through the sleeves of the chemise and pulled it over her corset, then she tossed the cloak around her, grabbed her handbag, and made her way toward the door. "I will be about twenty minutes." She turned the key and stepped into the corridor. "Lock the door behind me, Tempie..."

– T.G.L.

14.

A bigail looked down the shadowy hallway in the direction of the staircase and exit. She waited to hear the door lock and walked onward. As she neared the flat of Arthur Envy, she tried to give herself a multitude of reasons to keep going. But when she reached into her handbag, the scarcity of farthings reminded her that a pound could get her a long way. Envy proposed a figure that could easily treble or quadruple that.

Abigail's hand shook as she gripped the brass door knocker. She took a deep breath and knocked demurely, producing a gentle and elegant cadence. Abigail stepped back and peered around to see if anyone watched.

There was no answer.

She waited and contemplated. After a minute, Abigail took two steps away and then halted to look back at Envy's door.

Abigail could have kept walking and one could imagine what would have transpired if she did so on that afternoon so long ago; but the thought of trifle and making her daughter happy led cause for her to return to the door and knock on again. This time, the door opened in a slow and deliberate manner.

"Abbie." Envy smirked. "I knew you would come around."

"I am not here to exchange pleasantries with you…"

"That will do." He stepped aside so Abigail could enter. "After you."

"You best keep your hands to yourself." She pointed her finger.

"You have my word."

Abigail stepped into the flat at a gingerly pace, tense with each step that she took. Her shoulders hunched and prepared to swat away Arthur's hand in event he attempted to grope her.

"Ah, yes I see we are making new friends already." Another voice spoke from behind Abigail. This one was velvety in texture and had a refinement to it. Abigail turned to see a second man who stood about six-feet, two-inches. He wore a black top hat and matching suit with a most noticeable red tie. The gentleman removed his hat to show his manicured short strands of blonde hair. His green eyes grew larger at the sight of her. Abigail also was taken at the sight of him, her hand extended upward over her breasts.

"I see that Mister Envy is not very good at introductions." He extended his hand. "They call me Pride..."

"Abigail." She smiled and gave her his hand.

Pride kissed her hand. "A privilege and a pleasure, my lady." Pride placed his arm around her back. "Please, take a seat."

He had a commanding presence about him. It wasn't his residence yet he acted as if he owned it. The living quarters was built identically to Abigail's, a one-bedroom facility with a combined sitting, dining, and kitchen area. It featured the same vista of Manchester's skyline of smokestacks, factories, and mills with the same grey cloud of soot and smoke that hovered over the city's centre.

Envy's place of living was far filthier by comparison, however. Dirty dishes piled up in the wet sink. Soiled clothes were scattered over the floors. Papers lie everywhere.

Abigail sat beside Pride on a faded emerald couch that bore many rips and tears in the fabric.

"You will have to forgive the state of this place. Unfortunately, some of us are not practitioners of hygiene." Pride adjusted one of his cufflinks. "So, Abigail..." He turned his attention toward her. "I imagine that you would like this to be as brief as possible. From what from Mister Envy has told me, he proposed a partnership between the three of us."

"If that is how you define motting and showing off me nancy..." Abigail locked her fingers in each other.

Pride laughed. "What sort of chap, do you take me for?"

"To be frank, I don't know what you are"

"I like her, Arthur. A lot of moxie in this one."

"That's for certain." Envy looked across at Abigail.

"Call it what you wish." Abigail rolled her eyes.

"So, do you know how we would go about this?"

"May I take a wild guess?" Abigail studied her cuticle.

"By all means..." Pride smiled.

"I get myself to look like a bit of raspberries and seduce some unassuming bloke?"

"That is a good start."

"I bring the lad here, you charge him for an hour, and I lie there whilst I pretend to enjoy it." Abigail cringed.

"We could take that approach. However, if you are one that is looking to keep some purity about yourself you can simply lure them to our establishment instead."

"So, you are saying that I wouldn't have to..." Abigail cupped one hand and put her opposite pointer finger into the circle she created.

"Not unless it is something you are passionate about." Pride shrugged his shoulders. "Evidently, you struck me as more of a domestic..."

"Wait, but she was supposed to wear some sexy..." Envy sat up nearly infringing upon Pride's personal space.

"Do you have a mind for business, Arthur? Or is it that you are that desperate to see Abigail in her tights?"

Abigail smiled and covered her mouth.

"Now get a hold of yourself Arthur!" Pride raised his hand.

"Fifty-five percent was the final offer, as I do recall." Abigail crossed her leg. "But halves will do just fine, if there is some flexibility in my schedule and we start tomorrow evening."

"No." Envy nearly fell off the couch.

Pride placed his arm in front of Envy. "Done." The room filled with silence. After thirty seconds, Abigail got up from her seat. "If that is all, I best get onto fixing my daughter her tea."

"Oh, but of course." Pride rose to his feet. "Come Madame, I will be happy to see you out."

"You ought to take notes, mate. It all would have went off without a hitch if you took a leaf out of your mucker's book." Abigail teased Envy as she followed Pride to the door.

Envy shot up from his chair. "Do you not realise that this slag just mocked us..."

"What did you call me?" Abigail clenched her fist.

Pride stepped in front of Abigail. "Please forgive my colleague's poor taste."

Arthur stormed towards the two. Pride stood his ground and stared a hole in him. "If you take one more step toward her, I fear something horrific will happen to you..."

Envy froze in place, with a look that he was in fear of his life.

"Apologise to her." Pride's face shook as he issued the demand. "Now!"

"I am sorry," Envy stuttered.

"Go sit down, I will deal with you in a minute." Pride pointed toward the couch. Abigail watched on and felt a mix of emotions. She was frightened herself in many ways but also found the display of dominance very erotic. Pride smiled at Abigail and ushered out the door. "Once again, I am deeply sorry for his incorrigible behaviour. I assure you there will be no more tantrums on his part..."

She bent forward slightly. "I am not bothered. It was very entertaining to see you put him in his place."

Pride chuckled. "I do get a bit carried away at times but I am happy to please you. Can you be here for half-seven on the morrow?"

"Sure." Abigail smiled. "May, I ask you something?"

"Please..." He opened his hand to invite the query.

"You were just telling stories in there to hush him, yes?"

"In regards to what?"

"I was under the impression that when it comes down to it, I am going to have to grit my teeth whilst some dosser feels me up and Heaven forbid whatever else..."

Pride shook his head. "Not by the least."

"Then what is it? Swindling? Gammoning?"

"Most of the lot that we trade with are legitimate customers. What you bring to the table is what I'd like to call strategic marketing. Naturally, a maiden with your beauty and charm will compel many to call at our inn. It's not just adult entertainment that we specialise in. We run a book and imbibe our patrons, as well. You could have easily been a bar maid or a hostess rather than how shall we say, some of our other personnel who hone their talent in more frivolous amusements." Pride raised his eyebrows. "It was Mister Envy that expressed his earnest interest in you being a merchant of the flesh. Granted, I can see why..."

Abigail chuckled. "Nothing new under the sun, there. He has been trying it on for months."

"And that is the sort of reckless behaviour that will be his downfall." He shook his head. "I will be more scrupulous in our relationship. However, please do look your best tomorrow." Pride looked her up and down. "Though, I cannot surmise such a request being too difficult for you to fulfil." He smiled. "You are quite an elegant creature. Please forgive my eyes for wandering should they ever decide to marvel in your incredible physique..."

"Many thanks for your compliments." She batted her eyes. "For the record, I do not mind if you look."

"Though I am enticed, I do draw a line and forbid crossing commerce with hedonistic wants." He nodded. "Unlike my partner, I am not one to have my cake and eat it too." Pride chuckled.

Abigail's cheeks flushed as the conversation dissipated into silence.

"Well..." Pride cleared his throat. "You don't want to find yourself tardy due to our chin-wag."

Abigail's heart beat faster. She had butterflies in her stomach and a tingly feeling all over. "There is no delay."

"You do have a little girl, yes?" Pride smiled. "I anticipate she is expecting your return shortly..."

"She is a bit of a work at times but I love her to pieces." Abigail fanned herself. "If all should go well between us, may I keep my Sundays with her?"

"Of course."

"Thank you."

Pride bowed his head. "My pleasure." He threw his hands behind his back. "So, we shall see you tomorrow night then?"

Abigail smiled with a warmth; her eyes dilated when Pride's vision locked onto her.

"Excellent." Pride extended his hand to shake Abigail's once again. "It was truly a pleasure to meet you."

"Much obliged." She curtsied.

"I trust you and I will have quite the adventure together."

"I hope we do, Mister Pride." Abigail smiled with a gentle nod.

"Call me, Nelson." Pride bowed his head. "Good evening, my lady." He stepped back into the flat and slowly shut the door.

15.

17 *May, 1863*

I watched Mother gaze at herself in the looking glass as she curled her eyelashes and rouged her cheeks. She paid meticulous attention to detail and very much desired to be the portrait of beauty in her time; thus, the shade of her cheeks needed to match the tone of her lips. Mother always made sure her complexion was flawless and her snow-white pallor was maintained, she seldom went out into the sun without a parasol and would go as far as to occasionally place a piece of raw meat over her face to remove any blemishes. Truly, she was beautiful and I always tried to remind her, but I wondered if she actually believed it herself.

Mother's eyes streaked across the room from a dark patch of mould that spread on the ceiling in the corner of the bedroom and then back to her reflection. Perchance she believed looking perfect would free her from the imperfections of our flat; someone would notice her and sweep us away to a better place or so she always hoped as she swept a powdered brush across her the bare portions of her chest. Mother wore a pink silk corset that contoured to her abdomen up to her bosom, the laces clung to her shoulders and plunged toward her bust. It was quite a stunning garment and fit her marvellously. She plaited portions of her hair and wore it up, exposing the back of her neck. Mummy stood up and ran her finger down the sides of the garment, flicking at the blue fringes of her skirt. She glanced down her black-lace stockings and matching leather boots, ensuring every shoe-string was tied.

"Is a gentleman calling?" I bit on my thumb.

Mother smiled. "No, Tempie. I am going to a work do."

"Can I come with you?"

Her heels echoed against the cranky wood floor as she walked toward me. "Adults only, I am afraid." Mother reached down and picked me up, I carefully threw my arms around her neck. "I am sorry, darling." She rocked me against her and kissed my cheek.

"Dora will be here shortly. You like her?"

I answered with a nod. Mother looked nervous, I could tell by how quickly her chest was rising and falling.

"You look very pretty, mummy."

"Cheers, sweeting." Her eyes fluttered as she looked at me. "So, do you..."

There is nothing I could say to that, as I had my hair plaited in two and wore a bog-standard starch chemise with a grey cotton overskirt. I looked like any other girl my age in Manchester, Mummy looked like royalty.

The door knocked twice.

"That must be Dora." She placed me down on top of the red duvet. "You be good for her, dear."

"Enjoy your work, mummy."

We shared a smile as she made her way to the door.

ABIGAIL STOOD IN FRONT of Envy's residence. Her hands soaked in sweat as she reached for the doorknocker. Clamouring noises from inside the apartment repelled her fingers. She let out a deep breath and knocked on; a voice grew louder until the door opened. Pride stood in the entrance wearing a black top hat, matching waistcoat, white shirt, a purple cravat, a grey vest, trousers that matched the coat and hat.

"My lady." He tipped his hat. "You look extraordinary." Pride extended his hand to escort her into the flat, kissing her hand as she entered. "Come in."

Abigail curtsied and followed Pride in as she shut the door; she never left his arm. All Envy could do was frown in disgust, jealous that she fancied his counterpart. Soon after, Abigail escorted Pride to a public house called *The Haberdashery*. Located on Withy Grove, it evolved into a storefront that became a modern mystery in Manchester. The surrounding area, Friedrich Engels defined as "Hell on Earth" or better described it as "a pool of miasma that coalesced from a maze of rookeries, narrow lanes, and densely-populated cottages" complemented by "poor sanitation, flooded cellars, vegetable oils, and excrements scattered across the cobblestone roads." However, The Haberdashery would lead one to believe that no such a place even existed just beyond its walls.

The front of the premises reminded Abigail very much of the inn that Ernest welcomed her to when she was just a teenage girl. However, her surroundings were not rolling hills or woodlands but instead mills, factories, and a thick cloud of smoke that hung over the city like a bad dream. On some days, the smog itself was unbearable and even irritated the lungs of those that never had a cigar a day in their life.

Abigail stood beneath the hanging sign to the pub, confident in knowing she was never out of the sight of Mister Pride. All she had to do, was steer inquiring parties away from the front entrance to the secondary entrance in the back where "other things happened". This is where books were set-up and where male patrons could become "well acquainted" with some of the enterprises' female employees. Lady Lee's assignment was to offer them a possibility of spending time with her in the rear of the tavern if they would only just follow her. It seemed easy enough and it was a good bit of fun for Abigail. The bowlers that rejected any prospect of marriage to her could not resist her. Typically, Abigail was disqualified from being a suitable match due to her "lack of character". In other words, she could not be forgiven because she bore a child out-of-wedlock regardless of circumstance. However, in this instance Abigail was the most alluring maiden that the place had to offer; To the vagabond or toff a-like, she could be seen from blocks away. To the many, she did not seem unattainable, only instead requiring a fee, an investment that all vested parties were eager to make.

After nine hours, Pride escorted Abigail back to Envy's flat in Ardwick Green where the three convened. Envy carried a heavy cotton bag over his shoulder and threw it down on the coffee table. The sack clanged against the scratched wood surface. A few coins spilled out onto the stained green area rug beneath the table.

Pride placed a cigar in his mouth. "I'd say we had a profitable evening."

Envy wiped his forehead. "All thanks to Abbie." A smile shot in Abigail's direction.

"That's incontestable." Pride reached into his breast-pocket and removed another cigar.

"Cheers." Abigail blushed. "I reckon that all of the patrons had their fill of amusements…"

Pride walked toward Envy to hand them the other cigar while his still smoked in his left hand.

"I did not see any customer I attracted, exit once over the span of the night."

Envy looked up at Pride after he started to swim his hand into the cotton sack.

"I am equally surprised that none know of such a venue that creates such an unprecedented experience."

"Unprecedented…" Pride laughed. "That's one way to describe it…"

Abigail looked around the room in confusion. "Is there something I should know?"

Envy glanced at Pride out of the corner of his eye, awaiting guidance on how to address what seemed to be an invasive query.

Pride shook his head as a smile broke from his face. "...I believe you have the pair of us at a disadvantage."

Envy placed his knee on the lip of the coffee table. "we've never came into this amount of money previously." He looked at Nelson from the corner of his eye. "Could be our best take spanning the history of our partnership, correct?"

"That is a spectacular summary, Mister Envy." Pride turned around and placed the cigar in his mouth. He puffed once and blew the smoke toward the dusty brown rafters. "Abbie is going to be an asset to this enterprise." Pride looked down at the floor.

"Shall I fix her a beverage?"

"No, Arthur she has to return to her daughter." Pride smiled at Abigail. "To that end, we shall see you on Wednesday, Abigail."

"But tomorrow is Sunday." Envy scowled.

"And?"

"She just started."

Pride placed his hand in front of Envy's face. "She has a child to look after. Do you suppose she can hire a sitter on short notice, regularly?"

"Don't let her use her feminine wiles to get the best of you, mate." Envy teased. "It's not good for business."

Pride took two steps toward Abigail and about-faced to stare down his colleague. "As I recall Arthur, it was you that sought me out for my commercial acumen." He placed his cigar down in a chipped red ashtray on the coffee table. Abigail glanced down at the tobacco as it burned unusually hot for a brief second.

Pride's eyes widened "...or must I remind you of this, intimately?"

Envy's smirk evaporated into quivering lips.

Pride turned his attention back toward Abigail and smiled warmly at her. "Lady Lee, please allow me to see you out."

The two hooked arms again; Envy curled his fist as he watched both make their way to the door. Pride opened the door for Abigail and escorted her out into the corridor. "Once again, let me express my gratitude for your services, tonight."

The two were stood close to each other, nearly face-to-face. Pride looked down at Abigail with a slight smile while her eyes were lit up when she returned the look. The two locked eyes for a moment; Abigail's gentle smile became wider.

"Thank you for having me."

"It was truly a treat, in more ways than one..." Pride stroked a strand of hair that fell close to Abigail's eye.

"I had a wonderful time chatting with you throughout the evening." She started to breathe heavier and inch closer to him.

"As did, I." Pride reached into his pocket. "First thing is first though, before we take this any further..." He removed a gold money clip that held together a roll of banknotes. "Can you open your hand please..."

Abigail felt the notes and coins stack in her palm.

"We had an incredible night and thus as per our agreement we owed you half. That worked out to four pounds."

Two more-pound coins fell on top of her pay. Pride placed his hand over Abigail's to close it around the money.

"And the additional two quid?"

"Buy your daughter something nice." Pride rubbed Abigail's wrist. "I am doomed to violate my own rule of mixing business and pleasure, it seems."

Her eyes darted up to meet Pride's.

"Though we will not see you again until the middle of the week, I would be remiss to say that I do not long to see you before then."

Her eyes started to smile at him. It was a sight that seemed to penetrate Pride's soul, he was caught off guard by it; all he could do was tug his collar for a second. "I am down at The Hab, Mondays and Tuesdays from eleven to six. If you are about, please call."

"Would that distract you from whatever it is you are engaged in?"

"I welcome such a distraction." Pride inched forward toward Abigail and bended down toward her as if he were going to kiss her. She closed her eyes but her lips were never met by his. Instead, she felt his lips press gently against her cheek. Her neck started to collapse and her head tilted toward him.

"Good night, Madame."

Though her residence was just down the corridor, Abigail felt as if she could float to it.

WHEN I AWOKE IN THE morning, Mother was gone. I heard her come in late last night but fell back asleep, as soon as she climbed into bed. I imagined she must have been exhausted, spending all those hours on her feet in high-heels and much tidying still needed to be done. I jumped out of bed and cleaned whatever I could from top-to-bottom, I folded the sheets, scrubbed the work tops, and washed the dishes. I wanted Mummy to come back to a clean home with little work to do, if any. When I put the last dish into the cupboard, I heard the door turn and in walked Mummy. Her eyes lit up as she doffed her bonnet.

"Temperance Grace." Abigail doffed her bonnet.

"Yes, Mummy." I ran toward her and threw my arms around her, she knelt down and embraced me.

"I am gobsmacked." She her hands through my tangled cinnamon-auburn hair. "Well done, poppet."

"Thank you. I thought I could help since you might be tired."

"*Since you were so thoughtful, we have more time to have fun, today.*" *She pinched my chin.* "*What do you say we go for a walk in the park? Perchance, we can go see the Marple Aqueduct?*"

"*Beer and skittles.*" *I hugged Mother again and this time she placed a brown satchel down on the floor to hold me close to her.*

"*Where do you learn these terms?*" *She laughed as she stroked the back my head.*

"*It was written in an advertisement.*"

Mummy pulled back and smiled at me, baffled by my knowledge of modern slang.

"*Can we play jacks first, Mumma?*"

"*We can do, darling.*" *She tapped my nose and then poked me as she let out a growl.* "*But I am going to win though!*"

"*No, you are not!*" *I giggled and ran into the bedroom, Mother followed after she picked up the brown satchel; her fingers disappeared for a moment until they emerged with a music box in her hand. She cranked it as I knelt down picking up silver jacks off the floor. The music box began to play while the red ball bounced against the wood planks. From the corner of my eye, I saw her staring at her lovingly and tenderly at me. She placed the music box upon the nightstand next to the bed and kissed me on the top of her head. Then, she sat beside me and we played: Mummy let me win.*

Two hours later, we walked hand-in-hand through Ardwick Green until we came upon a green bench that overlooked a lake which ran the length of the park. The skies were blue without a cloud. Sun glistened against the still waters of the lake. Families sat atop blankets along the grassy inclines that extended from the pond, bathing in the warmth of the day; spring was in full bloom. Butterflies perched on snow-dips that sporadically sprung across the fields; hedges were filled with carnations of various pastel shades. The trees that lined the park were painted in vibrant emerald and olive hues.

Mummy and I sat beside each other wearing matching sunhats that each had a pink rose fixed to its side. Our white bodices glowed in the sunlight.

"Did you enjoy your work do, Mother?" I squinted as the sun was exceptionally strong that day. I could feel it pierce through the muslin.

"It went well, dear, thank you." She waved a black hand-fan toward us.

"You're welcome. Did all the work people like you?"

She smiled and put her arm around me. "I believe one lad in particular showed some fondness toward me."

I grinned and kicked my legs back and forth from the excitement. "He should."

Mother smirked at me as she looked me from the corner of her eye.

"He would be mad not to adore you, Mummy."

She smiled at the remark and pulled my head against her chest. "Thank you, dearest. It's wonderful to know you hold me in such high esteem.".

"Do you reckon a man will love me one day?" I wrapped my arms around her.

"I haven't any doubt, my love." Mother rubbed my back. "One day when you are older someone will shoot their cuff for you, Temperance." Her hands rose and fell with each breath I took. "And you will be successful in whatever you commit yourself to; you will have a home and a family of your own."

In many ways it seemed like an event so distant, perhaps never within reach. Then, I couldn't even stomach the idea of being away from Mother.

"But what about you, Mummy? I want to stay with you."

"As do I." She smiled. "Selfishly, I could keep you forever, my little dove." Her eyes watered. "But I will rejoice in knowing my little girl has made the most of all that life can offer." She looked into the pond. "That I fulfilled my purpose."

"*Do I have a purpose?*" *I looked up at her.*

"*We all do, darling.*" *She stroked my cheek.* "*And one afternoon many years from now you will come back to this park and remember this conversation.*" *She looked across the park at a little boy throwing bread to a swan.* "*This place will always be a special place for us.*"

"*But I don't want to leave you.*"

"*Temperance, when the time comes you cannot be afraid.*" *She removed my hat and pulled my long hair down.* "*You can always come back here. I will always be with you no matter what, my daughter.*"

I started to shiver and clutched her tight.

"*Fortunately, you are still just a little poppet...*" *She smiled warmly and reached into her handbag.* "*Close your eyes, Temperance. I've bought you a gift.*" *Ruffling came from the bag as I shut my eyes.*

"*Can I open my eyes now, mum?*"

"*You may, dear.*"

I opened my eyes to the sight of a black box on my lap which shined under the sunlight. My fingers untied the bow and I eagerly removed the lid. There I saw it for the first time, a blue butterfly hair pin set in a layer of white tissue against a folded leaf of paper. Mummy reached down and flipped it over on its other side. The initials T.G.L. were engraved into it.

My eyes enlarged as they filled with tears. "*It is beautiful.*"

"*I was certain you would like it.*" *She grabbed a hand full of my hair and set it in place.* "*There you are, sweeting. You are lovelier than a field of lilies.*"

"*Thank you, Mother.*" *I squeezed her tight.* "*I will treasure it, forever.*"

"*You're welcome, precious.*" *She glanced down at a leaf of paper inserted into the box and removed it.* "*Read this, it speaks into what we chatted about moments ago.*"

I carefully pulled the paper from my mother's hand and unfolded it.

"*To everything there is a season, and a time to every purpose under Heaven. A time to be born, and a time to die; a time to plant and a time to pluck up that which has been planted.*" A breeze our cheeks and once it passed, Mummy joined in reading the passage.

"*A time to weep, and a time to laugh; a time to mourn, and a time to dance.*" My voice faded out against Mother's which became more prominent. "It's a passage from the book of Ecclesiastes, my dear. I pray that your days are filled with much laughter and plenty of dancing." She clutched my hand. "May you always remember that our Father in Heaven placed you here to fulfil your purpose under Heaven. May it be as so and greater than you can imagine..." She pulled me close and embraced once again.

"I love you, Mummy."

"I love you too, darling." Her wet lips smudged against my forehead. "We best get on with our journey to Romiley, if you wish to see the grand aqueduct."

Minutes later, Mother hired a livery outside the park and we travelled to London Road Rail Station, from there onward to Romiley. It was warm the rest of the day, the sun shined extra bright at each of the sights we saw.

That Sunday afternoon so long ago, remains etched in my memory.
– T.G.L.

16.

Heels clattered against the cracked stone as Abigail ascended the steps of *The Haberdashery*. With each step she took, her nails clung to her dress to protect its navy-colour from being scuffed black and brown. Her eyes darted into the shadowy front room, hoping they would land upon Mister Nelson Pride. At first sight, there was no trace of him. She stroked her long auburn hair as her heart beat against her ribs. She imagined a large potted plant on the top of the steps to be Mister Pride, rehearsing all the possible greetings and things she could say to engage him.

A fly landed upon one of the potted Croton's dangling sun-bleached leaves. Abigail's mind settled for a moment as she watched the insect dash along the leaf before it flew away into the bustle of Manchester's city centre. Sunlight rested on her porcelain skin until it was overshadowed by a sweaty hand that squeezed her wrist.

"I remember you." Abigail looked down to the second step; a pair of almond-shaped green eyes were glued to the pink bow that draped from the neckline of her dress. The hand and eyes belonged to a man with a youthful complexion tucked underneath a layer of scruff. Sweat trickled toward his cheeks from below his black top hat.

"You are new here, I noticed you at past week's end..." He was close to falling off the step from wobbling. "...I have been waiting to see you again..." His delivery was slurred as he stumbled once more. The patrons' khaki-coloured shirt was unbuttoned and half-tucked into a creased pair of black trousers. Though he appeared dishevelled, his clothes appeared to be of fine quality.

"That's nice." Abigail reached for a matching pink bow she placed into her hair.

"What is your rate?" His brown loafers nearly crushed Abigail's toes as he tripped forward.

"Please, sir..." Her arm extended forward until she felt his chest press against her palm.

"Please, sir, nothing..."

"I seek no trouble. I am here to see Mister Pride on his invitation."

The man's fluid body movements stiffened. His flirtatious smile vanished and was replaced with a slack-jawed gaze of dismay. In an instant, he went from goofy and drunk to sober and solemn. Abigail felt the sun once again touch the area of her forearm where he had taken hold of her.

"My apologies, my lady." His head slightly bowed as his fingers gripped the black brim of the top hat. "Please forgive me for any injury caused by my unruly behaviour."

Between the abrupt shift in the punter's demeanour along with witnessing Arthur Envy's sudden loss of confidence every time Pride glared at him, Abigail wondered what power Pride possessed that enabled him to disarm men in a moment's notice.

"No injury given. Perchance it was one too many flashes of lightning." She chuckled to ease the tension. "You know what having too many gins can do."

"I appreciate your grace. You are a proper bit of soap, please make it known to your suitor." The man reached for the red cast-iron railing and descended the steps.

"Suitor?" Abigail mumbled the words as she watched the drunkard flee from a combination of fear and embarrassment. "I wish it were so." She made her way inside to make an inquiry about

Mister Pride's whereabouts. After being told to wait a few minutes, she took a seat at an empty table. Abigail was jittery and hoped to find a distraction to rest her eyes on until Pride emerged. The mahogany floors, matching tables, white crown mouldings, or low ceiling did not do the trick.

"Lady Lee." A voice called out to her with a hint of enthusiasm. Pride strolled into the front sitting room with extra vigour in his step. His fingers gripped the gold cufflink fastened to his starch white shirt. Everything about his appearance was well maintained; there were no creases in his black vest, his scarlet cravat-tie was placed perfectly in the centre of his neck, and his obsidian bowler hat had not one speck of dust or dander. Pride's shiny black shoes thundered against the floors until he stopped beside Abigail. "What a glorious surprise." Pride's fingers slid into Abigail's hands. With caution, he plucked her hands from the table and kissed her soft skin. "You look nothing less than divine. I am sure you have caused many cheek-aches today."

"Thank you, Nelson, you are far too kind." Abigail smiled. "I recall you said you were in on Tuesdays and I just so happen to be about."

"It is truly wonderful to see you." Pride gently released Abigail's hand, it swung back to his hip. "Can I offer you a drink?"

Sun peeked through the window into the blue of Abigail's eyes. Her hands shot up to shield her face. "It is too early for a beverage, I am afraid."

"Not to some." A smirk spilled across Pride's face. "For some, it is always the right time." His eyelashes fluttered as he leaned upon the flimsy wood table. "Where is little Abigail? I was expecting her to join you."

"The sitter happened to be passing by and knocked on."

"That was fortuitous." Pride raised his eyebrows.

"She was kind enough to have Temperance for a couple of hours so I could get out for some fresh air..."

"...And you came into town for that?" Pride chuckled.

"No..." A smile broke from Abigail's face. "...I came to see you." Her warm smile widened. "You invited me to call, did you not?"

"Absolutely, and I am glad you did."

In that moment, a glass shattered. The attention of all sitting at the tables was directed to a middle-aged man dipped in sweat that lie collapsed on the floor closer toward the front entrance. Beside him, a puddle of lager trailed away from the shards of the broken mug. The fallen punter and the spill were a considerable distance away from Pride and Abigail who sat nearer toward the bar.

Pride unclipped a silver pocket watch and examined the face. "Perhaps, I can take you over the road." He turned his wrist away. "My dear friend Mister Collier serves a delectable Madeira..." Pride smiled "...unadulterated, of course."

"That does sound inviting..." Her head turned toward the fallen patron. "...Is someone going to tend to that gentleman?"

Pride waived his hand. "That geezer is in here nearly every day of the week and he is overcome on half of them. One of the lads will sort him out and he will be quick to learn that we do not endorse his lifestyle choices." Pride hooked Abigail's arm. "Now how about we get off for some of that fresh Manchester air?"

Though it was only a five-minute walk, the two might could have journeyed to the other side of the world. At times, the footpaths were flooded with pedestrians. Foot traffic stagnated and the debris-filled streets of Manchester did not provide a better alternative of passage. Smoke blanketed the air that throbbed with chatter and trots that could never be silenced.

Nelson Pride and Abigail Lee found themselves sitting alone in a quiet place sharing a bottle of dessert wine. Across from them, an aperture provided a view of the massive gothic structure that served as the original Manchester Royal Infirmary and Asylum.

This building stood on the site of what many know today as Piccadilly Gardens. – T.G.L.

They flirted; they laughed; and shared stories about each other's past. It was difficult for Pride and Abigail to take their eyes off of each other. It was only when Pride glanced out the window toward the face of the clock on the infirmary that he realised three hours had passed.

Both Abigail and Pride were bashful at their negligence of time management. Still, they were so reluctant to bid each other farewell. The two stepped back into the front entrance of The Haberdashery with their arms locked as they had been when they left hours before. Pride invited Abigail to stay for a cup of tea in the front with him, before he reluctantly had to return to the back. Abigail obliged.

"Well..." Pride stirred the broth of his tea. "...I must confess that I have not had an engaging afternoon such as this, in a long while..." Nothing about him had changed from the moment he first greeted Abigail that afternoon. His tone did not alter, his tie was still tied tight, every button on his vest was still done.

"As did I, Nelson." Light combed the left side of Abigail's cheek. "Thank you for everything." Her spoon started to stir in her tea.

"The pleasure is all mine Abbie; I am glad to know you better..." Pride sipped on his tea.

"I love my girl more than anything in this world but I am already sad to go." She followed and took a sip of tea.

"Fortunately, you will be back with us tomorrow night."

"I am already counting down the ticks."

"As am I." Pride's fingers passed over Abigail's hand. "I must ask you. How is that you are not married?"

Abigail looked down to the ground. Her energy and vivacity had regressed into shame. "I suppose you already know the answer to that question." She looked up.

Pride's head shook "These primitives..." He kissed his teeth "...they think they observe etiquette by not so much even nodding at a woman that passes." His manicured nails itched against his cheek. "Yet if there were the slightest suspicion that a woman was not a virgin, these men will do a Dutch." He glanced at Abigail out of the corner of his eye. "...an expenditure cast unjustly in your daughter's name." Pride poured milk into his tea and circled his spoon through once more. "Still I find it shocking that not one bloke has ever made a bid for your affections, sans the lad who helped you conceive your little girl..."

"Unless you quantify your colleague's conduct as such..."

"Arthur..." He snickered. "...you best keep off the grass with the likes of him." A crimson handkerchief dabbed against his nose. "Nonetheless, I would have imagined any man would fancy himself fortunate to gain your hand."

"Well there is nothing stopping you is there?" Abbie smirked, placed her head in her other hand, and winked at Pride.

"Thankfully, no." He chuckled briefly. "So, what became of the father of young Temperance?"

Abigail sat back in her seat.

"Has he passed away?"

There were a million things Abigail could say but none could leave her mouth.

"I don't wish to pry." His free hand raised above the steam that danced from his teacup. "However, you never struck me as a left-hand wife..."

Abigail sighed. "On the short end of it, I was overcome, and this lad who was quite the dizzy had his way with me."

"So, you were raped?"

"That's the ticket." Abigail's replied with an air of sarcasm. Her long auburn hair tossed to the side as she glanced out the window at a passing trolley. "Though none believe me..."

"I do." Pride took Abigail's hand; her face turned to lock eyes with him.

A loud shriek echoed behind the bar. Abigail's head snapped back; her eyes bulged hoping it could detect the source of the racket.

"Don't mind the noise, it happens all the time." Pride wiped his hands against a pale-yellow napkin. "I reckon its time I see you out."

The side door to the back flew open and a woman fled through it. The lady was not much older than Abbie but she wasn't wearing traditional attire. Her alabaster skin was fully on display: all of her arms, most of her legs, and much of her cleavage. The lady's voluptuous figure was stuffed into a black corset and short petticoat. Her eyelashes were curled and embraced by mascara; her cheeks powdered in a thick layer.

A ball of fluff lay limp in her arms. Her lips quivered; her cheeks were red. She nearly fell on three occasions as she sprinted toward the table.

It was the first time Abigail witnessed Pride appear out of control. His facial expression was closer to the woman's: one of alarm and worry.

"So that's what goes on back there." Abigail raised her eyebrows.

"Mister Pride..." The woman stopped just inches before the table. "I am going to have to take a leave."

"Leave?" Pride scowled. "Tilly, I need you here tonight." The pitch of his voice became authoritative.

"My rabbit has died." She sniffled.

The rabbit's eyes were black and full of void. Its whiskers wilted, its head arched over her wrist, its body ready to spill toward the ground if it were released from her clutch.

"This furry thing?" Pride's finger came within an inch of the deceased animal's ear.

"Yes." Tears formed in her eyes. "I have to bury him."

Pride scratched his temple and peered back at Abbie. She looked at him as if she were evaluating his every move. His irritation transformed to a warm smile. "I understand, Tilly..." He sat up. "...but what if I told you..." He glanced around the room. "...I could resolve this right now." Pride's pointer finger once again came within inches of the dead rabbit. "Would you be able to carry on this evening, if I did?"

"This is no laughing matter."

"I am not laughing..." He waved his hands. "...give me the hopper."

Abigail leaned forward as Pride took hold of the rabbit from Tilly and placed the rabbit on the table as if it were a bag of groceries.

"Be careful."

"He's already dead, Tilly." Pride's eyes shut as his hands wrapped around the rabbit's throat. After a few seconds, his grip softened and the rabbit's black whiskers began to twitch. Abigail spit tea back into her cup, overcome by amazement. Tilly shared a similar look to Abigail, astonished at the feat performed before their very eyes.

The rabbit moved its head off the table. Pride stroked the bunny and helped it to its feet. It looked around, bewildered, and confused. The rabbit hopped once and looked directly at Abigail with its nose chattering. Abigail's extended her hand to touch the rabbit until it was violently scooped up by Tilly.

"Oh, Mister Pride!" She lunged toward him with the rabbit vibrating in her arms. "Thank you ever so dearly." Her lips pressed against his cheek. "I do not how I can repay you."

A pout formed on Abigail's face.

"It's no trouble, Tilly." His hands flicked dander off of his vest. "Fetch him a carrot and please be ready in a couple of hours."

"I will do, Mister Pride. I can start early, if you prefer." She sprinted off and shut the side door behind her.

"That would be lovely, Tilly." He smiled.

"How did you do that?" Abigail placed her palms upon the table.

"Do what?" Pride's hands fanned away specks of dust.

"Come off it, you just resurrected that bunny!"

He seemed unphased at the mention of it and responded with a stoic disposition. "I merely have a propensity for the veterinary arts."

Abigail sat back in her chair and crossed her arms. "Clearly, The Good Lord has blessed you with the ability to perform miracles."

Pride broke out in laughter. "The Lord, you say?" His thumb extended backward. A patron glanced at Nelson out of the corner of his eye, sipping on a bitter.

"Who else would I be referencing?"

"I have piqued your interest and I intend keeping it that way." His hands swept across the table to swipe away any remaining fur or hair.

"Are you going to tell me how you are able to do that?"

He glared at her with a blink of menace. Pride swallowed hard. "Normally, I would have nothing to hide but I am infatuated with you Abigail, so I prefer you don't take me a charlatan."

She leaned forward onto the table where her face was just inches from his. "If anything, it has made you even more beguiling..."

Pride's head nodded with a mischievous smile. "...You give me your word I can trust you?"

"On my little girl." She gripped his cheek.

He reclined against the chair. "You don't seem like one that would ever place their daughter in jeopardy."

"I have always looked after Temperance. It would be nice if someone endeavoured to look after me."

"Very well." Pride's fingers slid into the breast-pocket of his vest to remove a neatly rolled cigar. "Do you have any objections?"

Abigail leaned back in her chair and extended her hand. "By all means, Mister Pride."

Pride pressed the cigar between his lips and pinched the outside of it. Without any matches, a red glow emerged from the cigar's end. This spectacle was equally amazing to Abigail. Once again, she wore a look of disbelief similar to when he resurrected the rabbit.

"Right so how shall I put this?" He took a puff of the cigar "...a dear friend of mine granted me some extraordinary gifts."

"So, you are an angel?"

Pride snorted as he exhaled a plume of smoke. "That is the funniest thing I have heard you say yet." His ivory teeth shined from his guffaw.

"If you are not..." Abigail's pinpoint pupils implied her curiosity and intrigue were getting the best of her. "then, what are you?"

"You are an intelligent woman." He dabbed his cigar to let off some ash. "You have the brains to match the beauty. What would I be implying?" Pride fixed his eyes to lock with Abigail's. Her cerulean eyes were mirrored by his black irises which flared a reddish tint.

"You cannot be." She smiled. "You are really pleasant."

"And who said that we have to be these menacing, mean, and ugly monsters as we are often depicted. To be fair, you are only hearing one side of the story."

She glanced down briefly before meeting her eyes with Pride's again. "That side is the only one that matters, Mister Pride."

"Ironic that good-natured souls can have such a tyrannical view of things." A scent of burning wood filled the air whilst Pride's cigar hissed against the lip of the dining table. "Now, please don't go telling your neighbours wild tales." He rose to his feet. "You know what the proverb says about loose lips."

"I applaud your humour."

"If that's what you call it." Nelson made his way around the table and pulled the chair out from behind her.

"Thank you for a lovely afternoon, Nelson." Abigail's heel scuffed against the carpet when she turned. Before she could even fall an inch, a strong hand gripped her waist and pressed against her blue cotton dress. Her chest began to expand and rise at a rapid pace. She licked her lips as if it were a reflex, a recoil to hold her back from unleashing her affection upon him. "This proves my point, Nelson. You are far too kind and dashing to be one of them."

A smile swirled across Nelson's face and he inched closer. "Thank you, Abigail. I hold an even greater admiration for you."

Abigail inched closer and pressed her body against Pride. The two broke eye contact when Abigail looked away. Her body shook against Nelson's arm that remained wrapped around her waist. She took a deep breath and looked up at him.

"Your eyes are beautiful..." Pride glanced down at her.

"Thank you..." she replied in a breathy voice.

"It's like looking into Heaven itself." His face got closer.

"Maybe I can take you there sometime..." she whispered as her eyelashes fluttered like butterflies in a meadow. Neither said a word after that. Their faces drew closer until their lips finally met.

For the next month, Abigail used every excuse she could dream up to be at The Haberdashery, whether it be working more hours, assisting Mister Pride with an errand, or a spontaneous afternoon call. The wages were fabulous and the romance continued to blossom. Abigail bought her daughter new toys and she purchased herself fine clothing; She also took her daughter to all sorts of interesting places, such as when they went sea-side for the opening of the Blackpool Pier. Despite all the luxuries that Abigail indulged her and her daughter in, she still had funds to spare. Finally, it all seemed to be coming together.

17.

I awoke in the middle of the night with a soaring fever and searing
pain in my throat. Despite all the bedtime stories Mummy read to
soothe me, the pain was too overwhelming. It took three good-night
kisses for me finally drift off to sleep. Nevertheless, I had woken twice
and experienced explosive fits of vomiting.

At the first crack of dawn, a physician was summoned to evaluate
me. My tongue had turned a strange strawberry colour and my
condition deteriorated ever more. The medicines clearly had no effect.
Our worst fears came to fruition when the doctor said it was Scarlet
Fever.

There aren't appropriate adjectives that could sufficiently
characterise, the insidious beast that is Scarlet Fever. The vile wretch
rode a pale white horse into the homes of many families targeting the
youngest. It plundered nurseries, bringing caches of sorrow, misery, and
terror everywhere that it travelled. Many sad mothers and fathers were
forced to face the reality of children no longer present to open their gifts
under the tree come Christmas.

I was just a little girl with my whole life ahead of me. I still had to
blossom into a lady, fall in love, and have children of her my own one
day. I dreamed of having a man I could love madly and would love me
just as much. I fantasised the notion of having three little girls to help
me with all the errands around the house. Girls who would run after
him when he came home; girls who I could play with and spend warm
Sundays chasing butterflies in the fields; girls that I could watch become
remarkable young women. I wanted to be to them what my mother was

to me. At that very moment, it seemed that none of it would ever come to pass. The prognosis was grim as I had no more than a couple weeks unless there was a miraculous intervention. – T.G.L.

THERE WAS NO TIME TO wait. As soon as she was able to hire a sitter for a few hours, Abigail journeyed to The Haberdashery. She paid the sitter whatever she asked as she saw it as the most prudent investment she could make; she was buying the time to procure the services of a man that resurrected a dead bunny just a month before. Two weeks after the miracle performed, Nelson Pride confided in Abigail that he had stopped a cholera outbreak in a parsonage in the Midlands. Abigail was determined to not be visiting the grave site of her daughter in the future. Surely, Pride could help!

Abigail ascended the steps at a deliberate pace. The clang of her heels against the floor did not stop until she arrived at the bar. The front room was busy with patrons filling nearly every seat. However, none lined the bar to order a beverage. Her cream-coloured wrists fell upon the mahogany counter and her eyes scanned the area from side to side until one of the bar maids came forward.

"Hiya Abbie, are you all right?" The woman was not much older than Abigail and looked like her in many ways, as well. She had a fair and clean complexion and a round, soft face. Her eyes were an emerald green; her mousey brown hair was tucked beneath a white bonnet. "I do adore those earrings." She smiled at the glimmer of a ruby earing that dangled from Abigail's earlobe. They shined with a magnificent glow from all the gold that encrusted the large scarlet diamond. "Mister Pride gifted those to you, did he not?"

"Clemmie, where is he?" Abigail's palms smacked against the counter.

"I was under the impression that you weren't supposed to be in today." Her eyes lit up. "It is always a pleasure to see you, looking well."

"Something urgent has come up. I need to speak with him."

Clemmie glanced out of the corner of her eye.

"Is he in the back?" Abigail pointed at the side door and took one step toward it.

"He has been bobbing in and out, all afternoon."

"Can you notify him that I require his assistance, immediately?"

Clemmie shrugged her shoulders. "Honestly, I do not know where he has gone." The bar-maid shot an ice-cold stare. "He issued one order and that was to ensure no one was wandering in the back until he was no longer engaged."

"It's my baby girl, she's dire." Her hands slammed on the lip of the bar once again. "I need to have a word with him." She gripped the rail that ran along the counter; her fingerprints smudged the polished brass.

"The only solution I can offer you is to find yourself an open table and have a pint or two and whilst you wait..."

"Bloody hell!" Abigail threw her hands in the air. "I do not have the time to lounge about." She stormed out the front door onto the steps. Tears welled up as fear filled her heart. Abigail focused on her breathing for a moment in hopes it would allow her to ease the angst. She let out a deep exhale. Her hand gripped the railing as she stepped down onto the cracked pavement of Withy Grove.

Hours dragged until the last order bell pierced through the chatter at half-past twelve. The pub shut a half-hour later. Abigail was dressed in a black satin corset clung to her tight along with a short black lace petticoat. She also threw a black silk hooded-cloak over herself which made her virtually invisible in the darkness. Her porcelain hands were clad in black leather gloves. Abigail made her way into the ginnel along-side the pub, creeping through the shadows toward the rear service entrance.

Abigail turned the door handle with a gentle touch until it became ajar. In a swift motion, she slithered through the opening and shut the service entrance. She was in the office but it was pitch-black and silent. Abigail's hands swept the floor until they met a large wooden object. It was the desk. She prodded, poked, and waved her fingers until she discovered the open area she could hide under. There she would wait until Pride returned. Then she could reason, explain, and beg if she must.

About an hour passed. Abigail remained curled up under the desk and started to doze off to sleep until the door flew open.

"Are they in the back garden?"

Abigail's cheeks warmed as she heard Pride's voice ripple through the darkness.

"Aye, boss."

She heard a second recognisable voice: Arthur Envy. A faint flicker of candlelight danced into the office from the corridor. Pride's boots plodded against the floor and vibrated the boards beneath her. Given the firmness of his strides, Abigail detected a sense of urgency and perhaps even rage within him.

"Right, we will have to do this clean and quick."

"Just make sure you don't spill the beans to my fox of a neighbour," Envy simpered as his softer step was not nearly easily comparable to the might of Pride's.

"What occurs between Lady Lee and I is none of your concern, Arthur." The sound of wood sliding from a draw filled the room for a brief moment. "Let us not stand on ceremony due to your personal jealousies."

"I don't think women should know more than they should." He snorted. "Good job you didn't tell her about the bookshelf."

"Whilst she does not know, you must understand that Abigail is not just a woman."

She wanted to emerge from under the desk and reveal herself to him right then and there. But something told her not to. Abigail swooned in the words for a moment and rehearsed a scene in her mind where she tackled him to the floor and smothered him with kisses. Her fantasy was interrupted by the sound of a pistol cocking.

"I would bend her over that desk and make her call me sire." Abigail cringed as she squinted at the faint outline of Envy's stout and husky body. His posture swayed with a swagger.

"Would you deem that disclosure all the wiser considering the dynamics of our relationship?"

Envy's shadowy outline became rigid and stiff.

"Or shall I remind you of the consequence of coveting?"

A smell of burnt sulphur tickled Abigail's nose. She pinched her nostrils to ward off the overpowering scent.

"No lesson is necessary." Envy's tone of voice diminished to low-pitched and meek.

"A wise choice, dear boy." Pride's voice trailed across the room until it stopped where the candle flickered. A mute darkness consumed the room when the two men left the room and shut the door behind them. The stench also left with them.

Abigail slid out from under the desk and crept toward the door. She grabbed the handle with caution, listening for any footsteps in the corridor beyond. Her sweaty fingers shook as she twisted the knob. The door creaked as it opened into another abyss of darkness. Abigail tip-toed out into the corridor, swimming her hands in front of her to locate a wall that she could use as a guide. The floorboards squeaked with each step she took. When she made it around the banister of the stairs, a lit torch hung on the wall provided enough light to direct her down the hall. She plucked the torch from the wall hook, placing it in front of her to lead the way. Abigail traversed the corridor until she came to a bookshelf which stopped her in her tracks.

There was something peculiar about where the bookshelf was placed as it was moved from where it normally was. The torch shined against where the bookshelf originally stood and revealed a black iron door. Her fingers slid along the thick frame to uncover that it was ajar. Abbie's nails dug into the crease and pried it fully open.

A brisk breeze came against Abigail's face followed by another pungent smell. The stench was closer to death itself. She coughed and covered her mouth exerting the maximum effort not to gag. Across the room another exit was open which allowed fresh air to come in and alleviate the odour. A shriek echoed from outside. With haste, Abigail snuffed out the flame and slid along the floor until she could finally get a view beyond the exit.

Outside stood Arthur Envy holding another torch that lit up what a shadowy back garden comprised of stoic concrete. Standing beside Envy was another familiar face: the man that accosted Abigail on the steps just a month before when she called to visit. Her attention was interrupted by a wet substance that clung to her skirt and her forearms. She moved her arm close to her nose.

Blood. But she hadn't cut herself on anything. Her fingers crawled along the floor until it began to trace a stream of blood that flowed away toward a dark corner of the room. Her nose lifted in the direction of the stream of sanguine to a more familiar scent. *Maggots.*

"You failed to hark my word!" Her attention was directed outside toward her love interest's command. The rear of Pride's hand which was raised to silence any form of defence offered by the punter that was vaguely illuminated by the lantern light.

"Mister Pride, I am sorry." The once confident man was now very much afraid to even flinch. "I will pay you in full for the money you lent me." He wept.

"And what of the interest, Mister Thompson?"

"Name your rate." Thompson squealed.

"You had also promised us two caseloads of Chardonnay from Marseille and have yet to deliver. Funny, how you were quick to take my deposit but deliberate to procure the goods..."

"On my missus and my first-borne..." he pleaded.

"May The Lord spare yours such a fate."

"I'd say the writing is on the wall here." Envy cackled.

"I conquer Mister Envy." Pride did not reciprocate the laugher as he offered a more sombre reply to change the atmosphere in an instant. "You are aware of what I did to the last bloke that did not hold up his part of what was a mutually beneficial agreement?"

"I cannot offer you my soul." Thompson's voice cracked.

"I'm not interested in your soul, sir..."

"Please..." He wept. "...I do not want to die..."

Pride let out a laugh and discharged his pistol. Another scream pierced across the back garden but it wasn't Thompson. A large spherical figure obstructed Abbie's view of Mister Pride, it became larger as it approached the door until another gunshot fired and the silhouette collapsed on the floor in front of her. Abigail squinted to make out who it was, it was the same frequenter that fell in a drunken stupor the day she first sat and chatted with Pride.

Her breaths became shallow and rushed. Something touched her knee. She reached down to palpate her skin and rubbed her fingers together... it was more blood!

"Serves him right for pummelling his six-year old son on the premises..." Pride laughed "...coward."

To Abigail, Pride seemed justified. After all, she could never imagine striking her child who was only a year older than her sick daughter. Yet the deceased in his drunkenness had the audacity to beat his son mercilessly. In that instant, a smile came across Abbie's face. She saw her love interest as a noble protector.

"Shall I toss that fat drunkard with the rest of the bodies in there?" Envy moved his head in the direction of the room where Abigail was.

Pride paused. "I'll burn the bodies..." He continued to walk. "...there are already plenty enough in there." He cackled. "You do recall our policy for patrons that purchase our premium services?"

"Seize their belongings..."

Abigail's fantasy came to a screeching halt when the truth had reared its ugly head; she was luring men off the street to be robbed, beaten, and in many instances killed. Yet, there was no record of them. Or was there? She did recall Pride's furtive management of a ledger that had some pivotal details that only he knew what they were. How had no one caught on though? It was strange how so many could disappear there and yet the police never even lifted a tablecloth.

Abigail glanced down and flicked wet blood from her finger-tips.

"Can I share a secret with you, Mister Thompson?" Pride turned his head which allowed Abigail to look at his face when she glanced upward. A chill ripped through her, tearing into her bones. Pride's face had transformed into the head of a white sheep! Beady eyes glowed a malevolent red. Fangs descended from his mouth. He about-faced toward Thompson and let out a ghastly snicker. "I am already dead!"

Abigail froze with terror and closed her eyes. Thompson let out a bark of agony and soon after fell over dead. Blood trickled towards Pride's feet and dripped from his lips. Abigail screeched as she fled for the door but nearly slipped while doing so, causing her to kick over a glass torch and shatter it.

"Who's there?" Envy yelled inside.

A gunshot exploded and bullet ricocheted off the wall behind her. She didn't have time to think, only to run. Abigail tore open the iron door and sprinted toward the front exit of the premises.

A ghoulish gaggle echoed from the secret chamber. "Run, little rabbit, run!"

"Abbie, is that you?!" Pride called out.

She didn't want to look back, she just wanted to get away. Her prayers were fervent not to trip over anything whilst she made her escape. Abigail unlatched the lock of the front door and sprinted into the desolate streets of Manchester.

21 JUNE 1863

The door swung open and Mother came running in. She was breathing heavy and shut the door to the bedroom, locking it behind her. Given the time of night, I was fearful she was in some form of danger. I lied there in the darkness and listened to her undress: her boots, her overskirt, her top all falling to the floor, followed by hair clip pressing onto the night stand.

Her warm hands pressed to my cheek before she climbed into bed beside me. Her sweaty arms coiled around me like another quilt. I stroked her wrist, but Mother didn't respond to it. All I could hear were her sighs and deep breaths, fixated on whatever troubles were ripe in her mind. Though it were dark, I could see her staring at the ceiling, holding me to comfort her. I wanted to make her laugh and take away her worry. I rolled over and wrapped my arms around her, pressing my head to her bosom and rubbing my fingers across her navel. It didn't seem to provide her any comfort as it usually did. She had never seemed so pre-occupied; she didn't even realise I was awake or that I was trying to comfort her; Then I had another idea; a smirk formed on my face and I poked her tummy.

"Ohh!" She grunted in her breath as she flinched.

"Where is your corset now?" I giggled and jabbed her in the stomach again.

"*Ewwf!*" *She pressed her hand to her midsection. Mother always embellished when we had a rough and tumble to encourage and rouse me. Given the state of me on that occasion, I think she was trying to give herself as much hope as it would give me that the illness had finally passed...*

I jumped on her and started to tickle her chest, ribs, and legs, quickly gaining the upper-hand as Mother was hysterical laughing and squirming across the sheets to hold me off. I was happy to see her having such fun. After all, I wanted to cheer her up.

"*You little brat!*" *She guffawed and bopped my head to counter.* "*At least you have your energy again.*" *She growled and tickled me back which led to us wrestling about, the both of us laughing together as we tickled each other and play fought, until I expended almost all of my energy.*

"*I win!*" *I nuzzled my head against her bosom and threw my arms around her. Though we were both sweating, she felt far cooler to the touch.*

"*No, I did.*" *Mother kissed my forehead and held me tight against her.*

I poked her thigh, it seemed harder than marble. Nevertheless, Mummy screamed ouch as if they were delicate, then she smacked my bum playfully.

"*Hey!*" *I giggled and retaliated with a matching strike.*

"*Oww!*" *She yelped and laughed some more.* "*You will have to do better than that, darling.*" *Mummy teased as she swam her hands through my hair.* "*A few bumps and bruises won't put me off.*" *I felt her smile widen across my forehead when my little hand knocked against her ribs in a last stand of defiance before the tomfoolery came to an abrupt halt; my teeth started to chatter from cold chills that returned with a vengeance. I broke out in tears from the horror, needless to say I had never been more scared until then. I clung to Mummy and she re-assured me it will all be right. When my sobs passed, I was still shaking. Mother's cure was to hold me tighter until we finally drifted off to sleep in each other's arms.*

A few hours had passed; the glow of morning crept through the crack of the door. I shivered violently whilst Mother was doused in sweat. It was summer but it felt like the midst of winter.

"Darling..." Mummy whispered to me.

My shivers had intensified, I couldn't move to look at her, I felt like I swallowed a block of daggers. My ribs were sore, my back was stiff, and my veins felt as if they flowed with ice. It was a struggle to keep my eyes open.

"Mummy..." It hurt just to talk. "...I can't swallow."

She palpated my neck, my swollen glands seemed ready to burst from my throat.

"You poor thing..." Mother rose from the bed but I didn't want her to go. I felt more comfortable when she was there. "I will fix you something to drink and heat some rags."

"Come back..." I whispered before I let out a snort and fell back into a deep sleep. It was my only way to find relief. I had barely opened my eyes the following morning despite Mummy telling me we were taking a trip. Normally, I would be excited but the sickness made it impossible.

18.

I could have counted every trot upon the dusty country lane that seemed as long as the seven years since Mother had been in Leicestershire. She left Evington a girl, but now she was a woman with a daughter of her own. The coach turned to the left and headed into the direct sunlight. Mummy's aubergine bodice glowed in white. Every button was done, collar up, hair neat and tucked beneath a black bonnet. Her hands were covered in white gloves, her crème skirt fell to just above her black boots; no skin was exposed other than her cheeks and the front of her neck. An occasional jostle shook the carriage as it made its way along the tree-lined path toward a large stone structure that stood ahead of us.

"Is this your house, Mum?"

"Not quite, my love..." The back of Abigail's hand pressed against my cheek. "You've cooled a bit. All of that rest must have done you right..."

"I am still icky..."

"Well that is why we are here, Tempie." She stroked a strand of my hair back. "To get you better, dear daughter." Mummy ran her finger against my floral-print dress puddled to smooth out any creases.

In that moment, I felt the urge to hug Mother yet again and did so.

"I love you, Mummy."

"I love you too, sweeting."

The carriage came to a halt. The livery opened the door and Mummy stepped out, clutching her bonnet as a gust of wind blew past.

She extended her hand to help me step down from the carriage. After she shut the door, the livery drove on.

My fingers gripped around my mother's hand tight, my pulse soared and throbbed against her wrist. Something felt wrong.

"Mummy..."

"Yes, poppet?" She swung our arms in hopes it would poke a smile from me.

"Can we go back?" I hugged her legs and leaned against her torso, hoping it would impede us walking any further. "...This place is scary."

She knelt down and extended her hands to fit my cheeks in her palm. "You have nothing to fear, Temperance." Her thumbs stroked my cheeks to prod a brief smile from me. "Your mother has some old pals here. I am sure they would be delighted to finally meet you."

My lips started to quiver. "Can we go home instead and play uppy-downy?"

For a moment, she studied my facial expressions, I imagine they were a mix of confusion, terror, sorrow, and desperation. "Please, Mummy..." I let out a cough "My intuition tells me we should leave..." the coughs evolved into a violent spate of barks. The episode did not let up until I vomited on the gravel, narrowly missing her boot with a green cloud of throw-up.

"Right, we need to get you looked at, young lady." She patted my back until the gagging settled. My energy started to dissipate, I reached for Mother's neck and she placed her hands under my arms to lift me.

A lock unhatched, followed by the massive brown door swinging open to reveal a face that caused Mother to lower her lip.

She had blonde hair, a resting pout, and a tense demeanour. The woman wore a long black dress that concealed any prospect of complimenting her figure. Her face barely showed any signs of aging.

"Lord in Heaven..." The lady gripped her sleeve. "I must be seeing a ghost..." There was no outward display of emotion, just a stoic and reserved expression.

"Hello, Alice..." Mother held me tighter.

"Is she the Alice from that letter?" I pointed at her.

Mummy nodded with a smile.

"Good afternoon, sister." Alice replied.

"She's your sister?" I muttered. "Can I have a sister, Mummy?" My words started to slur as my breaths became slower and deeper. I had started drifting off to sleep on Mother's shoulder from the overwhelming fatigue that poured on.

"If you are a good girl, perchance one day, you will."

My eyes opened to Alice smiling at me.

"Can we call her Florence?" My impromptu suggestion forced a chuckle from Mother and a wider smile from Alice. "I do like that name..."

"She's very much your daughter, Abbie." Alice held her smile for a moment before returning to an ice-cold glare. "Nevertheless, you have a bloody cheek turning up here unannounced. How long have you been gone?"

"The circumstances are extraordinary; we are in great peril."

At the time, I didn't understand why Mother said that but she knew fell well what that entailed.

"What trouble have you gotten yourself into now Abbie?" Alice's crossed her arms. "It seems to follow you every you go."

"Can we put aside our differences for the sake of Temperance?"

Alice's amber eyes darkened from the fury that brewed inside her until she looked at me as I stood there on the balls of my feet holding Mummy's hand. Somehow, I disarmed her to a smile.

"She has scarlet fever."

A crow cried and a gust of wind blew.

"I will call for the doctor." Alice's eyes softened and she extended her hand to invite us in. "In the interim, I'll fetch her some of this remedy that helped us quell a cholera outbreak here not too long ago." She smiled at Mother and rubbed her cheek. "We'll look after you until she is better,

I pray." Alice kissed her on the mouth and embraced Mummy tight. *"It is well, little sister."*

I closed my eyes, feeling at ease for the first time.

"What are you doing, Alice?" The tone and timbre were masculine and forceful. My eyes flew open to an elder man dressed in a black tunic as he emerged from the entrance. His fingers were wrinkled; he had a full head of snowy white hair; his face was filled with spots up and down his cheek-line.

"Friar." Alice nodded. *"This is Abigail. She was brought up here."*

"I've heard all about her." He stepped forward and shot a menacing glare at Alice, then turned it toward Mummy. *"And what brings you about?"*

"Apologies, Father." Mother nodded.

"It's Friar."

"Friar." She feigned a smile. *"I've sought my sister's aid as my daughter is gravely ill."*

The friar placed both of his hands behind his back and kissed his teeth. *"Whilst I am sorry to hear that, I do not suppose we can be of service to you."* He shook his head. *"We've just had our struggles in dealing with a sickness that took two pour souls. I cannot take any chances with your afflicted bastard because you have had a day off from charving."*

Mother glared at the friar. *"Could you not refer to my daughter as a bastard?"*

"Friar..." Alice placed her hand between the pious patriarch and her sister. *"That little one is my niece."*

He raised his hand. *"Tales have circled about this convent for years concerning your little sister's gallivanting and what sort of individuals she associates with."* His eye twitched. *"This minx had the audacity to claim she was raped because she was gassed and cannot remember whose bed that she landed in."*

I stared daggers at the priest but Auntie Alice smiled at me with the hope it would distract me. Alice turned towards the friar. "With respect sir, my sister was not lying. However, since her daughter is present, can we discuss this at a more appropriate time, please?"

"Alice, I will decline the discourse. I have my sources into her diabolical affairs." He shook his finger. "I pray your daughter gets better and she finds her way from you."

Mother took a few breaths in a virtuous display of humility and restraint. "Sir, I humbly ask you in the name of mercy."

"There is no mercy for you, your sins are unforgivable."

I couldn't let him say such things about Mummy anymore. "She doesn't need you..." My hands latched to a thick lock of her hair. "...you mean old man..." I threw my tongue out at him. Auntie Alice placed her hand over her mouth to cover a brief smile. Friar Patrick's eyes bulged with fury.

"She's fresh, isn't she?"

"You insulted her mother."

I nodded and let go of Mummy's hair. A breeze tossed it to the side to reveal a love-bite. Friar Patrick's dark eyes focused on it.

"Are either of you familiar with the book of Leviticus?" He placed his hand to her collar to examine it further.

"God, The Lord is really nice. He wouldn't be mean to Mum like you have." My eyes filled with water as I threw my arms around Mother. Though I was a child, I was ready to protect Mother at all costs.

"Heart-warming..." He chuckled and put his hand at his hip. His attention was re-directed to me whence my teeth began to chatter "Alice, take the girl inside and apply the leeches. She's developing a fever..."

"Many thanks to you, sir." Mummy nodded and took two steps until his outstretched arm blocked her path.

"...whilst, I have a word with our guest."

This seemed like a troublesome predicament, this man didn't seem like someone who worked for The Lord. I couldn't trust him to be alone with her.

"I will not go without you, Mummy."

"Little Sister, I know we have had our squabbles in the past but you can trust me with her. Even if you view me an ancient tyrant, I have always placed your best interest first in all I have done." Alice took Mother's hand and shot a sneaky lour at the friar which quickly reverted to a warm smile. "I wish to shower my niece with the affection, I regrettably withheld from you at times."

She looked at Alice and then Friar Patrick. Both of their eyes told different stories. Alice's look was one of concern; the friar one of disdain. It was clear that Alice was on our side, I could not say the same for the friar. However, Mother's discretion ruled.

"Mummy will be right in, sweeting." *She kissed me on the cheek and handed me over to Alice with caution.*

"No!" *I squirmed but Alice was quick to place her thumbs below my eyelids to blot them.*

"Go with Auntie Alice whilst I speak to the friar about your condition."

"Please, I can't leave you out here with him..." *I wept. The side of my face was soon stroked by the warm and tender hands of my aunt. My ability to speak was soon challenged by violent shakes. I wanted to tell her that this could be a trap and that the friar could be up to a wicked scheme. But Mother would insist otherwise, as she saw this as a moment to win him over. I could not see that happening with the likes of him.*

"I will be right in, my dear." *Mother smiled at me and tickled me under my chin to coax a giggle.* "Alice will take you for some..."

"Marzipan." *She stroked me as I watched her wink at Mummy.* "This little cherub will love it."

She clasped her hands with a smile. "What a lovely surprise, indeed. You make sure to say thank you to Auntie Alice for her generosity, yes?"

I nodded with a reluctance and nervousness. Alice took me in her arms and carried her into the nunnery. I didn't take my eyes off of Mummy, until I could not see her anymore when the friar strolled toward the door and shut it behind us. If only I was there! – T.G.L.

FRIAR PATRICK SHUFFLED his steps with his back turned until he about-faced with a brandished pistol. The shiny silver barrel glistened under sunlight and forced Abigail to raise her trembling hands toward the sky.

"On some level, I do believe you adore your daughter." He tilted his neck to the left and right. "So, I am going to try to be as nice as I can about this..."

"If you do not wish to treat her, my sister will return her to me, and we'll be off."

The friar advanced on Abigail taking two steps until he was nearly face-to-face with her. The gun never moved from its encroaching position faced toward her abdomen.

"We will treat her well." The pistol shook in his hand. "In fact, I trust that your poisonous influence will fade from her, once we cleanse Temperance of your infidelities."

"If you touch my daughter..."

A finger tugged against her collar. Air swept along the side of her neck. Friar Patrick examined the blotch on her skin.

"Is this a flea bite?"

Abigail swallowed hard. "How did you guess?"

He chuckled as he yanked her dress and broke two buttons off. Abigail's bosom was exposed, her cleavage sprinkled by another couple of love-bites. She looked down at them and her face grew red.

"If I were a man of science..." The friar pulled back the safety on the firearm. "I'd say those are the marks of one's lips."

"And I mistook you for a preacher." Her whimsical smirk collapsed when the friar hurled his fist into Abigail's midsection forcing a loud moan from her. She doubled over and held her stomach; Her bonnet tumbled off her head onto the dusty ground.

"I should shoot you dead now, prostitute!" He pulled her hair and pressed the barrel against her head. "You cannot fool me!" She pressed the barrel harder against her temple. "You are just some filthy whore who lays with whoever she pleases..."

"Did The Lord commission you to abduct my daughter?" Abigail tried to catch her breath and held her stomach to soothe the strike. The back of the friar's hand smacked across her cheek.

"Your daughter?" He holstered his gun onto a belt under his tunic. "I'll tell you what becomes of your daughter." The friar clenched down on her long dark auburn hair and twisted it. "We will exorcise whatever demons you possessed her with. Maybe then she will grow into a proper woman unlike you."

Abigail ran her fingers against her lips to blot the blood that dripped toward her chin. She got back to her feet with a wince, still feeling the effect of the blow to the stomach. Her hair flung back.

"Perhaps when she is a bit older, if you haven't found yourself pregnant with six others like her, I will be kind enough to allow you to visit her." The friar lifted his tunic to once again flaunt the pistol holstered on his belt. "However, if you don't leave within the next five minutes, I will summon our curates Green, Bell, and Roland to escort you out of here. They are excellent at keeping the peace as The Lord has blessed them with exceptional abilities when it comes to their fists and other devices."

"Can't finish it yourself?" She spat blood from her lip and picked up her bonnet.

"Don't be coy with me, slut." The friar scowled. "Consider yourself fortunate that you weren't down London way and had to leave her at a foundling hospital."

"I promise you; you will regret this." Abigail brushed off her dress and took a few steps toward the tree-lined drive that led away from the nunnery. She stopped and glanced back at the friar, lifting skirt to expose the fair flesh of her bum. Abigail kissed her hand and slapped the cheek, giggling as she did so. Before she could drop the skirt, thunder cracked, and a burning sensation filled her glute, as if she had been stabbed by a hot knife that punched into the meat of her flesh. Abigail let out a loud whimper. She reached down and blood poured from an open wound, it traced back to a smoking handgun that the friar held with an expressionless gaze.

"Your sins will be your demise, so please allow me to bestow some wisdom upon you before you come to ruin." The friar advanced as he applied gold rings to several of his fingers. Abigail turned around, wincing from the pain that jolted through her as blood dripped onto the dusty lane from her. The friar hurled his fist at her jaw, but she managed to block the first attack and then the second, parrying with a jab of her own which recoiled the friar's head back. She connected on another blow to his jaw which caused him to stumble back a step. Abigail threw another violent punch at him which he caught; the friar smirked back at her. Before she could counter, the feeling of crushing metal crunched against Abigail's corset. There was no padding or armour to protect her ribs from bearing the brunt.

"Ewwf!" She doubled over and held her stomach.

The friar let out a shriek as he launched another hook into her body, crashing against Abigail's ribs.

"Owww!" Abigail moaned as she felt a bone crack. She couldn't breathe and her ribs radiated with nearly as much as pain as her wound. The friar's fist crossed her cheek and drew blood from her nostrils, sending Abigail onto her fours.

"The cost of your iniquities will be your daughter's inheritance." The steel toe of the friar's boot crashed against Abigail's exposed rib which was already damaged severely. She cried as she rolled into the dirt, coming to a rest lying on her stomach, a cloud of dust ascending around her. "I am merely collecting what is due." The friar cracked his neck and turned back toward the convent, as the cries of her daughter for her mother screeched into the country air. Abigail was bruised, beaten, and desperate; time was working against her and she had to do something.

19.

A bigail pulled on the pewter handle of the metal service entrance and stepped into The Haberdashery. One candle stood lit on Pride's work desk; papers and documents were scattered across the face of it with a large burgundy leather-bound ledger offset in the right corner. Beside the desk, his lime green leather chair was swung out and empty. Mauve curtains were drawn over the bars across the small indent windows, filling the office with shadows.

Various sized boxes were stacked toward the ceiling. Many were stamped *Handle with Care* in red stencil. All had black scribble written on each of the panels. Knowing the activities Pride and Envy were involved in, one could only imagine what sort of contraband were inside the boxes. Abigail's eyes surveyed the room until it halted at the sight of a painted portrait of a woman. Though it was merely a painting, the subject of the painting was quite beautiful. The woman had a huge head of whitish-blonde hair, she had cream-coloured skin, a fair complexion, cupid's bow smile, and rosy cheeks. Eerily, her face bore a semblance to Abigail. Her eyes were a sapphire blue shadowed by a large flower hat that tilted toward one side. The woman's corseted figure was clad in a gold bustier with a draping white overskirt; dressed like someone who had lived perhaps 100 years before.

"That there is a Countess, a daughter of an Earl from Aylesbury." Pride pulled out a drawer from his desk and removed a decanter of whisky.

"I was told by one of the sisters when I was younger that I was born there."

"Perhaps, there is some distant relation..." Pride removed a cup "...Though I doubt that is the case, since the fellow she married was called Taylor..." He looked over at Abigail who had her back turned to him as her sight remained fixed on the portrait. As if she were a piece of exotic jewellery, Pride revelled in Abigail clothed in a lavender-coloured ball gown and matching scarf that wrapped around her neck. He stared at the tress that draped to the ground and the fringes that flowed with her figure. Her auburn hair was plaited in a bouffant and the excess flowed down her back.

"And how did you come to know her?"

Pride poured whisky into the glasses. "Care for a drink?" He removed a second cup from the drawer.

"Lord in Heaven only knows what dodgy scheme you immersed yourself in." Abigail turned around to look at Pride for the first time as he sat on his desk. Nelson was dressed smart but had a casualness about him. He wore black pants, a crimson shirt, and a silver tie.

"I believe your characterisation of me is askew." Pride took a sip. "A colleague offered to help her through a rather tumultuous period of her life." He pointed toward the portrait with his cup. "Charlotte wasn't treated too well by her husband, you see."

"Charming. Did she find herself in one of your brothels?" Abigail sneered.

"Given your tone, I believe you have already arrived at a conclusion." Pride handed Abigail her glass of whisky. "Presumptuously, of course..."

"I am not one to be tricked." She crossed her arms. "What levy must these takers pay for your gratuities?"

He chuckled. "Spare me your misgivings, Abigail, if you felt that I did not have something to offer you then you would not be here." He took a larger swig of his drink. "I concluded that we had seen the last of you after you dropped in our conference with Mister Thompson." Pride glared at her. "And don't you dare lie to me and say that you weren't there."

Abigail looked down defeated; All she could do is try to appeal to his sentimentality.

"I am in dire need of your assistance." She took a sip of the whisky and cringed at its strength.

"And how can I do so?"

"It's..." her lips trembled.

"Your daughter?" He smirked and pressed his glass to his lip.

"Yes." She winced at a sharp pain that pierced below her ribs.

"And what would I get in return?" Pride grinned.

"If it is my body you want." Abigail gritted her teeth as she reached behind her to grab for the laces that tied the bodice together. Her ribs seared from a crushing sensation.

He raised his hand. "Though I would enjoy such a treat, it's not what I ask..."

"If you do not wish to bed me..." Abigail threw her hands at her hips. "Then what is it that your desire?"

"Your soul will do just fine." Pride grinned.

"Quite a shame that you do not have authority over such matters, sir." Abigail shook her head.

"I am rather fastidious in these affairs." Pride took another sip and placed his drink upon the desk. "Plus, you can master a variety of gifts and abilities these pathetic humans cannot." He stood upright. "...and you can save your daughter's life."

"It seems then that my precious girl is to be no more." Tears flowed from Abigail's eyes. "Owww." She groaned under her breath; her aching ribs aggravated by her sobbing.

Pride glanced to the floor; a trail of dripping blood followed Abigail. "Are you wounded?"

"Yes, badly so..." Abigail caressed her rib, the laces of the corset seemed to compress the ache associated with the injury sustained.

"How did that happen?"

"I returned to where I was brought up, hoping to find help. Instead, they have taken Temperance off of me..." Tears poured onto her cheeks. "To do abominable things that I cannot imagine..."

"Who are they?" He took another sip of whisky.

"The friar, primarily..."

Pride laughed. "These wolves in sheep's clothes that pretend to serve God." He necked the rest of his liquor. "So, I take it these gentle souls are the source of your injured ribs, as well?" Pride laughed briefly. "I expect nothing less from them." His eyes moved toward the decanter on his desk. "I recall you telling me that you were raised in a rectory in Leicestershire, yes?"

Abigail nodded.

"And why did you journey there so hastily?" Pride marched toward her. "Were you afraid that we were going to pay you a visit after we learned of your snooping?"

"Please, Nelson..." Her hands shook causing her to drop her glass.

"Do not fret about the spilled drink." He pressed his fingers against her lips and he embraced her with a gentleness. "I practice grace unlike those you had a flutter upon. Mister Envy, however..." His hand rubbed Abigail's back as she shook "...he is far more choleric toward your recent behaviour."

"Will you help me?" Abigail stuttered. "I do not have time to faff about!" The bitter taste of her tears overpowered the dampness of the room. "Owww." She grunted when Pride's hand touched her rib, gritting her teeth from the sharp pain that filled her.

"If you do exactly as I say, she will be back in your arms before the morrow." The pain started to fade through a warmth that came from his hands. "Free of her sickness and full of spirit like any other young bonnie lass, but you must give me what I ask..."

Abigail pulled her head away. "Will I be damned as you are?"

The warm feeling radiated throughout Abigail's body, it was euphoric, sensual, and filled her with pleasure from her head to her toes. She threw her arms around Pride as she could barely stand from the feelings that were flowing through her. A smile smothered the distress on her face.

"Does it feel like you will be?" Pride whispered into Abigail's ear and nibbled on her ear-lobe.

"No." She moaned.

"Well then, why not make this vow official."

Abigail took a deep breath and looked deep into Nelson's eyes. "How do I know this is not deception?"

"You don't." Pride chuckled before he returned to a straight face. "It's a matter of faith, is it not?"

Her eyes widened.

"And all I am asking is you place your faith in me." Pride stroked her cheek. "It isn't as you imagine, it would be more than your soul being bound to me." His hand gripped her cheek. "We could be together. The three of us..."

A sigh escaped Abigail's lips.

"Truth be told, Abigail, you are the sort of woman I want to build an empire with."

"Do you really mean that Nelson?"

"You didn't need to run; I was preparing a place for you." He looked into her eyes. "Alas having to do this would have been inevitable." His hands locked into hers. "At least now it's for good reason..." Pride reached under Abigail's skirt and fondled his finger against the wound. "The contract requires a dab of your blood; your poorly bandaged wound will suffice." He smiled and placed her head against his chest. "Now all you have to do is declare your soul is mine before those that bear witness and we will bound together." Pride rocked her. "We will be bound and my gifts will be yours."

"Before all those that stand witness I vow, I am yours in spirit and body. My blood is your blood; my flesh is your flesh."

"Just like wedding vows." Pride sliced his finger with a dagger. "That will do." Pride held her tight against him as her hands gripped his back. "My blood is your blood; your flesh is my flesh." Abigail fainted into his arms.

"Now for Little Miss Temperance." Pride ran his hands against the wound while he kept his other arm tight around her. Then, they disappeared.

ABIGAIL AWOKE FEELING disoriented and sat up slow. After her blurred vision cleared, she saw Pride standing over her holding the severed head of Arthur Envy. The sight startled Abigail to rush to her feet.

"No need to fright my dear, all is well."

"What have you done?" Abigail kept her sight fixed on the lifeless face of Envy and his eyes rolled into the back of his head with the tongue hanging outward.

"Long before I encountered you, Mister Envy here..." He dangled the head. "...was of the opinion that I could bring him wealth, prestige, and prosperity. By you giving me your soul, you liberated me from my bind to him. Now it is you that are under my dominion but I am using this freedom you have given me to help you get your daughter back. But the only way we could do that is by destroying the greatest obstacle toward meeting our mutual goal..."

"Utter madness." Abigail breathed heavy as she reached against the wall and felt the stone brush against the bare flesh of her buttocks and arms. "This is not up to dick."

"This was a necessary evil." Pride threw Envy's head into a basket. "I will have no rivals for your hand."

Abigail looked down to see she was her arms and legs were bare but the rest of her body was tucked into a figure-hugging one-piece garment that wrapped around her neck. She was also clothed in matching knee-high boots and open-finger gloves to complement the attire.

"What am I wearing?"

"You will need something more comfortable to wear in your adventures. You can use your svelte physique as a distraction."

"I won't be seen in such despairing attire..." Abigail threw her hands on her hips. "I prefer andante in shaded lilac or my little girl's favourite, ghastly lilac..." She threw her hands to her side.

"How about agony in red?" Pride smirked.

"With a hint of pink..." Abigail clapped her hands. "...and please let me design it myself...."

"As you wish." Pride nodded.

Abigail focused on the candles that lit the room. In that moment, fire started to form at her finger-tips. "...Butter upon bacon."

"Fascinating isn't it?"

"How in the world?" The flames grew the more she looked at them.

"You have the gift of pyrolysis which can render your skin scorching to the touch of any that dare try. You can also burn whatever you have mind your set upon within the bounds of reach, of course."

She locked eyes with Pride, her disbelief was replaced with confidence, moxie, and a menacing grin. "I am reborn, aren't I?" Her tone lowered.

"And with your new talents comes strength that can overpower any and cat-like agility." Pride brandished a firearm. "You will also note that your gunshot wound has healed..."

The flesh where Abigail had sustained a bullet wound was fully repaired as if it never happened. When she stretched her arms and bent downward, there were no feelings of pain in her ribs, they were fluid as if they were never bruised or fractured in any way.

"Am I immortal?"

"The only weapon that will prosper against you is Holy Water itself. Thankfully for either of us, we do not congregate near any cathedrals." Pride twirled the gun and holstered it. "Some of your adversaries may attempt to burn you, punch you, kick you, stab you, and it could hurt severely..." Pride approached her and ran his right hand up her thigh. "...but it will not kill you." His fingers continued to wander until they cupped Abigail's cheek. "However, you should always be prepared for the unexpected." Pride met Abigail's lips and the two shared a deep kiss until he pulled away. "We best get on with saving your daughter."

20.

To this day, I find it funny how the quaint vicarage could have been mistaken for a citadel guarded by sentries. However, whatever measures they took against the infection seemed to work. I felt energetic, vibrant, and healthy again. All I wanted though was my Mummy. The thought continued to cycle through my young mind throughout the evening until I heard a skirmish unfold outside. It must have been Mother, I thought. She had finally come to rescue me. My hopes were answered when I heard a ladder crash against the window and I saw her climb into the room.

"Mummy!" I jumped into her arms.

"Tempie, I am so happy to see you." She embraced me tight.

"They told me you were gone." I sobbed.

"I would never let anything happen to you without having a say in it." She undid her cloak and wrapped it around me. "Are you alright?"

I nodded; it was the first time I saw this rather fashionable outfit she was wearing. I couldn't see it under her crimson cloak initially but when she opened it was raspberry-coloured skin-tight, sleek and shiny ensemble that contoured to every curve of her bust as well as her navel, her toned core, and her firm legs. Her arms, cleavage, and neck were all bare. As always, Mother looked beautiful and I definitely wanted to have one of my own. It appeared more comfortable than the heavy white nightgown I was forced to wear.

"Where is Sister Alice?" She licked her thumb and rubbed off the ash that was applied to my forehead in the shape of a crucifix.

"They killed her! They were going to do an exorcism to me but she tried to stop that mean priest."

"What have they done?"

"They put her on fire." I gulped, caught in a brief reverie of the horrors of watching her dress set alight until the silhouette of her body was engulfed in flames. "They said she was a witch..."

Tears swelled in Mummy's eyes. We embraced and shared an unplanned moment of silence for her until Mother's outfit provided an escape from the sorrow.

"Why are you wearing that?"

"I usually wear gowns and skirts but..." She smiled as if it were another game we would play, no question that this time it was for her to relish in our reunion and equally to escape the pain of Alice's demise. "your Mum is no ordinary woman." Mummy raised her eyebrows. "I have been blessed with extraordinary powers; you see." She stroked her hair. "This costume helps me to use them." She kissed me under my eye. "Do you like it?"

"I love it." I twirled my hair. "You look stunning, Mummy!"

She smiled warmly and squeezed me tight against her. "Thank you darling, that means the world to me."

"So, are you a hero, then?" I glowed at her. "Because you are my hero, Mum."

At first, she didn't respond but I knew the words had left a mark on her, as if they had fulfilled her for all that she must have endured just to be there with me.

"Right you are, but you cannot tell anyone..." She raised her finger. "You are the first to know my secret." I nodded in agreement and noticed a nasty patch of black and blue on Mother's thigh. It wasn't from when I hit her in our play fight the previous night.

"Mummy, why do you have a bruise on your leg?"

"I slipped on a rock."

"Is that why you have blood on your head?" I pressed my hand to her wet hair and felt a bump beneath it.

"I am all right darling, I promise." She winced and placed her hand to her stomach for a moment.

"I do not feel poorly, anymore."

"That's my brave girl." She took her cloak and tied it tight around me. "Shall we go home, lovey?"

I hugged her tight and nodded, I was afraid to let go because I feared it would result in me losing her again. She had to unlatch my fingers which pried to her.

"Let's get off then."

When I lifted my head, I watched the door creep open. A gun came through the sliver followed by a pale, bony, and aged hand that clutched it. Friar Patrick's pimply face tensed with rage.

"Mum, watch out!"

His flowing white hair fell below the white collar of his black tunic was the last thing I saw before Mummy pressed me against her to shield me. We shook in each other's arms as we heard him squeeze the trigger once, twice, and thrice; but it had never fired, the gun had jammed.

"I should have taken the Holy Water with me but foolishly I did not. Between your victory against our curates and your capacity to swiftly recover from any damage you sustained, I know now that you could only be one thing..." There was no remorse in his cold blue eyes. "...A demoness."

"She's no demoness, you imbecile..." I snarled. "She's a heroine."

Mother pressed her finger to my lip.

"She is a chip off the old block, isn't she?" The friar laughed condescendingly. "I reckoned you would be paying us a visit this evening and took all necessary measures to safeguard all that reside here, including your daughter who will soon be an orphan."

"You give it your best go but I don't fancy your chances."

"Shut up, you wicked slut." The friar flung the gun at her.

Mummy swatted the pistol to the floor as she got to her feet. The friar was eager to land the first attack with an attempted cheap strike. She blocked the first punch and side-stepped the second. Mother threw a punch with her right and connected on his jaw causing him to stumble backward. She landed a second punch on his nose and continued the attack. She jabbed him twice more and hit him with a haymaker that caused him to sway; but still he did not go down.

She glanced back at me and for that moment, I was at ease because she was in control. Nevertheless, butterflies filled my stomach with every second that passed in the conflict. I didn't want this to go on a second longer, I wished he would collapse so Mummy and I can run off into the night, both of us unharmed.

Mother continued to dominate as she took a step back, planted one of her long legs, and extended her other leg into the friar's jaw which sent him flying forward face first into the desk across the room. He caught himself on the yellow placemat that sat upon the mahogany, only inches from smacking his face against the desk before he held himself up against it. She advanced and reached down to tug the priest's collar but was instead met with an elbow in between her nostrils that made her hair splash across her face. Her nose wrinkled and her eyes teared from the impact of the blow. Needless to say, I felt the sting of that strike as much as she did.

The friar grabbed a white china plate that sat on the desk and swung it at Mummy's head. She ducked and threw a punch through the dish shattering it in his hands and striking his jaw to knock him backward. He wore a look of amazement as she smiled back at him. Mummy kicked him in the midsection and punched him in the face causing him to fall backward toward the desk. She went for a third punch but missed and instead connected with the wall which flung dust into the air. I would have thought that would have hurt her hand from striking the hard surface but she threw another jab unabated. However, on this occasion, the friar caught her fist and tried to squeeze it. Mummy *smiled back at him with confidence, obviously unaffected by the pressure applied. I hopped up and down once, it appeared that she was going to win with little trouble. However, I spoke to soon as the friar drove his toe into her abdomen. The blow collapsed Mummy's diaphragm and caused her to let out a loud grunt and double her over. He yanked her towards him and drove his knee into her stomach, forcing a louder grunt out of her. I cringed and tensed with each blow she took. The friar took hold of her hair and wrapped his arm around her throat, launching his fist upward toward her rib cage. That one seemed to hurt her the most.*

"Argh..." She yelled and bent over at the waist.

"How are your ribs?" The friar clutched some of her attire above her backside. However, his offense would be halted there. Mother performed another amazing feat when she lifted the friar off the ground and crashed him down on his back, bridging her legs as she did so.

"Never have I been better." She executed a handstand and got back to her feet. "Are you ready to surrender yet?" Mummy breathed heavy. "It is only going to get worse from here for you." She laughed. "Come on then..." She stepped away. "I best teach my poppet a few tactics at your expense."

"He has no chance, Mummy!" I clapped my hands, taking notes of the exhibition that I just witnessed. I confess then and there, I wanted to emulate this at some point in the future. Women weren't supposed to be confident and strong like Mummy. Yet, she made it look easy.

The priest's eyes were filled with rage. He was incensed, antagonised, and utterly manhandled. He rose from his feet and charged, throwing another careless punch. She blocked the first and then the second with a smile on her face; then she caught the third one and put the friar's arm behind his back. He agonised from the submission hold applied. Friar Patrick pivoted on his foot and fired a punch into Mummy's midsection, I closed my eyes at first until I heard her giggle. The second attempt also had no effect, she had flexed her abdominal muscles and welcomed the strikes. He threw a punch that crossed her jaw and no damage was done. Mummy stroked a displaced strand of hair back behind her ear. Friar Patrick appeared helpless, demoralised, and embarrassed. On the contrary, I was both relieved and amazed.

"Not like this afternoon, aye?" She clenched down on his arm and dropped him to a knee. He was met with a vicious knee strike before she placed one hand upon him and threw the friar across the floor, as if he were a toy. I continued to cheer and Mummy acknowledged my steadfast support.

"He's lost, my love." Mummy laughed as she stood over him lying flat on his back looking up in bewilderment. Mother pressed her boot against his tunic, the friar's movements languid with his eyes shut. "He's no match for us, Poppet."

The friar's eyes flew open as he twisted her ankle; my smile disappeared as she bellowed in pain.

"One of you is enough as it is." The friar grabbed her shoulders and smashed his head against hers; the dastardly ploy bought Friar Patrick a moment to reach into his boot and remove a small silver dagger. Tears filled my eyes as I watched the knife slice through my mother's midsection. She screamed and bent over, holding the wound, her hands filled with blood. The friar twirled the dagger in his hand and plunged it deep into her thigh. Mummy writhed in agony from all of the punishment, but the friar did not relent. He reached down on the floor and picked up the pistol. He squeezed the trigger twice until it finally let off a shot, the third time. A bullet flew through Mother's heart and exited out of her back.

"Mummy!" I screamed.

The friar threw the gun at the wall above the bed narrowly missing me. I took cover behind and a pillow. Part of the metal chamber broke off from the impact and came to rest beside me.

The friar clenched his hands down over Mummy's throat. "Now it is time to finish you." He lifted her off the ground and planted her onto the bed next to me. The vicar dug his hands deeper. "Unlike you, I have divine power. I can overpower you at a whim, you fragile little flower!"

"Stop it!" I snapped out of a frozen state of shock.

The friar ignored me as she gagged.

"You are going to kill her!" I smacked his arm twice, hoping my words would conjure some sympathy.

"God willing, Hellspawn!" His black eyes bulged toward me.

I looked down at Mother who was struggling to move her eyes from having her air cut off, I had to do something.

I bit his hand as hard as I could until blood was drawn. Lightning flashed in the distance when my teeth gnashed against his flash.

"Ahhh!" He growled as he was forced to release the hold and tend to his bitten hand with his other. The duvet was smeared in red and yellow from a combination of sweat and blood that seeped from her.

The priest raised his hand and I braced myself to be struck; it never happened; Mummy took control of his hand and immediately his flesh began to scorch. All of her strength returned and she yanked him by his black tunic, tearing his top. Smoke billowed from around him as the stench of burning flesh filled the room. "For my sister and my daughter..." Mother locked eyes with him "...This is just a taste of what the Good Lord has in store for you."

Mummy lifted him off the ground and deposited him out the window. Before I had time to process what transpired, she collapsed on the bed. I curled up against her and cried in her arms.

"You are safe now, crumpet."

She groaned as she lied on her back holding held her stomach. A dagger still protruding from her thigh as blood flowed across her sweat-soaked skin. Mother rested as my tears dripped onto her. I kissed everywhere she had been wounded with a hope it would make her better. "You need the doctor." I yanked the dagger from her thigh.

"Ewwf!" She grunted and sat up quickly. Mother cringed and set her eyes upon me. "Ouch..."

"Sorry, Mummy."

Alarm filled her at the sight of the blood-soaked dagger in my little hands. "Give me that!" She opened her hand. "...you'll cut yourself."

I handed the dagger over to her slowly and she tossed it aside. She briefly stumbled as she walked. That was enough to invoke tears from me.

"Don't cry, my love." Mummy pressed her lips to my forehead. "Because you are my daughter, you have these powers too..." She brushed my hair back and dried my tears. "...you can help me..." Mummy extended her hand. "Lock your hand in mine, poppet."

I placed my fingers crusted in her dried blood into her hands which seemed to get warmer. Mother placed both of our hands on her abdomen and then her thigh as I sat beside her. The wounded areas accelerated in their healing as the temperature of her hands continued to rise. She unlocked her hand from mine and reclined onto the bed. "Keep your hands on me, they are healing my wounds."

Somehow it seemed to work! So, I continued to move my hands up and down her ribs, midsection, chest, and thigh.

"Good girl." Mother sighed with relief. "You are restoring me..."

I pulled my hands away for a moment. Nevertheless, the bleeding slowed and the flesh continued to repair.

"Go stand by the window, my love." She rose to her feet. "It's time for us to go home." Mother pulled a key ring from her boot and removed a gold mortise key. "I am aware you are afraid of heights but we are going to have to climb out that window."

I couldn't go out the window. Heights terrified me; I was always afraid of falling. So naturally, I shook my head and resisted her request.

"You can hold onto me and I will climb down for both of us." Mummy placed the key into the lock walked back toward me. "I won't let you fall; I promise."

I nodded again.

"Mummy you are still healing and I am not using my powers." I touched her thigh which had fully repaired. "Are you sure it's not just you with the powers?" Only dried blood spots remained near the areas she had been wounded. "I am better now because of you." She smiled at me. "Stand close to the window, love..." Mummy pressed her hands against the duvet on the end of the bed closer to the door. I backed away from the bed as flames began to kindle. I didn't know what to make of what I was witnessing. "Now let us move along, we have much travelling to do." Mother snuffed out the fire by flicking her finger.

"Can you show me how to do that?"

"Another time, dear..." She stepped out the window and made her way down the ladder to the fourth rung. "We must hurry." She placed her hands firm on the sides of the ladder to ensure the hooks were snug against the windowsill.

"Come toward me, please." She climbed up to open her arms to me. I scurried over to her with the cape dragging on the floor behind me.

"Remove the cloak."

"But I want to wear it!" My feet stamped against the floor.

"Now is not the time for you to get shirty, young lady." She spoke to me at length. "What if you trip over it as you step out?"

"Sorry, Mummy." I untied the cloak and threw it out the window toward the base of the ladder.

"...We'll fetch it at the cloak at the bottom..." Mummy wrapped her arm around me and held my head against her chest. "Hang on, don't be afraid...." She descended the ladder with me snug in her arms as flames and thick black smoke rolled out the bedroom window.

21.

I burrowed my head into my mother's bosom as she climbed down; I couldn't watch. I trusted that she would not let me fall and refused to move my eyes until we reached the ground. When I stepped on to the ground for the first time, I saw the blackened corpse of Friar Patrick burning in the hedge to the right of us. To the left was Mother's cloak, I ran and collected it for her.

She crouched down. "My turn to wear it, sweet." Mummy grabbed her hair to expose the nape of her neck, so I could tie it around her. "Marvellous." She rose to her feet once again.

"Can you make me a pretty costume like yours?"

She adjusted the butterfly hair clip in my hair. "It will be better than mine." Mother joined my hand and led us down the hill into the dark night.

"It has to be lavender, lilac, or a pink-violet, so our colours match each other..."

Mother smiled back at me. "You and I will be the most glamorous and unstoppable team, poppet."

"Abbie" A man called out.

"Who is that?" I looked up as we waded through taller grass.

"There is no need to worry, he is with us."

"There she is!" Another voice echoed from the distance.

Mother about-faced and looked back at the convent. Flames continued to roll out of the window where I was imprisoned. In the room next to it, stood two shadowy figures. Near to where we escaped on *the ladder, three more figures stood along the ridgeline, their silhouettes pointed in our direction.*

"Here." A blonde-haired man emerged and handed Mummy her bow with a set of arrows. "Allow us a minute to have a word with those two."

"You what?" She gazed at him with confusion.

The man vanished into thin air.

"Make ready!" A voice commanded from the three men that stood near the ladder.

"Tempie, get behind me." Mummy fastened the arrow to the chord of the bow. I placed my arms around her waist and rested my head against her lower back. Mother squinted as she focused on the three henchmen that loaded their guns. Her fingers snapped and the arrow ignited in flames. Then, she released it.

Like Mummy's beauty, the arrow had a ferocity and grace about it. It flew through the air and hit its mark with precision. The flaming spearhead crashed into the shoulder of the lead henchman and sent him tumbling over. The two other men halted to tend to their fallen comrade who was submerged in flames.

That strange man materialised behind one of the two men that stood in the adjacent window. Mummy released another flaming arrow. The second projectile soared towards the three adversaries and landed in the leg of the second belligerent, bringing him down immediately.

"Tally-ho, mum."

"Many thanks, my dear."

Mother reached for another arrow until we both froze at the sound of a gun discharging from the room followed by a bulbous man being thrown from the window. He screamed as his straw-bottom hat flew from his head, his white tunic the only discernible garment seen crashing to the ground. The mysterious man that had just vanished appeared at the window, laughed at the sight of the carnage.

Mummy equipped another arrow as the last henchman ran toward the rifleman that was thrown from the window. Once again, she ignited the arrow in a bath of flames. "And one more for safe measure, chaps." She released the arrow and hit his shoulder mid-sprint to send him to the ground. Abigail released one more flaming arrow, it flew high into the air and made its way through the window where the two riflemen stood until the man intervened. She did not know exactly what it hit but it crashed into a stack of oiled hay. The room filled with flames in an instant. Moments later, the man re-appeared beside us.

"I told that porky slob the grey mare is always better than the horse." He laughed.

Mother dropped her bow and jumped into his arms.

He held her tight and kissed her working his hand up and down her back. "I was gravely worried about you. Are you all right?"

"I am worked over quite a bit." She pecked his lips. "I am much better now, though..." She moaned from pleasure and rested her forehead against his. Mother seemed smitten by him but I couldn't bare his sight.

"Who are you?" I crossed her arms. "Why are you kissing her?"

Mother turned to look at me after the two had another kiss. He did not acknowledge me as the two remained wrapped in each other's arms.

"I am terribly sorry, lovey." She took hold of my hand and looked up at this man who wore a fake smile that pretended to be a gentleman. He could dress and look as he did, I however was not fooled.

"Temperance, this here is Mister Pride..."

I couldn't take my glare off of him.

"...Mister Pride is Mummy's..." She looked back at Pride queuing him to say something but he did not answer. "He is a very dear..." Mother struggled to form the sentence as she hoped that he would say something romantic. She was entranced by angst and infatuation.

"Friend." Pride took a step forward. "Your Mum is a very dear friend." He stressed the word friend which caused her to blush from *humiliation. She looked down at the ground disappointed. I saw the confusion written all over Mother's face and how bad she had it for him. As such, she couldn't see him for who he truly was.*

"It doesn't seem that way to her."

"Mindful you are." He bent toward me. "It is a pleasure to finally meet you, Temperance. Your mother has told me all sorts of wonderful things about you."

"I don't like you."

"Temperance Grace!" Mother wrinkled her nose in response.

"You don't love Mum. You don't care about her, one bit."

Her cheeks flushed. "I do not know where she came up with that."

I squeezed Mummy's hand tighter and stepped in front of her. To me this bloke was no different than that evil priest, only he was more cunning and crafty in his wretchedness.

"Mummy, I see how you look at him and he doesn't do the same. Don't be tricked, he is bad."

"Oh, Temperance I fear you are wrong." She stroked my cheek. "He came here with me to rescue you."

"Then why did he leave you to fight all those bad men on your own? Why didn't he help you or climb up with you to get me?" I scowled. "Why didn't he try to heal you like I did?"

Mother stood up with both her arms around me. "I am so sorry, Nelson. She is usually very cordial to any that she meets." She looked down at me, her pleads for my cooperation all but on her lips. Nevertheless, I wouldn't acknowledge them. Only a true gentleman should court my mother and he definitely was not one.

"Children say uncanny things." Pride chuckled.

When Mother wasn't looking at him to kiss my head, he shot me a dirty look, his eyes turning a beady red. His gimmick didn't intimidate me though, it just confirmed what I already knew. When Mother looked him, he faked his smile once again.

"*Perhaps you will feel differently, when you are better acquainted with him.*"

"*Did you not just see what he did?*"

Pride raised his hand. "*Abbie, I can imagine you are fatigued as is your daughter. It has been an eventful evening to say the least.*"

"*I am not going anywhere with you and neither is Mum. She got hurt bad trying to save me and might have gotten killed, but she has powers.*" I pressed my hands into her arms. "*You just stood here the whole time; which means you don't care for her or you're a milksop.*"

"*Hold your tongue, Temperance.*"

"*Yes, you ought to mind your mug and your business, tinker.*" Pride barked.

"*Don't you dare speak to my child like that.*" Mother raised her finger at Pride which caught him off guard. "*You are not her father so you have no place to reprimand her, do I make myself clear?*"

He was at a loss for words. In his arrogance, he assumed that she would turn against her own daughter. For the first time, things did not go according to plan for Pride who seemed to believe he was in command of every situation.

"*I am sorry.*" He adjusted collar. "*You are right; I should not have said that.*"

"*And it will be the last time, I assure you.*"

I shot Pride a contemptuous smile.

"*I understand my daughter to be quite a sharp-witted filly at times but she raises a valid point, Nelson. We have witnessed you dissipate into the thin air, materialise on the first floor, overtake the two lads, and do so before you could wish them olive oil. I on the other hand endured a series of gruelling battles.*"

"*I already explained why I left you to it, I need not repeat myself...*" Pride crossed his arms. "*...you need to know how to use your powers.*" He paused "*...on your own.*"

"Does it not upset you they put their hands on me? There are some men in this world that would never be able to catch a zed for the rest of their days if they knew that someone struck their woman."

"I am not your keeper, Abigail..."

"Assuredly, you would be so chivalrous to do all that you can to prevent any harm from coming to the pair of us. Clearly, I mistook you..."

"Correct me if I am wrong, friend." Pride once again stressed the word "friend" as some form of a weapon to gain the upper-hand in the argument as he knew it deflated her when she heard him refer to her as such. "I have not called you my wife nor my lover. It was imperative that you used your powers successfully and completed all the trials." Pride looked at me then turned his attention. "There is no time to argue, we must go before the constables arrive and we have a whole new set of troubles to tackle. I see fire behind me and lightning ahead of me." He squinted at a flash along the horizon behind the treeline in back of Mother. "A storm is travelling here; we must make a hasty departure."

She looked back in the direction that Pride was. When she took her eyes off of Nelson, he once again slipped a dark grimace at me, this time a set of fangs descended from his mouth to match the haunting red eyes. I stood my ground and stared back at him until I was abruptly overwhelmed by intense malaise, vertigo, and nausea.

"Mummy." I swallowed hard. "I feel icky, again."

"Oh dear." She rubbed the bottom of my chin. "As soon as we get back, I will fix you a meal and we can have a lie down."

"I am going to faint." My words started to slur and I wondered whether it was the sickness or the works of this trickster? My mother was an intelligent woman, surely, she must have known that he was not human, not of this world, and the embodiment of impurity and iniquity. How could she be fooled so easily? My deliberations were put to a halt when my legs felt ready to give out.

"I need you to be strong for me, darling." Mother cradled me against her and placed the back of her hand behind my forehead. "She is febrile." She picked me up and started to run with me on her shoulders.

"We can take her to a ward in Nuneaton that I know of which is ideal for this scenario." He glanced at the burning convent.

"In Warwickshire? that's miles away!"

I drifted out of consciousness as Mummy sprinted until we reached the wood.

"Tempie." Mother gave me a slight tap on the face to orient me. "You must awake, my dear."

"I am sorry, Mummy." I murmured.

"You have nothing to be sorry for." She held me against her as I heard her sob. "How could she take such a drastic turn for the worse?" Mother's shrieks filled the fields as she started to cry hysterically. "Her cheeks are usually so rosy and red; they have gone lifeless and blue."

"Don't cry, Mummy." I opened my eyes and smiled at her. In my moment of weakness, I mustered up the strength because I wanted to take away her pain.

"You can remedy this!" Abigail point her finger toward him. "No more piddling about, Nelson. Do you think I have forgotten about Tilly's bunny?" Mother roared. "I vowed you my body, blood, and soul! Either you will help her or you can burn in whatever cauldron you came from."

"It isn't that simple, I am afraid." Pride's response was calm and collected, as if he had no palpable emotion to all that was occurring; as if he were not alive.

"Then I shall take her to the first physician I come across..." Mother's reply by contrast was animated and full of passion. "...I will nick your colt, if I must!" Mummy shouted back at Pride over her shoulder. Tears ran off her nose onto my lips. "I need you to stay with me, my love." She cradled me tight in her arms as she lifted me.

"*Thank you for saving me, Mummy.*" I expended the last of my energy to touch her cheeks and to dab her tears. "*I love you so much...*"

"*You are the sunshine of my existence; I would do anything for you...*" She watched over me. "*I love you, Temperance.*"

My eyes shut...

That was the last time I ever saw her. – T.G.L.

VOLUME III

22.

"That's all for now." Temperance pressed her hand over the stack of loose leaf.

"Is there more?" I pointed to the crinkled document under her hand, accompanying them were several more pages with sentences scribbled, crossed out, and some had large "X's" drawn across them.

My beloved froze for a moment until she bowed her head with a smile. "Heavens, this is a rather large garment. I could have easily mistaken this kit for a dress, it is surely long enough." She laughed, glancing at the white Georgia Bulldogs jersey draped down just past her elbows and a black number 27 sagged against her arms.

"Well they are your team, my queen."

"If you say so." She smiled and rolled her eyes. "What do you reckon?"

"The Dawg jersey looks great on you..."

"No, you spoon." She slapped my arm playfully. "...The story."

"It is well-written but really upsetting. I hope that lowlife got what was coming to him."

"Oh..." Temperance grinned. "He gets his come-uppance."

"I can also see where you get all your manners, etiquette, and good graces from." I shook my head. "Your Mom just wanted to do right by you and be loved for who she was."

Temperance didn't respond, she bit her lip and appeared to be holding back tears. "Temp, every time I look at you, I feel the guy in the *Twilight Zone* with the magic typewriter" I rubbed her shoulder. "...as if my heart dreamt you into life."

A smile escaped from her pout; my goal was achieved.

I remember the first time I watched that episode with Temperance and was taken back. It reminded me of my love for her and I too was reduced to tears just as I was then. Temperance hugged me tight and started to cry. "I wish I had that typewriter so you could see your mom again..." My fingers blotted her tears and wiped her nose.

"So, the last time you saw her was..."

"She's gone..." Temperance glanced down to the floor. "...Mother left me at an orphanage in Nuneaton and all I could do is watch her leave with Pride as I could barely keep my eyes open..."

"I am so sorry, sweetheart." My face turned slightly to peck her nose. "I wish there was something we could do..."

"Well we cannot." Tempie rose from the couch. "That's all left to the imagination, now..." She took hold of my hand and pulled me up.

"I have more one question." I swung her hand.

She raised her eyebrows to acknowledge.

"Are you still afraid of heights?"

Temperance smirked and snapped her fingers. Once again, she was clad in the skin-tight lilac garment she wore when she first revealed her powers to me. This time she also had a pink satin cape tied around her neck, draped behind her. My jaw dropped at how incredible she looked, mystified as to how she can perform the feat.

Temperance pulled me close to her with little effort and wrapped her arms snug around me, placing my head against her breast. Then, she lifted me with no strain and rose off the ground. We levitated in thin air.

"Do you fear enclosed spaces?" She smiled and glanced down at me.

"Not anymore." I kissed the top of her breast and then her neck, exciting her to close her eyes and breathe heavier.

"You are going to make us fall, if you keep doing that..." She opened her eyes briefly and shut them again when she clutched my jaw to press her lips firmly to mine.

This kiss turned into a tight embrace which culminated with us on the floor, making love for an hour that seemed like seconds. Though we had every inclination to set off for our day trip, Temperance and I lay in each other's arms wrapped in a quilt. Temperance shut her eyes and rested her head on my chest but I could not relax. *Was she going to walk off one day and never come back? When was she going to leave me?* It kept racing through my mind.

"What are you thinking about?" She pressed her hand to my chest and looked at me with concern.

"I was just thinking about how grateful I am to be here with you now." I kissed Temperance on the head. "Thank The Lord."

"Do you ever think about what would have happened, if we never met that day?" Temperance curled her head against my chest. Though her question was as innocent as her, it took me down a pathway that was nothing short of malevolent. A world that I used to dwell in that I feared returning to. Nevertheless, I can feel myself sitting back on that bench, smoking Marlboros like a chimney, craving a drink because I was desperate to numb out what I felt; perhaps I'd have gone back to the Aqueduct and stepped to the edge or maybe I would have gone back to the flat and drew the kitchen knife, contemplating whether or not to stab myself in 30 different places; maybe I would have bashed my head a dozen times. In a moment, that trapped, claustrophobic feeling descended upon me, it was around me again, and pulsing through my veins; I couldn't breathe; I couldn't think; I couldn't see anything; I couldn't reason; I was met by the hopeless, noisome, despairing feeling that only pain and turmoil waits around every corner and that the best thing for me to do is get out.

"Your heart is racing, my love." She ran the back of her hand against my ear, drawing her head close to mine.

Why was she here? I wasn't supposed to be happy, the very idea seemed like something out of reach, something like Temperance herself and yet she was touching me. Temperance is a charming old house set upon a hill flanked by a willow tree and I was no longer out in the cold wondering what it was like to be inside its warm walls.

I closed my eyes ran my hands through her hair, embracing her tight against me. "That's a scary thing to think about."

We shared a hug.

"You smile every time we embrace." She spoke to me with a jubilant inflection. "I can feel your lips arch."

"I treasure it." I cupped her face with both my cheeks.

"As do, I." She kissed my cheek and patted my thigh. "So, you never answered my question."

"I rather not answer that, Honey Bee." I put my arm around her and looked up at the ceiling, focusing my eyes on the gold chandelier and its gooseneck candelabras. "It's like asking you if we hadn't, would you have been hiding away in this house until you felt the compulsion to move on?"

"What other choice would I have?"

"I was thinking the same thing when I went by the aqueduct." I laughed.

"That's nothing to make light of..." She looked at me with concern and anger set in her eyes. "Suicide is a serious matter."

"My friend said the same thing..." I looked back at the ceiling. "...but I always thought the greater tragedy was the trajectory that leads someone to such a state."

"It is." Her gaze fixed to me; the words coming from her mouth clearly directed toward me.

"You have to understand something..." I sat up. "None of these people care. They will leave you to stew in your own moroseness and try to sweep away their apathy with sweet words."

Temperance raised her eyebrows, as if she were my mother and I were her son, a cool gaze that urged me to tranquilise.

"You know I meant what I said, right?" I smiled her. "You are my best friend."

"You are my only friend." A smile escaped her for a moment and then the same look of concern returned her. "I have been alone and miserable and I have lived far longer than you in such a state." She ran the side of her finger against my cheek. "I cannot contemplate the violence that you considered wielding against yourself." She plucked at my eyelash and flicked something away. "I never questioned your regard for me, it is how you regard yourself that concerns me..."

I rubbed my nose in a circular motion, fixing on my socked foot close to the twinkling brass bedpost. The thought injected adrenaline into my veins, my shoulders tensed.

"I would have thought you'd be still considering all the love we just made." She stroked my head. "...you seem quite perturbed..." Her warm hands rubbed against my bare chest. "...this anger you hold onto; you must let go of it; it plagues you..."

"It's not anger...." I let out a deep breath.

"I know..." She smiled warmly with a sympathy that radiated from within her.

"I always thought it was going to be the death of me one day, you know..."

"So, you don't know how to live without it, is that the way of it?"

"No." I shut my eyes and glanced up at the carvings in the white crown mouldings.

"I recall the other day when we were watching that *Wuthering Heights* on the tele..." She placed her stockinged foot against mine. "...you found it mirthful when Heathcliff raised a fire poker to

Linton after he drew him to the floor, as if you were living through it vicariously..."

"I will tell you Temperance of my tempestuous exertions..." I feigned an accent to imitate Heathcliff, letting out a laugh at my own created dialogue before slipping back into my normal way of speaking "How can you not love that guy?" I laughed some more. Temperance looked over at me as if I was someone different that she didn't know.

"Is that how you envisage yourself?" She crossed her arms. "A tyrant?". Temperance arched her eyebrows with her lips stiffened. "...For the life of me, I cannot understand this fascination you have with these dark and wonton lost souls who desire nothing more than to wreak havoc..."

"Am I not a lost soul?"

"You are nothing like them, darling..." She flashed a smile at me.

I glanced back at her and a brief smile broke from me. "You make me very happy..." I kissed her nose and moved my head back to stare into the blue of her eyes. "...However, if I was to ever lose you..." I gulped. "...I too would get revenge."

"Against who?" Her tone shifted to defensive. "...Me?"

I shook my head. "I could never bring myself to do anything to harm you..."

"Then who would be the target of this plot for vengeance?"

"Everyone else..." My hand brushed across the air "I'll go hustle a boat load of money and use it to torment all these people."

"That makes no sense at all." She stroked my cheek. "Why commit yourself to such a wayward endeavour that would bring you no peace?"

I didn't answer; I just looked up at the ceiling and tracked all the black spots that throbbed in front of the light. It was unusual for me to feel content like I was there. I was often maligned; from the outside looking in, no one understood what was going on inside of me and how on some days I had to will myself out of bed just to take a shower. It hadn't happened since Temperance came, I barely slept but found my youthful energy that I thought had been lost.

I felt her hands softly cup my fist which had started to unfurl upon her touch. I looked at her gently, my eyes beholding her; she who brought light to a misery which was ceaseless and unrelenting; a dark abyss of riptide and stormy clouds that lashed with unrelenting gales. She was the sunshine that pierced through the shadows and calmed the seas.

"You can read minds, can't you?" My finger rose and Temperance coolly pressed it down. "Surely, you know I am a caged dog, Temperance."

"Must you speak so contemptuously?" Her voice shifted to a maternal tone. "You are so sweet to me, you are lovely with children, kind to animals, and respectful of your elders." She rose to her feet and threw my football jersey over her. "You are no caged dog nor are you a villain of any kind..." Her eyes fixed on mine. "Contrary to how you perceive yourself, you are a wonderful man, treacle..."

"Thank you, I'd like to be." I looked down. "But I am too troubled to ever be the person I hoped to be."

"Well, I have faith that you will exceed expectation."

I felt understood and appreciated. "But you know what it's like to feel trapped though..." I sighed. "That is your existence too, is it not?"

"You know nothing of my existence, sir!" Temperance roared at me and turned her back. Her shift in mood was startling and prompted me to sit up at attention. The room went silent; I was afraid to open my mouth as I deliberated over what she would say next.

"...I am terribly sorry; I should not have scolded you like that..."

I took her hand. "I didn't mean to..."

"It's not your fault..." She kept her back turned to me. "At times, I reckon you place me on a pedestal that is not fit for purpose. I am not as virtuous as you believe me to be..."

"Well, you are not a good person, Temperance."

She turned around to look at me, she looked deeply wounded.

"You have wealth, beauty, intelligence, and all sorts of supernatural abilities that people would do Lord knows what with..."

Her eyes enlarged as she pre-empted my next remark, readying herself to come back at me with a witty and elegant rebuttal, if she needed to.

"...but despite everything you've endured, you are tender, caring, understanding, gentle, and generous."

She appeared confused now as she perceived I was verbally attacking her, moments ago.

"You were never good..." I smiled. "...but you've always been great."

Her cheeks turned red and her eyes watered up.

"I wish I could be more like you because I could never be half the person, you are..."

She took my hands and embraced me tightly, her prompt squeeze indicating the effect my remarks had on her, over any words. "You need be to loved." Temperance rubbed her cheek against mine. "As do, I."

I held her tight as she drew her lips close to my ear.

"You are like a fire; a blaze that grows intolerable in its neglect and desires to consume all that surround it in its heap of passion..." I listened on as she spoke softly, in awe and admiration of her usage of metaphor and the advanced intelligence that she so effortlessly demonstrated. "...but if one was there to tend to it, feed it, and bask in its glow, it will thaw the chilliest sepulchre, brighten the darkest of rooms, and warm all those about to a cosiness only found at home..."

She moved her head and pressed her lips against my cheek. "I am here..." Temperance whispered softly. "Now let's go home, my dear."

23.

Temperance and I sat in silence, listening to music as I drove. I held her hand as I sped along a road that hugged the coastline, Jimmy Eat World's *Sweetness* blared through the speakers as the interlude reverberated through the car.

Temperance gazed out the window at the green dunes that screened us from the beach and water behind it. Her blue eyes matched the colour of her bonnet, fixed to the top of her head. She wore her hair up in an ornate configuration of plaits, twists, and curls held in place by several obsidian hat pins which protruded outward slightly. The hat boded a medley of roses of all hues at the front and side. Wherever Temperance's eyes landed, it was as if she were analysing the landscape comparing it to the last time that she saw it, taking note of any changes. Houses passed us on the right, large stucco and brick inspired villas discernibly a new addition to the old thoroughfare we were travelling down. Stray stands of Temperance's hair flicked in the breeze that came through the open window; freckles formed under her round eyes as she squinted modestly at the passing dunes. The music playing seemed to flow around her, as if it were a symphony designed to radiate her soft skin, accent the freckles beneath her lashes, and illuminate the sparkle in her eyes.

A signpost soon emerged welcoming us to St. Anne's on the Sea, I clutched Temperance's hand harder, she matched the intensity. A few minutes later, a series of signs directed travellers to local attractions, one of which was St. Anne's Pier. We came to a halt at a traffic light and Green Day's *Brain Stew* came on the radio. The outro comprised of mighty power chords blasted through in full effect.

"Do you mind if I turn this?" Temperance spoke over the music and covered her ear with one hand. Before I could respond, her porcelain fingers twisted the volume dial of the stereo.

"Albeit it's not that screaming racket [A Temperance-ism for music of the hardcore rock genre] you enjoy..." Her eyes shut for a moment. "...it is still giving me a blooming headache."

"I am sorry, darling." I rubbed her forehead. "Put on whatever like..."

She snapped her fingers and *Sweet Escape* by Akon and Gwen Stefani came on.

"Really, Honey?"

Though Temperance tried to remain reserved, sitting upright, with her other hand placed over her lap, a smile briefly streaked across her face.

"I was looking for Tarzan Boy but this will do..."

"Great choice!" I turned up the volume and started to scream the intro Temperance pressed her hand to her head as she broke out in laughter; then she joined in.

She sang the lyrics to the chorus back to me as she looked at me out of the corner of her eyes, her smile arched in my direction. Temperance paused to nod demurely at a family that watched us drive by, visibly impressed by her hat.

"To think the song is already eleven years old...."

The words seemed to freeze her in place. In an instant, the music fell silent and her smile was gone.

"Has it been that long? it seemed like merely a second." Temperance stared blankly down the road. She appeared lost; perhaps somewhere between 2006 and 2017 but it looked as if she were re-orientating herself in the present after visiting some distant point in the past. "Goodness me, it only goes faster...." Distress consumed her gaze until she looked up at the approaching pier on our right. "Park by the bandstand, please..." Temperance pointed. "...we can promenade for a bit."

Moments later, we rolled into an empty car park. I stepped out after turning off the ignition and opened the door.

"My lady." I extended my hand to Temperance and she stepped out from the vehicle, parasol equipped in her other hand.

"Ta, my dear." She bowed her head and kissed my lips; I closed the door behind her. Temperance adjusted her hat on her head and looked up toward a massive structure that stood ahead of us, a Tudor-style edifice with a clock fixed to the centre. In front of it, a green panel anchored by frieze and sunburst panelling. In gold leaf lettering on the panelling itself written was *Ice Cream, Beach Goods, Taxis, and Amusements*. In the middle above the front entrance, *St. Anne's Pier* was written.

Temperance wore a blue and white day-dress with gold buttons that were done down the centre of the bodice, resting neatly over her midsection. A blue brooch with a gold star circumnavigated her throat, a matching sky-blue bow tied and draped over her bodice. The gown descended to her knees in a blue and white striped pattern. Pantalettes emerged from beneath the sea-side day dress and tied off at her knees. Starch white cotton stockings covered her shins that tucked into her royal blue pleather boots. The wind flicked the blue and white stripped ruffles of her bodice, her white chemisette beneath the bodice glowed in the sunlight.

"Are you sure you want to go here, my love?" My arm hooked hers as I brushed off my white polo-shirt and then my blue trousers. "Blackpool is only a ten-minute drive."

"We'll save that for later." She tapped my arm with white gloved hand.

"Yeah but with everything that happened here previously..."

"This place is vaguely recognisable compared to as it was on the night of that gaff..." Her hand moved toward me. "And I have you here to make sure I am safe." Temperance smiled sweetly.

"Let's go take a walk by the water, then."

Temperance looked at me with a tight-lip.

"I mean let's go promenade." I made quotations with my hands.

"Hush your mush." She giggled and briefly pressed her lips against mine. "It is warmer here than in Crete today, we best take advantage of this rare treat, as snow is forecasted on the morrow." A wind blew and draped her dress tight to her figure. She held her hat and walked beside me, our hands clasped together. Even there in an empty car park and vacant promenade, there was a propriety, elegance, gracefulness, and femininity to how Temperance moved. In everything she said and she did, it was full of beauty, charm, deportment, and magnificence.

"You know; I saw a video from 1903 of the high street over there." I moved head into the direction of St. Anne's Road. "All these folks walking around not knowing that over 100 years later, some guy like me would be watching them on some video on the internet." Our shoes scratched against the gravel as we approached the entrance of the pier. "They were like you and I, just going to the sea for the day, living their lives, and not thinking much."

Temperance's eyebrows lowered as she listened to every word I said. "I always wished I could be like that, just live out my life in fullness and peace, before going back home to our Father and Lord in Heaven." I glanced at the concrete steps that led to the beach. "Unless I wrote about all of this, they'd never know. From a far, I'd just be some guy wandering around that vanished into obscurity."

Temperance dimples formed the cupid bow smile. "In any era, you were never meant for obscurity, my profiterole."

We stepped onto the sand; the beach was all but ours. A woman stood far away from where we were, where the tide had wet the sands just hours before. She tossed a tennis ball as a spaniel dog scampered in pursuit of it. To our right, the pier extended outward like a fist into the bay. It wasn't remotely close to the picture from the turn of the century when it was at its peak. A smaller and more modernised attraction with white plastic sidings and seafoam green roofing.

"Mitchell and Kenyon." Another breeze blew and tossed the navy ribbons at the back of her hat into the air for a brief moment. "There was an electric tram that ran through here and they were filming it." She looked up at the pier. "It was a lovely May day like today but there was something missing...." Her head turned toward the sun. "I surmise I was waiting for you..."

"Well I finally got to the right country, thank The Lord." I smiled. "I would have needed a time travel machine for the other part to get to you otherwise." My smile grew wider until I got lost in my thoughts. "*Elite Syncopations* was published in 1903. I could see it playing in the background whilst you saunter around in black and white picture. You would look over your shoulder and then a smile would creep across your cheeks as you twirl your parasol. Birds would be flying around, ladies pushing their prams, kids playing badminton, and like I said none would ever suspect that over a century later someone would be watching them on a handheld device. The idea would seem preposterous."

Temperance set her gaze was set upon me, inviting me to say all I needed to. "You know, you could have gone on about the rest of your day and done some routine errand and never knew that in the twenty-first century I would be watching you and wishing I could just spend a day with you like we are now." I glanced up at the clock face in the entrance building. "I'd tear through the time-space continuum just to touch your hand." I threw my arms around her and squeezed her tight, I would have been content to never let her go. Temperance stroked the back of my head and held me, until she pushed my shoulders back to look at me.

"Anonymity has always been my most steadfast friend and ally...." Her eyes enlarged; I saw my reflection in Temperance's irises. "...until now."

WE WALKED UNDER THE ironwork of the pier until Temperance and I stood upon a firmer part of the beach where shells and rocks had formed in wet sand to make the surface firm and not oppose every step we took. Temperance placed her hand over her brow and beamed at the sight of a duck wading along. She whistled at it and it approached her, allowing her to pet it for a second. The occasion brought delight to her as she knelt down and rubbed its head with a gentleness, calling it all sorts of affectionate nicknames as she did so. Soon after, seagulls perched on the beach face and cawed in a cacophony. My beloved imitated the birds and cawed back at them, as if she were little child again.

"Did you see that seagull? He stole that doughnut." I chuckled.

"Jam Rolly Polly flavoured." Temperance led me by the hand toward a rusted jetty which stood marooned in the sand. "For a known scavenger, the gent has exquisite taste."

"You can't go wrong."

We shared a laugh as we neared the eroded pier, a collection of broken and petrified wood anchored with a series of iron bars that corroded from over a century of exposure to the elements. At either end of the jetty stood a tower with a globe ornament.

"This is all that remains from what you read." She glanced at the structure as she grabbed her hat. The wind had started to pick up and roar. "This here jetty and me..."

I didn't say anything but she could detect I was tense.

"It was all a show." Temperance put her hand on her hip. "The IPN were a rather nefarious outfit that catered to an unscrupulous audience." Temperance tapped the sand with the tip of her parasol.

"...these proper gentlemen, many of whom were married, had a fetish for women in revealing attire finding themselves in peril..." She smirked. "Ironically, subverting the notion of chivalry." Temperance held her hand out and inspected her nails. "Even to the little ones, it was a form of entertainment that seemed to excite them." I leered at the pier and listened to Temp speak.

"If I took a blow to the body and doubled me over, they loved it." Temperance picked up a rock and skipped it into the ripples. "If I tore my suit, bled, or split my lip, the IPN would exhaust the subject." She glanced back at the pier closer to the coast. "They all swooned over the sound of my groans, grunts, and moans when I got hurt or beaten up a bit..." Temperance threw a smaller pebble. "They fantasised in me prevailing and overpowering the threat in a display of supremacy." She shook her head with a smirk. "Nevertheless, the more damage I took, the more it got their cockroaches."

"Got their cockroaches?" My fist curled around a larger rock.

"...Masturbate..." She rolled her eyes. "It was erotic to them after all, so I played to it to tease them..."

"I don't know how it's erotic because I hate the thought of you in any kind of danger." My shoulders tensed up. "I would literally take someone's life from them, if they tried to hurt you."

"Don't be angry, Butterscotch. It was amusing for me." Temperance cupped my hands. "Here I stand, a chaste woman, a virgin, who never even kissed a boy prior to you and I had the opportunity to expose these quote-un-quote married family men who pretend to demonstrate such valour and gallantry without even needing to flirt." Her hand cupped my chin. "I revealed their true character with very little effort on my part, all I had to do was wear a revealing ensemble and make dramatic sound effects whenever I was struck..." She smiled. "On some occasions I was actually hurt but you know that I recover rather quickly." Her head turned out to the water which started to creep toward us. "I found vindication given how they treated Mother and I as a result of having no father on my birth certificate."

"They missed out..." I launched the rock out to the sea as if I were throwing a baseball or football, providing me with a release from the pent-up agitation. "...it's impossible not to love you."

Temperance smiled and led me further from the structure and into the cool waters which kissed our feet. She stopped and stared into my eyes as if she were addressing my soul. "From the first moment we locked eyes, I knew you were unlike any other man I had ever met previously."

Her candour sent ripples through me; my eyes felt as if they were going to water. She knew she touched me and that spurned joy to well up within her.

"You are going to make my cry..."

"I could see your soul, I could hear your heart, and I could navigate the labyrinth of your mind." Temperance looked down at her reflection in the water. "And the way you looked at me, the way you speak, and the beauty that resonates from within you..." She stood tall and radiated an inner strength and nobility that was never forced, it's just who Temperance is.

"I was taken by it and it still scares me..." Temperance continued to lead me further down the beach into deeper water. "I was filled with the notion that I could never get close to anyone." She looked up at the Blackpool Tower which poked above the horizon in the distance "After the incident here, I was frightened of being exposed and went into hiding for a bit." Temperance waded her foot through the water. "Incessant solitude seemed to be a cast-iron guarantee."

"I can relate to feeling alone and as if it will always be that way. It's why I considered walking into the sea and never coming back."

Temperance pressed her lips to my hand. "Alone we are not, any longer." She swung my hands. "I could not manifest the progression of events on that day in Marple we met, that's why I trusted it."

A smile broke across her face. "You, me, how it all unfolded." Temperance swam her foot through the water. "You say it was a dream for you but it was also a dream for me." Her eyes went out to sea as her fingers started to tremble. "We are soulmates in the most absolute of physical, emotional, and metaphysical terms."

"I knew it from the moment we met." My eyes cast out to sea landing on the same ship that Temperance watched steam by. Like us, the vessel was trying to find its way.

"So, whatever happened to that guy and his sicko sister?"

"Broadhurst?" Temperance tilted her to the side, I confirmed with a nod.

"I was pursued by a mob of ruffians and escaped from the pavilion via crashing through a third-floor window. I endured a series of nasty bumps and fell through a table until I came to a rest on the pier." She cringed. "I admit I sustained quite a bit of damage to my body and it also tore my suit." She bit her lip. "As I was healing from the bumps, a sweet little boy came tended to me and sent the mob in the wrong direction. I picked myself up, reset my shoulder which was dislocated, winked at him, and ran off until I encountered two men who attacked me with umbrellas further down the way." Temperance looked back at the boat jetty. "...I was able to overcome them with little effort, only to find myself wounded thrice by a gun fired from Delia's hands. Needless to say, I evaded any further injury and much to her chagrin I overpowered her with ease. She hit me in the stomach and I didn't flinch; she was perplexed whence I smiled back at her, considering blood was still seeping from my wounds onto my leotard..."

A lump formed in my throat had cut off my vocal cords, until my rage pushed words forward. "You know I'd never hit a woman but if one tried to harm you, I would..." Temperance touched my fist. "Shhh...." Her hands stroked my trembling hand. "...it's past it now."

I let out a deep breath and listened on.

"...Broadhurst fell off the pier onto rocks there..." She pointed to an area of sandy beach. "...After I defeated his sister, he attempted to charge me and I leapt to the side." Temperance glanced at seaweed that washed in from the surf. "His momentum took him over. Then, I had to fight my way off the pier through all of his henchmen. Needless to say, I left with a split lip and a sore midsection, spending the better part of the next day bathing my wounds and rubbing my bruises. But I prevailed..." She tapped the butterfly pinned to her bonnet with a smile. "The result for those troublemakers was supremely demoralising as they were humiliated and dominated by one lady in tights. It languished them for the rest of their days and moreover destroyed any notion of credibility they had worked their socks off to cultivate." Temperance smirked for a moment and glanced down. "The travesty in it is that I had no want of such events to unfold." She looked up at me. "I do not know what became of Delia or Ada Louise Broadhurst and I found that odd considering all that Delia knew about me." She glanced back at the remnants of the pier. "Still, I cannot express how terribly sorry I am for how it all transpired with Ada's father." She shook her head. "I endeavoured to establish a small account for Ada to ensure she had all she required but it was impossible to locate her whereabouts. I assume her aunt took on custodial duties."

"But that wasn't your fault." I took her hand. "That guy killed himself trying to do something horrible to you..." I felt a smirk form. "...He did it to himself..."

"Yes, but every girl needs a father." She removed her hat. "...Heaven knows I would have loved one."

"You do have one." I pointed toward the sky.

Temperance sulked. "I was under the impression I am considered an abomination..."

"I can't imagine that would be the case."

"Anyways..." She let hair fall down her back. "Fancy taking a dip?" Temperance took a few paces to dry sand to place it upon her parasol. "We can contravene the term mixed bathing" She unbuttoned her bodice.

"That water is freezing."

"I've hatched a plot to ameliorate that." She stepped out of her day-dress and boots. I took off my shirt and trousers and threw them on top of her clothes. All that remained was her upper body clad in a white corset and her "bloomers" snug to her legs.

"That's a lovely corset, Mama."

"To be fair, they can be quite comfortable." She raised her arms. "Can you take it off me, please?"

I walked to the back of my beloved and unlaced the white strings of the undergarment until the small of her back and the curvatures of her shoulder blades were fully visible. The scent of salt water filled my nose as a breeze brew across the nares on the back of her neck. I pressed my lips against her back and wrapped my arounds around her. "You can wear my shirt, if you'd like..."

"We are both not wearing our tops, that will suffice." Temperance took my hand; her pace accelerated as she skipped and giggled until we dove into the frigid waters. My beloved let go of me for a moment and swam around me. The waters started to bubble and flash with purple light, the temperature rose from paralysing chilly to lukewarm and rejuvenating. Temperance emerged from beneath the water and leaped into my arms.

She laughed as she wrestled me into the surf. I picked her up and she squealed, she retaliated with a splash and a giggle. We frolicked and rough-housed in the water, cackling like hyenas as we splashed at each other.

My beloved swam up to me and threw her arms around my neck. I swung my hands down into the water, aiming for Temperance's white pants that were refracted under the ripple of the water. Our wet bodies coalesced and wrapped in each other's embrace. We held each other for a minute and listened to the waves break.

"How is all this real?" I kissed the side of Temperance's head, tasting salt as my lips pressed against her wet hair. "What if one of us is really just dreaming right now?"

"Dreams do come true, Butterscotch." She pulled her head back, water dripped down her face, her eyes matched the sea.

"I mean this is all like a fairy tale, it seems like there can be a happy ending."

"All things considered, I am old enough to be your great-great-great grandmother and if there is any wisdom, I can impart upon you, it's that happy endings are real. As a writer you know better than anyone as you commit your imagination to them."

"But what if we are dreaming right now and we wake up?" A sense of panic filled me; my head swivelled from side to side. "What if my mind created you as an escape from the suffering it causes me." My hands gripped Temperance's hips. "What if this is like the *Twilight Zone* episode with the Stop at Willoughby?"

"One can always conjecture and circumspect on the basis of what ifs." Her hand rubbed up and down my back. "What if I am an anachronism and this is my dollhouse that I can always play in but never exit?" Water burbled as the tides encroached us. "What if several narratives are unfolding concurrently and only one is the timeline you live in? Then who's to say which one is real, but let me ask you this..." She placed her hand to my face "Does this feel real?" Her lips forcefully pressed against mine.

"More than anything."

"Then believe in it, my dear..."

Our kisses grew deeper, our lips locking, and tongues dancing in each other's mouths as the sea moved with our hands concealed beneath the water. She straddled me and I threw my arms around her. Temp looked pensive, as if she were about to weep.

"I know you are like a combination of Mary Poppins and Catwoman but I would die for you..."

"Well what if you never had to?" Her hands swam against the nape of my neck. "What if I told you that as an alternative, you and I could live beside each other happily..." She pressed her forehead into mine with a gentleness. "Forever..."

"I'd love that..." My arms curled extra tight around her.

"Your diabetes..." She held me tighter. "What if I could make that go away too?"

I opened my eyes to look at her. "You already make it..."

"I am serious, dearest." Her eyes glassed up. "I am not pawning off an old mule." Her fingers made their way into my scalp; they vibrated with a low heat. "All you have to do is what me Mum did or I can do it for you..." She smiled and lay across me as I held her tighter. "...we can have our own world and we can dance every night under moonlight knowing we are truly together for all eternity..."

"There is nothing I would want more, but what about The Lord?"

"What about Him? Wouldn't He want us to be happy?" She pulled a wet strand of her hair from my lip. "Besides you wouldn't be selling your soul for riches." Distress poured across her face. "Moreover, it's not fair, I never did a deal to begin with." She embraced me as if I was a stuffed animal. "Oh Butterscotch, just think of all the fun we can have together; all the places we can go; we never have to worry about a thing..." Her face pressed against mine. "...we can run away and live in the countryside, a long way from anyone. Nothing but our love and green meadows for miles."

"Sounds like Heaven." I rubbed her cheeks with the back of my hand.

"It would be..." She closed her eyes and whispered.

I didn't say anything for a minute but just soaked in the sound of the waves crashing behind us.

"We could have it all, all we would have to do is sort you out..." A slight sigh escaped her lips.

"I love you, Temperance. You make me believe that there are things in this world that are beautiful, good, and true. I could never be half of what you are..." I kissed her forehead. "I can never have enough time with you, I'll always want more."

"I love you too, my darling more than you can ever fathom." Her words were sped up from eagerness. "But we don't have to worry about time anymore!"

Butterflies filled my stomach. "It's not that I don't want to, but what if it backfires?"

"It won't, trust me." Temperance's eyes glassed up. "It went without fail when Mumma did." She looked like a lost little girl trying to find her way home in the pouring rain. "I can be Lady Pride, the pathetic and selfish villainess that corrupted a man by the purity of his love..."

I shook my head. "You are the most wonderful person that I have ever met, I just hope you don't change your mind about me in 92 years..."

"Why would I ever change my mind, Butterscotch? You know everything about me. All of my secrets, my strengths, my weaknesses, my very hopes and wants. I wouldn't make a damp squib of it..."

"Think about what you are saying here though."

"I am sorry but there is no alternative, otherwise we are ultimately bound to head in opposite directions."

The thought haunted me; I didn't want it come to that. I couldn't bear the thought of losing her.

"You can move in with me and all your finances will be taken care of." She smiled. "You can quit your flat, we can sort out any paperwork you require, and you won't have to worry about a thing." She clapped her hands with a juvenile smile. "Any requests that you have I will see to, and it shall be done."

"That's really sweet of you honey." I smiled at her. "...but as long as I have you, I have all that I want." My arms wrapped tight around her.

"Well now you won't have to resort to that college football betting racket anymore to subsidise your income."

"Honey, that's not the not the only thing I do..."

"And now you don't have to do it any longer." She spoke with authority.

"But I like to buy you gifts and surprise you with things." I stroked her cheek. "...you know how much I enjoy bringing you stuff, just to see you smile..."

"You do spoil me...." She looked back at the dune. "...perhaps I can spoil you for a change." Her eyes locked back on me. "Please, just do as I ask..." Her eyes glassed up. "...I have been wanting to share all that I have for the longest of times..."

"I just don't want you to labour, as a result."

"Nor will I." She kissed the side of my cheek. "I've made some sound investments and my finances labour for me at this juncture..." Her eyes squinted as she analysed the words forming on my lips. "...unless that's not the real issue?" She glowered. "Do you not fancy the idea of a woman looking after you?" Temperance swirled her tongue in her mouth. "Perhaps you fear it makes you less of a man, is that it?"

I shook my head. "It's just, I can't sit around and do nothing..."

"Is that what you think I do?" She replied with a hint of defensiveness in her tone.

"No, it's just I want to contribute..." I stroked her wrists. "...and when I am idle, my mind starts to mess with me..."

"I can understand that sentiment..." She nodded and smiled. "...so do your writing..." She kissed me again. "...and when you become a renowned and famous author, you can buy us a big old house from my day." Temperance moved her head back and stroked the sides of my arms.

"I'd love to do that."

Any romance or progress in the discourse came to a screeching halt when her disposition grew serious again. "...but first we must deal with the pressing matter before we carry on any further..." Tension and anxiety filled her.

"What if there is another way to deal with this?" I threw out the idea with the hope it would steady her.

"Must you dither?" She loured. "The sooner accept what I propose, the sooner we can quell all this uncertainty." Her intonation accelerated. "...Something haunts you, please tell me..."

The town of Wigan flashed across my mind for a brief moment and the feelings of loneliness and heartbreak, a time before Rachel. A time where the grief was even more profound, my mind circumnavigated to the subject at hand.

"What if The Lord can help us?"

"We are enjoying a day out, so we can table it..." She placed her head on my shoulder. "I will ask you once more tomorrow." Her arms wrapped tight around me. "I trust you will do what is right..." Temperance's lips puckered against my cheek. "...for both of us."

24.

Temperance opened her wooden chest and her hands sifted through a collection of memorabilia. I walked over to stand behind her, her eyes lit up as she removed two Punch and Judy puppets. She grabbed them and scurried off until she ducked behind the couch and only the puppets could be seen.

"Dah, duh!" The Judy puppet bowed. "Hello, boys and girls! Today's word of the day is incontrovertible."

The Punch puppet moved across the top of the couch and spoke in a man's voice. "Doesn't that mean when we are motoring in one of those upmarket luxury cars with the roof cut out?"

"Not by the least!" Temperance raised the pitch of her voice and rendered it to sound less mature. "You are referring to being in a convertible, dear."

I laughed.

"Incontrovertible means without a doubt. For example, it is incontrovertible that our friend Temperance used to loved her mother's rag pudding for tea when she was a little girl." She swapped to a gruff male voice. "It's also incontrovertible that Temperance loves...." The puppet paused. "...now what's he called?"

I laughed some more.

"Now that is terribly rude, Mister Punch." She swapped back to the higher-pitched female voice. "He is watching the show..." She whispered and gestured discontent with the puppet.

"I am so very sorry." The puppet turned toward me. "Hey Judy, why don't you spell that word out for all the other good little boys and girls!"

"Incontrovertible, I-N-T-R-O-C-O-N-T-R-O-V-E-R-T-I-B-L-E, incontrovertible." My eyes glanced over at the stack of papers I noticed the day before. What was most peculiar was that some of the leaves appeared extensively aged followed by ones that seemed brand new. "Yayyyyyyy!" The puppets hands clapped in a high-pitched squeaky exclamation. I leaned over and tried to make out what was written on the but could only determine it was another chapter. "And that's the way you do it!" Temperance emerged from behind the couch with a child-like smile on her face.

I clapped my hands and she bowed.

"We need to do a proper play; I'd have a ball with this."

"I have had much merriment with these." She placed the puppets on the couch. "I also had a doll named Hortensia and a stuffed elephant named Mister Ruffles." Temperance placed her hand on her hip. "They were my mates." She was imbued in nostalgia. "...oh how, I miss them terribly."

"So, is that the next chapter?" I pointed at the sheets of paper.

My lady lost her tongue for a moment as if something urgent had crossed her mind.

"It is nothing worth having a nose over."

"Are you sure?"

"Do not read the blasted thing..." Temperance pointed her finger at me until she feigned a smile. "Forgive me, I do not mean to be cross..." She stared into space as if she were recapping a series of events over and over again. An awkward silence filled the room until Temperance slapped her knee. "Right, I am going to have a bath." She pecked my cheek. "Join if us, you like." Temperance walked toward the bathroom, turned on the switch for the hot water, and shut the door behind her. I was tempted to follow but curiosity got the best of me; I wanted to know what else she had written. Instead, I made myself a cup of coffee, sat back down on the couch, grabbed the collection of papers, and read on.

The events were hard to follow but seemingly they culminated in Temperance's mother disintegrating the house into flames. Apparently, she had fled to Long Beach, New York after helping the Union win the Battle of Gettysburg. On additional pages, more notes and prose were written in correlation to the composition. They chronicled the Firefighter Christopher Parsons taking Abigail on a date and the truth of her powers being revealed. The young firefighter who was smitten with Abigail despite learning her story, warns her of the danger should she stay around, and then gives her money to take a ferry back to England to find Temperance. The fireman never revealed how he felt, he sat on his feelings for her and let her go, settling for a kiss as she got into the coach to head towards the port of New London. What struck me most was how incoherent and incomplete the narrative was; it seemed as if it was thrown together frantically in an emotional state.

Given the recent crafting of these narratives, I wondered if this exercise wasn't a symbolic representation of what my beloved thought would transpire between us. I reflected upon it further but my thoughts were soon interrupted when a finger glanced my shoulder.

"What do you have there?" Temperance stood over me in a long purple dressing gown. Her wet hair wandered across her back and chest. She gripped the paper and studied the content; Her cheerful disposition turned cold with each breath she took. "You defied my instructions..." She reached for a silver hair brush in the same box the papers were in. "How much have you read on?" The silver brush navigated through her wet thick hair.

"A fireman from New York..." I chuckled. "...The whole story seemed like a re-creation of you and I..." My smile was soon met by a menacing pout of rage from Temperance. I took a deep breath and changed the subject with a hope it could de-escalate the tension.

Her brush strokes became more aggressive.

I moved my fingers into hers. "Let me brush your hair for you, my love."

She handed me the comb. "To be fair you aren't a foozler, just yet..."

I kissed her head and slid the comb through her hair. "If you need help writing a scene with fires by the way, you can use that job I told you about where we had the flames rolling out the windows..."

"It's you, alright?!" Her shoulders tensed. "Tis you and I, but I cannot complete it!" Her voice raised. "Is that what you want to hear?"

I raised my hands in surrender.

"As for my mother, I cannot say what happened conclusively. I carried out extensive research and some accounts have led to a woman of my mother's likeness last seen in Unionville, New York near to where Christopher and his fire brigade were in operation. Other sources suggest she perished in the town of Long Beach in a fire; none have recovered her body. Some claim she never existed..." She huffed. "Despite several fact-finding and research excursions, I can only conjecture..." Temperance pulled the butterfly bobby pin from her hair "...the only material evidence I can recover." She carefully placed it on the table "... mysteriously discovered in St. Anne's..." Temperance looked around the room. "And I had to endure a gauntlet just to regain it..."

"Them again." I stopped brushing her hair and froze stiff for a moment. "I really ought to get over there and frog-stomp someone..."

"Bottle that..." Temperance turned her head back to me. "Can you not see at this point that you can hurt me more than anything those men did to me?" Her lips quibbled. "Can't you see that you can mortally wound me? And as to why Christopher is a re-creation of you?" Her eyes widened and her tone of voice raised. "I will call a spade, a spade." She looked away; her cheeks flushed red. "The other firemen in the story are based upon your pals in your old company from when we had that video chat."

A smile unravelled across my face, amazed at the sheer creativity. "You imagined all this from a Skype call?"

Temperance's eyes darted back and forth across the room; her eyes fluttered with a nervous energy.

"You are a genius, Miss Lee." I laughed. "You can create a whole tale based on a few facts and simply imagining the rest..."

"Isn't that what you do when you take a turn for the worse?" She snickered. "You escape into your own little world."

I brushed off another jib as the strands of her wet auburn hair shook in my hand.

"On a page I skimmed over you had your mom leaving town and Chris felt something for her but didn't do anything, he just let her go..."

"What difference does it make?" Temperance glared at me out of the corner of her eye. She seemed more disposed toward taking comfort in my brushing of her hair. For a minute, I said nothing and watched her shut her eyes and drift into her thoughts.

"Well, it's very Victorian..." I laughed with a tremor of nervousness, hoping it would ease the tension once again.

"You're apt..." Temperance eyes slammed open and she sat up. My shirt dampened from her wet hair pressing against my chest. "...since I am a Victorian woman..." Her eyes became wet. "And clearly you are a massive fan..." Temperance got up and placed a white bow in her hair. "Shall I reprise my role as the angel in the house for you?"

"What's up with you?" I placed the brush down on the table. "Talk to me, Temperance..."

"I prefer not to discuss the matter."

I put the collection of papers on the glass table. I rose and placed my arms around her, my lips pressing against her below the white bow she had placed in her hair. She remained stoic and motionless, not sweet and bubbly like she normally was.

My hands moved up and down against her stomach. "I will listen for as long as you need me to."

"I appreciate that but I've already told you that I am not bothered." Temperance drew her arm at length. "Can we move onto a better form of conversation, please?"

"Very well, what would you like to discuss?"

"Your decision, no more postulating." She pulled away. "Please tell me you are going to make the right choice."

"Temperance, I...."

"Save it then, I know what comes next."

"Hold on..." I raised my hands. "I haven't seen you this tense before..." My fingers extended toward her shoulder.

"I am full of surprises, am I not?" She shrugged my hands off. "If you persist acting a nuisance, I'll feel inclined to leave you with a face like a bulldog chewing a wasp."

"Isn't that a good thing, Go Dawgs?" I smiled, hoping to make light of the situation.

"Oh, clear off with that flaming hand-egg gobshite..." She turned around.

"I was trying to make you laugh."

Her hands choked the handle of a coffee mug. "I didn't find it humorous." The cup clanged against the wash basin.

The sound of Temperance scrubbing the coffee mug with forceful strokes. and running water filled the flat.

"Why just let her go, though?"

"Isn't that what you will do with me?" She looked over her shoulder. "Classify my writing exercise psychodynamic, but I have re-imagined history to prepare myself for what seems to be inevitable." Temperance laughed. It was eerie, nervous, and masking pain. "...as was drafted, I come forward, you free me of my past, the trough will remain between us for aforementioned reasons, and then you'll let me go to burn in my own misery..."

"I would never leave you..."

"Will you not?" She swung her head and glared back at me. "Prove it, then..." her blue eyes looked right through me. "Heed my word and do as I say!" The despair kindled behind her serene irises. "We can resolve the issue but you refuse to cooperate!"

The stereo started to play in the background it was Cream's rendition of *Crossroads*.

"I am supposed to sell my soul?"

Temperance wrinkled her nose.

"It's not mine to sell." I cupped my hands. "And to who would I be selling it, you?"

"I suppose so..." She glanced back at me. "Fearful that I will imprison you for eternity?"

"I think we should take our case to a higher court to the king that would handle this situation best." I took a step behind her and slid my arms around her hips.

"If He hasn't condemned me already..."

"Why would He?"

Temperance let out a brief laugh. "Since you read on, you should know the answer!"

"What if we got married?"

She remained silent and obstinate, breathing heavily. My sense of urgency prompted me to continuing throwing out alternatives.

"What about the fluid bonding?"

"Fluid bonding?" Temperance glared at me from the corner of her eye. "That terminology sounds quite contemporary for a traditionalist..."

"Your mother and Pride exchanged blood without any barrier, that is a form of fluid bonding." I kissed the back of her head. "So is intercourse without any form of protection." I rubbed her stomach. "We've done that and far more already..."

"So that's it?" She tittered. "you believe praying about it or making love without contraception is going to sort this?" Temperance simpered. "...quite a higgledy-piggledy plan that..." Her wet hand plucked my fingers from around her. "Just say you no longer wish to reconcile the issue; you needn't be polite about it..." She waved her hands through the stream of water. "The hours we spent by the fire reading all those blooming novels and you remark how you would never do what the so-called Victorian protagonists had done, and that you would actually fight for the woman you love..." She shook her head "...and I believed you and imagined you would be my knight..." Temp rolled her eyes with condescension. "...Alas here we are and you do bugger all!" Her voice rose. "Mister Never Give Up, himself!" She snickered. "Similar to the Victorian protagonists you are not, you are far worse..." Temperance exclaimed. "You roar as a Markham when in fact you whimper like a Linton!"

"What in the world is that supposed to mean?" I threw my hands out in protest.

"Bray Wyatt?!" Her voice rose louder "Heathcliff?!" She clenched her fist. "Indeed, you are just like them as they speak grandly too but do nothing when it actually matters!"

"What's with all the trash talk?"

"It seems to me you have tucked into your swan song..."

"And when did I do that?" I snapped back. "There is no need for insults."

"Well you insult me!" Her back rose and fell with the rapid breaths that passed through her. "Have you provided any alternatives to what I suggest?" She hunched her shoulders, tense as if she were a cat ready to pounce. "No, you babble about fluid bonding, all here-there-and everywhere, whilst you defer in proposing a deuced solution!" Temperance scolded. "Are you gormless?"

"I didn't know you were in the business of harvesting and reaping souls, Temp..."

"How dare you!" She scowled. "Pray you listen! I never asked you to wrestle a lion or face down highwaymen that wish to beat me." She scrubbed another mug with force. "You are willing to do that but you refuse to grant a simple request!" The mug banged against the sink and dropped into the water. "For mercy's sake!" She covered her mouth and waved her finger.

"Have you hurt your finger, my love?" I reached for her hand.

"I am fine..." Temperance shrugged my hand off. "...Right, my dander is up." She about-faced and flicked her hands free of the excess water. "You should go..."

"But why?"

"Because you are acting a proper plonker!" Her voice raised.

The words cut like daggers. I had never seen her so angry before. It was nerve-wrecking; I didn't want the woman I love to have such ire towards me.

"Can we talk about this, please?" My hands shook as they reached toward her.

"No, I told you to leave it!" Temperance rolled her shoulder. "Now, do one!" She pointed toward the door.

"Please, I am sorry, I don't want you to be mad at me." My voice cracked. A million rehearsed scenarios began to materialise in my mind. I had been in situations like this before and they always resulted in heartbreak and anguish. I didn't care if she was mad at me, I just wanted to talk this out somehow.

"Blimey." She pulled a wool coat from one of the silver hooks on the back of the door, nearly ripping it from the screw. "I am at wit's end. I shall take my leave and go have a wander..." Temperance placed each arm in her coat. "Once I return, you best have flocked off."

"Sweetheart..."

"I will not entertain your moaning." She plucked the bow from her hair and tossed it on the floor. Temperance removed the butterfly bobby-pin as well, sobbing as she did so. "You are sending my head west, you." A hair tie exited from her coat pocket and ended up between her lips. "Overegging the bloody pudding." She mumbled.

In record time, she threw all of her hair into a pony tail. "Sort your head out, then dash..." Temperance opened the door and stepped out into the hall, slamming it behind her. The force caused the walls to reverberate. I looked around for a moment thinking of what I should do next but that was easier said than done.

25.

I ripped open the door and followed Temperance out into the frosty night. Her plait bounced with each step she took, her back hunched from beneath her coat. I wasn't dressed appropriately, running out in the snow in a t-shirt and basketball shorts.

"Can you hold on for a minute, please?"

She stopped at the gate and shot me a look of fury. "Lend me your ear, yea? It was berries and cream until you came around and proceeded to muck up my life!"

You could see the pain behind her eyes and it ripped me apart inside. All I wanted to do was wrap my arms around her and take it away from her, even if she pissed me off with her snide remarks.

"I was happy as Larry until that day I saw you sitting on that bench along that stupid canal."

"Were you actually happy, Temperance?"

"It doesn't matter now, does it?" She yelled. "It's all gone pear-shaped regardless, so I would have been better off passing along the High Street instead."

"Why, would you say that?" I placed my hand on her shoulder. "Then I would have never met you."

"What if my mother turned back in Nuneaton?" Her round eyes seemed to bulge.

"And what if I went home the day, I met you?" I reminisced of an afternoon before I met her, when I was mesmerized by a painting of a woman that looked just like Temperance, hung on the wall of

270

a parlour in a Victorian museum in Buxton. "What if I jumped off the aqueduct instead?" I swallowed. "What if I missed you by five minutes sitting on that bench?" It was then that I felt woozy and the crushing sensation in my chest again. "What if I just let you walk by, and never said nothing because I was petrified to do so?" I shrugged my shoulders. "I could be back in my flat, rotting away in my bed."

Temperance's lips shook.

"...perhaps there are parallel worlds where we learn the answers to all of the what-if's, but thankfully those are mere questions in this existence. Did you not say something similar to this on the beach, just yesterday?"

"Whilst it is a riveting investigation of chaos theory, I was ready to plod on through the rest of my miserable existence on my own..." Temperance shrugged my hand off. "This is all your fault!" She pointed at me. "You made this go all to pot!" Her voice accelerated with an angst. "...I reckoned I would have never had a bleeding shag until I were married but then again that would never have happened otherwise?" Her voice continued to rise. "After all, who would be chuffed with a lass that does not age or die? A pile of a rubbish, I am!"

"None of that is true, let's go to Stockport Town Hall and get married..."

"Now, you are being a goose." She growled.

"I'm serious and you don't even give me a chance to get into that..." I opened my hands.

"Well, it appears futile..."

"It's not, Temp..."

"Why are you so dogged?" She countered and crossed her arms again. "Why do you bash on with this pertinacity?"

"I can ask why you are so stubborn and be more open-minded?"

My beloved shot me a dirty look.

"...There need not be any questions about the future, instead we can share the rest of this existence together." I looked deep into her eyes. "Remember, everything we discussed?" I reached for her hand.

She shot me daggers again.

"I want to have that with you..."

Temperance gritted her teeth. "I was in over my head!" She waved her hand. "I had not written a word in three-quarters of a century either but you managed to rouse all of that as well." Her finger pressed against my chest. "Whilst I have divulged every detail about myself to you, you are also the only one to know that I am just a little pebble stuck at the side of the river with nowhere to go." Her hands flew to her side. "Can't you see? Everything that I do means nothing." She let out a heavy breath through her nose. "But, you." Temperance glared at me "...look at me in a way that no lad or geezer ever had previously! You look at me as if I am the greatest thing The Lord ever made."

I reached for her hand again but she swotted it away. "...as if I meant the world to you..."

"But you are the world to me."

"Nevertheless, thanks to you, I have to live in constant worry now. Perhaps that I will lose you or even worse..." She looked away.

"Even worse, what?"

"That despite all of these grand proclamations, you will ultimately betray me and vanquish me into nothingness."

That comment hurt more than all the others combined. Temperance knew she took it too far, her eyes softened as soon as she finished what she said.

"Why on Earth would I ever do anything to hurt you? I would risk my own well-being to make sure nothing ever harmed you."

Her tone became gentle. "Box off my reaction as a mild case of hysteria. That is how the so-called experts would decipher it back in my day." Her eyes intensified again and looked as if lightning bolts were ready to fly from them. "Nonetheless, your time here is limited whilst mine has no end. Henceforth, this little romance between you and I is going to end..." Temperance's hand clasped together. "...somehow, someway."

"Who said it's going to end?"

"Oh, come off it, love. You may very well find a better match for yourself."

"Find someone better when I said I would marry you and lay my life down for you?" I pointed back at the canal.

"No matter how you cut it, I have been bequeathed my mother's powers and that means the only ways you and I could truly be together forever are for you to sell your soul, I pull whatever trick that was done me mum on you against your will, or I decide to render my own fate and top myself with a flask of Holy Water." She simpered. "If none of those are conceivable, maybe our pal upstairs quits us all and perhaps then we can be merry in peace..." Temperance glared. "Would you truly risk everything for me?"

"I already have and I always will. Everything is for you, Temperance."

Every reassurance I offered her was met with a look of doubt. My heart pounded from seeing her in such a passion.

"Tell me, what was your dream before you met me?"

"To meet a woman like you."

"Because of your novels, yea?" Her eyebrows rose. "Maybe you are not in love with me but rather the idea."

"No, Temperance it's you." My tongue swirled under my lips. "Since I was a kid it's true, I wanted to meet a woman just like you. It was my dream in life, it kept me going, and that's why I came here..."

"Utter bollocks." She shook her head. "Albeit, why would you want to be with me anyhow?" She clenched a fist. "I cannot offer you what you really desire." Temperance squeezed her fist tight. "What a cow, I am."

"None of that is true, darling."

"I must congratulate you on busting my velvet. Soon enough you will have a mooch somewhere else when this all goes stale."

"Stale?" I swallowed. "I don't think you realise what seeing your face, hearing your voice, holding your hand, or being in your presence means to me." I opened my hands. "If you don't want to have sex, I don't care. It's not about that, I just want you."

Temperance sniffled. "You've read it previously, all I ever wanted was to have a home with a man I love and daughters to help me to fold linens on a Sunday morning. One little one called Henrietta, ideally." A flicker of light came from near her hand. "However, I cannot have that either, can I?" She let out a brief laugh. "Things will never change. Eventually, I will be alone again and left just as I was when I was a little girl..." Lightning began to flash from her fingers. "...never knowing me pop and being a bastard that is a product of rape with a mum that is gone and never coming back..." Her eyes bulged as she finished her sentence.

"Honey..." I grabbed her wrist.

"Reply at your own peril. I advise you to choose your words carefully as I can electrocute you at any given moment."

"You would actually do that to me?"

She pouted.

"Last time I checked you always used your powers for good. You are the noblest and sweetest women I've ever known, so lay off the thug shit, 'ight?"

"Cheerio, I will not put some high voltage in you." She mocked me. "But you can peel off, you wanker." It was followed up with a two-finger salute.

"Yo, why don't you chill out?"

"Why don't you chill out?" She flicked her pony-tail and did a smug impersonation of me.

"Screw it, if it'll make you feel any better then go ahead." I opened my arms. "Do it!"

"Shall I carry on with running a current through you, then?"

"Yeah, let's go."

"I am not having a knee's up." She laughed with an air of menace. "Don't push me..."

"Do you think I am afraid?" I shrugged my shoulders. "I wanted to off myself on several occasions."

She bit her lip with a palpable umbrage.

"...if shocking me will help you feel better, then go ahead."

"Be careful what you wish for, you may just get it..." Another flash of light sparkled from her hands.

"Like you?" I smiled at her. "You can beat me to a bloody pulp and I'd never a lay finger on you, ever..." I stressed the word. "...but I ain't intimidated..."

"Fair play to your resolve." Her nod of approval was met with smug intonation. "It's not like you can offer much opposition."

"Well I am a tough out." I took a stab at an untimely joke but she didn't laugh in response. "I must warn you though, electrocuting me would mess things up royally. I suggest you consider an alternative."

She reached for the brass handle of the gate. "And I suggest that you learn when it is time to relent." Temperance swung the gate open. "I've swotted up."

Once again, I watched for a moment to collect myself. Temperance walked down toward the cobblestone path. Her hips swayed from side-to-side, frustration steered each step she took. I stepped out and followed her until she got close to where the canal widened ahead of the walk.

The trees were covered in snow on both sides. There was no sound just the sight of the orange glow of the gas lamps glimmering against the darkness of the canal. She kept walking and I ran to catch up. I didn't care that I was nearly an ice cube at this point; I had no regard for the possibility of slipping and falling into the canal either. "Temperance, I love you!"

She flinched, as if she had been pierced by an arrow. Temperance stood shivering; in a matter of moments she held her head in her hands. I walked over to her and placed one hand around her back, her sniffling and sobs became more obvious as I approached.

A palm struck my face. "Why must you say that?" Another hand flew it at me but I caught the next attempt.

I yanked her towards me and wrapped my arms around her. She wept and gripped me tight. Her sobs grew louder and more violent as she clutched my shoulders. I rubbed her hair and back. She rested her head against my chest, curling up in the comfort it seemed to provide her. Her hands clasped my collar.

"I am sorry." Her words were muffled between her sobs. "That was wrong and uncalled for. You should leave me for it."

"I forgive you." I brushed the snowflakes off of her. "I am sorry for upsetting you."

"You have nothing to apologise for."

"You should not have run after me." Temperance sniffled. "You can catch a lurgy in this cold dressed as you are."

"It's worth it."

"Don't be wonky. I am not worth it at all." Her thumbs pressed against my cheeks and wiped some water than ran from under my eyes.

"You are worth all the trouble in the world, my love." My teeth started to chatter.

"Oh, dear." Temperance unbuttoned her coat and wrapped her coat around my back and tightly embraced me. Her body against mine felt like embracing a hot mug of tea. I extended my arms around hers, it suddenly felt like spring day. Temperance pulled her head back to look at me. A brief smile escaped her until her eyes watered up again. "I am sorry; I cannot do this any longer." She backed away. "It's for the best." Temperance turned her back toward me and traversed the snow-covered slate path toward the front door of her residence. All the windows of the adjoining houses were all illuminated, all those who dwelled in them cosy and warm inside.

Temperance grasped the brass doorknob from the outside and turned back to face me. "Do not call, do not send any overtures via text message, do not pen me any poems, just forget about me..." Tears poured from her eyes. "...please."

"I can't do that." I stepped forward with urgency toward her with a hope I could dry and catch those tears, but once again I was met with a hand.

A lump formed in my throat. My eyes sagged, water filled them, my lips begun to shake. I don't really care with any of you twenty-first century tough guys think either about it, you aren't strong unless you can show your weakness. It's called being real and for what it's worth, this woman could level me anytime she chose. There is no shame in admitting it either, because what is life without love? It isn't about you after all.

"Do not make this any more difficult for me." Her finger pointed toward the end of the lane where it converged on Stockport Road. The hissing of passing car through the slush rippled down the lane. "Do not be obstinate, do not be melodramatic." She pointed toward Stockport Road again. "Just do as I told you."

"And then what?" I threw my hands out in protest. "You wander down to the pub in a month's time and some lowlife moves in on you when you are vulnerable..." I orated and shook my hand once again. "And just like that." I snapped my finger. "You are gone." I leaned forward. "Is that how you are going to play it?"

Temperance glared at me, but said nothing.

"Lose you to some apple jack drunk fake who has no appreciation for anything?"

She kept her glare upon me until she calmly broke her silence. "Do you presume that I would dispose of you so carelessly?"

"What do you call what you are doing right now?" I turned my back for a moment and collected my thoughts as I listened to the water trickle through the locks." ...Just know..." I turned back around "...that I will relinquish you to no one..." I pointed at her.

"I defy you to remove your finger from my face..." She spoke coldly. "You read in my diaries what I did to a foolish bloke who dared do such a thing previously..." Her demeanour shifted to aggressive and menacing. "...Do not point at me..." Temperance yelled. "Do I make myself clear?"

"Don't threaten me." I dropped my finger out of respect.

"If you take offence and wish to test your luck." She smiled back at me "...Have a go..." She snickered.

"You've already won..." She looked on confused for the first time, unsure of where I was going with this rant. "...you torment me on a daily basis and I will never put up any opposition..." I started tapping my finger against my skull. "...this is the monster that I fear..." I laughed as I tapped my head harder. "...I have no choice but to fight it every day..." my nostrils flared. "And at times, it's made me feel as if I hated myself..." I chuckled and threw my hands out. "...But you..." I paused; my arms were longing to reach out to her, my lips aching to smother her sour and pouting face with a kiss. "...I love!" I emphasised the word hoping it would get through to her. She remained stoic, reserved, and resolute. "And my love for you as Charlotte Bronte once put it is, a tyrant-passion!"

She rolled her eyes in response, seemingly humoured whilst pooh-poohing it at the same time.

"You confounding woman!" I raised my voice. "Are you still looking to be troublesome, even now?"

"You best knock it on the head..." She screamed back at me. "...as I don't care to entertain any of your previously exhibited bellicose rhetoric..." Temperance spat at me. "...I will relinquish you to no one..." She mocked. "The gall of you to presuppose that you possess any form of dominion over me..."

"This coming from the same woman who acts so imperious..."

"Imperious?" She crossed her arms "...perhaps appropriate as I will have the last word here, thank you..." Temperance's tone became all the more snobbish. "You can go now..."

"Well I guess you are your mother's daughter, then..."

"And what is that supposed to mean?" She snickered.

"You give up on those that love you when it matters most." I looked away in shame at the untimely remark; when I looked back at Temperance her eyes and hair turned a luminescent white.

"Temp, I am sorry..." I took a step toward her. "I shouldn't have said that."

"Be gone." She screamed; lightning formed around her finger tips. "Leave at once, stroppy boy!"

I looked around at the windows, concerned that a nosey neighbour may peer through the windows at our argument and see Temperance's powers now on display. She however did not seem to care at this point as her fury was fixed on me.

"Very well, suit yourself." A current of light crashed from her finger and blackened the snow a few feet beside me. The crash created an explosive sound as if fireworks were set off. It was then that the curtains started to draw to from a few windows along the row of terraced houses. I had to get out of there before anyone grew suspicious of her. If anyone asked, I'd play it off as thunder snow.

I took a step back with Temperance's coat still in my arm. Her eyes dimmed down. "Never come back." She sobbed and kicked snow. Tears trickled from my eyes as I opened the gate and took one more look at her. Temperance never looked more beautiful and I never felt more hopeless. She plucked open the door and slammed it behind her. I walked down to the end of the road, lost and not knowing where to go. Everything from the day that I met her came rushing back to the surface. I hadn't felt pain since I had met her, but now it's familiar face smiled back at me.

The first thought to entire my mind was to jump off the aqueduct. I walked around Marple for an hour and I found myself back on the same snowy lane outside her home. The iron front gate banging against the lock from an occasional gust of wind. There, I collapsed on the pavement in a surge of tears. Once the worst of it had passed, I covertly stepped into the front garden and looked up at the window of her flat. There were no lights on, but a window had been cracked open. It was now Temperance who was crying, I heard her from standing out there in the cold. My heart broke at the sound of it; I couldn't leave her. So, I slept in the car parked outside, I didn't manage to get much rest that night.

26.

I awoke to the sound of snow blowing off of the tree into the canal. I rubbed my eyes and stepped out of the car. The sun had not risen yet as it was the fleeting moments before dawn. My eyes glanced up at Temperance's window, my breath tracing through the frosty air with every scattered thought gusting through my mind. I stared out to the snow-covered hills in the distance and found myself lost again not knowing what to do. Falling asleep though briefly, gave me a moment of respite from the anguish that was burning in my heart. On some days, only death seemed to offer liberation and refuge from the prison of my mind. Steadfast, I always prayed for moments of joy, faith, Kingdom come, and hopes fulfilled.

All Temperance had was her secrets and temporal moments always fleeting whilst she steadily remained. Her prison had walls that even a woman as mighty as she could not scale, fly over, or bowl through. Nevertheless, wherever she be, I wanted to be there beside her.

I stretched out some soreness and started the car. The windscreen wipers tossed off the snow accumulated on the glass and I went out for a drive. The first thing that crossed my mind was the manuscript I was working on which was about how and when I met Temperance. It was saved as a file on my laptop which was still in her house, but I also had written pages which I was planning to have bound for her. I yearned to hold the very pages that chronicled our love, as if I were holding Temperance once again.

When I arrived back at the flat in Audenshaw, I couldn't be there for more than five minutes as it was silent, bereft of the laughter that filled it whenever Temperance stayed over in the past. All those nights, I fell asleep with her in my arms as she sang to me. I never took it for granted.

We had talked about living together and I was days away from giving my notice to give up the flat. Now, it was just like that Autumn day when I first met her. I fled to the canal to escape the woe and anxiety; that led to me to Temperance. Like before, I was overcome by despair and once again without her.

I got back in the car and drove back to Marple, I had to be close to her. What if she should ring me, text me, or magically appear should she have a change of heart? I parked the car back in front of Temperance's house, the blue door looking back at me the only impediment between her and I.

I wondered what she was doing inside. Watching her perform even the simplest things such as cutting bread was a spectacle in itself. Part of me had hoped she heard or saw the car park and that it would coax her outside. The image of her face would drown me in ecstasy. Patiently, I waited for a good ten minutes until nothing came of it.

Dawn had finally arrived and I was back in the ASDA; purchasing a pack of smokes and some Budweiser. About an hour later, I found myself sitting on a bench by the River Goyt, not too far from the Roman Lakes. In my travels, I passed by the ruins of the mill where Temperance had worked long ago. The mill was nothing more than a collection of stones beset in the Earth. But Temperance still stands.

I imagined her on a hot summer day making her way up the ruined steps, lost, confused, and hopeless; desperate to find a way out as if she were about to burn to the ground like the mill eventually did. Then I was haunted by another notion: what if Temperance was now just another picture of a woman from long ago, faded into history, and never coming back? The idea brought tears to my eyes.

I reached into my pocket and removed my phone, glancing at the screen with a hope she would have sent me a message or attempted to call. Instead, I had received a text from Pete timestamped minutes before which said: *"My nan was right about your missus?!"*

Alarm filled me. I put down the bottle of beer and unlocked the phone, I pressed the green button hard to initiate the call. The speaker rang twice before Pete's voice usurped the ringing sound.

"You alright?"

"I've had better days." I bit my lip. "What's the deal with the text message?"

"Temperance isn't twenty-eight, is she?"

My heart raced as I was in between a rock and a hard place. I didn't like to lie but I had to protect her, even now.

"This is not the right time for this. I just got into a bad fight with her and she's gone."

"I am sorry to hear that mate but if it is true, her secret will get out regardless."

"And if anyone wants to mess around with her, they are going to be dealing with me personally." My fist balled up. "Regardless..." My nostrils flared. "...now I need people to back up off her, do you understand me?"

"So, you know about it?"

"I know that she has been through a lot in her life and that no one needs to bring any more misery into it with such absurd accusations. And if you or anyone else tried to do anything that would harm her, I will mop the floor with every last one of you!" I shouted and caught my breath. "I don't care who it is or what it has to come to, everything is on the table..." I held for a brief pause of silence. "...and I am cool with that." I spoke calmly. "Now, leave her alone!" I slid the phone screen down to the red icon, ending the call.

"Clown..." I placed a cigarette between my lips, lit it, and gripped a sweaty bottle of Budweiser and twisted it open. The puffs and sips, a medicine to soothe the absence of Temperance but insufficient as a suitable alternative. I sat upon the bench, back in my comfort zone, drinking, smoking, and listening to my music as I watched the river bubble and flow onward. This is what I was used to doing: sitting there, brooding, and numbing my mind with the substances I listed. I listened to Bryan Adam's *"Have You Ever Loved a Woman?"* and then a bit of Chopin, followed by *Sun King* by The Beatles, Oasis, and finally Joplin; all haunting in their own way given their relevance to my muse. At least, then whilst listening I was in a temporary stupor. Nonetheless, at some point, I'd have to feel alone, gloomy, like I didn't exist, and that I was on a one-way journey through melancholia until I eventually perished. But in that moment, I didn't have to; I could numb it. I didn't half to deal with what just happened with Temperance, I could simply drink.

My eyes streamed up to the large stone rail viaduct that towered over the river and then to the small hut that used to be a tea room in the Victorian times behind me. Smoke filled my throat and expelled into the air. In that moment I was released from my sorrow, distracted by the sounds, smells, sights, and sensations. I looked toward the banks of the river and saw three mallards nibbling on pellets of bird feed. A man stood by the river with his arm around a woman's waist, her long blonde hair cupped in the hood of her red cotton coat.

I plucked the headphones from around my ears and watched as two little girls scurried back to the man, who carefully placed more bird feed into each of their small porcelain hands. The man rubbed the woman's back as they watched the girls skip toward the banks, both warning the children to be careful as their blonde hair tossed behind them when they skipped toward the ducks. Both girls pirouetted as they threw the bird feed into the River Goyt and ran back to their father, their eyes sparkling with energy and love as they threw their arms around his waist. The man reached down and kissed both on the domes of their head, swimming his arms around their little bodies wrapped in purple and pink winter coats. The sight flooded my eyes with tears.

I sniffled and blew my nose, a burst of warmth rushed from my nostrils. I put the headphones back onto my head, hoping to find refuge. I stared back into the river as *She's A Star* by James surrounded me. Immediately, my beloved's face filled my thoughts as soon as the chorus rang the first time but the lyrics in succession seemed to twist the knife. My lips quivered as tears started to stream down onto the dusty ground below me, my cries now audible as I paused the music and collapsed my head into my hands. The misery overwhelmed me, my heart had set Miss Lee as its North Star, not a shooting star that I only cast a wish upon.

I was torn between ending it now in the river or marching back to her house and proposing to her; I couldn't give up; I couldn't leave her. I believed that marrying her would still resolve the issue that wedged between us, I had faith in the miracles that come from above and the miracles that love which comes to us from above can cultivate. My cries intensified as I wept her name: Temperance.

"Hello, friend."

I looked up and sniffled. A man stood to my right, near to the open portion of the bench. His plump lips formed a warm smile that radiated through his snow-white beard. It contrasted with the dark colour of his bucket hat and winter coat. His trainers were a pristine ivory shade without any blemishes, his khaki trousers were without a crease. In one hand, he held an aquamarine travel mug with the message "God Loves You" inscribed in white script.

"Why the tears, son?" He sat on the bench.

I feigned a smile and sat up. "I was moved by the sight over there."

The man's blue eyes locked in on the family by the banks of the river. "A father playing with his daughters?" He smiled at me.

I nodded.

"Do you have a daughter?"

"No..." I sniffled. "I have always wanted one though." I threw another smoke in my mouth. "So has Temperance..." I reached into my pocket for a lighter.

"Temperance." He took a sip from his mug. "...beautiful name, one you seldom hear in this day and age."

"And where is your better half?"

"How do you know she isn't my sister?" My cigarette pressed to the flame until it started to smoke.

"I have known brothers to dote on their sisters, but I can't imagine that being the reason for a man sitting alone in a park, having a beer before breakfast."

I looked over at him and took a puff. "Touché..."

"Your voice softened when you said her name." He smiled. "Only a man in love does that."

"Yeah well, I don't think she wants anything to do with me anymore."

"And why is that?"

"We had an argument." I spat and took another puff of my cigarette. "...she revealed some things which I am not at liberty to discuss..."

The man raised his hands in acknowledgement.

"...but with respect to these revelations, she feels that we cannot overcome them, and that I won't do what is required to do so..."

"Well, would you do what you needed to do?"

"It's complicated."

"Have you tried to talk to her?" He took another sip from his mug.

"Yeah and that went south quick." I took another drag of my cigarette.

"Don't give up." His hands pressed to my wrist, it felt soft, warm, and tender in its touch.

He looked into my eyes. "...I know what you are willing to do for her." He sat back. "Don't let her go..."

I smiled and took another puff before letting out another huge of cloud of smoke from my mouth. "I didn't plan on it."

"Good." He nodded. "What they don't tell you on those new-fangled dating apps is that it's the beauty of going through it together so all those ordinary, routine, everyday moments are so special..."

I reached into my pocket searching for my phone. Instead, my fingers gripped a chain and I removed a set of keys from the pocket; they were the keys to Temperance's house! I must have placed them in there when we argued and then forgotten all about them in the chaos.

"What do you have there?"

"The keys to her house."

He chuckled.

"I have her coat in my car too, she forgot it in the midst of it all the arguing."

The man sat up and patted my thigh. "Women are very intelligent creatures, if she wanted you to be gone, she wouldn't have left those with you." He rolled his eyes. "Now put down the booze, forget the cigarettes, go back there, and talk to her."

"I told her I would marry her and I would die for her, and still she told me to get lost..."

"Then try again. If you are willing to die for her, why not take another shot at working it out?" He took another sip from his mug. "That seems far easier." He chuckled. "Besides, you don't strike me as a guy that ever quits."

I stood up and took another puff of my cigarette.

"Do something different..." He extended his hand outward. "...write down your thoughts and give them to her..."

"The novel..." A smile unfurled across my face. "I was going to surprise her with it..." I put the cigarette out against my shoe.

"I knew you would figure it out." He stood up. "Just have faith."

He smiled at me. "It will all be okay, son..." He pressed his hand on my shoulder once more. "...anyways, I best get off, I have to finish making my rounds."

"Thank you for being a friend to me, today."

"Don't thank me, son." He twisted his mug to where the *God Loves You* inscription faced toward me. "I am happy to be here for you..."

"I am sorry; I didn't get your name." I extended my hand toward him. "I'm..."

"I feel like you and I know each other well.'" He smiled back at me and shook my hand. "It's not too late you know..." He paused for a moment. "...for you or her..."

I squinted at him.

"Thinking about what I am saying to you..." He patted my hands and released me. "...should you need me; you know where to come."

He sat up, readying to go.

"May The Great Lord bless you, sir."

He remained on the bench and smiled. "May He bless you as well."

"Can I ask you something?"

"Of course, you can." He grappled with his hat.

"If someone loves The Lord but sells their soul to save someone they love or to be with someone they love because they want to be there for that person, does that make them bad?" My fingers ran against my forehead. "What if a mother did such a thing to save her sick child?"

"Well, at least she wasn't looking to give away her soul to drive one of those Lamborghini Diablos." He laughed. "She loves her child and love will motivate people to do all sorts of things..."

"I love Temperance and I would do anything for her." I looked him in the eye. "But I told her that I believe The Lord could resolve this issue I mentioned to you, and I have faith that He would."

"With Him all things are possible, so whatever it you are both facing, He will be there for you."

"I tried telling her that, but she is just lost..." I got up and walked over to the river, my back to the bench.

"She believes that The Lord has condemned her ... I don't believe that."

"She is precious to you and loved greatly. She is a ball of lightning but Tempie has a wonderful heart..."

Tempie; No one has called her that since she was a little girl.

"Hey, how did you know?" I turned around to look at him. He was gone. I looked back at the river and a smile widened across my face.

27.

For the first time, I felt a spark of hope since Temperance and I fell out. I just needed to convince her that everything was going to be alright. I had to show her the manuscript, so she could see with her own eyes that my love was unyielding. I swung open the gate, it whined as I closed it behind me. I looked up to the window, all of the windows were cloaked in curtains. This time, Temperance was not looking down at me from the bedroom to greet me. It was, as if, she had withdrawn completely into the shadows.

I placed the key into the hole but it wouldn't turn the handle. I stepped back and glanced at the blue door with a peculiar stare and tried again. Once again, the handle wouldn't budge. She must have put her key in the lock from inside. However, I would not be deterred. My fingers gripped the icy door knocker and I tapped twice.

My heart skipped a beat hearing my beloved's voice echo through the door as she hummed and sung words that I could not make out.

"Honey bee!" Cold smoke escaped from my mouth as I yelled. "please let me in..." I pleaded as I banged on the door. I waited for a couple of minutes but there was no sign of her. I knocked on again and still no response. *Mozart's Piano Concerto #20 2nd Movement* started to play from inside the house, the ghostly piano notes wafted from her house into the frosty Marple air.

Tears filled my eyes as my heart crashed against my chest. I walked across the lane to one of the locks, desperate to catch my accelerating breaths. I sat down and took out my phone and sent a text message to her, that way I could guarantee she knew that I had come back. *Honey, I am outside yours, I will wait however long I must, but I must show you something. Please give me that chance, I beg you. I love you more than life itself.*

I sent the message and placed another cigarette into my mouth, reclining against the cold metal piling. I closed my eyes, breathing in the smoke to gain a moment of relief, and immerse myself in the music.

I was transported to the beach in Blackpool, standing under the shadow of the Tower. Perhaps, I had gone back in time and was there with Temperance in the 1800's, walking with our arms locked on the beach as the music played in the background; a warm and sunny day with a faint breeze. Oh, how I could be there with her forever! My eyes opened when I heard the song *Only Time* by Enya playing. *And who can say why your heart cries,* I turned back to stare at the blue door, hoping that she would just come outside so I can see her. *When your love lies.* As the music played, my eyes filled with tears as I glanced around the quiet lane longing for a glimpse of her. *Only time.* I looked up to the window of her house and didn't see Temperance looking back at me; my heart felt ready to disintegrate into a million pieces. When I heard her voice harmonising with the melodies that played, the majesty of it filled me with awe as if I were ascending to Heaven and she were singing amongst the angels. Chills shot down my spine and hearing her, brought the glimmer of her smile cascading through the trees; down the line; and searing through the trickles of water flowing through the locks. Desperation filled me, I had to touch her! I had to feel her. I just wanted to hold her again and never let her go. A sudden eruption of anguish filled my throat with an acetic taste; it became unbearable. My eyes turned to a beer bottle lying against the kerb, I squeezed it and smashed it, a thousand pieces of glass flying in a multitude of directions, as the tears started to pour from me.

Profanities and vulgarities roared as I hurled my fist into the grass over and over again, sending mud and wet strands of grass airborne as I threw blow after blow. I reached down to take hold of a broken brick; the next projectile primed for launch in my tantrum. When I looked up, I saw a sight that disarmed me in an instant: Temperance.

She was clad in all black bombazine, her piercing blue eyes watching my every move behind a black lace veil. Her expression was an eerie one to take in, her lips were shut and firm, her eyes flaring with an inner vexation that was bubbling to the surface. I on the contrary, was overjoyed to see her.

"So, this is the lad I that I fell in love with?" Temperance's held one gloved hand in another, standing at attention with a demure posture. I quickly threw the brick to the side; it clunked against the grass beside me. "...Mister Markham, pardon me, Mister Huntingdon. It's lovely to see you, so kind of you to join us..." Her crass tone delivered her sarcastic reference to *The Tenant of Wildfell Hall*. It was meant to be an insult but I didn't let it get the best of me.

"It's nice to see you too, Helen..." I attempted match her wit; she glowered at me in response until she broke the silence.

"Have I not done enough to drive you away?"

"You could never do that." I shook my head, my response serious in contrast to the previous banter.

"You're pathetic." Temperance simpered.

"Whatever..." I was stern in my response. "Just hear me out, please..."

She walked across the street. "I knew you would be back." Her velvet glove took hold of my hand. "It's who you are..." she raised it to look at the blood that seeped from my knuckles. "We best clean this."

"I am not like you..." I smirked. "...making dramatic video game sound effects every time I get poked by something..." My fingers swam into my pocket to pluck out my packet of cigarettes. "Obviously I will protect you with my life, but for argument sake you'd make a great fighting game character..." I laughed as I put the cigarette into my mouth. "I mean you are super strong, really athletic, control lightning, and wear lilac-coloured tights."

Temperance stared a hole in me. "And yet if I was wearing them in this very moment, you would be gagging for it."

"I absolutely would be." I smiled and winked. "...your butt looks amazing in them, you hot tamale."

I was hoping she would have laughed from my childish antics but instead Temperance remained unamused.

"I see the perversion hasn't desisted." She plucked the cigarette from my lips. "You shouldn't be having these..." The tobacco paper crushed in her glove. "I shall not permit it."

"Thanks Mom."

She grilled me. "Clearly, you have been drinking, as well..."

"Since daybreak actually."

"So, we are off on a benjo, now, are we?" She snickered. "Is this what you wanted to show me?" She shook her head with contempt. "I must commend you on this riveting exhibition you are putting on." Her voice filled with a condescending timbre. "Coming to my gate with your swizzles and smokes..." Her voice rose as she continued to yell. "...whilst wearing that absurd coat and that dire winter hat that you could live in!"

I had no idea what was wrong with I was wearing; it was literally just a standard black puffy hooded winter coat and a matching thermal hat. If anything, she normally liked that look and how this was pertinent to the situation, I could not figure out. However, anything was possible now as the woman was clearly in a heated passion.

Temperance took a step toward me and her tone quickly shifted back to sardonic and smug. "How I pine and yearn to respond to your sweet musings with evermore alacrity!" She about faced and paced back toward the gate. "Waste my time, you shall not!"

"Temp, that's not what I came here for." I extended my hand to wrap around her belly but she pushed it away.

"You could have fooled me." She stomped through the snow.

"Why are you dressed in mourning clothes?"

"Before I bore witness to whatever this is..." Temperance waved her hands up and down. "...I was off to Church."

"For who's funeral?"

Her eyes watered up, the sight of it prompted mine to follow. My imagination filled me with some gut-wrenching ideas. "Were you going to go and attempt to vanquish yourself with Holy Water?"

Temperance shed a tear and pressed two fingers to her forehead. Instinctively, I wanted to grab her and comfort her. When I reached for her, she took a step back. "Or do you already have it?"

"That is none of your concern at this point." Her words muffled by a snivel as she removed her hat.

"With respect to what you are trying to achieve, that wouldn't have resolved anything."

My response invoked an ire from her, her eyes bulged with fury. "Look who's talking!" She smacked me with her hat. "Bloody hypocrite!" Temperance shouted. "You should follow your own advice and dare not amble near any aqueducts, should you?" Temperance tried to whack me again but I covered up.

"I don't believe that you are 152, because you act like a five-year-old!" I yelled back at her.

"Says the lad who spat out his dummy, just moments ago." Temperance clenched her fists, pink shimmers of electricity formed around the knuckles. "...Come here for Round Two, have you? I warn you not to peg away any longer!" She pointed toward Stockport Road. "...Go home!"

"I am home!" The words flew from my chest. "I am with you."

The electricity which had started to turn purple and become more radiant had vanished in a flash.

"Why has it come to this? We've always been kind and caring towards each other..."

She huffed and puffed but would not respond. However, she appeared remorseful and ashamed, as if the anger had settled for a moment and she reflected on how things have gone.

"Why are we fighting in the first place?"

Temperance placed her finger under her chin. "We'll let's see... As I recall, you pinched my memoirs and read them without my permission. From there, you essentially told me that you don't wish to reconcile the very problem that is coming between us."

"You were asking me to sell my soul and for what it's worth given how you hard you pushed it, what if you were manipulating me?

"Manipulate you, how so?"

"You go from wearing that sexy Incredible Temperance costume and being all sweet and loving to flipping out when you didn't get what you wanted. Could it not appear to be a classic case of manipulation?"

Temperance's eyes seemed to zero in on me, as if her irises were dilating at what I said; she was aghast as if a grand accusation was leveraged against her and she was eager to defend herself.

"I wear my costume because it's snug; I also wear it because you fancy it." She stressed the latter. "I remind you that for anyone else that sees me in it, it usually means I have come there to thwart them..." She let out a deep breath. "I confess that I do love the attention because it's a welcomed change to feel genuinely wanted..."

Guilt washed over me; what she said revealed more than anything she ever wore.

"...believe me when I tell you, if you were in the fire brigade, I'd want to see you wearing attire of that trade, as much as you wish to see me in mine."

"I would do that for you..."

"Thus, my motivation precisely..." She curtsied slightly. "...I would wear it every day, if it would make you happy..."

"Would you really?" My mind diverted for a moment to a pleasant image but my heart was overcome by her wanting to please me. It spoke further into the true nature of the woman that captured my heart; a thoughtful and gentle soul.

"Yes!" She replied strongly and brought my attention back to her. "...I'd do anything for you."

These statements were sincere, as she said them calmly. Nevertheless, they made my heart want to burst. "...and as to my affection towards you, it is entirely sincere and as a result, my love for you puts me in a rather precarious predicament." Her voice started to raise and accelerate. "...That is why when you offer some absurd pseudoscientific alternative, it puts me in a passion!"

"Clearly, as you threatened to electrocute me with a lightning bolt."

"Only after you made a snide remark about my mother preceded by you pointing your finger at me and said you would relinquish me to no one, as if I were some object you were attempting to subjugate."

"I am sorry, I lost my temper, but for the record I was never trying to control you..." I swiped my nose. "...I just don't ever want to lose you to anyone or anything..."

"Then why won't you do what I suggest?" She crossed her arms.

"Because I have a better plan, if I am honest."

She chuckled. "Since you are an expert on my supernaturalism, you who possess over 120 years of experience on the matter..." Her tone lowered and slowed, it was up and down like she was. "...please do not persist in antagonising me, do you think I didn't observe you sleeping in the parked car outside last night like some wayward stalker?"

"I heard you crying and I didn't want to leave you. I couldn't bear the sound of you in such agony..."

Her eyes softened and then watered. Mine soon followed.

"...I'd freeze if I had to but even if I was in a cramped in the car, I wanted to be there in case you needed me..." I sniffled. "Even if you broke my heart, I still love you and would drop everything to be there for you..."

We looked at each other, as if it were a stalemate in a chess match one pre-empting the other to make the next move. However, this wasn't a competition. I wanted reconciliation; I was on her side and wanted her to be by mine.

" I don't want to fight; I just want to talk this out; please..."

She shed another tear and placed her hand between two fingers. "Will you come inside, please?" Temperance raised her hand and looked at my bleeding knuckles. "...To be fair, your hand needs cleaning..." She took my hand and led me to the gate.

"I was praying you would say that." I followed until I remembered the manuscript; I stopped for a moment and released her hand. "I've brought you something, it's in the car..."

Temperance looked at me over her shoulder. "Go get it, then..." A smile broke from her face briefly; its brevity was enough to inject me with new hope.

28.

When we stepped into the house, I was met by a dark, shadowy, and musty catacombs that was atypical to the bright and lively environs which characterised Temperance's house.

"I best fetch some hydrogen peroxide and cotton from the medicine cabinet." Temperance picked up her music box and wound it up as she walked toward the bathroom. I glanced around the sitting room and my eyes were immediately transfixed to an item that caught my attention: a vial of Holy Water.

I listened for her boots which thundered above me and made my way toward the vial which sat on the mantle. I heard her at the top of the steps and before I could grab the vial, I retreated to the couch. She descended the steps rapidly and I hastily made my way to curtains to fling them open. A moment later, she stormed in from the bathroom with a vial of hydrogen peroxide and cotton swabs, placing them on the table beside her.

"What are you doing?"

"Letting the light in."

A white column of sunlight cascaded into the sitting room.

"Give me your hand." She summoned in a serious tone and I obliged. Her attention focused on pressing a warm rag wet with hydrogen peroxide against my knuckles. "We best stop the bleeding and prevent infection..."

"The Holy Water wouldn't have worked you know..."

"And punching the ground doesn't resolve what angers you." Temperance glanced up at me and swept my knuckles with a cotton swab. "Yet here we are."

"Holy Water doesn't work on angels..."

She dropped the swab and gaped at me. "You dare say that even now?" Her hands clutched mine.

"...I do..." I rubbed her finger and she pulled away. When she removed her hands and the cuts on my knuckles were completely healed.

"Why didn't you do that to begin with?" My jaw dropped at the sight of the feat. Her cheeks went flushed.

"I wanted to stroke your hands without causing a stir..." She shrugged her shoulders. "...sue me." Her fingers swept her nose. "If you'll pardon me, I must empty my stomach again." She dabbed another tear and about-faced, her shoulders trembling as she took two steps.

Once again in roundabout fashion Temperance was diverting so she could regain her composure; the woman was obsessed with presenting this outward appearance of strength and resolve, but she needed to know, she didn't have to do that with me; I love everything about her and it was safe to be vulnerable with me.

I ran forward and intercepted her, embracing her tight in my arms. I closed my eyes and clutched her hair as I pressed the corner of my lip against her temple. I cherished holding her again.

"I owe you an apology for having a fit." Her eyes meandered out the window toward the canal. "I was a proper brat."

"It's all good." I kissed her forehead. "I said some things in the heat of the moment which I shouldn't have and I am sorry for that."

"I cherish your forbearance and discretion." She released me and walked forward toward the couch. "Nevertheless, I do not deserve you."

"Temperance, you are far greater than I could ever be..." I spoke to her tenderly. "Talk to me, tell me what is truly on your mind." She about-faced and headed for the couch again; Temperance pushed her bustle down and sat on the corner of the cushion, I joined her.

"I awoke one morning with these powers and I matured well ahead of schedule." A tear fell from her to the carpet. "...I don't know how or why..." Her eyes shot back at me. "I can only derive a notion that whatever ties Mother had with that villain also had an effect on me." She removed her gloves and placed them on the table. "The nurses in Warwickshire reported I was dead but they went to their graves knowing that wasn't true." Temperance looked out the window. "You will recall from a diary that an account was established by Ernest for a clandestine child born in a workhouse..." I squinted at Temperance and rubbed my lip, reflecting back to the first time I read of it. "That was me". She swallowed. "The solicitors struggled to identify me and when they had done, Mother had fled and I was already in the orphanage." Temperance sniffled. "I inherited a large fortune and ran away from there as fast as I could...."

"And yet you helped so many people..."

"All women go mad of the want of something to do..." A smile broke from her lips. "Florence Nightingale said that; and since I have been gifted these abilities, I felt it was incumbent of me to use them to make the world a better place. I never had anyone to share my money with anyhow, so I put it in a savings account, left it to collect interest, and focused on honing my talents to benefit others..."

"Thus, proving that you are the extraordinary woman I know you are and why I don't think you will ever turn into black ash..."

Temperance smiled for a brief moment and looked out the window. "Nevertheless, I am all fur coat and no knickers." She shut her eyes. "No one can know the truth about me and that is why I never truly committed to anything or formed any long-lasting relationships." She glanced out the window again. "You are not the only one that could never fathom the idea of someone loving them."

"I am sorry, if I ever made you feel like I was going to leave you." I took her hand. "...you will never be alone again...."

She pulled away and looked up at me with intent. "Perhaps, we can be friends and have a clean breast..."

"Friends?" I opened my hands. "That is a demotion."

"Evidently, you object."

"I can't just be your friend, Temp." I looked out the window. "I am in love with you, I cannot be without you..." I sighed. "I'd never know happiness again..."

"I love you, K- ".

It was rare for Temperance to call me by my name; it was common for her to use a pet name or some term of endearment. Hearing my name on her lips meant that was she serious.

"...but with all the factors given due consideration, you are better off."

"Better off? That's like saying Thanksgiving was made by the Reptilians..."

"Reptilians?" She broke a smile for a brief moment "...you are the all or nothing sort..."

"That's right" I let out a deep breath. "I am a winner; I am going to win."

"What?" She squinted at me with confusion.

"...I have faith The Lord can make a way and I pray here and now that He does..."

Dust particles danced in the sunbeam between her and I.

"...When I was at The Roman Lakes today, it's like I was talking to Him. This dude showed up out of the blue, he had all the answers and seemed to know so much about you, and he reassured me..." I paused and looked up at her "...us...that we're loved and all we have to do is pray about it..." A tear trickled down her cheek into my finger which reached to catch it. "...and to go through with the plan..."

"Would you care to explain this plan?"

"I would but if I went into detail, it can ruin something that is meant to be very special..." My reply was skittish. "I am asking you to trust me..."

An awkward silence filled the room.

"...can we go for a ride? It won't take long to do it..."

"I need some time to think about all of this..." Temperance swiped another tear from her eye. "...and mull everything over..."

"But literally it will take ten minutes..."

"I need time..." She shook her head.

"How long?" My heart started to race.

"I cannot say...." Her attention fixed to me when my breaths became more audible.

"Please..." I fell to her feet and took her hand "...I beg you..." Tears started to flood my sight. "...I am sorry; just please don't do this to me ..."

I felt her hand stroke the back of my head. "...Loss is a constant with me..."

"But it doesn't have to be like that for either of us..." I started to weep; my head soon rested against her skirt. "...I've heard this all before, please, I don't want to live this nightmare again..."

"What distresses you so much that you feel the need to beg?" Her hands slid down to catch my cheeks and pull my face up. In that moment, I flashed back to Mesnes Park in Wigan, standing in front of the pavilion on a warm spring day and watching families have picnics in the lovely weather whilst I was lost, trying to convince myself to not end my life. More of the memory continued to flashback, the deeper this went. I had completely blocked it out with Rachel but it seemed to re-surface more and more, the disagreement with Temperance continued. I have always been terrified of happy endings because I didn't think they were real, after all, it's always been abuse and being left with a shattered heart. I was scared that this would happen with Temperance, the one who I love most of all.

Her empathy was resonant in her eyes, as she looked like a mother comforting her child. "I would never abandon you; I promise..." She pressed her hands to my cheeks. "...an Englishwoman's word is her bond..."

When our eyes locked, I felt trust. Even if my world was crumbling beneath me, a part of me wanted to try to believe that she was different and that this was different. I sniffled and nodded; I looked back and grabbed the manuscript.

"This is what I wanted to show you..." I extended my arm forward to her with it in hand.

"Time and Temperance?" She looked at the first page and took it from me.

"It's a novel I have been writing about you..." I drew her attention to a pink sticky-pad that protruded from the stack of papers. "I bookmarked this particular passage I want you to read..."

Temperance held the novel on her lap and flicked through the pages.

"Will you read it, please?"

She nodded.

I went into embrace her and she stopped me at a handshake. I took her hand and kissed it.

"I will fight to the end for you, Temperance." I released her hand. "I am not going anywhere." My eyes wandered to the door handle until I turned back once more to take another look at her, sitting on the couch with her puffy eyes now escaping form the parted veil.

"I don't want to be someone you look back at two hundred years from now and reflect on what could have been. On the Day of Days, I'd want to be able to tell My Father in Heaven if He would be so kind the hear the words of one of his sons who loves him that Temperance Grace Elizabeth Lee is my soulmate and that everything I did ultimately was to honour his word about love and giving it to his greatest of angels..." I gripped the door-handle with a sweaty palm. "...I will do whatever it takes to make it as such...." Tears flooded my ears as my lips started to quiver. "...I just hope I will see you again, after this..."

"You will do..." She looked across at me. "...I promise you that too."

And then I did as she asked, even if tormented me. I took one more look at her and exited her house. A wave of fear, uncertainty, and anxiety washed over me. I struggled to make it to the gate before I started to break down and cry. What if that was the last time, I ever saw her? What if something happened to her? I'd give her a week and then I'd call her. If I had to, I would confess what I was planning, but I really wanted to do it the way I had imagined... Hopefully, she wouldn't block me; but if she did, I would come back. I didn't want to smother her but at the same time I was going to fight for her, at all costs. I had spent so much time with her and been so deeply connected to her, that being without her seemed like being deprived of oxygen.

29.

I had leaned against my car for a good ten minutes, crying and sobbing uncontrollably as a cigarette burned in between my fingers. It seemed like the beginning of the same bad dream or perhaps it was the time I spent with Temperance that was the dream and I would awake back up on the same couch with the same cigarettes, alcohol, and decay that I had thought I finally escaped. Maybe, I had never left, but when I realised that the novel I wrote had come and gone, it was sobering.

I had to get in my car and retreat back to my flat. When I arrived back, I would go collect some cans of beer and wait; I imagined what lie ahead, the constant checking my phone for any updates, hoping that a text had come through from her. Wrestling with the fear that I missed the notification even if the sound was fully on and the mobile itself was practically glued to me. How long would it last? How long would I wait before I return? A week? It will all seem like one long day, anyhow. I'd put on the Georgia Sugar Bowl from 2008 and eat a load of junk; taking comfort in the sugar rush and in knowing that the bowl game concluded in a glorious ending.

The mobile chimed once and adrenaline shot through me. I grabbed my phone from my pocket, only to notice it was a text from Martyn. My emotions had full control of me and had hoped it was Temperance but then again, texting wasn't really her style. Besides, I literally just left, but the heart has a funny way of making one think so wistfully.

She said she wouldn't abandon me, so I trusted her word. Nevertheless, I had the urge to end it and not find out whether that was true or not...after all, they never came back previously but maybe Temperance would. A fear gripped me to find out; on the contrary, maybe it would be different in this occasion.

The ambivalence paced through my brain and soon my veins throbbed in my skull; a sharp pain filled me. My head collapsed in my hands and tears started to stream down my cheeks, my breaths became shorter and my cries became louder. I threw the cigarette and fell onto my knees again, crying as I banged the asphalt. I took a deep breath and got back to my feet, I finally unlocked the car door and opened it.

"Wait!"

I turned back and looked in the direction of the voice that called out, it was one whose timber, accent, and tone was one that my soul raptured at the sound of. It was Temperance!

She had undergone a wardrobe change; auburn spirals of hair wrapped around her head and descended down to her shoulder in a voluminous flow. A black bowed brooch tied around her neck, its tail draping down into her busty cleavage, a black cloak draped across her shoulders. A violet corseted dress clung to her chiselled core and navel which was perceptible through the sleek and shiny fabric, a black lace emerged from the centre attempting to silhouette her enormous round breasts which rose from the corset and showcased her hour glass figure. Her bare pale chest glowed under the sunlight and shined from oil. Her long flowing dress descended to the floor, segmented by the presence of her belt that she wore on her adventures with the pink T buckle. In one hand she held the manuscript, in the other a pink sunhat.

"Oh wow..." I let out a deep breath, as her beauty was overwhelming in the moment.

"May I have a word with you?"

Though she looked to die for, she had a stoic look that could be construed as a desire for confrontation. I shut the car door and returned to the front of the gate.

"How did you change your clothes so quickly?"

"You already know the answer to that." She opened the manuscript and flipped through the pages.

"...I've never seen that dress on you before..."

She continued to move through the manuscript.

"...you look absolutely breath-taking..."

A smile briefly shot from her face at the compliment, but she remained focused on the text. "Why didn't you tell me about what happened in Wigan?" She was breathing heavy. "...you wrote of it, here..." The anecdote accompanied the passage I steered Temperance to read.

"I have kept some things to myself, too..." I watched a lone finch perch upon a rhododendron bush. "...they are quite painful too bear and this scenario has an eerie semblance to it..."

"Tell me about it." She opened the gate. "There are no secrets between us."

I stepped in and shut the gate behind us. We stood in the front garden, just feet apart from each other.

"I know I told you about my most recent ex before I met and the other that abandoned me, but I never spoke of..." Her name started to form on my lips.

"I don't require her name..." Temperance tapped my wrist gently. "...tell me what happened..."

"I met her on a dating app..." I reminisced. "We exchanged details and spoke on the phone for hours, before we finally met in person. In a matter of weeks, we were in love, and it seemed like she and her daughters were going to be my future. She was an hour's drive from here but I moved to Chorley to be closer to her and the girls..."

"How old were they?"

"Eight and six..."

Temperance placed her hand over her chest.

"They were adorable..."

"And how did things end?"

"She left me after I was in Wigan for two weeks and completely cut off contact with me...." I ran my hand over my head. "...I knew no one up there and I was completely on my own. I remember walking through Mesnes Park feeling like I was the only person there despite everyone being out with their families on such a pleasant spring day..." I watched the finch hop on the ground and leap toward a purple pansy. "...I must have called Samaritan's ten times over that period..."

"It all makes sense, now..." She looked down and turned her back. "I realise that you have suffered greatly and you must have been in torment."

"I've been having flashbacks to that day in the park, as of recent..."

Temperance turned around. "...In my own sordid methods, I felt as if I am trying to do what is right, by setting you free..." She looked down. "I also realise that this whole experience could conjure some skeletons in your closet, I would know as I always fear abandonment myself." Temp looked at me. "Nevertheless, I cannot bear the thought of you potentially harming yourself, as this could trigger such an event..." She re-opened the novel. "Moreover, losing you would always haunt me..." Her finger stopped on the passage that was bookmarked. "So do tell me, do you really mean this?"

"Temperance saved my life, by simply being in it. She doesn't realise that her most supernatural gifts are her heart and spirit. With everything my beloved had been through in her existence, she is noble, kind, caring, and supremely affectionate. With everything that she has, she could have been corrupted or overly proud; Instead she is gentle,

gives all of herself, and leads by example. Her intelligence, her beauty, and her character, all shining examples of the heroic woman that Temperance is. Temperance is my hero. I am madly in love with her and it is my dream to marry her, so I can have the honour of calling her my wife, and the mother of my children....I don't care what becomes of me doing so..."

"Every single word."

"So that's why you said you wanted to marry me..." A glow formed with her smile.

We locked eyes and mine started to fill up with tears. Hers soon followed; her hand extended upward to the side of my cheek, as if she were readying them to catch the tears. I started to shake some more but reached for her side, until she skittishly turned.

"Hitherto, I understood that I have to make a choice and though I care for you because you are an important person to me, I do appreciate that my desire to reconcile coupled with an aversion toward any form of romantic attachment would be duplicitous." She curled her fingers under her chin and looked as if she were deep in philosophic though." I understand a friendship would be out of question for a superfluity of reasons, though I do want to be there for you desperately."

"You covered all of this in the span of ten minutes?"

She shook her head nervously. "No, I've been pondering this for some time but recent events have brought it to the forefront." Sweat started to build in her cleavage and on her cheeks. "...I want you to know whether you realise it or not, I would be lost without you. You saved me, as well..." She looked at me with that same youthful, optimistic, and bubbly smile that caused me to lose many chess games against her. "I recognise you are modest and sadly may take this as hyperbole, but it is the truth... Temperance's looked down. "When you walked out the door and the silence started set in, I languished just as I did all through last night..." Her eyes fixed back upon me. "I would be yours until the end of the time..."

I reached for her hand but in her animated state she pivoted away from me unknowingly. "However, I do not want to be selfish and force you to endure all the meagreness that I have..."

"Mama..." I took hold of her hand, interrupting her discourse. It was a strange transaction; she was clearly overthinking everything and I was calm and steady. It was as if we had swapped personalities. Temperance's eyes darted up to meet mine, hanging on what I said next.

"I love you..."

"I love you, more." Temperance burst into my arms and pressed her lips against mine; I kissed her with force as my arms coiled around her back and she jumped on to my hips, straddling me.

A powerful volley of kisses ensued, as she forced me against the door of the house; she bit on my lip and I gently pushed her up against the wall, kissing down her neck as I massaged her bosom and tugged on the front lattice. She started to moan as my lips made their way down her chest, until she squeezed the back of my head and our foreheads gently pressed against each other as our breaths flowed into each's mouths.

"Stay tonight, will you?" She whispered. "I'll order us some pizzas for tea..."

"Well if you are going to bribe me with pizza, now I have to stay..."

She chuckled and our lips smacked together again. "...I believe we may need a few, after we are through..."

"I'll get us some Oreos and milk, for dessert..."

"For pudding, you mean?" She smiled and pecked my lips. "Good choice of biscuit, that..."

"Honey..." I moved my head back. "...for the last time, they are cookies..."

"I am not arguing semantics with you..." She playfully jabbed me. "We've bickered enough..."

"Okay, guy..." I teased her and poked her playfully in the stomach, she embellished and slapped me back, giving me the mischievous look that she often did before we played around, which is what exactly happened. She giggled and grappled my arms but I shook one loose and tickled her, Temperance started to laugh and retaliated; our faces drew closer together in the intimacy of the ensuing play fighting and escalated into vigorous kissing as my hands stroked her up and down in a soft and sensual fashion, undoing her belt, as she removed my shirt. Her hands ran into my pants as mine meandered under her skirt before we had all but disrobed each other fully.

"Do you wish to wait?" I pressed my lips to her body and wandered down toward her navel. "Today is the exception..." She gasped as she guided my head down further. "I wasn't *planning* on it..." The mention of the word prompted an urgent matter that engrossed my every thought.

"The plan!" I spoke at length. "Honey, we have to do it..." I grabbed my shirt and threw it over me.

"Right this instant?" She sat up.

"We can't wait any longer..." I handed her overskirt to her and reached down for her corset.

"We were making up..." Temperance fitted her corset to her waist. "...we were nearly there..."

"...we can make up all night." I fixed her fastenings. "...it'll be even better after this." I stroked her sides. "...please trust me, this is going to be special..."

"You truly have a skill for timing, I must say..." Temperance appeared flustered as she put her overskirt on.

"I have to take you somewhere important..." I extended my hand down to her to her.

"But you've hardly slept..." She looked up with me defiance and took my hand reluctantly as I helped her to her feet. "...and I am not dressed to have a day out..." She brushed herself off.

"You look absolutely beautiful..." I took her coat and placed it around her "...please wear the dress, it's perfect for the occasion." I threw on my coat and scooped her in my arms, which enticed her to shrill. "And then once we've completed the plan, we'll come back here and finish what we started..."

"At this point, I wouldn't dare attempt to impede you..." She smirked as she threw her arms around my neck in a cordial yield of acquiescence.

"...good, because we'll have much to celebrate..."

She gleamed with excitement. "And what are we celebrating, exactly?"

"That's up to you, my love..." I kissed her once more and carried her toward to the door. "Now to carry out the plan..."

SUN TWINKLED AGAINST the snow that blanketed Ardwick Green. Ice melted away as faint strands of grass poked their heads dipped in frost. The park was empty. It was only Temperance and I.

"I have come here countless times and hoped to catch just one more glimpse of Mummy. I would be thrilled." She removed her bonnet and let down her cinnamon-auburn hair. Her face moved left to right at all the buildings tucked behind the iron fence which enclosed the park. In that moment, she appeared to be searching for something in the landscape. "Mother and I loved it here..." My beloved smiled for a brief moment. "We used to live there." Temperance pointed to an empty green field pitched beyond the park and street behind it. "The council has long cleared the buildings." She gazed at the empty parcel of land. "The flat had a lovely view of the pond that used to be here." Her finger moved in the direction of a listed factory house at the other end of the park. "The drinks manufacturer is still here though; they were called Jewsbury and Brown when I was a little girl."

"I take it there was no Apollo Theatre, then?"

"No, that would have been mint though, wouldn't it?" She chuckled as she ran her finger against her plum shawl. "Though I always preferred the Empire when it was in operation." Her lips pressed together as she reminisced. "...This was a very thoughtful gesture by you. However, we could have gone here anytime; is there more to this grand plan?"

"Are you familiar with Ezekiel 18?"

"You brought me here to quote me The Bible?" She looked back toward the house she grew up in.

"I prayed for you, I prayed for us, and I pleaded for you before The Lord. I poured my heart before Him about all of this..."

"No one has ever prayed for me since the incident..." Temperance squinted at me. "Go on..."

"Behold, all souls are mine; as the soul of the father, so also the soul of the son is mine..." I smiled "...declares, The Lord." My eyes wandered to where hers were. "...Ezekiel 18:4." I redirected my smile towards her. "I recommend you read the whole chapter; it is very pertinent to this situation in entirety."

She titled her head and shrugged her shoulders.

"You can't sell your soul, my love. Your mom and Pride took a vow and essentially got married." My hands gripped her shaking fingers. "That must be how it all happened." There was a conviction in my tone, it was far more compelling compared to my fluid bonding hypothesis which as recalled was vehemently rejected. "your mom just did it with the wrong party..."

"So, what is it you are suggesting?"

"If we took an eternal vow before The Lord and got married, He will see us through." I glowed. "Let us be bound through and to Him."

Temperance scratched her forehead.

"Either you won't be able to shock any people anymore or I might be like you..."

Temperance reminded of the little girl that I read about back in 1863. The sweet and innocent daughter that sought answers from her mother. Once again, her blue irises cried for hope.

"Do you have faith in The Lord Jesus Christ?" I gazed deeper into her eyes and gripped her hands tighter. "Is He your Lord and Saviour?"

"Yes." She nodded with her lips stiffened. "I fervidly seek Our Father in Heaven's grace and mercy. I earnestly wish to be his daughter and friend."

"You already are..." Adrenaline dripped into my veins. "...and He will help us, there won't be any of this you and me separated forever unless a deal is contracted with dark powers mayhem."

Temperance's eyes swelled with tears.

"If I am wrong, we'll do it your way. I have that much faith."

Joy filled her face.

"God is love and with Him all things are possible. By His grace and mercy, our love and bond will prevail." I looked up to the sky, in that moment the sun cascaded downward against Temperance's face covering her in a piercing light. The violet of her ensemble seemed to glow like the wings of a monarch butterfly.

"You have to receive His love, Temperance, we both do..." She glanced at me and listened on. Normally, Temperance was one to instruct and in many ways lead. This time, it was my turn. "...and we need to receive each other's love; in many ways we haven't done either yet. But if we do here and now, the plan will work..."

She nodded back at me.

"And when we have a daughter named Henrietta, we can hand her the finished novel, combining your story with mine that chronicled everything leading up to her birth." I glanced at the factory and then back at Temperance. "...including this day and the day we became husband and wife."

In that moment, I thought to myself how I wished her mother could have been here. Ardwick Green was the place where she prophesised that her daughter would one day grown into a woman, get married, and become a mom; where Temperance would find fulfilment.

"Since you speak of it so frequently, I must ask you..." Her fingers squeezed mine. "Would you really marry me?"

My response was silenced by the sight of a woman standing near the iron fence that traced the perimeter of the park. She stared at Temperance and I standing across from where my beloved lived as a child. The woman had long dark auburn hair that fell over her bosom and back. The wind tossed her crimson cape-like shawl behind her revealing a pink corset underneath. A translucent black-coloured skirt danced alongside the shawl in the breeze. Her attire was reminiscent of someone from Temperance's time. In many ways, she looked like Temperance with a darker shade of hair.

"Yes, I really would." I dropped one knee to the concrete, cold rock pressed through my baggy jeans against my skin.

The women caught the corner or my eye. I looked over at her and she gave me a thumbs up. It was if she were giving me a sign of approval and Temperance were her daughter.

"There would be no greater honour than to call you my wife." I pulled a hand away to take hold of the artefact nestled in my pocket. "I wanted to marry you when I first saw you." My fingers wrapped around the velvet ring box and slid it out. "I won this at Coral Island over a game of basketball." The box opened and inside rested a silver ring. A sapphire-coloured heart framed by small diamond butterflies glistened under the sunlight.

Temperance's lips had opened, her jaw descended toward the floor.

At a deliberate pace, I slid the ring onto her finger. Temperance's breaths accelerated as she looked down at the ring, tears streamed down her cheeks. "You didn't win this shooting baskets." She whispered.

"No." I chuckled. "But I love you Temperance Grace Lee and whether it be the next sixty, sixty-thousand, or six-million days, I want them only with you." I took a deep breath. "I brought you here today to this special place to ask you one thing. I hope and pray you will make me the most blessed man on the planet..." My eyes locked with hers. "Temperance Grace Elizabeth Lee, will you marry me?"

It appeared she had so much to say, yet all she could do is open her arms, nod, and utter one word being overwhelmed by the moment. "Yes."

Blood rushed to my head as I jumped to my feet to embrace her. We burst into each other's arms and I lifted her off the ground; we kissed with passion and intensity until we stopped to hold each other.

"Bravo, this is quite the plan..." She ran her hands up my back. "I've been given a day that I could have never imagined..."

"Same for me, my love..." I kissed her forehead. "And we'll have many more, I pray..."

Temperance nodded and smiled before she burrowed her head into my chest and embraced me, as I held her tight. We didn't speak after that, but just took in the moment together.

Once again, my line of sight re-directed across the park toward the mysterious woman. Her smile was as large as ours. It was evident she had been watching the whole time, her hands were clasped against her cheeks and she were glowing as much as the two of us. It was as if she were Temperance and she had just been proposed to.

I covertly put a thumb up behind Temperance's back toward her, the woman threw back a jovial smile and clapped her hands.

"Is someone there?" Temperance released me.

The blue of my beloved's eyes became the centre of my vision. In a weird sort of way, it was as if the woman by the fence were face-to-face with me. Temperance turned her head to look where I had and the unknown lady had disappeared without a trace.

"I felt as if Mother were here..." Temperance surveyed the area with a look of confusion, it was if she could hear or see something but not detect the source. "...it was quite strange, really..."

The daguerreotype of Temperance's mother, Abigail flashed in my mind as a crimson cloak blew across the park.

Later that day, we went back to Temperance's house and made love all night while eating pizza and Oreos in between, as we planned. The next day, I gave my notice to quit my flat and I moved in with her permanently.

On the first day of Spring, Temperance and I got married at an old church near Knutsford. Though we dressed for the occasion, we wed with just the two of us present. We escorted each other down the aisle and gave each other away to one another. Temperance's surname has a special meaning to her. It survived so much spanning nearly two centuries, naturally she was reluctant to give it up. So, when we married, I defied convention and took her surname. From there, we spent a week by the sea filled with enough love, romance, and passion to span a dozen lifetimes.

30.

I parked our pick-up in the drive and emerged with removed four bouquets from the back seat. I shut the front gate and walked across the front yard of our home. A breeze kissed the leaves of the willow tree, birds chirped, and the fragrance of flowers filled my nose. Sun bathed the yard in warmth, my grey polo shirt, dark blue baggy jeans, and charcoal-coloured shoes were all accented by the sunlight. The final twenty-five seconds of Scott Joplin's *Treemonisha Overture* belted out into the yard from the piano in our sitting room before transitioning into *Pine Apple Rag*.

I swiped my fingers across the top of my forehead and looked back to the gate; there were nothing but green fields and flowery meadows pitched beyond them across the road. In the distance, a sign post pointing to Goostrey and Twemlow. I turned back and glanced up to a small window in the top floor of our home. The aperture was canopied in a white Victorian façade. Above and to the right was a capstone with *Sycamore Grove, 1875* etched into it. The house was made of a red brick; its most notable features, a turret structuring to draw the eye upward toward steeply-pitched slate roofs with signature finials featuring large bay windows extending out from the sitting room and the bedroom above it. These Victorian architectural nuances were accented by cream-coloured moulding. Double hooded windows matched the ivory-shaded roof façade and entrance overhang. A large green door with a stained-glass window greets guests. I looked up toward the central second floor window, Temperance hummed and whistled along as she folded a towel, I smiled as I watched her, brushing away a tear as I did so.

"If God grants me grace, then He will show me the way, and I pray I will be singing this song." My beloved's voice overtook the piano with a smile on her face. Butterflies hovered around the moulding of the window. Temperance extended her hand to catch one of the butterflies, smiling sweetly at the creature as it perched on her knuckles until it wafted its cerulean wings and gently flew away. Two doves perched on the gable above her, a lilac strand of lightning formed in her hand as she continued to sing.

I proceeded to watch Temperance, until our eyes locked like that day when I walked up the lane in Marple on the day I first told her loved her. Temperance drew a handkerchief across her cheek before electrical bursts formed a pink heart in front of my beloved's lips. It descended from the window as she blew a kiss toward me, and wafted through the air until it dissipated around my cheeks, tickling them with a warm and gentle sensation. I looked up at Temperance and blew a kiss back to her despite the urge to sprint toward the house, scale the side, climb up to that window, and give her a most passionate kiss. However, another face joined my beloved at the window, the same piercing blue eyes, followed by the same bright smile, our daughter Elizabeth.

"Papa's home." Bet exclaimed, her mahogany hair flicked behind her as she fled away from the window. The piano stopped playing.

The door flung open and out came our daughter Henrietta. Her butterfly bobby-pins danced across her dark auburn hair; her joyful blue eyes lit up as she sprinted toward me like when she was younger. Her long blue skirt and the short ivory sleeves of her blouse whisked through the air as she ran toward me.

"Happy Birthday, Papa!"

I placed the bouquets down and opened my arms to her. She crashed into my embrace and I scooped her up and spun her around, eliciting a squeal from her.

Elizabeth soon followed after; her plaid hoop skirt flicked in the wind as her black high-heeled shoes rummaged across the grass. Bet's hair was tied in a pink bow with the remainder of her mahogany hair falling down the back of her white blouse that matched Hetta's. Her eyes also sparkled like her sister.

"Did you really think you were going to sneak past us?" Bet jumped into my other arm and kissed my cheek.

"I could try..." I pressed their heads against my chest. "But I don't think it would be possible..." I kissed both of them on the domes of their head. "I am amazed at how much you have both grown."

"I've gotten a lot stronger, too." Henrietta batted her eyes and flexed her bi-cep.

"I guess you didn't get that from playing the piano, Hen?" I felt a bulging muscle emerge from beneath the soft flesh of her arm. "You know you girls are truly a spitting image of your mother in more ways than one."

"Funny, you should say that." Bet looked to Henrietta. "Many reckon we are Mummy's sisters."

"Your hair is more of a cabernet tone." I winked at her. "Otherwise, it would pass..."

"Well you would know that, wouldn't you?" Elizabeth made a funny face at me. "Having you wrapped our fingers, as we do..."

"Whatever you say, Elizabeth Grace." I teased and she responded by slapping my arm playfully.

"Just the other day if I was asked if I was Papa's sister." Henrietta giggled. "Gobsmacked, when I said I am his daughter."

"Pooh, as if we cannot hit a growth spurt like Mother did when she was our age." Elizabeth gleamed. "We are only her twin daughters, after all..."

"Fascinating to see what happens with Giggle, as she is only a few years younger than us..." Henrietta's words swam into the spring air. "She is already exponentially stronger and more athletic than anyone close to her age..."

"Please sweetheart, don't give her any ideas..." I raised my hand. "To quote Mummy, Georgie's never been shy when it comes to monkey tricks..."

My beloved walked onto the porch in a long flowing paisley gown. A black brooch tied around her neck to complement an ivory cameo near to the centre of the collar. Her sunhat was neatly placed upon her head, her posture up-right, dignified, and elegant. As always, my dearest looked impressive and graceful.

"Happy birthday, Butterscotch." Temperance beamed as she sauntered toward me with a series of gentle and demure steps. "Welcome to the Good New Old Days" She removed her hat and her palm gripped the side of my face as she stared into my eyes and let out a child-like smile. "You look just as you were on our Wedding Day, ever so handsome." She pressed her lips against mine.

"And you are more stunning every time I look at you." I wrapped my arms around her. "Old woman..." I smirked at her and she shook her head defiantly with a smile back at me. We chuckled and then I kissed her forehead and pulled her close to me. Our two girls smiled as they watched.

My beloved glowed with pure joy and ecstasy. "He's paved a way."

"Indeed, He has." I smiled back at her with equal radiance. "The Lord has blessed you with the gift of making the impossible, possible..." I held her and stroked strands of her hair. "You are an inspiration to us all, my love." I locked my hand in hers. "You deserve to have a book written about you."

"And thanks to you Papa, Mummy does..." Elizabeth stepped back to the porch and took hold of a book bound with a brocade cover. The title *Time and Temperance* inscribed in Victorian gold-leaf lettering shimmered under sunlight. It was the first copy I had bound for my beloved.

"I love how it starts on the day you and Mumma met near that aqueduct yonks ago." Elizabeth clutched the book against her as it was much a coveted trinket of her history as much as her mother or I.

Temperance threw her hand at her hip. "You two have been rummaging through my memory chest again, I see."

"To be fair Mother..." Henrietta blushed. "...the title is apt considering the circumstances..."

"...Indeed, you look well for a Victorian woman, Mumma..." Elizabeth batted her eyes. "Evidently, you have rubbed off on Father, as well."

"Many thanks, poppets." My beloved chuckled.

"...I dare declare, all of us...." Bet smiled.

"Papa, do you still carry a lock of Mummy's hair when you go on the fire truck?" Henrietta took my hand.

"And when I do poetry or novel readings too."

"I will have to fetch a pair of scissors and cut a lock of my hair for you to take with you." Hetta smiled.

"And I." Bet placed her arm around me. "And Georgiana, so you can have all of us with you."

"I'll proudly carry you all with me, my lovelies." I embraced the three of them.

"You bought us flowers on your birthday?" Bet laughed and pointed at the bouquets resting on the grass. "Typical, that."

"I don't need a reason to bring my wife and daughters flowers now, do I?" I winked. "The four of you are my greatest gifts, every day." I smiled at them and each of them beamed back at me lovingly. "Speaking of which, where is Georgie?"

"Baby Sister is slopping about." Elizabeth raised her brow. "Lying in wait to surprise you when you least suspect it."

"Sounds like two other girls, I know." I looked away with a smirk.

"Georgiana is preparing her gift for you." Henrietta smiled. "It's so bloody adorable how excited she is to give you her present."

"It's supposed to be a surprise, Harriet." Elizabeth teased. "You do recall Baby Sister's request, right?"

"Well how dare I forget?" Hetta bantered. "Thank you for reminding me, Eliza."

Bet wrinkled her nose at Henrietta.

"Now Papa, we wanted to make today special for you because you are special to us..." Henrietta grabbed my hand and tugged me toward the front door.

"We went full hog..." Temperance smiled. "I am sorry to say but your birthday is no longer just another year that passed by..."

"Mumma is right, Papa..." Elizabeth rolled her eyes. "...you are supposed to celebrate your birthday." She stressed the word celebrate, referencing my lack of enthusiasm for birthdays when I was under the surge of depression. To me, my birthday was normally a day just acknowledging that I didn't die. The girls however had other ideas. Their thoughtfulness was needless to say very touching and also reflected the kind nature of their mother.

"Come now..." Temperance clapped her hands, emanating glee as she did so. "...I cannot wait for you to open all the presents, we've gotten you."

"We got you some cool stuff..." Henrietta impersonated my accent. The antics cracked a chuckle from both Elizabeth and Temperance. "...Papa." She slipped back into her natural accent which sounded identical to her mother.

"Let me get the door for you all."

"Always doting over the four of us, allow us to spoil you for a change..." My wife tugged me back as Henrietta strolled forward to open the door.

"We've baked you a cake." Ellie's eyes lit up as she grabbed my arm.

The girls' steps thundered against the carpet as they yanked me toward the corridor.

"Victoria Sponge..." Henrietta hooked other my arm. "Your favourite..."

"Glossed in vanilla icing." Bet clutched my hand.

"Sprinkled with nonpareils..." Henrietta arched her eyebrows.

"It's a good thing that when you married Mumma, you were miraculously cured of your diabetes, aye?" Elizabeth nudged me. "That worked out well for you." She poked me with her elbow. "Plus, you got me out of the deal." She bantered. "I know Harriet and I came as a package but she is a break-even, if you ask me."

"You are a cheeky bugger, Little Sister..." Henrietta feigned shot a contemptuous look at Elizabeth.

"Aye..." Bet shrugged her shoulders with a smirk. "It's the consequences of you having an eleven-minute head start on us, Bubble.

A smile broke from Henrietta's face and they both shared a laugh.

"Happy Birthday, Daddy!" Georgiana leaned over the banister of the stairs, stopping us on our way to the kitchen. She looked like my wife when she was a child, imbued with long poinsettia-coloured hair, fair skin that freckled when she was excited, cheeks that turned rosy in the sun, and blue eyes that sparkled with love. Her hair was parted by a pink bow and fell down her back. Her black boots scampered against the wood as she held her striped dress with each step she took. When she reached the fourth step, she stopped and rolled up her white long sleeve undershirt which matched her stockings. Judging by the wide smile on her face, I knew what the look meant; she was going to jump.

I opened my arms because I knew it was already too late to tell her otherwise. Georgiana leapt off the steps and flung herself toward my arms. I caught her safely and secured her against me, letting out a breath of relief. "Sweetheart that frightens me, can you not to do that, please..."

"But I can fly, Papa." Georgiana wrapped her arms around my neck and pressed her lips against my cheek.

"Of course, you can, baby girl."

"Look at what else I can do." Georgiana's hands cupped around my face, bristling against my whiskers. Gee snapped her fingers and she transformed into an entirely different outfit. Georgiana wore a shiny sleeveless spandex pink leotard tucked into heliotrope pleather briefs which had a pink G on the back of them. A silver belt wrapped around her waist boding a white medallion buckle crested with a pink-coloured G to bring the ensemble together. She also wore white wristbands, lilac gloves, and pink pleather boots. Her hair was plaited in two down her back.

"I am like Mummy!" Georgiana glowed as she plucked one of the straps and it popped as it snapped back against her shoulder. "She made this specially for me!"

Henrietta and Elizabeth glanced back at me with apprehension, as if this was an unplanned addition to the festivities. "You look fabulous, sweetheart." I adjusted her on my hip and smiled at her; she returned the smile. "So, was the big surprise you diving off the steps onto me?" I tickled Georgiana's stomach and she giggled.

"No!" She shook her head playfully and palmed my cheeks. "I made you something."

"Well, I need to see it then!" I Eskimo-kissed Georgiana and she pressed her lips to mine.

"Okay!" She exclaimed "...and after we can have pizza with marshmallows and watch the Bulldogs since you said they are named after me..."

"That Hoo-Ha..." Henrietta rolled her eyes as she was first to enter the kitchen. "According to Papa, every street, village, queen, and duchess is named after we four..."

"That's because they are, darling."

Henrietta shook her head.

"Daddy, how much will the Dawgs win by today?" Georgiana smiled.

Temperance interjected. "Georgie dear, do you really wish to excite your father with that blinding football team?"

Georgiana nodded and threw her arms around me. "The Georgiana Bulldogs will crush them!" She growled and clenched her teeth, before finally letting out a childish laugh and pressing her face to mine.

"Infecting the youth with your antics, I see..." Temperance snickered. "Good job that, Butterscotch." She started to whistle the fight song *Rambling Wreck* of one of our arch rivals, Georgia Tech. I stared at her with discontent. Georgiana and Henrietta also frowned in her direction.

"Quite a catchy melody, don't you think?" Temperance smirked.

"That's the wrong team, Mummy..." Georgiana scowled.

"Mumma's lack of discretion is utterly abhorrent...." Henrietta threw her hands at her hip. Temperance opened her hands and gave Hen a playful dirty look.

"Good choice of word, Hen." I smiled at her; she gleamed and nodded once.

"Victorian woman you are indeed, Mother...." Bet squinted at Temperance and laughed to herself for a moment. "your sense of humour is bloody dark." Ellie crossed her arms. "The song that is supposed to be sung is *Baba O'Riley*." She smirked at me. "Naturally, just before the Bulldogs kick off..." Her smirk widened. "Not that I have any interest in that hocus pocus, of course..."

"How did that work out for you the last time you started up, honey?" I bantered.

"I cannot recall what you are referring to." She grinned.

I shook my head and chuckled. "I love you more than anything my dear, but why Georgia Tech?"

"Yea." Georgiana looked over at my beloved with a look of displeasure. "Why, Georgia Tech?" She embellished her tone in her interrogation. A smile formed across Henrietta's face, followed by Elizabeth, and then Temperance who had to hold back laughing altogether from Georgiana's cheekiness.

"I am not supporter of the team by any means, poppet..." She shrugged her shoulders with a smirk. "...I just enjoy winding your father up..." A smile poured from her face.

"Mumma, can you and Papa do a show with the puppets when the game is over?" Georgie formed icicles between her finger tips.

Temperance and I smiled at each other.

"I reckon your father and I can sort something."

"Daddy, you and Mumma are the best team." Georgie waved her hand and a flash of light sparked.

"It's your all Mom, Gee." I placed Georgie down. "...she just makes me look good."

"Flatterer." Temperance blushed.

"Can we go to Styal too?" Georgiana stood on the balls of her feet. "So, we can watch the airplanes take off?" She hopped off the ground and flew around in a small figure-eight for a split second before placing her feet back down in front of me.

"Sure, sweetheart." I stroked her head. "That's a great idea."

She pressed her head against me and hugged me with a smile.

"Love it there, I do..." Hetta twinkled and brushed off her blouse. "I remember when you would set me on your shoulders so I could see the airplanes speed down the runway."

"Why don't we all go, then?" I cautiously plucked a stubborn piece of scarlet string on Henrietta's sleeve and smiled at her. "We can throw some blankets down on the hill and watch."

Elizabeth snorted and let out a laugh. "Sounds like a picnic, that."

"Bet, you liked it most of all." I reminisced. "You were so adorable when you used to throw your arms out and pretend you were an airbus for British Airways..." She blushed in response to my reference to her youthful exuberance. Henrietta burst out laughing, Bet retorted with a defiant look in her direction.

Georgiana let go of me and moved out from under my arm. "Here, Papa..." She plucked an item from the steps and handed it to me, it was a folded piece of paper which she rendered into a card. "This is the surprise."

I leaned down to her and took the card from her. "Oh wow, Georgiana..." She had drawn a picture on the front page in crayon. In black she wrote *Happy Birthday, Daddy* and there in the drawing was a sun in gold with a squiggly smiley face. Two clouds hung over a likeness of our home. The accuracy was exceptional, as Georgiana had matched the colour of the roof and the side profile of our home perfectly, detailing every hooded window, every brick pattern, and some of the ivy trellis that grew up the side; the large willow tree in the front garden was also featured. Beneath it, a stick figure rendition of what was supposed to be our family, Georgiana drew herself in a purple dress with red plaits holding the hand of what was supposed to be me, wearing a red shirt that says Daddy on it. Holding the hand of the incarnate of me was Temperance who Georgiana drew in all lilac with her hair up. Two twin stick figure girls, one in purple, and one in blue held each other's hands; one of which held Temperance's other hand.

I looked up and smiled at Georgie. "...this is amazing, honey."

"It's from when you just were outside with Mummy, Hetta, and Ellie..."

I flipped the page and looked inside at the message written, it said: *I love you so much, you are the best Papa ever, I want to make you happy as much as you make me. Happy birthday, love, Georgiana.*"

"Thank you." I closed the card and pulled her in for a hug, kissing the side of her face. "I love you so much, baby girl."

I looked up at Henrietta and Elizabeth and walked over to them and embraced both of them and gave both a kiss on the side of face, as well. "Hen, Bet, I love you so much."

"I love you too, Papa." Hetta nestled her head on my shoulder. "You are my hero."

"Me too, Papa." Elizabeth put her arm around my back. "I love you dearly."

"That means the world to me, girls..." I cupped Bet's face and smiled both of them, holding back tears. I kissed them once more and let them go.

"Georgie is quite the accomplished artist, isn't she?" My beloved ran her hands through the top of Georgiana's hair.

"Indeed, she takes after Bet in that regard...."

"That's because I am the cool older sister..." Bet stuck her tongue out at Hetta in gest. "Right, Giggle?" Elizabeth winked at Georgiana.

"You are both gifted; Henrietta is more of a writer, like me..." I smiled at Hetta and whispered to her "I could never draw like either of them..." We shared a laugh and I took one more look at Georgie's card, my eyes made their way across the sketch to the rear of the house. Georgiana had drawn the other large willow tree in our back garden, beside it was a woman with dark red hair, a pink dress, and a crimson cloak; a most peculiar addition.

"Georgiana, dear..." I knelt down.

"Yes, Papa!" She enthusiastically came to my side.

"Who is that?" I held out the card in front of her and pointed at the unknown figure she drew.

Georgiana looked at the figure. "My friend."

"Well, why don't they come and join us?" I smiled at her.

"She would have done but said it would be rude of her to interrupt." Her eyes lit up. "...Personally, I believe she is a bit shy."

I chuckled. "And what is her name?"

"Abbie..."

"Abbie?" I looked over at Temperance who appeared puzzled. "As in..."

"Nana?" Elizabeth's eyes flickered red for a moment.

"Bet..." I shook my head at her.

"I am just saying, Papa." Bet threw her hands out in protest. "Considering the state of our family, is it really so inconceivable?"

"Papa..." Henrietta placed her hand on my shoulder. "Ellie could be right...."

"Thank you, Big Sister." Elizabeth nodded and Hetta smiled back at her. But that was always the story with the two of them, they were always in cahoots. No matter the weather Elizabeth always came to Henrietta's defence and vice versa, even if they were teasing each other or had an argument just before. They were twins but also best friends; affectionate and loyal to each other.

"...do you recall when we were Giggle's age a few years ago and saw someone that looked like Nana standing just across that field over there?" Hetta motioned her head in the direction of the front window. "Initially we thought it was Mumma playing tricks, but realised it was not when you and her were having a kip together on the couch ..."

"Abbie said she likes you Daddy, because you really love Mummy and take care of us." Georgie smiled. "She also said that Mummy is quite incredible and a lot of people said that about her in the past..."

Her smile widened. "I told her of course Mummy is incredible, she is a superhero!"

Temperance normally would have been supremely flattered at our daughter's display of reverence toward her. Instead, she appeared haunted.

"Of course, she is, Mummy is the greatest superhero!" I dabbed Georgie's nose and glanced over at my beloved. "And Mommy really appreciates your compliments, darling." I put the card down on the side table pressed against the staircase. "...in fact, she's speechless that's how moved she is by your kind words." My eyes steered toward my beloved again who stood frozen; her state of shock was clearly evident. "This was very thoughtful of you and I must say that you have quite the vivid imagination, my beautiful."

"But I am not pretending, Papa." Georgiana insisted. "She was standing in the back garden whilst all of you were out front..." She glanced at her mother. "...I was chatting to her from my bedroom window."

Temperance and I both locked our eyes on Georgie.

"...why do you think it took me so long?" She pleaded as if she were fearful of being in some form of trouble.

"Sweetheart..." I shot her a re-assuring look. "...is she there now?" I peered over at my beloved, Henrietta and Elizabeth had drawn to her sides and stroked her arms to ease her tension which radiated off of her.

"I cannot say when she will be back..." Georgiana looked down. "She is playing hide and seek and is very good at it..." An eerie silence filled the room until Henrietta spoke.

"That's because she doesn't want Super Georgiana to find them." She wrapped her arms around Georgie's ribs and growled. Temperance and I smiled at Henrietta's show of affection for her little sister and seemingly all was forgotten. Perhaps, Georgie's curiosity led her to look at some at old photos or diary entries, and her imagination got the best of her. After all, she was dressed like a superhero because she loved to pretend that she was my beloved's sidekick; Hen and Bet did the same in the past.

Elizabeth and Henrietta nodded at each other before Bet's hand locked in mine. "Papa, you are always there for us." She led me toward the kitchen. "You always try to make us happy, and you always make us feel safe, loved, treasured, and protected."

"We want to thank you..." Water dripped from Henrietta's hands as it poured into a vase. "Squeak, if you'll please." She flicked her hands free of water and lifted the full cake off the table with one hand. The cake was not small by any means, yet it was if it were a feather to her. "With pleasure, Sister Dearest." Elizabeth stared at the candles on the cake and placed her hands over the wicks, in a flash they were flickering with flames.

Henrietta reached for the light-switch in the kitchen. "Allow me, lovely." Temperance snapped her fingers, the bulbs shut off. The kitchen became a shadowy rendition of its former self which was illuminated formerly by the brass chandelier glimmering from the breach of daylight.

"Our daughters are multi-faceted, aren't they?" Temperance blew electric sprites into the air, all differing in hues and brightness. The sprites danced into the sunlight until I was looking down at the River Goyt again from the top of the aqueduct. My head lurched over the stone wall to the water below and I felt both dizzy and nauseas, as if I was falling. Two warm lips pressed against my cheek and two arms wrapped around me from behind, as if they were pulling me back from the edge and enabled me to fly; those arms were Temperance's. The water at the base of the aqueduct were replaced by the blue of my beloved's eyes.

"Are you all right, darling?" She smiled sweetly. The lights had gone back on and I hadn't realised.

"I am now." I embraced her tight when I pulled back, I had noticed Temperance had undergone an instantaneous wardrobe change. Her hair was up under her blue butterfly hair clip. She was in the same lilac leotard that she customarily wore and it was tucked into corresponding heliotrope pleather leggings with the pink front lacing over the crotch. She also sported the belt which boded a white medallion buckle crested with a pink T whilst also wearing her white open-fingered silk gloves and pink boots.

"You look immaculate, my queen." My hands stroked her stomach until they came to a rest snug against her ribs.

"It is your birthday..." She winked and drew close; our lips pressed together as my hands moved down around her waist. My beloved looked over her shoulder to peer at the girls engaged in conversation. "Do tell me when are we calling at the fire station next..."

"Let me know what works for you and we'll put it on the calendar..." I kissed her neck and covertly pinched her bum while Henrietta and Elizabeth were putting some final touches on the cake with Georgiana.

"Naughty boy." She spoke under her breath as she smirked. "Save that for later when the poppets are off to bed..."

We shared a laugh and kissed again, holding each other until I felt a tug on my arm. Georgiana looked up at me, her blue eyes shining back at me like her mother's.

"You see, Papa, our outfits have matching colours!" Georgiana pressed her head against Temperance's stomach and wrapped her arms around her thighs.

"Of course, we do, treacle." Temperance scooped her up and levitated with Gee in her arms. "We are a team."

"Watch this!" Georgie moved her arms around Temperance's ribs and slid underneath her armpit until she perched on her back with her one arm below my beloved's neck and the other over her bosom. Her feet clenched against Temperance's ribs as she threw her hands out. "Look! No hands!"

"Impressive you are my dear, but keep those arms around me." Temperance's tone implicated concern. "We don't want you to have a fall and hurt yourself."

"But Mummy, I am like you..."

"Georgiana Rose, must I repeat myself?" Temperance looked back at her from the side of her eye.

Georgie adjusted her feet and moved her arms around Temperance to hug her from behind.

"Good girl." Temperance placed her boot upon the ground and put Georgie down gently, sending her off with a stroke of her hair.

"You look absolutely beautiful, Mumma." Henrietta put her hands together. "I've always adored those leggings!"

"Thank you ever so dearly, Bubble." Temperance rubbed Henrietta's cheek with her thumb. "They are quite the enhancement now, as I have reservations with anyone seeing my legs except your father."

Bet pressed her finger to her tongue and rolled her eyes.

"I am honoured but I have no authority over what you wear, my love. Besides, at this point, it's just something for you and Georgie to wear around the house for fun, anyhow."

The girls and Temperance looked at each other for a moment, their eyes seemingly delivering surreptitious messages to one another.

"I must say Mother; I wish I had a core like yours." Henrietta ran her hand along Temperance's belt-line toward her navel. "Proper powerhouse you are with all the squats and crunches you do." Hetta gently on knocked on Temperance's abdomen, at this point she was flexing her stomach muscles.

"Look!" Georgiana's finger erected and poked into her midsection. Temperance grunted slightly from the sensation of the jab. "one..." Georgie's finger prodded into each abdominal clearly visible from the skin-tight fabric. "Hmph!" Temperance's grunt was more pronounced. "two..." Georgiana counted all the way up to six and poked each muscle, as she did so; a couple of the prods forced a wince from Temperance.

"It's like a brick wall!" Georgie glowed.

Temperance doubled over for a moment, pressing her hand to her stomach. "It's a good thing, we trimmed those fingernails yesterday, otherwise that would have really hurt..." She held her abdomen with one hand and glanced over at me.

Gee looked up with concern and remorse, looking ready to cry. Before she could say anything, my beloved stooped down and kissed the dome of her head. "All is well, my love..."

The two smiled at each other, but each in a different way. Temperance doted on her youngest child who hung on her every word; Georgiana was deep in awe and idolisation of her mother.

"...before we turn the lights off and sing for Papa, can you help Bubble with the forks and napkins, please?"

"Sure, Mummy!" She scampered off.

"She's strong, her." Temperance spoke inaudibly to me and smiled at Georgie with pride as she helped Henrietta set the table.

"That was like taking six punches to the body." Temperance placed her hand to her stomach once more and let out an exhale of relief.

"As powerful as you are, Mumma..." Elizabeth giggled. "...you are still no match for me." She jeered.

"Is that so, Squeak?" Temperance smirked and jabbed Bet in the shoulder playfully. "Oww!" Bet yelped and held her arm. Temperance crossed her arms and smiled back at her. A loud smack filled the air when Elizabeth's hand crashed against the Temperance's back.

"Ouch!" Temperance yelled out. Though it appeared she were embellishing, the slap sounded hard; a large red mark crossed the exposed areas of skin on her shoulder blade where Bet's hit landed. "You best run now, daughter."

Elizabeth squealed as she fled, but Temperance pursued her and there wasn't much room for her to go anywhere. In seconds, my beloved wrapped her arms around Elizabeth and retaliated with a bum smack which forced a yelp from Bet; She proceeded to tickle her adversary up and down her sides. Ellie pivoted and burrowed her head into Temperance's bosom and tried to turn the tables by tickling Temperance under the armpit and under the neck. Temperance squirmed and squealed for a moment but very quickly took control of the bout. Both howled and guffawed throughout, as they always did whenever they "larked" or had a bit of rough and tumble. Temperance seemed to enjoy it as much as Elizabeth did (or Georgiana when applicable) as it invoked memories of when she was a child and romped with her mother.

"You little rascal, I am no match for who?" Temperance rapidly transitioned from tickling Ellie into submission to gently embracing her.

"I almost had you..." Bet threw her arm around her mother's waist and rested her head against her; both had worked up a sweat from their short yet intense grapple; the red mark from Ellie's slap had since vanished.

"Call it a draw, poppet..." Temperance pressed her lips to Bet's forehead. Elizabeth kissed my beloved's cheek and placed her hand over Temperance's stomach. Temperance placed her hand over Elizabeth's hand and held her tighter. Both smiled with their heads pressed together and their eyes shut; Henrietta soon joined the affectionate embrace and nestled up against her mother, as well.

"My precious babies." She kissed Hetta on the head and cuddled both girls against her, in all her glory exuding sheer delight. Georgiana scurried over to join the trio, I watched with joy; It melted my heart to witness the love and bond between my wonderful wife and our three spectacular girls.

A sense of urgency swept over Georgiana; she snapped her fingers and reverted back to her day dress as she scampered off into the sitting room; her red hair trailed behind her like flickering flames.

"Everything's ready, Mumma." Henrietta broke the silence but my beloved responded with a rub to Hetta's back, keeping her eyes shut with head pressed against both her and Elizabeth as she held them close to her; savouring every moment. Seconds later, Georgie sprinted back from the sitting room. "...Mummy! Look at what I have!"

Temperance opened her eyes and glanced down at a stuffed toy elephant that rested in Georgiana's arms. A look of alarm swept across her face, vanquishing any notion of the preceding merriment.

"Is that Mister Ruffles?" I took my beloved's hand.

Temperance looked at me out of the corner of her eyes and nodded. She snapped her fingers and reverted back into her gown. The room once again filled with an eerie silence.

Temperance knelt down and hovered her hand over the trunk of the long-lost companion she had when she was Georgiana's age, long ago.

"Where did you find this, Georgeanne?"

Two sets of knocks thundered against the front door prompting the hairs on my neck stood to stand at attention. Temperance tucked her trembling fingers in my hands, I pulled her close to me; her skin felt plush, warm, and soft against me, as if it were a pillow. Georgiana placed the toy on the couch and ran under my arm.

Another set of knocks came, demure and elegant in cadence, nevertheless strong with intent. Elizabeth and Henrietta huddled with us and stared at the door.

"That must be her." Georgiana smiled.

Don't miss out!

Visit the website below and you can sign up to receive emails whenever K. Scott Fuchs publishes a new book. There's no charge and no obligation.

https://books2read.com/r/B-A-HCTAB-TQUOC

BOOKS 2 READ

Connecting independent readers to independent writers.

Did you love *Time and Temperance*? Then you should read *Six Months in Wigan*[1] by K. Scott Fuchs!

A collection of poetry about love, failed romance, loss, depression, and finding peace.

Read more at www.kscottfuchs.com.

---

1. https://books2read.com/u/mvBEn2

2. https://books2read.com/u/mvBEn2

Also by K. Scott Fuchs

Six Months in Wigan
Time and Temperance
Poetry from Ryecroft Hall

Watch for more at www.kscottfuchs.com.

About the Author

K. Scott Fuchs is a novelist, poet, and performer. Time and Temperance is his first novel released; the follow-up prequel sequel, Mrs. Coleman of Coalbrookdale is set to be released in early 2024. He is also the author of the poetry compilations, Six Months in Wigan and Poetry from Ryecroft Hall which are also forthcoming.

Read more at www.kscottfuchs.com.